Praise for

PATRICIA WILSON

'Full of raw emotion'
SUNDAY POST

'**I was engrossed** and hanging on each and every word. This
book will leave a lasting impression . . . [and is] one that
I will find myself recommending to everyone I meet'
REA BOOK REVIEWS

'We race to the end with our hearts thumping . . . **Terrific stuff**'
LOVE READING

'A **beautiful, heartbreaking story** of sacrifice and
love in the face of evil'
FOR THE LOVE OF BOOKS

'Full of raw emotions, family vendettas, hidden secrets
and three very strong women'
THAT THING SHE READS

'The **perfect blend** of fiction with historical fact'
SHAZ'S BOOK BLOG

'Day by day the story unfolds . . . secrets are revealed, feuds
revisited and three generations of women reunited'
PEOPLE'S FRIEND

'Beautiful and evocative'
IT TAKES A WOMAN

'I loved it'
ECHOES IN AN EMPTY ROOM

'I absolutely **LOVED, LOVED, LOVED** this book . . . I can't wait to read more from this hugely talented author'
GINGER BOOK GEEK

'A very **dramatic** novel, one you **cannot put down**'
SOUTH WALES ARGUS

'Thoroughly researched and **very well written**'
THAT THING SHE READS

'The author writes in such an **evocative and emotional** style that the reader cannot help but get totally lost in the book'
KIM THE BOOKWORM

'Attention to detail is second to none . . . **I cannot praise this book enough** and just hope that the author writes another book soon'
BOON'S BOOKCASE

Summer In Greece

ABOUT THE AUTHOR

Patricia Wilson was born in Liverpool. She retired early to Greece, where she now lives in the village of Paradissi in Rhodes. She was first inspired to write when she unearthed a rusted machine gun in her garden – one used in the events that unfolded during World War II on the island of Crete.

www.pmwilson.net
🔹 @pmwilson_author

Also by Patricia Wilson:

Island of Secrets
Villa of Secrets
Secrets of Santorini
Greek Island Escape

Patricia Wilson

Summer In Greece

ZAFFRE

First published in the UK in 2021 by
ZAFFRE
An imprint of Bonnier Books UK
80–81 Wimpole St, London W1G 9RE
Owned by Bonnier Books
Sveavägen 56, Stockholm, Sweden

A CIP catalogue record for this book is
available from the British Library.

ISBN: 978-1-83877-489-9

Also available as an ebook and an audiobook

1 3 5 7 9 10 8 6 4 2

Typeset by IDSUK (Data Connection) Ltd
Printed and bound in Great Britain by Clays Ltd, Elcograf S.p.A.

Zaffre is an imprint of Bonnier Books UK
www.bonnierbooks.co.uk

For nurses everywhere

ODE TO *BRITANNIC'S* BELL

Beneath a sea of turquoise karma
Lies a wreck with silenced drama,
HM Hospital Ship *Britannic* sleeps alone.
Crusty groupers watch and wait
Like Churchill, tired of the debate,
Did mine or missile send this fated lady home?

Gone are those for whom we weep
Those great explorers of the deep,
With tanks and fins and masks carefully cleared.
We're thrilled, quite blown away,
How well-preserved *Brit* is today,
She fights the rusticals that scientists had feared.

To raise her up they say
Would not be the proper way
To remember all those souls so sadly drowned.
In a sea, that's salt with tears,
On sands of time for countless years,
With coral garlands she is gloriously crowned.

Inside, explorers carefully glide,
Find safety doors are open wide
In firemen's tunnels like a giant yawn for breath.
The current's pulling like a gale,
The diver's fins against it fail,
Another tragic ghost remains there after death.

Now time has trickled by,
'Where's the ship's bell?' the diver's cry.
More than a hundred years have very slowly passed.
Then we hear a diver screech,
For lying just below his reach,
At great depth he found *Britannic*'s bell at last.

Patricia Wilson

PROLOGUE

Dover, December 1916.

FROM THE LADDER OF HIS pigeon coop, Doctor Charles Smith gazed over white-frosted farmland. The sun peeped over the horizon, then slid into the full glory of a new day, setting dull clouds ablaze. Rich golden light painted the windows and thatch of a distant tied cottage where his patient lay sleeping – the family inside that humble home would treasure their baby boy for the rest of their lives.

After twenty-four hours attending a difficult confinement, the local midwife, Fanny Eccles, had sent the young woman's father, Jacob Boniface, to knock the doctor from his sleep. In that vacant hour before dawn, Dr Smith saved the exhausted young woman's life with a simple snip, and later, a few stitches. Now, mother and baby were sleeping peacefully. In a whimsical moment, the doctor imagined an angel heading for Bethlehem, stopping off to illuminate that humble dwelling in Dover. He yawned, then smiled, uplifted by the Yuletide scene.

He glanced across the frozen furrows of a turnip field and gave thought to all those men serving. Christmas or not, they'd be too busy killing each other with the newly invented machine guns in the Great War. He sighed wearily, hoping for an hour's sleep before leaving for his surgery.

These days, too many of his call-outs were under more ominous circumstances. The gangrenous limbs of war amputees, or sepsis, were often the forerunner of yet another premature funeral. His morphine and syringe were always to hand.

He shivered, tugged at the corduroy collar of his waxed jacket and stared at the sky, searching hopefully for his best birds. A month ago, ten homing pigeons had left for the Somme in wicker baskets strapped onto the backs of British soldiers, the Pigeon Corps. Military leaders waited for the birds to carry crucial information home from the front line.

The trill of a bicycle bell broke his thoughts. Turning on the ladder, Dr Smith peered over a hedge. Albert, local telegraph boy, pedalled helter-skelter down Lighthouse Lane, his bright grin challenging the doctor's frown. The doctor had delivered Albert fifteen years ago and had hardly seen him thereafter, yet this would be the fourth time the boy had thumbed the gate-latch in the past six months.

He turned and stared over the Dover cliff top, across the English Channel to the grey line that hid France, and beyond, Greece.

'Doctor! Dr Smith!' Albert shouted, abandoning the bell to wave a message over his head. 'News from Athens!' The boy wobbled, then clutched the handlebars and returned to bellringing.

He hurried down the ladder. Earlier in the year, Charles and Martha had dealt with the sudden sacrifice of their other two children, Arthur and Sissy. Two weeks ago, another telegram had arrived, this time concerning their youngest child, eighteen-year-old Gertie.

With deep regret we must inform you, after the sinking of HMHS Britannic in Greek waters, VAD Gertrude Smith is listed as missing, presumed drowned.

Those first three words hurt like a knife in his chest. He didn't need more information, and was left stunned. But, as the days passed, he found he was desperate to know every detail of Gertie's passing. He wanted to take his girl's place, absorb her pain. His whole life had been spent fighting death, and he had won more battles than lost. Was this the grim reaper's revenge? If he hadn't been a doctor, would his three children be alive today?

This would be simple confirmation.

His heart squeezed. How would he tell Martha? She sat quietly in their empty home, torn between hope and despair, hardly having eaten or spoken for a fortnight. His throat stiffened again. He patted his pocket for the thickness of a freshly ironed handkerchief.

Albert skidded to a halt, his back wheel overtaking the front. He kicked out the bicycle-stand but after a tremulous moment, the heavy frame clattered to the ground. The boy ignored it and rushed up the path. 'It's just arrived, sir!' He panted dramatically, delved under a clumsy gas mask in his box-satchel, then thrust a receipt book and pencil towards the doctor. 'Sign here, please.' The proud apprentice rubbed his knees, eyes sparkling with excitement, red cheeks glowing from his freckled face.

Hadn't the lad realised, telegrams in wartime meant unwelcome news? Charles rummaged in his pocket for a halfpenny. Albert beamed.

'Go!' the doctor said, reluctant to read the dispatch while the boy gawped.

Martha appeared in the cottage doorway, her hair tied in rags and covered by a robust net that reminded Charles of the trout in Parley Brook. Her eyes had that same blank stare of fatality.

He would need to fish later, to be alone to cry, to come to terms, and to gather his strength to support dearest Martha.

'Go,' the doctor repeated. Albert lolloped back to his bike. As the gate slammed behind him, a cloud of pigeons took to the air, wings applauding. They circled, then settled in a discontented line on the roof, watching, waiting.

Charles ripped open the telegram, knowing it was futile to hope. He read the single line, then reached for his handkerchief.

Martha, face ghostly pale, rushed to his side. Her nails dug into his arm, clinging to hope and her husband. 'It's about Gertie?' she whispered. Now, her eyes sparked with hope, or fear, he couldn't tell which. She peered up into his face.

He nodded. His throat tightened so much he couldn't speak. Despite his efforts, tears brimmed, then overflowed. Martha let out a howl so heavy with grief that the pigeons took to the heavens again.

Charles wrapped his arms around his wife and pulled her fiercely against his heaving chest. He swallowed hard, took a deep breath, and forced the words he had to say.

'Don't, Martha. Don't. She's safe. Our Gertie's safe.'

CHAPTER 1
SHELLY

Dover, present day.

A WHITE CHURCH WITH BLUE domed roof dazzled against a backdrop of the Aegean Sea. The glossy travel brochure lay on the kitchen table. Shelly Summer placed a hand flat on her chest and turned away to suppress anxiety palpitations. At the kitchen window of her cliff-top cottage in Dover, she gripped the edge of the porcelain sink and peered out across the grey English Channel.

Shelly knew how people saw her: a busy vet who was respected and admired. But she needed an escape – to be alone for seven days, to lie on a sunbed and lose herself in a good book. To swim in the warm Mediterranean and dive to an abandoned wreck. If only she could come to terms with what happened . . . She tried, really she did, but it still haunted her. She could not forgive herself, and wondered if David would, if he could. But, it was too late for that. Twenty years too late.

She would embrace Greece, love every moment of her great escape; the beaches, villages, food, music and perhaps even find a little romance. Then return home refreshed, ready to face the obligations of another year.

Now, there was an added complication. Her father, Gordon, always grumpy in the morning, was becoming so forgetful. He was a constant worry, and perhaps even a danger to himself.

Gordon ignored the brochure and set about consuming his boiled egg. The only sounds were the clock ticking towards 8 a.m. and the wind whistling under the kitchen door.

Shelly kicked the old sausage dog draught-excluder into place, then sat at the table.

'Sleep all right, Dad?'

He grunted and without looking up, asked, 'You going away, then? 'Oliday, is it?'

He'd spotted the brochure.

'It's Eve's. She said I have annual leave from last year and I thought, perhaps, a week in Greece. Will you come?' A flurry of wind and rain hit the window. She tried to keep the desperation out of her voice. 'Wouldn't it be nice to get some sun on your shoulders, Dad?'

Gordon didn't reply.

'It sounds really lovely. Listen to this . . .' She flipped the brochure open and read from a random page, injecting a wistful tone into her voice.

'*The island of Syros, heart and soul of the Cyclades, sits under the blue brilliance of a Greek sky. Crystal-clear water and deserted beaches await. More traditional than its famous neighbours, Santorini and Mykonos, Syros is a working island that preserves the glamour of a bygone age. Villages nestle in the natural landscape. Alleyways wind around white houses where plumbago and bougainvillea emblazon picturesque hamlets.*'

She glanced at him. He'd stopped eating.

'*The capital, Hermoupoli, is dotted with churches and cathedrals, both Orthodox and Catholic. Majestic buildings of outstanding beauty and architecture tumble down the hillside and look out over the warm Aegean Sea. Among sponge divers and shipbuilders, and fishermen and florists, tavernas await with their gastronomic delights and amazing hospitality.'*

She looked up again. 'I've just thought, wasn't Syros the island we all went to when I was a little girl?'

His eyes narrowed, peering into the depths of a distant memory.

'My first holiday, Dad. You and Mum nearly wet yourselves laughing when Gran Gertie tucked her skirt into her knickers and held my hand while we paddled. Don't you remember? I tripped and grabbed her skirt and nearly pulled her pants down.' Shelly stopped and smiled. 'There's a photo somewhere.' She studied his face, looking for some recall. 'You bought a white hat that said KISS ME QUICK.'

A smile spread over Gordon's face. 'Oh . . . yes.' The toast popped up.

'I couldn't read "quick", remember, Dad?' Overwhelmed by the happy memory, joy had been a rare visitor in that kitchen for so many years. She slathered her toast with butter and jam. 'You'd ask, "What does my hat say, Shelly?" and I'd read so carefully, spelling it out. "Kiss – me—" and you'd sweep me up and kiss me all over and blow raspberries on my belly until we were all exhausted from squealing with laughter.' Amused, then saddened, she remembered the big, generous man with a wide smile that her father was in those days.

They sat, lost in reminiscences, lonely in the brick cottage until Shelly continued. 'I told Mum she looked like a film star in her white bikini and she said, "Thank you, you look like a princess in yours." I can hear her voice . . .' Silence united them again then Shelly said, 'It's an odd thing, Dad, but I've forgotten almost everything from before . . . you know, and then that holiday comes back as clear as day.'

Gordon grunted. 'It was Gertie who insisted we went to that island, Syros. It was really important to her, like she was on a pilgrimage. On most days, she'd disappear after lunch, and return all red-eyed and clearly upset at dinner time. Your mum tried to get her to drink a strong cup of tea, to calm down.'

'Wouldn't she say where she'd been?' Shelly asked.

'No, not a word – but wait, I haven't finished tellin' yer. Gertie nabbed the waiter and said, "Young man! Forget the tea. Bring me a double gin!" with no notion of foreign measures. When the Greek waiter, who seemed to be rather fond of her, asked, "What would you like in your drink, madam: orange, lime or tonic?" Gertie would say, "I'm partial to a splash of lime, but that would be fresh lime, young man, like we had on the *Britannic*, not that cheap cordial they serve in the bar, thank you." He would make a little salute, then bow, which cheered her up a lot. He'd go to a tree in the street and pluck a lime especially for her.'

'The *Britannic*? Never heard of it. What is it, an island?'

His head came up with a slightly surprised look. 'No, it was the largest hospital ship in the world, ever.'

'A hospital ship? You've lost me. Was she taken ill abroad or something?'

'No, she was a nurse in the First World War. Anyway, Gertie always refused to talk about where she'd been on those afternoons, but she repeated the same routine every day.'

'I don't remember any of that, but I was very young. What a mystery. I wonder where she went.'

'So did we. When I offered to follow her, your mother insisted we respect her privacy. Every morning she'd come to the breakfast table, take aspirin, drink strong black coffee, and squint murderously at us all, but she never divulged where she'd been.'

'How would she even know where to go?'

'Well, she'd spent time in Syros before. During the war.'

'Gran Gertie was a nurse, on a ship, in the First World War? Well, you live and learn. I'm quite shocked that I didn't know.'

'Why should you know? Most people don't know what their grandparents did, never mind their great-grandparents.'

'That's fascinating, don't you think? I'd love to go back to Syros, wouldn't you, Dad? Will you come with me – please?'

He sniffed hard. 'I'm not up to it, Shelly. Not without your mum. It's no good hoping. You go, love. Have a smashing time, you deserve it. You don't want a miserable old beggar like me tagging along. Besides, I can't leave me birds,' he said, bringing her back to Dover and his precious pigeons on a miserable Monday morning.

'I see . . . never mind. I might not go. It was just an idea. A silly whim.' No point in making him feel bad if he didn't feel up to it, she thought. Nevertheless, she tried one last time. 'It's just . . . well, the brochure looked amazing after all the rain we've had.' Her eyes flicked up to his face. The silence stretched out and the room closed in. Shelly had to get away before she suffocated.

*   *   *

Sunshine and smiles in the Med were like balm to her troubled soul. A week of photography and scuba diving would anchor her for another twelve months. They had been David's two greatest pleasures, too. He and his best friend Simon used to dive wherever they could. It was an odd thing, but when she returned home, Shelly felt cleansed and guilt-free for a while. As if she had lived a small part of David's dream. If she left the brochure on the table, Dad might realise how desperately she needed a break. He would never say he didn't want her to go, but she sensed he

9

was uncomfortable about being left alone for a week. Old age was catching up, and about time, he was eighty.

She closed her eyes and imagined sliding into the sparkling turquoise Aegean, the delicious tingle of saltwater cooling her bronzed skin. Then her shoulders dropped.

Gordon stared accusingly over his glasses. 'I know what you're thinking – that you can't leave me alone for a week – but I'll be fine, Shelly, honestly.' He pushed his breakfast plate away. 'I 'aven't quite lost the plot yet, you know? You go while you can. God knows, you work hard enough all year. I can always get Bill Grundy to stop over for a few days if it will make you feel better.'

Shelly's jaw dropped. 'You will not!'

'Why's that then? You afraid we'll have too much fun?' His white eyebrows were bobbing. 'Spoilsport!'

She stifled a laugh, then her heart melted. What was this, her dad making a joke? 'I'm afraid you'll use my pressure cooker to try and build a still in the kitchen again. You're like a pair of naughty kids when you get together.'

Despite the banter, her concern remained. Last month, he had set fire to the chip pan and could have been badly burned if she hadn't stopped him tipping blazing oil into the sink. Only a week ago, she had returned from an evening call-out and found he had gone to bed and left the back door wide open.

She tried again. 'Think about it, Dad. It would do you a lot of good. When was the last time you went away?'

'Bruges, on the coach with the club, just before . . .' He stared at the half-eaten boiled egg with a sudden look of disgust, as if staring into a crystal ball, seeing the worst of his past right there in the golden yolk. Startled for a second, they glanced at each other, then both turned their eyes to the toast. 'You know, your mum . . .'

'That's more than twenty years ago, Dad.' Gordon Summer had never moved on from his wife's death. Consequently, the widower's wounds had never healed. She wondered if her father would consider going for some grief counselling, but the subject needed time and persuasion and she was already running late.

'Is it really that long, Shelly love? Seems like yesterday.' His voice faded to almost a whisper. 'Still hurts like yesterday too.' His wide eyes stared into the past. 'I guess it must be. Same year as my sixtieth, wasn't it? Remember that party she put on?' He tilted his head to one side, eyes misted for a moment, then a look of intense joy filled his face. 'Bloody marvellous, wasn't it?' he whispered. 'Remember the cake? All my friends from Dover Homer Club . . . and me mates from the docks.' He gazed around the kitchen, grinning at their ghosts, the light in his eyes shining right into Shelly's heart.

She stood still for a few seconds, enraptured, and reluctant to distract him from the wonder of his daydream. Perhaps she should do a party for his eightieth. But the kitchen clock drew her attention and the moment faded.

'Of course, that was when I still had a job, Shelly,' he grumbled.

'I'd better go, Dad. Busy day at the surgery. Lunch is in the microwave. Four minutes. It's all set, just press the start button, OK?' She kissed him on the cheek.

Reaching for his e-cigarette, he noticed the fluorescent-pink sticky-note on the microwave door. She caught his withering *I'm not stupid* look right between her eyes and decided to ignore it.

'See you later, Dad.'

* * *

In the surgery later that morning, Eve ran an artistically painted fingernail down the appointment book. 'Holiday all booked then?' she called to Shelly.

'I wish! Dad hates the idea of flying, and he won't abandon his pigeons. I can't leave him on his own for a whole week. God knows what catastrophe I'd come back to.'

'Have you thought about renting him a room at The Rose and Crown?'

'I did, but he'll just go home once I'm on the plane.'

'Can't someone stay at yours?'

'That's what he suggested, but how would you feel about Bill Grundy scratching and farting in your bed?'

Eve hooted with laughter. 'Not the dreamboat I'd imagine between your sheets.' She did a little shudder. 'Have you joined that dating agency yet?'

'Oh, stop it!' Shelly rolled her eyes. 'I filed the brochure in the kitchen bin, where it belongs. Talking of romance, we've got three cat neuters this morning, better crack on, so to speak. If you prep the anaesthetics, I'll shave them and do the job once they're under the influence. That leaves you, Miss Glamour-nails, free to man the counter and do the paper-work. OK?'

'Sounds like a plan.' Both women set about their respective jobs until Eve broke the silence. 'Anyway, I thought your cottage had three bedrooms. Couldn't Bill Grundy sleep in the other one?'

'It's full of junk. Dad's become a bit of a hoarder since Mum died. That's not a bad idea, though. I might tell him I'll go on holiday if he lets me clear his rubbish out of the spare room, so that Bill can sleep there.'

'Get someone in to do it; those house clearance people.'

'Ha! He'd have a hissy fit! Besides, Mum's clothes are still in the wardrobe. I don't know how he'd feel about getting rid of them and, to be honest, I'll find it pretty hard myself.'

Eve raised her head. 'Sorry, really thoughtless of me. But I could come around this weekend and we'll do it together. And you'll owe me a pub lunch, right?'

'Thanks, you're very kind, but I'll get around to it, honestly.'

'Listen, Shelly, I don't mean to be blunt, but you've had more than twenty years.'

Shelly slumped into a chair. 'I don't know where the time's gone, Eve. I should move on, I know it, but I can't seem able to let go. The truth is, I don't want to . . . I'm still hanging on to every memory.'

Eve frowned, sat beside her and placed a hand on her shoulder. 'Shelly, come on. Is this about more than your mother's clothes? Please don't tell me you're still blaming yourself . . . you were sixteen!'

Remaining silent, Shelly went to the sink and scrubbed her hands viciously.

'Perhaps you should talk about it?' Eve said. 'You know I'm always here for you.'

Shelly peered into Eve's eyes, opened her mouth to speak, but felt tears rise. She wanted to talk about it, to tell those close to her what had really happened that awful year, the whole story from beginning to end. It had shredded her life and made any future relationship impossible, simply because she could never forgive them; never forgive herself. Never.

She snapped her mouth shut and shook her head. 'No, I'm fine, really.'

Eve sighed. 'OK, say no more, but I *will* be around on Sunday to sort that bedroom. We'll photograph everything too, just for the memories. Scrapbooking, you know? And then I'm starting on you, madam. Hairdressers, nail salon, and some new clothes, right?'

'Thanks, but really, I've got better things to do with my money.'

'Shelly Summer, you've no right depriving the world of that beautiful woman you're hiding! Come on, what do you say? Just do it to please me, then we'll go out for a meal and a drink for my birthday.'

Shelly frowned. 'Your birthday's in October.'

'So what? You'll be early for once.'

'Bollocks . . .' Shelly said, then laughed. 'And if we don't move ourselves, the owners will return to find the cats still have theirs.'

Eve giggled. 'OK, I get it, change the subject, but I'm not giving up,' she promised.

* * *

Shelly and Eve became friends in school but lost touch when Eve studied in Liverpool and Shelly at Oxford. They became partners in the veterinary business, and got on tremendously well. Quite remarkable for two opposite people.

Eve was all glamour and high-maintenance. She would never admit to being past thirty-five, and due to the Botox, hyaluronic acid, lash and nail extensions and laser treatments, she looked less than thirty. She knew every new exercise regime, diet, and fashion trend, and had built-in radar for detecting wealthy, handsome men from a hundred metres.

Shelly, on the other hand, was not interested in her looks, men, or fashion. Shelly was an achiever. She collected skills, certificates, and awards like Eve collected lipsticks and perfumes.

* * *

That evening, when her father had gone to bed, Shelly opened the door of the spare room and surveyed the contents. There were boxes everywhere. It seemed like a mammoth task but if she did one box each evening, six would be gone by Sunday. She lifted a large shoe box off the Lloyd Loom bedside cabinet, took it downstairs, and used a damp cloth to wipe away a thick layer of dust. That box would do to start with. Probably full of rubbish for the bin.

She lifted the lid, puzzled by the contents at first, then she recognised the ancient cassette player and collection of tapes. It had belonged to her great-grandmother, Gran Gertie. The tapes were labelled THE MEMOIRS OF GERTIE SMITH: TAPE 1,2, and so on.

She plugged it in, loaded cassette one, and pressed play.

CHAPTER 2
GERTIE

Dover, 1990.

MY NAME IS GERTIE SMITH, and I'm recording my life story on these cassette tapes for my darling family, especially Margarete and Shelly, my granddaughter and great-granddaughter. After a happy life at White Cottage, I'm now living at The Gables Retirement Home, in Dover. I've been blessed with great love in my life, and also some heartbreaking sadness. You will learn that where there's passion there's pain, especially regarding those we hold dear. I hope by telling you my story, showing you what I overcame, I might give you a little extra strength when *you* need it. I found the most difficult thing we have to learn in life, is to let go. Let go of guilt, anger, and blame; and the hardest of all is to let go of those we love, my darlings. But this is something we must do, for their sakes, and ours.

My story starts on Wednesday, 5 August 1914, with the outbreak of the First World War, though we called it the Great War in my day.

I was born in The White House, now known as White Cottage, on Lighthouse Lane in 1898, and had a happy childhood with my older siblings, Arthur and Sissy. My father, Charles Smith, was the local doctor, and my mother, Martha, was a saint who took care of us all. They were good parents and I loved my family dearly.

Like any sixteen-year-old, I wanted to stay in bed that fateful morning, but my father's raised voice drifted upstairs. I slipped into my robe and slippers and hurried to the drawing room where my family gathered around Father, looking over his shoulder.

GREAT BRITAIN DECLARES WAR ON GERMANY
The following announcement was issued from the Foreign Office at 12.15 a.m. Owing to the summary rejection by the German government of the request made by His Majesty's Government for assurances . . .

Father fell silent for a moment. 'Never mind what's happening abroad, we've got our own problems here with the crisis in Ireland!' he boomed, shaking his newspaper the way our turkey-cock shakes his feathers when a hen comes near. He dropped the broadsheet onto the coffee table and started pacing.

'This is Churchill's doing, and Grey's speech in the house, yesterday! They've led us into this ridiculous state of affairs!'

Arthur picked up the paper. 'Look, Father, there's a call for military volunteers to serve Britain. I'll sign up, of course. It all sounds rather exciting. It will be over by Christmas, surely.'

Mother's hand went over her mouth.

'Don't look so worried, Mother, we'll soon show them what's what,' Arthur promised.

Fully dressed and perfectly groomed, Sissy sat stiffly with her hands in her lap. When she spoke, it was with a certain aloofness. 'You see, Father? If we women had the vote – and were represented in parliament – we would have objected to a war. I wonder what Mrs Pankhurst has to say about the matter.'

Oh, how I adored my courageous sister! One day I would be exactly like her, brave and bold and a champion for all women.

Father glared at her. 'Don't talk nonsense, Sissy. This is not the time for your games, and parliament's not the place for girls!'

Mother put her hand over her mouth again to muffle a whimper, then, as if catching a little bravery from her daughter she spoke tentatively. 'Now, now, dear. I think Sissy is making the point that she's on your side.'

Before Father could roar again, there was a tap on the door and Mrs Cooper, our three-day-domestic entered, springs of ginger curls escaping her starched white cap. 'I've watered the horse and fed the chickens. Eggs are in the larder, ma'am. Can I get on wi' the beds?'

Father placed his fists on his hips. 'Do you know we're at war with Germany, Mrs Cooper?'

The smile fell from her apple cheeks and her jowls quivered. 'War, sir? I heard some such gossip over the bank holiday. Demonstrations in Trafalgar Square and the like reported in the newspaper. But I ask you, Dr Smith, will it stop the hens laying? I think not.' She smoothed her spotless apron and folded her hands over her round belly. 'Mr Cooper can't see as it will make any difference to 'is pigs but, to be honest, I'd be worried if I had a son of soldiering age.' She glanced at Arthur.

Father patted his cravat then slipped out of his smoking jacket. 'We're an island, therefore in danger of siege in the event of war reaching our shores. I'm going to take you all into town to buy as much sugar, tea, bully beef and flour as you can carry before it's in short supply. Starving people out has won many a battle and we must make sure it never happens here. Gertie, go and get dressed right away.'

Though reluctant to miss the conversation, I did. Breakfast was rushed, then Father took us into town in the automobile. Dover thronged with like-minded people. Both lower and upper decks of the trams were overflowing, and one would wonder how the conductor got around. Queues of shoppers snaked out of doorways and onto the streets. Posters, pasted onto walls and windows, called for able-bodied men to sign up and defend the Empire. Everywhere buzzed with excitement, fervour, urgency.

*　*　*

Arthur came home that evening and at dinner announced that he had joined the army. 'I'll work two weeks' notice at Frister & Sons, then I'm off to training camp. Honestly, I won't miss being an accountant one little bit.'

Mother, who was serving squab pie, clattered the dish to the table. 'No! You could get shot by one of those nasty Huns. Father, tell him he can't go, you won't allow it.'

*　*　*

Sissy went into town with Arthur the next morning, the first day of his official notice at Frister & Sons. According to Arthur's account over dinner that evening, she marched into the office after him and spoke boldly to Mr Frister Snr.

'I've come to offer my services, sir,' she said, looking the old man in the eye. 'I'm prepared to work with my brother, without pay, until he leaves, then step into his place until his return at the end of the war.'

'Have you lost your senses? This is no place for a *girl*. Go home to your mother!' demanded Mr Frister.

'With respect, sir, whoever replaces Arthur is also likely to sign up before long and, as a consequence, you will be obliged to start training someone new again. The sensible thing would be for you to employ me, I'm a quick learner and will be a loyal and trustworthy employee.'

Mr Frister blustered and glared at Arthur. 'I'll thank you to accompany your sister to the door, Master Smith, and bid her *not* to return. We've wasted too much of the morning already.'

'Yes, sir. Sorry, sir.'

Sissy was so furious that Arthur hadn't backed her, she locked herself in the bedroom and refused to dine with us.

The next day, the National Union of Women's Suffrage Societies announced that it was suspending all activity until the conflict was over. Mrs Emmeline Pankhurst encouraged suffragettes to focus on the war effort. She asked women to take up the roles of men in factories and, on 10 August, we learned that our government was releasing the thousand incarcerated suffragettes from prison.

'Hurrah!' Sissy rejoiced. 'It takes a *war* for our leaders to see sense. The same men that got us into this horrible situation, now see us women as useful human beings!' she cried. 'I'm applying for a job, immediately.'

Mother had taken to whimpering every time one of us spoke.

'Don't be ridiculous,' Father boomed. 'What can you do?'

'I can drive as well as any man!' Sissy proclaimed.

'Impossible! You've never been behind a wheel, never mind tackled the gears.'

'With respect, Father, neither had you until you acquired our marvellous Model T.' She met his eyes. 'Or I might train to be a doctor, like you.' She gave me a quick glance and I sensed mischief. 'You're admired by everyone, Father, and I would be proud to learn your skills.' Another glance came my way. 'Just imagine, if Gertie and I followed in your footsteps, you could hang a sign over the surgery: DR SMITH & DAUGHTERS.'

Father's face turned puce.

* * *

Two days later, Sissy and I signed on for our St John Ambulance training. I dreamed of being a nurse, and Sissy hoped to be the first woman ambulance driver for the Red Cross. Father and Mother were shocked. This was not the behaviour of 'nice' young ladies. However, much to Father's surprise, we both achieved our certificates in first aid, and also understood a great deal about the workings of the human body. Meal times were most entertaining as my sister pestered Father with medical questions. He, in turn, gave up trying to remind Sissy of her 'place', and I do believe he was secretly quite proud of her.

My darling brother had his inoculations, which gave him a horrible scab on the top of his arm and made him feel quite wretched for a few days. Then, he went off for training on Salisbury Plain where, he told us later, he spent most of his days digging trenches, learning to clean and fire his rifle, and polish his boots. He was sent to fight in a major battle – Mons, Belgium, on 23 August.

Sissy, who was itching to do something, anything, managed to get employment at a distant munitions factory. She promised to write, and two weeks after her departure, I received a letter.

My dearest sister, Gertie,

I miss you terribly! I am writing you a different letter from Ma and Pa because I don't want them to worry.

The munitions factory is buried between sand dunes and surrounded by a trench. It is forbidden to say where in case Kaiser

Bill gets our post. All of us women workers stay in a hostel which is awfully basic, a mile away from the factory. Life is hard! We're not allowed to wear anything metal, no hooks, or metal bones in our stays, so most of us have abandoned this undergarment. Oh, the joy of being able to breathe and not have your middle pinched into pleats!

They wake us at 5 a.m. to break the ice on our water jugs. Breakfast is bread with lard and sweet tea. We walk a mile to work in our khaki uniforms, which are not too bad, and a heavy cape which we clutch around ourselves against the bitter cold. Our boots are diabolical, unladylike and uncomfortable. Thank God for Vaseline which we smear on our heels and bunion-bone to prevent more blisters. We must wrap our hair in muslin, so we look like dumplings ready for the pot.

We slave through a twelve-hour day, all windows closed, and the silence is peculiarly sinister as we pack these instruments of death and torture. I fill sixty-pound shells with TNT which are ammunition for some great cannons that are bound to bring victory for our brave soldiers.

I often think of Arthur and hope a German woman is not packing shrapnel into a shell that might harm him. Although I'm determined to serve my country, I hate to think of the distress brought to some mother in our enemy's country by the bombs I help to put together.

A woman died from TNT poisoning last week, Gertie. The girls in one section turn yellow from the explosives – even the whites of their eyes – and twenty workers were killed on Thursday in an explosion. We were hurried into the surrounding trenches for fear of a massive detonation but the trenches were not wide enough so we had to squeeze in. Then we realised, the mud walls teemed with slugs! Cripes! How I wished we wore trousers.

Yesterday a government photographer came around – we were all afraid his flash would blow us to Kingdom come. He was terrifically good-looking, so you can imagine the smiles from two thousand women blinding the poor chap. The gossip is, Lloyd George himself sent the photographer, though we're not sure if it's for the Pathé News or the broadsheets. I'll let you know when I hear.

There is a whisper they're building a military hospital nearer home, so I will apply to nurse there. It's my dream to take care of our wounded soldiers.

I hope everything is going well for you, dearest Gertie. Try and stand up to Father once in a while. Do write back!

That's all for now.

Love from your devoted,

Sissy

I touched my cheek remembering Sissy's goodbye kiss. Oh, I missed her terribly. The correspondence trembled in my hand. I quickly dried the letter when a tear splashed onto her precious words and puckered the paper.

* * *

When Arthur and Sissy came home on leave, we sat around my brother in the parlour, enraptured by Arthur's stories. He fed Mother all the best bits of army life, and kept the less savoury morsels for himself.

'Greece is terrific, Mother, it's easy to see why kings and queens go there to take the waters and watch plays by Sophocles and Euripides in the ancient amphitheatres.' She would lower her embroidery hoop and gaze at him. 'The great marble auditoriums are always outdoors, Mother, and on summer

23

nights they're filled with thousands of people. Their perfect design means everyone can hear the actors and music with no need for a single microphone.'

Mother's eyes widened in wonder, Sissy and I exchanged gleeful glances.

'Tell us more, dear brother!' Sissy cried.

Arthur smiled softly at Mother and at that moment, I loved him more than ever.

'Greece lay beneath a sky bluer than anywhere else in the world. Magnificent marble temples with columns double the height of this house strewn all over the city.' He kissed Mother's hand and bowed, as if she were royalty. 'One day, after this war, I'm going to take you to see the Parthenon, a great temple on a mountain, right in the centre of the city of Athens, Mother.' Enraptured, her face shone with love for her son. 'I will take your hand and lead you down the centre aisle as if you are the Goddess Athena herself, the Queen of Athens . . . the Queen of Greece.'

When I look back, I remember poor Arthur's hands trembled sometimes. A distant stare in his eye preceded an unexplained look of revulsion. Later, I discovered he was in torment, remembering the battle of Gallipoli. What a noble gesture, to fill our mother's heart with glory when he was suffering horrors too diabolical for us to imagine.

* * *

Both Sissy and Arthur came home for Christmas that year and we planned to have a wonderful time together. I had no true concept of what 'war' meant, or where it would lead, or how it would change our lives.

On Christmas Eve, a plane flew over and dropped a bomb on Dover. Mother and I had spent all morning baking mince pies for the carol singers when there was a terrific explosion outside.

Mother grabbed me and pulled me under the heavy kitchen table. She crossed herself and recited the 'Hail Mary' while I trembled with fear.

After a few minutes, Mother placed her hand on my cheek and whispered, 'Don't be afraid, we'll be fine.' She reached up and retrieved the cooking sherry, and there we sat for an hour, sipping the mince-pie-plonk. All my fear of being bombed was taken away by the wonder of my mother treating me like an adult . . . like an equal, for the first time in my life. For me, it was a wonderful moment of closeness that I'll never forget.

'Shall we go and look, Gertie, while we can still walk?' We both giggled nervously, then rushed out and peered over the cliff to see if there was a German gunboat pointing its cannons at our home. There were no ships to be seen, but still, Mother rolled her sleeve up and shook her fist across the English Channel.

'Don't you ever dare frighten my daughter like that again, Kaiser Bill, you dirty devil, or you'll have me to deal with!' she cried, and I could hardly walk back up the path for laughing. Still, we managed to finish making the mince pies, and nobody seemed to notice the lack of sherry, or that the pastry lids were askew.

CHAPTER 3
SHELLY

Dover, present day.

'YOU'LL BE LATE, GET AWAY with you,' Gordon said gruffly, as Shelly came downstairs for work. 'Can't afford you slacking, *and* taking exotic holidays.'

She smiled, kissed his cheek, and hurried out, almost bumping into the postman.

'Morning, vet. I've got a letter for you.' He thrust it towards her and glanced into her face with a flash of adoration.

'Thank you, Malcolm. Very kind of you to cycle all this way.' A tinge of pink brightened his plump cheeks.

'It's nothing, m-miss.'

Shelly glanced at the envelope, saw the Cambridge postmark, and felt the blood drain from her face.

He's found me then . . . after all these years, he's returned to his roots.

'Not bad news, I hope?'

Shaking her head a little too fast, she shoved the letter deep into her pocket. 'Must run, Malcolm. Busy day ahead.'

'Fancy a cuppa, Malcolm?' Dad called.

'I don't mind if I do.'

* * *

Shelly hurried outside into a bright, blustery morning. She watched a gull out over the cliff, wings spread, heading into the wind. Almost stationary, it floated on air, free, determined to be where it was. Captivated by the magnificent views and the dramatic light of stormy weather, she was reminded of her good fortune.

With her father's help, White Cottage had been mortgaged for the funds to get her through college. Evening education followed, while she gained experience as a low paid junior veterinary. The property was also surety for the funds she needed to open the practice and although people sometimes commented about their high veterinary bills, they had no idea of the costs involved.

Nevertheless, business was good and she would soon be in the clear, reaping the benefits of her many sacrifices.

Before turning the ignition, she squandered another precious minute gazing back at the cottage. It had once been The White House, a grand, five-bedroomed family home built by an ancestor. She could imagine horse-drawn carriages, and Model T Fords pulling up outside.

In the Second World War, a bomb caused dangerous cracks in the masonry and a portion of the house had to be demolished. With post-war austerity, the family decided the building was adequate with three bedrooms, so the brickwork was tidied up and the house renamed White Cottage.

She pulled the envelope from her pocket and stared at the handwriting, presumably his, DJ's. Shelly pressed it against her cheek.

Oh, if only she could see him again!

But she had to think of the long-term consequences; what good could come from digging up the past and all the pain that went with it? She had enough to deal with. What effect would it have on her father – after all, it was his fault that DJ went away. Returning the correspondence to her pocket, she started the car.

Perhaps she would open it this evening, depending on how she got on with the spare-room spring-clean.

* * *

Years back, Shelly had made a feeble effort to empty the crammed wardrobe, but within ten minutes, she was in tears. She promised herself then, she wouldn't try to sort her mother's things until she had forgiven herself for that terrible Christmas. Her mother's elegant dresses brought back many beautiful memories, but each one loomed like Marley's ghost, pointing the finger at her. A room full of hobgoblins and heartache.

She was only sixteen, when it started, and by the time she was seventeen she had lost three people she loved more than life. Now she would have to face the first of them, in the dust and gloom and memorabilia of the spare bedroom.

Perhaps the time had come to put everything right. Starting that very evening.

Shelly stood tall, ready to face her demons. She needed to move on and live her own life, free to love again, and be loved.

She set to work. Boxes of jumble that her father had shoved in there over the years were destined for the charity shop. She dragged cartons onto the landing, making space to investigate. The Women's Institute ladies had come over after her mother's funeral and packed Mum's stuff away.

Memories tumbled into Shelly's head, she must have been six or seven when her great-grandmother would gather herself up and struggle onto Shelly's bed. There, they would listen to story tapes, transported into the worlds of *Jungle Book*, *The Borrowers*, *Charlotte's Web*, and *The Snowman*.

28

Those stories were sorely missed when Gran Gertie went into the residential home. She felt a rush of love, tinged with pain at the memory.

With sudden yearning to hear Gran Gertie's voice, she fetched the tape player and listened to the next episode of her great-grandmother's memoirs.

*   *   *

Half an hour later, stunned by what she had just heard, Shelly sat on the edge of the old bed and gawped at the cassette player.

CHAPTER 4
GERTIE

Dover, 1915.

AFTER THE MINCE PIE INCIDENT, Father had the cellar cleared out and put a few essentials down there, like water and candles and a couple of old chairs just in case Kaiser Bill got more accurate with his mortars. The exercise meant that Mother could rest assured; whatever the war brought upon us, her husband and children would be safe.

When another explosion rocked our house a week later, Father ordered, 'Everyone down to the cellar, we're being attacked!'

We lifted the trapdoor and hurried down the wooden steps. After an hour with no more disturbance, Mother, Father, Mrs Cooper and I emerged with a list of things we needed if the worst happened again. A primus stove, books, crayons, paper, a jigsaw, blankets, a bucket, another jug of water.

That incident had been the first of nine thousand German bombs that fell from planes onto British soil in the Great War.

* * *

Who could have foreseen the way our lives changed over the next two years? The war gained momentum. Fokkers and Zeppelins flew over Britain dropping their payloads of bad-will and bombs. National conscription started. The government insisted that all able-bodied men join up, and Sissy's dream of being a nurse became a reality. Her letters were terrifically inspiring. Whenever I felt lonely, I'd go and sit under the big oak tree and study her correspondence. Her sense of glee shone off the page as I read.

Gertie, you're terribly lucky! How everything is changing for us women. We can become anything we choose, and isn't that absolutely spiffing? Can you imagine how terrific it would be to drive a bus, Gertie? You must imagine, yes, imagine, because that is the first stage of accomplishing your dreams. Or, you could learn to be a welder, dear sister, or a brick layer, or at worst, go and work in a factory. Stay away from the munitions factories, though. They're awfully dangerous.

I carried her letters around in my pocket and read them over and again. How could women do welding, were there no end to our skills? Just the idea made my skin tingle. Some women cut their hair, some even wore trousers! We joined together in support for our men and our country and succeeded in surprising even ourselves.

Arthur returned home on a few days leave every three months. He told us horrific stories when Mother was out of earshot. There was a haunted air about him in mid-December. We gathered together for a pretend Christmas Day. Mother, determined to spend every moment with her son, fell asleep in the chair after we'd swapped presents and eaten.

My darling Sissy was also home. She wore bright red lipstick and drew a black beauty spot on her jaw, which Father objected to, saying she looked common. She sat on Arthur's lap and threw her arms around his neck.

'Come on, Arthur, tell us what's really going on?' she said quietly. 'Ma's asleep, and you know we won't breathe a word.'

He sighed, weary and depressed. 'If it gets out that I've told you, they'll execute me, you know that?'

Sissy and I exchanged a horrified glance, then nodded.

'It's the Gallipoli campaign.' We frowned at him. 'On the land and the sea between Greece and Turkey. Turkey's on *their* side and we're supporting the admiralty, allowing allied ships to pass through the Dardanelles. They're desperate to capture Constantinople and knock Turkey out of the war, but it's not going well. If it wasn't for the Aussies, and Kiwis, we wouldn't have hung on this long. Godawful trench warfare. Gas that literally melts your eyes and lungs. Bodies everywhere, wounded and dead. Trenches running with rats at night. The casualties are unbelievable.'

'What? Real dead bodies?' I said, unable to imagine such a thing.

'Yes, Gertie, real dead bodies!' I could hear the irritation in his voice. 'That's what the rats come for, running over us when we fall asleep in the trenches.'

'Rats?' Horrified, I couldn't imagine.

'Despite the rain, it's so bloody hot there.'

I clasped my hand over my mouth and glanced at Mother. Oh goodness, if she had heard him use that language!

Arthur snorted good-humouredly when he realised he'd sworn, but then his face softened and a sad look came to his eyes. 'Sorry, darling Gertie. You're so innocent, dear sister. You wouldn't believe how often I think of you when things get too bad. When the trenches swarm with flesh flies. When there are sheets of maggots. When everyone's sick, shell-shocked, or suffering from trench foot.' He stopped and stared, trance-like. 'You see, we're not really in this war for our country, Gertie, or for King George; we're fighting for our mothers and sisters.'

We gazed at him, sadly silent until Sissy asked, 'What about food, Arthur? What do they give you?'

'The food's infested, yet we have to eat. We're all horribly weak, and tired, and so outnumbered we can hardly advance.' He shook his head. 'The situation's impossible. They say half a million casualties have gone to the hospital sorting station on a Greek island. Lemnos, I think it's called. Not too far away, but it's understaffed and overcrowded. Now the rainy season's with us, wounded men lay dying in the mud as they wait to be collected by British hospital ships.' He sighed so deeply he trembled. 'We're all doing our best, but . . .' He shook his head again. 'It's futile. We're bound to retreat before New Year. If the worst happens, Gertie, I'll remember how much I enjoyed this Christmas dinner. Promise you'll toast me every Christmas in my absence, preferably when you set the figgy pudding alight and swig the brandy.' He grinned at us all, his eyes bright with a sort of madness that I didn't understand.

That was the last time I saw my brother, Arthur. When I woke the next morning, he'd gone already. He never came back. We learned he'd died of shrapnel wounds at the hospital he'd told us about on Lemnos, waiting for a ship to bring him home.

The telegram boy came belting down Lighthouse Lane ringing his bicycle bell. I'd never seen Father cry before. The silent tears that trickled down his face were more painful than my mother's wailing as he pulled her tighter into his arms.

Sissy came home for a week.

In the misery that followed, we received a formal letter from the battalion adjutant which Father read to us all. Our darling Arthur was part of a thrust forward on the front line. We were told that his group of brave soldiers had become separated from

the main drive and came under fierce shelling. The men ha
fought bravely.

Remembering the things Arthur told us when Mother fe
asleep, I wanted to yell that it was all make believe. I was cry
ing with anger to think he had died for me! My poor brothe
had been mortally wounded in the squalor of trenches that h
himself told us swarmed with flesh flies and rats!

The letter went on in its polite, remorseful way to say tha
Corporal Smith suffered a severe head wound and was take
by hospital ship to Lemnos. Despite every effort to revive him
Corporal Smith passed away.

In the aftershock, I wondered if it was an error, perhaps ou
Arthur was still alive. 'It's a mistake,' I whispered. 'Father, surel
he can't be dead; the army must have made a mistake! So man
people dying . . . such a common name, Smith.'

Father had trouble speaking, which somehow made m
angrier. Sissy pulled me into her arms. 'No, they have tag
around their necks. There's no mistake. But remember what h
said, Gertie? He said it for a reason.'

I shook my head. 'No, no! He can't be dead, Sissy, he's m
brother! Brothers don't die!'

'Listen to me!' she continued, shaking my shoulders befor
turning to our parents. 'Mother, Father, when our Arthur wa
home, he said this: "If the worst happens, Gertie, I'll remembe
how much I enjoyed this Christmas dinner. Promise you'll toas
me every Christmas in my absence, preferably when you set th
figgy pudding alight and swig the brandy." So come on, let's pou
a tot of brandy now, for everyone, just like Arthur told us to.'

When we had charged our glasses, Father said, 'The toast i
the last line of the letter. The adjutant assures us that: Corpor

Smith has been a great asset to his country and a gallant and universally liked soldier.'

*   *   *

Sissy returned home from the munitions factory and, on her twenty-third birthday, she applied to join the Voluntary Aid Detachment. More than ever, she wished to become a nurse and soon signed up for training.

'Promise you won't go overseas, Sissy!' Mother begged.

'I promise, Mother. Many wounded soldiers have been shipped home and need help right here.'

Yet after a terrible battle on the other side of the Channel, my darling sister volunteered to nurse the wounded in France. She wrote every week and I kept all of her wonderful letters.

*   *   *

The shortage of doctors meant we hardly saw Father. When we did, it was clear that Arthur's death had taken its toll. Gone was the bombastic man who laid down the law. He quietly withdrew into himself. I took over his beloved pigeons when he hadn't the time. Since the start of the war, his birds had been used by the Pigeon Corps. Often, theirs were the only form of correspondence received by our leaders at home, from the officers on the remote front line.

The coop was built onto the outside of the house, with steps leading up to it, as the attic was Mother's sewing room. A maid's bell in the kitchen was attached to a wire across the coop entrance and when it rang, I climbed the ladder, found the bird, removed the canister from its leg, and cycled hurriedly to the police station.

Every fortnight, a despatch rider would arrive on a motorbike and sidecar. He'd take a dozen birds away, and I'd await their return. I was paid generously – twenty shillings a week – and they also supplied a sack of corn for the birds. I loved my job, although sometimes the young policemen would tease me and make me blush. I wanted to follow Sissy and be a nurse and there's no place for shyness in nursing, so it was vital I gain control of my fiery cheeks as soon as possible.

Life reached an uneasy harmony, but then we received a letter from France. Sissy had come down with the Spanish influenza, which was killing people faster than the war. We were all afraid and watched each other for the symptoms: headache, temperature, dry cough.

Please, Sissy, get better soon!

I was sitting under the tree, about to read one of my sister's letters. In my mind's eye, I could see her smiling face and hear her so clearly.

It's a brave new world, Gertie. Make the most of it.

I must have been staring up the lane because suddenly I realised the telegram boy was cycling towards me but I could still hear Sissy's voice.

Don't be sad, Gertie. We'll meet again, I promise you.

I jumped up to run indoors, not wanting to sign for the telegram while Father was out. Before I'd reached the door, I turned and hurried back to the gate, my heart thumping. Unable to speak for the pain of holding back tears, I took the envelope and signed the receipt. There was no way I wanted to put Mother through the agony.

When I turned to walk away, Albert said, 'Sorry, but you should read it, miss, in case you want to send a reply.'

I stood there like a fool – what should I do?

Albert said, 'Do you want me to read it to you?'

It was too much. I shook my head and tore it open.

It is with deep regret . . .

The influenza had quickly turned into pneumonia. Despite the doctors' efforts, in a matter of days Sissy had passed away.

The following weeks were dark and empty, and my parents were bleak with sorrow. The funeral drained us all, we felt such loss. Mother continued to set two extra places at the table, and Father withdrew further into himself. I became most aware of how sacred, yet fragile, life is. Despite the continuing bombing raids, life went on without our brave Arthur and my darling Sissy. I searched for a way to make up for my parents' loss, but all I managed was to feel an immense sense of loneliness.

*   *   *

A poster on the police station wall caught my eye. Three women in starched white aprons and clipped veils stood side by side.

VAD. NURSING MEMBERS urgently needed. Apply inside.

Trembling with excitement, I felt Sissy's spirit rise inside me. I had to try! For the first time since my sister's death, I felt a glimmer of true purpose.

'Your father's not going to be pleased, Gertie,' Sergeant Miller said, handing me the form. 'Fill this in and submit it, along with any other relevant papers, at the town hall.'

I raced home again, the wind coursing through my hair. I snatched my St John certificate and my French and German schoolbooks, tossed them into the wicker shopper on the front of my bicycle, and pedalled like fury back into Dover.

My heart was thumping by the time I reached the town hall. I retrieved lipstick, powder, and a compact from under the gas mask in my saddlebag – there was no need to rouge my glowing cheeks but I applied the lipstick.

With all my heart and soul, I ached to nurse the sick and injured, to be the heroine of my own life and the lives of others. To be remembered for who *I* was, to demonstrate to my parents that I was as valuable as my sister and just as capable of performing noble deeds. Having worshipped Sissy until the day she died, I knew the time had come for me to rise up and prove myself. I hurried up the town hall steps as fast as I could.

My age, eighteen, was a problem, so I lied at the desk. 'Twenty-three, sir,' I claimed, knowing this was the minimum for female volunteers. Lucky to be taller than most eighteen-year-olds, I stretched up and proudly lifted my chin.

Had he recognised the lie?

Breathe, look confident, be Sissy! It's all in a good cause.

'I'm quite capable, sir,' I said boldly. My heart thudded as I handed over my papers and flung my shoulders back. 'I passed my St John exam with merit because my father's a doctor. Also, as you can see from my notebooks, I am fluent in French, and German.' This was a gross exaggeration. 'As you know, sir, these languages are a great advantage in these difficult times.'

I could not believe I had spoken to him like that!

His eyes narrowed as he studied me, then he nodded and handed over a list. 'These are the things you'll need for training camp, young woman.'

Back home, I considered my actions. I was fulfilling Sissy's dreams. She wanted me to be bolder, to fight for equality, and stand up for my rights. But what about my dear parents? My heart was breaking for them. Their dread would be devastating, especially my mother's who believed everything came in threes. From the cliff top, I gazed over the English Channel, watching ships, trying to visualise what it would be like to work on one as a warrior in the war for my country. Mrs Pankhurst would be proud, and once my parents had got over their fears, they would be proud too.

I informed Mother and Father of the application at dinner that evening. Father shouted and banged the table top so hard, the salt cellar toppled. Mother cried and begged me to withdraw my application, but I explained that I would help save the lives of young men like my darling brother. Perhaps, if there had been one more pair of hands, my sister may not have been so terribly tired and overworked. If she had been stronger, she may not have caught the influenza in the first place.

Father stood and banged his fists on the table again. 'How dare you use your departed brother and sister as a weapon to get your own way! You will never attain the skills and self-discipline to step into their shoes!'

His words felt like a knife had been plunged into my chest.

I looked him straight in the eyes. 'I know, Father.'

The room fell silent. Ashamed of using my siblings to change my parents' minds, I felt abandoned.

I retired to my room, where I cried and cried, proving my father right. Sissy never cried; she would throw a tantrum.

After much thought, I decided to take the first step and train. After all, I may never be accepted into the Voluntary Aid Detachment, I explained to Mother.

'You can't go, Gertie! I forbid it!' she said the next morning. 'I haven't slept a wink, nor shall I if you persist with this madness.'

'Mother, you can't deny me my dream. Besides, I must do it for poor Arthur and Sissy. It was Sissy's dream too, remember? What Father said hurt me terribly, Mother, but what I said was true, if there'd been one extra pair of hands in the hospital, Arthur might have made it. Or at least I could have done my best – instead of doing nothing.'

It was difficult to hold back tears of frustration, but I had to. 'Do you know how hard it's been, growing up in the shadow of two such wonderful people? Now I have a chance to shine, and perhaps help some other mother's son. Would you deny me that chance? Would you deny that mother of another wounded soldier the chance of getting him back alive? Please, the last thing I want to do is hurt you or Father, but you can't keep me locked away, like a princess in a tower, forever. I know you love me and want to protect me, but I need to grow, Mother.'

Our eyes locked, wide and hard in an effort to hold back pain.

'All right,' Mother said quietly after a long silence. 'I'll help you.'

We went up to the attic, her sewing room, where she removed a crystal vase of dried honesty and a lace doily from the treadle-top, then set up the Singer. In the corner stood a wooden chest where Mother kept assorted linens and special materials. Next to that, a canvas-covered dressmaker's form with a beautifully turned walnut neck and stand.

Together, we sewed the things I needed, finally embroidering my name on everything in neat chainstitch. We hardly spoke, both of us full of emotion. My name anchored, tightly stitching my spirit to those earthly things. So long as my name was there, it felt as though everything would work out.

I recall it was an odd list:

One calico bag – six feet four inches by three feet – to be filled with straw at camp.

A pillow-bag.

Two blankets.

A Macintosh rug, if available.

Two towels, a duster, and two tea cloths.

Besides these things I had to take a set of cutlery, a shoe brush, a bicycle or candle lamp, an enamel basin, cup, saucer, two plates, and a block of soap.

'Here,' Mother said. 'Sissy would want you to have this, Gertie.' She placed Sissy's silver fob watch in my palm. My parents had bought it for her when she signed up to train as a nurse.

I read the inscription on the back. *For our daughter, with love.*

'Oh, Mother, can't you see that I have to take this step for Sissy too.' Then, I was in my mother's arms and we were both crying. 'I'll wear it for Sissy and treasure it always.'

CHAPTER 5
SHELLY

Dover, present day.

DESPITE THE DUST AND GLOOM, a spark of excitement tingled as Shelly remembered a trunk of memorabilia under the bed. Better to go through that on her own in case it made her emotional. If there were any clues to her own personal tragedy in there, she didn't want Eve seeing them.

A moment passed before Shelly realised the kitchen phone was ringing. She hurried downstairs and picked up.

'Hi, it's me, Eve. Sorry to let you down at such short notice, but I can't make it today.'

'Is everything all right?'

'Absolutely, more than all right. It's just I'm running a bit late, and now I have to cook breakfast for someone.' Her voice trailed off to a whisper. 'Nudge-nudge . . .'

'Shameless!'

'Listen, don't forget to get that holiday booked! Blue skies, turquoise water, remember? You've got all day, Shelly, no excuses now!'

Shelly laughed. 'I will, no worries. See you tomorrow.' She hung up; the smile still on her face.

'Who you seeing tomorrow then?' her father said with a hopeful glint in his eye as he entered the kitchen. 'Boyfriend, is it?'

'No, Eve, at work. She was going to come over to help me clear out the spare room, but she's been side-tracked.'

'Clear out?' he exclaimed, the mischief falling from his face. 'Shelly, you won't throw any of your mother's stuff away, will you? I couldn't bear to part with it, let alone imagine some other woman touching her things.'

It's been more than twenty years.

'Of course not, Dad. Don't worry. I'm sorting it into boxes and we'll go through each one together, OK?'

His shoulders dropped. 'That Malcolm's a nice young man, don't you think?'

'The postman? Yes, he's sweet.'

'You won't mind if he comes over once in a while then.'

'This is your home, for goodness' sake. You can bring your friends over any time. Listen, did you know Gran Gertie had recorded her memoirs?'

'I did. They're for you when you grow up.'

'Dad, I'm thirty-seven years old. When were you planning to give me the tapes?'

'I forgot about them. It's probably safe for you to listen to them now.'

'Safe?'

'Well, you need to be a bit, um, broad-minded, like.'

'Are you blushing, Dad?'

'No, yer daft bugger!'

* * *

Gran Gertie had been Shelly's constant companion in her early years when Mum was postmistress in the village. She recalled the family matriarch's silver hair, always pulled back in a bun, and her chin lifted so she peered down her nose. Gertie's soft, freckly hands had oddly shaped knuckles and gentle fingers that dabbed Magic Milk on Shelly's scraped knees. Gertie removed splinters, sharpened homework pencils, and plaited her long hair before school. Those hands also tucked her into bed before a bedtime story each night.

Shelly smiled, Gran Gertie's fairy tales always had a naughty elf that said the forbidden words – shit, fart, and bugger. She could hear her great-gran's voice.

The wind whispered through the treetops like a sprout fart after Sunday lunch.

They would giggle together, eyes fixed on the bedroom door in case they were caught being naughty, the sense of conspiracy making her feel secure. Her great-grandmother knew everything, and if Shelly ever strayed from the facts, Gran Gertie fixed her in a stare and slowly pulled in her chin. Shelly's heart would pound and in seconds she would breathlessly blurt out the truth, regardless of the consequences.

When times became difficult, Shelly would scramble into Gran Gertie's lap, her head resting on that pillowing bosom as she stuck her thumb in her mouth. Gertie was the only person in the world who didn't tell her off for sucking her thumb. Shelly still smiled at the thought of her.

She stared into the junk room. Her mother's treasured doll's house, the ivory teething ring with a silver teddy dangling, a box of diecast cars, and the brass steam engine that really worked were loved toys.

'They'll be worth a few bob now,' Dad had muttered, but he still packed the toys away. She slid the lid off another box, and found a pile of seasonal sweaters.

*   *   *

Physically and emotionally exhausted, Shelly slipped into bed at midnight and quickly fell to sleep thinking about that last Christmas. For the three days of the holiday, Mum made Dad wear a different Christmas jumper. Shelly felt a giggle hopping around in her belly as she remembered how he hated them.

'If you love me, you'll wear it,' Mum challenged as she tugged the green crewneck that bore a ridiculous, grinning Rudolf with square, white teeth over his head.

Their happy marriage was glued together by compromises. 'I'll only do it if . . .' was commonly uttered, and Shelly was captivated by the sometimes bizarre deals struck to secure their relationship.

However, Shelly was not granted this bargaining power, she simply had to do as she was told.

'Mum, I'm sixteen! I did realise some time ago, there isn't really a Santa Claus, you know!'

Mum threw her head back and laughed. 'Shelly, darling, stop being a pain! You can pout all you like, you're not coming into town with me.'

'But why not? We always shop together on Christmas Eve. The sales will be starting this afternoon.'

'I'm going to pick up a special present and I don't want you around. That's the end of it. I'm leaving you in charge of the mince pies. Take them out of the oven when the timer goes and pop them onto the wire rack. Mind you don't burn yourself. I'm just going to have a word with your father.' Her big brown eyes sparkled with all the merriment of Christmas as she pulled on her coat. 'He's around the back, having a Christmas jumper sulk and picking sprouts for dinner tomorrow. So, give me a kiss, my darling daughter, and don't let the mince pies burn.'

Mum was gone in a flash, and as Shelly hovered, horrified, on the borderline of her dream, she knew what the next ten minutes held. She tried, and tried, to shout a warning – to change the future – but her words were never voiced. Through the front window, she could see the back of her mum's red wool coat as she walked away, heading for the bus stop.

Shelly could see her so clearly and, though sensing it was a dream, she was filled with horror. Could she stop it, change it, after all, what were dreams for? Surely, they were warnings. 'Don't go, Mum!' she tried to shout, but her mouth was glued shut and the words were nothing but a muffled mumble. She tried again and again, her mother getting smaller in the distance, the red coat, the bus stop . . . she mustn't reach the bus stop!

Then, as if Shelly had broken through into another dimension, she found her voice and yelled, 'Don't go, Mum! Don't go! Don't go! Mum, please!' She tried to run after her, but her father held her back, she could feel his hands on her shoulders and hear his voice, but still she shouted, 'Mum, don't go!'

Dad cried urgently, ''Ere, don't, Shelly. It's not real, love. Wake up now. Wake up!'

A moment of confusion tangled time and place, like in one of those films played backwards, making no sense until it's played forward once again. Her father was patting her shoulder. 'Come on, love, you're havin' a nightmare.'

'Oh, Dad, it was so real. I was there . . . you know?' She sobbed as she surfaced from the heartbreaking drama, drained, and oh so sad. 'Will it ever go away? It's been such a long time now.'

'Put yer dressing gown on and come down. Let's have a brandy-cocoa and a bit of a chinwag.'

She looked at him, saw the pain in his eyes – he was still suffering too.

*   *   *

At the kitchen table, Shelly poured the cocoa and her dad slopped a large measure of brandy into each mug.

Gordon spoke first. 'I know, love. It's the same for me. I have . . . well . . . oh God. Why is it so difficult to talk?'

'I don't know. It just hurts too much, I guess.'

'We've never really spoken about it, have we, Shelly love? I reckon we should have done, long ago.'

'It won't go away, Dad. I don't know why I can't just accept what happened and move on.'

His forehead puckered. 'I've given this a lot of thought too,' he said. 'I think it's because we've both shut it up inside ourselves. We *can't* let it go. In truth, we don't want to let my Maggie go, and why would we? We both want to keep her with us because we loved her so much. But I have to confess, I was shocked before when you said it was more than twenty years. It's time to move on, Shelly love. More than time, especially for you. Life's passing you by.'

Shelly couldn't hold back her tears. 'I loved her so much, Dad.' She knuckled her tears away. 'And I never told her. And it was my fault.' She closed her eyes and tried to quell her sobs.

'Don't fight it. Let the grief out, Shelly. And you didn't have to tell her you loved her. She knew, just like you knew she loved you.'

She had never thought of that before. Looking up, she saw tears had settled into the crags around Dad's eyes too.

'When the bell rang that day, I thought she'd forgotten her keys,' Shelly said. 'I was going to pull her leg, you know, tease her. I knew we'd laugh about it for ages.' She shook her head. 'I pulled the door open and saw the policemen . . . well, I don't know, I thought she'd organised some kind of joke. Like a novelty telegram or something, and when it wasn't, when they asked for you . . . I felt guilty for grinning at them, and for thinking such a thing.

'Why did it happen, Dad? Why us? Why Mum? Teenage boys don't drive into women standing alone at bus stops on Christmas Eve; they crash into lampposts, they crash into other cars, they don't crash into other people's mothers.'

Dad swiped a finger under his eyes. 'I ask myself that same question every day, love; and the answer is, I don't know. He was drunk, the boy. His first job, first car, first Christmas as an adult. At first, I wanted to go out in my car and find him. Revenge, you know? Then I wanted to find his parents and bust my knuckles on their faces. The consequences of not being a disciplined parent, of not teaching your children right from wrong, are too high. His parents are partly to blame, and the barman, and his mates. And me . . .'

'How could you be to blame. That's nonsense, Dad. It was my present she was going for.'

He took a gulp of his cocoa and stared ahead for a moment. 'Funny, don't you think, that in a moment of acute crisis you remember all the small details? Things that don't matter at all stay in your head forever.'

'I know what you mean.'

'I was in the garden, filling that cream enamel colander with sprouts for Christmas dinner. I remember a chip near the handle. It would go rusty there and I'd have to give your mum the money for a new one.' He shook his head, staring through the table top into the past. 'Money-wise, that year was difficult with me being laid off from the docks. Yer mum refused to skimp on Christmas. "I'll go without all year, Gordon, but Christmas is Christmas, so don't make me call you Scrooge in December, dear," she'd warned me.' He dropped his head into his hands and hauled in a great breath. 'God, how I miss her!'

Shelly's heart ached. She reached for the kitchen roll, tore off a couple of squares and pushed them into his fist. He dried his face and stared at the table for a long time.

'It's all my fault, because—' His tears gathered again. 'You see, what you don't know is – what I've always been too ashamed to tell you is – your mum came down the garden and asked me for the taxi money. She was running late and the buses might have been on Sunday service, with it being Christmas Eve. And the thing is . . . the thing is . . . I refused. It was me, you see, that told her to get the bus. Too bloody mean to give her five pounds for a taxi, but what was the real cost? I'll never forgive myself—' He squeezed the tissues tightly and punched the table so hard, Shelly feared he might have broken something.

'Dad, stop! It wasn't your fault, or my fault, or even the boy's fault. If we're going to heal, we have to stop looking to blame. I just want the hurt to stop. It's not fair; and it will never be fair no matter how hard we try. I want to help you, but I have other demons to deal with, remember?'

Gordon's mouth turned down. 'I might not talk about it, Shelly love, but I haven't forgotten what happened after your mother's death. I just want to say one more thing tonight.' He looked up, straight into her eyes. 'I am truly sorry, Shelly. Perhaps I made a mistake, but it was with the best of intentions. I couldn't see any other solution.'

Shelly dropped her head into her hands and gave up trying to hold on to her composure. Eventually, she got up, wrapped her arms around her father, and kissed his wet cheek. 'Thanks, Dad, that meant a lot to me. I'm going to bed. Don't stay up too long. Night, now.'

* * *

Although emotionally exhausted, Shelly went back to bed feeling lighter than she had for years.

She lay on her back, and imagined herself floating on the flat, turquoise water of the Aegean. Under a cerulean sky, the dazzling sun warmed her to the bones and the softest breeze whispered over her skin.

A lone seagull flew overhead. From the distant shore, she could hear bouzouki music drifting towards her from a beach taverna. Delicious smells perfumed the air – succulent lamb chops roasting on charcoal, pungent garlic bread sprinkled with fresh oregano, toasted to the point of perfection. She imagined crispy Greek salad with fat, sweet olives and salty fetta. She always fell into a deep relaxed sleep long before pudding.

* * *

Morning broke with memories of that awful Christmas Day. Gordon returned from somewhere – the police station or the mortuary, she didn't know – and ripped down all Mum's lovely Christmas decorations. He stuffed them into the wood burner and set fire to them, all the time sobbing and shouting obscenities. Instead of opening presents, an endless stream of Mum's friends and neighbours passed through and said how sorry they were.

Shelly snapped out of her recollections when her dad wandered into the kitchen wearing a bewildered expression. 'I've lost me glasses.'

'On your head.' She turned and picked the phone up on its second ring. After a minute, she bid the caller goodbye and hung up. 'Sorry, I have to go in early, Dad. A dog in collision with a car, poor thing, needs emergency surgery.' She pulled the dresser drawer open and handed her father a box and a booklet. 'Here, have a read of this while I'm out. If you get Alexa to understand your voice, you'll find it useful while I'm away. It's fun too. You can ask her absolutely anything you like.'

* * *

After dealing with the unfortunate dog, which was beyond surgery, Shelly returned to her car. Delving into her pocket for the key, her fingers touched the unopened letter. Before she turned on the ignition, she stole a moment for herself and tore it open. Her suspicions, aroused by the Cambridge postmark, were correct. It was from *him*, DJ. She had left DJ in Cambridge nearly twenty years ago, and had never seen him since. However, she'd never forgotten him, or stopped loving him.

CHAPTER 6
GERTIE

Dover, 1916.

AFTER MY INDUCTION TRAINING, I had the dreaded interview before a selection committee. Two men and two women, all very stiff and even older than my father. That afternoon, I returned home to await the result. If they rejected me, at least my parents would be pleased.

I washed the dishes while Mother pegged out the bed linen. Tuesday was Mrs Cooper's day off. The postman came through the gate. Mother abandoned the laundry, took the post, and came indoors.

'This might be it, Gertie,' she said, holding out a white envelope – her smile tight – her face pale.

I reached for it, but she kept hold of the corner and in a desperate voice said, 'I'm sorry. I know how badly you want to go, but I hope they don't need you, darling.'

I opened the envelope carefully, raced down the letter searching for the words *accepted* or *rejected*, but saw neither. Confused, I read through it quickly until reaching the line: *Report for duty . . .*

Overloaded with emotion, I couldn't speak and felt a tear trickle down my cheek.

'Oh, Gertie, I'm terribly sorry.'

'I got in, Mother. I made the grade.'

'Oh!' Mother pressed her hands against her heart and stared at me, her only remaining child. She scooped me into her arms with the fiercest hug, then raced out of the door.

I went to the kitchen window and saw her standing beside the wicker laundry basket, staring across the landscape, fists balled at her sides. She picked up a pillowcase but the wind caught it, blew it across the garden until it lay pinned vertically to the hedge. Mother hurried after it, peeled the pillowcase off the laburnum, then she grasped it against her breast and rocked from side to side. I knew she was crying.

Over the next week, I had my typhoid and tetanus injections, and a smallpox inoculation that produced a horrible scab like Arthur's, and made me feel wretched. Life at home became difficult – my damp-eyed mother hugged me too often, Father hardly spoke. Mother knitted mittens, socks, and balaclavas at a furious rate, as if the more soldiers' feet she saved from trench foot, the more favour she would gain with God to keep her daughter safe.

* * *

My application to assist the Queen Alexandra's Imperial Military Nursing Service was approved. Orders arrived telling me to join the hundred and one qualified medical staff on HMHS *Britannic*, in a few weeks' time. It is impossible to describe how thrilled I was.

When I broke the news to my parents over dinner, Father finally snapped.

'Right, young woman. You learn to swim before you go anywhere near that ship, otherwise I'll make you a ward of the court and you won't be going anywhere until you're twenty-one. Do you understand me?'

In dismay, I stared across the table at Mother who lowered her eyes and passed the gravy boat. Neither of them knew I'd lied about my age in order to be accepted in the VAD. 'But how shall I learn to swim? Can you swim, Mother?' I asked, breaking the silence.

'What a ridiculous question, of course not.'

'I'll teach you, Gertie,' Father said, sticking a finger inside his starched collar and giving it a tug. 'Do you have something appropriate to wear?'

I felt the heat of a blush in my cheeks.

'I'll sort something out, dear,' Mother said quickly. 'I've seen the bathing dresses young people wear these days. I'm sure they'll have one in the emporium.'

'No, no, not a bathing dress, that's no good for swimming. The skirts'll sink her. Abandon the corset, Gertie, and put on a pair of my woollen combinations. We'll start at dawn. Make sure you're up and ready at five o'clock.' He stared at the table top for a moment. 'Martha, is that cork protector still under this cloth?' Mother nodded. 'Then roll it and tie it like a breast of lamb to keep your daughter afloat while she learns.'

'Yes, dear. Do you want me to come with you?'

'I certainly do. Bring towels and brandy.'

Before dawn the next morning the three of us hurried along the treacherous cliff path that led down to St Margaret's Bay.

'If we hear any planes,' Father said, 'I'll blow the lamp out and we'll have to stand still until there's enough light to see where we're going. I don't want anyone falling down the cliff. Is that understood?'

Father led the way, holding the lantern high. Shadows danced around our feet making it even more difficult to see where we were stepping. To the rear, Mother struggled with a bulging carpet bag. I felt ridiculous in my father's underwear and my mother's second-best coat. Thank God it was dark. I strained my ears for the sound of a plane, hoping for once that Kaiser Bill would save the day.

At sunrise, my father and I entered the freezing water. I had never been in the sea above my knees before. Terrified, but determined, I obeyed Father's instruction and lay belly-down in the shallows, the cork roll across my chest and sticking up from under my arms. Father's hand cupped my chin.

'Come on, Gertie, kick those legs!' he boomed.

After fifteen minutes, I stood and said, 'Surely that's enough, Father, I'm freezing to death.'

He gave me such a shove that I staggered and lost my balance on the uneven stones. In a moment, I went under. Father came after me, I thought to help me up, but he shoved his big hand over my face and pushed it under the surface. I caught a glimpse of him through the water, lips tight, cheeks red and blown out. He was drowning me! I struggled against his hand, grasping his wrist, kicking furiously, my lungs bursting.

Just at the moment I couldn't hold my breath any longer, he pulled me up. Tugged into his arms, he held me tightly. Though I was crying, I could feel his chest heaving against my cheek and realised he had held his breath as long as me.

When he could speak, he said, 'Forgive me, but I have to make you understand why you must keep trying. You must be able to swim, my precious child. I could not bear to lose you too.'

Mother dropped everything and rushed into the sea, the bottom of her skirts so wet and heavy she could hardly walk.

Father commanded her to leave. 'Mind your own business, woman!' he shouted. 'I'm trying to save your headstrong daughter's life!'

Despite my fear, coldness, and aching body, I was terribly proud of my darling father.

We continued with the lesson, but at one point, a wave dragged me from him. Mother screamed and rushed to the water's edge again. I clung to the cork and yelled, 'Father! Father!' He stumbled after me, grabbed the back of my sodden long johns and hauled me into shallow water. 'Keep kicking!' he cried. 'Never give up! You won't be able to take a break when you're in the middle of the ocean.' I heard a heartbreaking tremble in his voice. 'Promise me! Promise me, you'll never give up, Gertie!'

'I won't give up, Father, I promise.' I made a determined effort to kick harder.

By eight o'clock, we were drinking beef tea and eating dripping on toast at the kitchen table. Every muscle in my body ached and I was exhausted to the core.

'Rub wintergreen into your calves and shoulders and we'll try again this evening,' Father said before leaving for the surgery.

Mother fell into a chair most ungraciously. 'You could have both been swept away, then where would I be?'

*　*　*

I'm proud to say, by the middle of the second week, I could keep my head above water without the cork. Mother had ordered a modern, knitted swimming suit with three-quarter legs and arms, and I promised my father I would practise swimming whenever the opportunity arose.

The summer passed quickly. My work experience took place at our local hospital, where I occasionally saw my father and caught his flattened smile and glint of pride.

We all held our breath as the war gained momentum throughout 1916. By October, a great sea battle took place right off our coastline: the Battle of Dover Strait. Father and I watched from the cliff top for most of the night. At the time, we didn't know who the burning or sinking ships belonged to: us or them. I'd always loved watching the ships, but to see those great vessels explode into fireballs, lighting up the dark – and for a few second the boats and lifeboats around them – was heartbreaking. To hear the distant cries of men calling for help, clearly some wounded and many in the sea, was too terrible.

The next morning, Mrs Cooper brought the newspapers in. Nothing of note said about German losses, which we took to mean there weren't any. Our navy lost seven ships and six were damaged, and the loss of life was appalling.

'BRITANNIA RULE THE WAVES! Bah. We're a disgrace!' Father bellowed over his breakfast. 'How are we supposed to win this war if we can't even scuttle a few ships on the doorstep of England?' He glared across the table at me. 'Go and dress in your uniform, Gertie, and be ready in fifteen minutes. You're coming to the hospital with me.'

Mother gasped. 'But why, Father?'

'It's about time our daughter saw some real casualties of this war. The tragedy of men with their arms and legs blown off.' He turned to me. 'Do you know what they're known as?' I shook my head. 'Basket cases! Basket cases, do you hear me? Because there's so little left of them, that's how they're transported, in a basket!'

Father's plan was to horrify me so much I would give up my 'harebrained scheme' as he called it, to work for the Voluntary Aid Detachment. I'd show him I could be as strong as anyone.

Although, when I glanced worriedly at Mother, who was practi
cally trembling at that point, I feared perhaps I might not be able
to take whatever he had in mind.

After losing Arthur and Sissy, his bombastic personality
almost faded away; but now it was back with a vengeance.
understood that he wanted to keep me safe, and I loved him for
that; but here was the odd thing: the more he tried to force his
will on me, the stronger I became.

* * *

We arrived at the hospital and met Staff Nurse Cuthbert, in
whose charge father left me. There followed the most disgust
ing four hours imaginable. I was ordered to perform the most
sickening tasks.

'Very good, Miss Smith,' Staff Nurse said, her voice as cold as
the sweat on my forehead. 'You realise, as a VAD your life will
mostly consist of bedpan duty?'

'Yes, Staff Nurse.' I nodded, suspecting that she'd caught my
loathing of this chore. But I would rise above this station, and new
recruits would take my place at the bottom of the nursing ladder.

'Then you may wait for Dr Smith at the hospital entrance.'

I stood out front, wrapped my cape around myself, and
watched the arrival of military ambulances. The stretchers
four to a vehicle, were pulled out and lined up outside the hos
pital where orderlies took over. Casualties from the night's bat
tle streamed in. Young men in a terrible state.

'Nurse! Nurse, please help me,' one young seaman cried. 'My
hand, please . . .'

For a moment, I wanted to run away, but his pleading tone
brought out the pity in me. I could hold his hand for a moment

The sailor was held to the stretcher by two heavy straps over a blanket that covered all but his head. One strap pinned him across his chest, and the other over his thighs.

I knelt beside him. 'Take it easy, sailor, they'll soon fix you up.' I eased the blanket back to take his hand in mine . . . there was no hand, just a bloodied stump at his wrist and a tight tourniquet. The shock caught me by surprise and I almost cried out. I fought to keep the horror and fear off my face, but the hardest part was to speak to him with a steady voice. I turned my head away, thought of our Arthur, then called on Sissy for help.

In a moment, I had regained control of my voice and was able to calm the young man. 'This is one of the best hospitals in the country, sailor. They'll take very good care of you, I promise.' I talked to him, told him about my brother, but not that he had died.

The orderlies came for him at the same moment as my father appeared.

I tucked the blanket back under his arm and patted his shoulder. 'Good luck, sailor,' I called, my calm voice seeming to come from somebody else, my insides shaking like Mrs Cooper's blancmange.

'Thank you, nurse,' the sailor called, his voice a little calmer now. 'I'll never forget you!'

In father's car, I turned away from him and, peering out of the window as he drove us home, broke down. I wept for a few minutes, then dried my eyes, blew my nose and threw my shoulders back.

Father never spoke of the incident, yet I sensed he was quite aware of my emotions.

That evening at dinner, Mother got herself in a tizzy about everything, saying it just proved how much danger I'd be in on the high seas, but Father sternly reassured her.

'She'll be on a hospital ship. Nobody's allowed to fire at hospital ships, ours or theirs. She'll be safer than you are in this house, Mother,' he said.

I was shocked by his sudden change of attitude. The hopes and dreams I'd held in my heart while gazing from the Dover cliff top were about to come to fruition. I would work on the greatest transatlantic passenger liner ever built, HMHS *Britannic*. To be honest, the ship had never actually traversed the Atlantic because our government acquired it before it had a chance. In consideration of my mother, I decided not to mention the vessel was sister ship to *Titanic* that sank only four years earlier.

'The largest British ship afloat, Father!' I said at breakfast. 'She's already made several rescues in the Mediterranean, saving the wounded of Gallipoli.' My thoughts went to Arthur and Sissy, how I missed them. Maybe I could save the lives of those who would otherwise perish?

Mother touched Father's hand. 'Can we go to the port and see her off, dear?' I had to report to Southampton at eight o'clock on the twelfth of November.

'Most certainly.' He stared at me for a moment before he swallowed hard and said, 'I'm proud of you, Gertie. I admit, I had my doubts, but I am convinced you will be a great asset to this country and our wounded soldiers.' He glanced at the two unused place settings at the table. 'Make sure you take good care of yourself, Gertie. We could not bear to look at another empty plate.'

CHAPTER 7
SHELLY

Dover, present day.

THE LETTER FROM DJ TREMBLED in Shelly's hand. She had resisted opening it all day, but now, sitting in the car outside White Cottage, she could put it off no longer.

He had found her after nineteen years. She stared through the windscreen, remembering every detail of him, but especially his wide, pale blue eyes. Then an echo of her heartbreak returned with such a fierce stab, she whimpered.

She said goodbye to DJ exactly one year and one month after her mother's death. That tragedy had turned the father she adored into a bitter and cynical old man. He blamed everyone for his loss, once he knew about DJ, he made Shelly's life miserable. Gordon Summer had had no idea how to deal with an errant teenager, he had no one to support him in his grief, and was too proud to ask for help, or admit he needed it.

Shelly's final words to DJ came back. 'My father's right. It's the best thing for both our sakes.' The words nearly choked her. 'I'm just seventeen, my whole life's ahead of me, and I have to admit that you're better off with her. She's more mature, and it's clear to see that she loves you as much as I do.' She curved her arms, remembering how she held him, never wanting to let go. Then she had walked away so that DJ wouldn't see any more of her tears. She had felt the same sense of loss when her mother died.

Shelly hadn't seen him since, apart from in her dreams. Often, she had thought about him, wondered how he was doing, where he was, who he was with, if he was happy. With the development of the internet, she had toyed with the idea of looking for him on a social network, just to see how he was doing, but it would only lead to more pain. Her young heart took an eternity to accept that she had to live without him. He belonged to another and later, she heard, they had emigrated to Australia.

However, according to the postmark on his letter, DJ had returned home.

But should she let DJ back into her life? She had been replaced nineteen years ago. Yet she could still feel his cheek against hers, tears dripping down her face. 'I swear, I'll never forget you,' she had whispered, then turned and walked away.

Swallowing hard, she opened it and began to read.

Dear Shelly,

I hope you don't mind me writing to you, and I hope it isn't too much of a shock to hear from me after all this time. The fact is, I've been in Australia. I have just returned to Cambridge.

I would really like to meet up, if that is possible, just to talk. I have some questions, of course. I'm sure you understand. I was thinking of a café, perhaps in Dover if that would be more convenient for you. Or, perhaps you would prefer somewhere more private?

Here is my phone number, please call me if you agree, and let me know a time and place that would accommodate you,

Best wishes,

DJ

She placed a hand over her heart. If she didn't deal with it today, the letter had the power to destroy her concentration, and with a tricky operation scheduled for the next morning, she needed a clear head. She took a calming breath and punched numbers into the phone.

She mis-dialled twice. What should she say . . . her first words after nineteen years? What would he hope for her to say? Her mind was paralysed. She stared at his writing. Blue ballpoint in loopy, open script that suggested a big-hearted person, generous, honest . . . but who really knew after all this time? The ringtone thrummed. She might be sick. She ended the call and sniffed back tears, disgusted with herself. Now, she wanted to speak to him so badly it hurt. But after what had happened all those years ago, perhaps she should not.

She wiped her eyes, flicked her dark hair back, and breezed into White Cottage.

'Everything all right, Dad? How are you getting on with Alexa?' She picked up a leaflet and started reading.

'He's givin' me a real hard time.'

'It's a she.'

'Silly bloody name then, ain't it?'

Shelly frowned, looked up, and said, 'You're pulling my leg?'

She caught a flicker of concern that was quickly replaced by a grin. 'What's for dinner? Us technology wizards need to keep our energy levels up,' he said.

'Hotpot with cheesy dumplings and a side of pickled red cabbage.' She started the microwave.

Gordon's eyes widened. 'Will this Alexa be able to cook like you, while you're away?'

Shelly laughed. 'Almost. She'll tell you what to take out of the freezer in the morning, and how many minutes to heat it in the evening.' Shelly smiled. 'Do you think you and Bill will manage, Dad?'

"Course we will. We've got a poker school going one night, a couple of strippers on night two . . ."

'You're too naughty, Dad! Now wipe that silly grin off your face.'

The microwave went, *bing!*

* * *

After dinner, Shelly returned to the spare bedroom. Too exhausted for any more sorting and too emotional to listen to another of Gran Gertie's tapes, she closed her eyes and recalled how she had first met David. David, the love of her life. A fortnight after her mother's funeral, Shelly had waited for her dad to leave for the pigeon club. When she had the house to herself, she started to box up some of her mother's possessions – it was an odd feeling to go through her mum's handbag; it was there, in her purse, that she found the ticket.

The collection slip said: H SAMUEL, JEWELLER's. COLLECT BEFORE 3.30 ON 24-DEC-2000.

That Saturday, dressed in her finest, with make-up, nail polish, everything, Shelly set out on a pilgrimage with only her mum in mind. For the first time since Christmas Eve, she really wanted to look her best. She walked to the bus shelter, as her mum had done, and sat alone trying to imagine how it had been that day. She flinched each time a car came racing around the bend, afraid that in some way she was invoking a re-enactment of the past. Thinking about death, she wondered if her mother could see her there, at that moment.

'Don't leave me, Mum,' she whispered, aware of the space around her, feeling her tears rise, then remembering she was wearing mascara and sniffing hard. The bus came, carried her into town with her mother's ghost beside her. Shelly stared at her knees. She could feel her mother's arm against hers, sensed her sparkling smile, her pride and her love. In moments like these, it was so easy to imagine Mum was still alive. But the bus journey came to an end, and so did the dream, for a moment.

She headed straight for the jeweller's shop, once again, imagining her mum walking alongside with that proud, *this is my daughter* air. That look always made Shelly smile when they were together.

At the high street, Shelly sat on a bench, watching the shop for a long while. She didn't know why, only that she somehow expected her mother to come out of the door, and Shelly would understand it had all been a terrible mistake. Perhaps *she* had been with her mother at the bus stop on Christmas Eve, Shelly reasoned. Perhaps *she* had been hit by the car and everything she knew from then on had been a drug-induced dream while she lay in a coma in hospital. When her body was repaired, the doctor would wake her . . . her mother would be sitting at her bedside telling her everything was all right now – and her father would be smiling, like he used to.

Fantasies like this kept her lonely sixteen-year-old heart strong enough to continue under the weight of her grief.

She took the ticket out of the purse, marched across the pavement and straight into the shop. A man at the counter, in his fifties, looked up curiously.

'Can I help you?'

'Er, yes, please. I've come to collect this.' She passed the ticket over.

'I see. Are you Mrs Summer?'

Shelly wondered if he was being sarcastic. 'No, she's my mother. She was . . .'

'I'm sorry, miss. We can only give it to Mrs Summer, unless you have a note from her and proof of identity . . .'

All the horrible hurt was gathering in Shelly's chest. 'But . . .'

'Sorry, it's the rules. Nothing I can do.'

It had been so hard to get this far. Her bravery was all used up. Anger and frustration escaped in an explosion of distress. 'She's dead!' she interrupted loudly, hysterically. 'She was waiting for the one o'clock bus to come here on Christmas Eve when a drunk driver mounted the kerb!' She was really shouting now, fury holding her tears back. 'Did you hear me? My mother's dead! Dead!'

Her chest was heaving though she could hardly get her breath. She slapped her hand over her mouth, her eyes wide and glaring in a struggle against tears. She swallowed hard, lowered her hand, and whispered, 'Whatever it is, it was my Christmas present.'

An older man came out of the back of the shop. 'Is everything all right?' The assistant told him what had happened. He looked at Shelly in a kindly way, which made her feel even closer to tears. 'Do you have anything to prove who you are, or anyone we can phone, young lady?'

She shook her head, pulling her purse out of her pocket at the same time. cMy dad's at home, but he gets upset. Anyway, he'll be in the pigeon loft. He stays there most of the time since it happened. I've got my bus pass, will that do?' She put it on the counter. 'And there's Sergeant Edge at the police station. He gave me his card and said if I had any problems at all, I could call him.'

The older man looked at the younger one. 'I don't think we need to do that. Let's see what we have, shall we?' He took the collection ticket and went into the back of the shop.

She could hear what sounded like a filing-cabinet drawer open, then two thumps of a stapler. He returned to the shop holding a midnight-blue-and-gold paper bag.

'There you are, my dear. Just sign for it. There's nothing to pay.'

Outside the shop, she took some deep breaths and walked a little way down the high street. The air was crisp, cold, and the town still busy with bargain hunters in the January sales. As the late-afternoon light faded, she saw herself in the shop windows, alone.

What she really needed was a friend to talk to, or just to be silent with. Shelly wished there was someone who could sit with her while she opened the bag. Her emotions were so exhausting that she felt weak most of the time. Looking around, she realised she'd entered the pedestrian area and faced Gerrard's Cake Shop. Suddenly starving, she bought herself a sausage roll and a cola and sat on a bench that wrapped around a tree trunk.

Fortified after the food and drink, she pulled the jeweller's bag from her tote. What could it be? She eased the staples open and pulled out a box in the same colour scheme. With butterflies in her tummy, she slid it open, then gasped at the simple beauty of a beautiful, silver, teardrop-shaped bangle. 'Oh Mum . . .' she whispered and looked up, in her mind's eye seeing her mother in her Burberry raincoat, with her furled umbrella and shiny old leather satchel bag slung across her body. 'It's beautiful.' Then she saw the writing engraved inside.

TO THE MOON AND BACK, MY DARLING. 25.12.2000

How often had her mother asked: *How much do I love you*? Shelly slipped the bracelet on and whispered, '*To the moon and back.'* Overwhelmed, her tears came fast and free. It was such a relief to be able to cry without the fear of her father hearing. Lost to grief, she felt herself cleansed in some way, then something cold and wet touched her arm and made her jump.

Her eyes flew open and she found herself staring into the big face of an old Golden Retriever. Its big brown eyes peered with sympathy. The dog dropped its head into her lap and continued to gaze up.

She scratched behind its ear. 'Sorry, old girl, I'm a bit upset.'

The Retriever cocked its head slightly and made an odd mewling sound.

'Hey, are you all right? Here, take this,' a male voice said as a hand came towards her with a McDonald's napkin.

'Thanks.' She glanced up and saw he was a little older than her, with sandy hair and blue-grey eyes. 'Thanks,' she said again, feeling snotty, and imagining the state of her mascara.

'Sorry about my dog, she's a sucker for tears. What's up?' he asked. 'Can I help?'

'Nobody can help. Please, I'd just like to be by myself.'

'Ah, sorry, I do understand – but it's just that I'm the opposite. I really need to talk to somebody.'

'Look, I don't mean to be rude, but I'm not the person to unburden yourself onto.' She found herself stroking the dog. The comforting weight of its head, that intense sympathetic stare, and its silence, was exactly what she needed at that moment. 'Your dog's lovely. What's its name?'

He sighed. 'It's my dog that's the problem. I've a terrible decision to make and it's just too difficult.'

'Really, I'm the last person to help you!' She would have walked, right then, if it hadn't been for the dog's head still in her lap. It seemed so sad and lonely that she hadn't the heart to shove it away. After peering into its eyes again, she relented. 'I give in. What's the matter then?'

'She's sick,' he said gently. 'Terminally ill. Should I take her to the vet and . . . you know, or let her hang on to the end? It would be kinder to take her to the vet, but I don't want to let her go. Everyone says it's up to me, but I can't sleep for the worry. It's the most terrible decision.'

'You're serious? You mean this lovely old dog?'

He nodded.

'No, poor thing, that's too awful.'

He nodded again. 'Her name's Pat. Pat the dog, get it? I can't decide, I can't even sleep for fretting about it.'

They remained silent for a while, then Shelly spoke. 'You must spend a lot of time with her.'

'In the week I do. I work from home building travel websites, so I'm always around.' He glanced into her face, looking for approval, perhaps, caring what she thought. 'But at the weekends, I'm a life-guard at the sports centre. I hate to leave her, but I'll lose my job if I don't go in, and the websites don't pay that well while I'm build-ing a name for myself.'

'That's where I've seen you. At the baths. I used to go every Saturday afternoon, but I haven't been since Christmas,' she said, taking another glance at his face and decided he was even better looking close up.

He frowned. 'Then I must have seen you there.' Again, he studied her face. 'But I don't recognise you.'

'I wear a yellow swim cap and goggles.'

'Ah, that's you?' He grinned. 'You're good, fast, strong, but you need to work on your turns.'

'You've been watching me? That's creepy.'

'Not creepy at all. It's my job to watch the swimmers. That's what I'm paid for.'

CHAPTER 8
GERTIE

Dover, 1916.

THAT AFTERNOON, MOTHER AND I stood before Sissy's grave. 'Promise you'll come back, Gertie. I don't need a hero.' She took my hand and squeezed it. 'You're my only child now. I couldn't bear to lose you too.'

'Mother, it's the safest ship on the water, ask Father. Nothing bad is going to happen. Stop worrying.'

The last autumn leaves tumbled down around us in a sudden gust. I peered into the bare branches and wondered if Sissy was sending her blessings. 'I won't let you down,' I whispered.

'I know,' Mother answered, dabbing her nose with a lace handkerchief.

* * *

Back home, I went straight to my room and pulled the Huntley & Palmers tin from the back of my writing desk. Inside, lay all Sissy's letters from the munitions factory, and from the isle of Lemnos, before her sickness and death.

I'd read them so often the corners were dog-eared. With the tin in my lap, I sat quietly, recalling how pleased she was that women were at last stepping up the ladder of equality. I unfolded the top letter and heard her sweet voice as I read.

Dearest Gertie,

How I miss you! I wish you were here in glorious Greece. There are beautiful beaches and beautiful men, and days of endless sunshine. You would love it. Life is very different here in the field hospital. All day yesterday and through the night we heard the boom of guns, and the night nurses say the windows in the surgical hut rattled. It was the loudest I have heard so far, and every time I hear them, the words of one of our patients come to my mind: 'Some poor devils are going to keep you busy.'

Soldiers from the front say there'll be a big push in a few days. God knows how we'll cope. We have fifty beds in our hut. We ease their pain, then send them to tent wards.

After work, at midnight last night, I went down to the receiving tent to see how the incoming wounded were handled. The big marquee had two feeble electric lights. Some doctors had electric torches. We're told when a convoy is on its way. The stretchers are laid on the dirt floor, close together. The injured have a ticket on their coat assigning them to a tent where men with similar conditions also wait: shrapnel wounds, gas, blindness, limbs missing, gunshot and trench foot. I think about Arthur often, Gertie. Sometimes, a soldier will come in covered in mud . . . and for a moment I am fooled. Hope that there has been a mistake rises rapidly and leaves me breathless. Then my heart is broken all over again. At those times it's difficult not to show affection for the poor blighters. They are all some mother's son, aren't they?

Volunteers hand out hot soup, usually pea with horsemeat. Unless they're in agony, we bathe the men, put their clothes in the fumigator, then let them sleep. The doctors talk to them a little, but they don't examine them. For those desperate darlings who will not make it through the night, there is morphine. A high dose.

The soldiers say very little. They're exhausted, traumatised, and in terrible pain, but they're also brave beyond measure. When I ask how they feel, torn open or limbs missing, they answer wearily, 'Not too bad, nurse' or 'A bit rough, to tell the truth.'

I love them all, Gertie, although there are terrible repercussions if any nurse is found fraternising with a patient. However, I do occasionally sneak a small square of Mother's chocolate in for a terminal case or two. God help the poor devils.

One patient was caught in an explosion and thrown onto an entanglement of barbed wire between us and the enemy. He had to stay there, exposed to gunfire, hunger, and thirst for twenty-four hours before anyone could get him away. He caught some shrapnel and several bullets, but I believe he will recover.

Another was shot in the hip and could only drag himself a few inches at a time between the trenches. He was out there, bombs and bullets passing over him, for three days. He took water from the canteens of dead soldiers until he was eventually rescued.

There was something about him, Gertie, something terribly special; my heart went right out to him. Thomas, was his name. Oh, my goodness. What a brave soldier! The light from his eyes shone right into my heart. When I cleaned the mud from his face, I gave him a fleeting kiss on the lips. This was such a forbidden gesture that I could have been expelled right there and then. Thankfully nobody noticed. 'Do you believe in love at first sight, nurse?' he asked. How I wished I could know him outside of this hellish war. I wanted to bathe him, tend his wounds and ease his pain. When I came back on duty, I brought him a square of treasured chocolate, but he had gone. Gone to heaven, Gertie. I wanted to be with him, in every sense of the word, so much that my heart broke into a million pieces. All I am left with is his name, Thomas . . . my Thomas.

I lie on my cot at night and hear the marching feet of new soldiers heading for battle. I wonder how many will come back incomplete – with limbs left in the mud on the front line – and how many of those marching feet will end their journey toes up on some foreign battlefield, never to return.

In the back of my mind, I can hear all the weeping mothers. You can't get away from the tragedy of it all. It is with you every waking minute, and in your ears as you sleep. The boots go on marching, marching, marching. Never so many, and never so firmly, when they return.

Enough of this misery. I am honoured to be here, helping our wounded. At least I had a choice and can leave whenever I wish. Not so for our poor men.

One of the greatest things about being here is meeting so many kinds of people. The Australian sisters are here, and the New Zealand nurses too. Without them, heaven knows what we would do. We all suffer the same discomforts and eat the same food. It's not too bad, and keeps us going, but we have lost much weight.

I've reached the end of my news, dear Gertie, but I will write again the moment I get a chance.

Love and kisses from me, your dear sister,
Sissy

My darling Sissy was my inspiration. I may never be as bold, brave, or intelligent as my sister, but I would try my best, and all would be done in her name. On 12 November, I stood on Southampton's dock, antlike in the shadow of HMHS *Britannic*, my skin tingling with excitement. Sissy's inspiration and my St John Ambulance certificate had carried me this far, the rest was up to me.

I squinted up at the majestic white ship. A broad green stripe ran around the hull, amidships, broken in three places by the universally recognised red cross. Low winter sunlight caught the great sign causing it to glint and flash, and confirming in our minds that nothing bad could ever happen to such a magnificent vessel. Breathless with excitement, and proud to be seen in public wearing my new uniform, I smiled at everyone who glanced my way.

'Smith, wipe that grin off your face, you're not a showgirl!' Matron ordered as she rounded us up on the quayside.

'Yes, Matron, sorry, Matron.' I removed the smile, but it was impossible to dampen the sparkle in my eyes. We VADs and new nurses were ordered aboard. My heart thumped with pride. Most of us rushed to the rail and peered down at those on the wharf below. We were so high, they looked small, but how desperately I wanted to see my parents ... wanted them to see me. I searched and searched, gripping the rail and leaning over as far as I dared, hoping to stand out in the sea of uniforms. Then, I caught sight of my father's face, upturned, luminous with worry and stern as ever. Mother stood beside him, dabbing her eyes with one of his large white handkerchiefs. She held it in the air, fluttering it as if flinging her tears my way. I jumped up and down, arms thrust above my head, they *had* to see me! A voice came from behind.

'Miss Smith, decorum, please!'

I turned. 'Sorry, Matron. I got carried away.' Clearly, I was destined to be scolded by Matron on a regular basis.

'Do remember, we represent our king and country, so we *will not* behave like children at a Punch and Judy show.'

'Yes, Matron. It won't happen again.' But I could not contain my grin. 'It's my parents, they came to see me off! There, Matron, down on the portside.' I pointed.

She raised her eyebrows and stretched her neck. 'An ladies don't point unless it's an emergency. What is the worl coming to?'

I dropped my arm. 'No, of course they don't. Sorry, Matror I am too excited.'

Matron peered down her nose and shook her head in despairing manner, but as she turned away, I caught the glimme of a smile.

Down on the dock, people gathered in likeminded cluster: Some younger people cheered rowdily, whistling, and wavin little flags or handkerchiefs up towards us. Other assemblie were subdued, saddened, clutching each other, gloved hand flapping awkwardly towards the ship.

The point of no return came at two fifteen in the afternoor My heart thumped as the stevedores lifted rope loops off th mooring stanchions, severing the umbilical to my motherland

I was on my own now. An adult at the start of a new life. Ou of the nest, I was about to test my wings. Could I fly without m father there to catch me? With Sissy's spirit behind me, I woul help to save the life of some other mother's son, and make m family proud.

With the lines slipped, the great vessel eased away. The clan of the ships bell added to an atmosphere of celebration. Shri farewells rose on the air, then they were drowned by an uproari ous rendition of 'Rule, Britannia!', played by a local brass banc My ebullience at embarking on this great adventure swiftly mor phed into a feeling of loss and loneliness. My country, and m dearest friends and family, slipped away from me.

Low sunlight hit the promenade, stretching shadows int thin grey ghosts on the pale cement. They grew smaller an more distant by the second. People moved away, heading fo the public house, or home. My eyes fixed on my parents, still as statues, and I understood every bit of their sense of loss. At that moment, it matched my own.

* * *

The purser – a short, dapper man – told us of the incredible power of HMHS *Britannic*'s engines. He caught my eye, and I sensed he was trying to impress me, which made me blush.

'The *Britannic*'s stronger and far safer than her sister ship, *Titanic*.' The purser presented facts and figures that meant nothing to me before he handed us over to Matron. I tried to memorise the things he told us, thinking I could put them into my first letter home and impress Father.

I imagined him looking up from the page. 'You see how much she has learned already, my dear. Our girl has a good head on her shoulders.' And Mother would be amazed.

Matron Merriberry, a powerful woman who carried the weight of middle age with dignity, led us around the vessel.

'Pay attention, ladies,' she boomed, glaring at each of us, then her face softening. 'We're honoured to be given this vessel for our work. The *Britannic* would have been the most luxurious passenger ship of the White Star Line, and indeed of the world. However, for the moment her more ornate fittings, and her magnificent pipe organ, lay in storage. That space is taken by operating rooms, surgeries, and wards with over three thousand beds.' She threw her shoulders back, then continued. 'Before you descend to your designated cabins, follow me around the ship and familiarise yourselves.'

We walked behind her, all eyes on her rotund *derrière* for a moment. Clearly, Matron was not fond of a tight corset. She swung her wide hips with the vigour that made me proud to be a woman. Mother would be shocked, but then Mother didn't think we should be fighting for the vote, or saying one single word against sending our brothers to be blown to pieces in the war, or objecting to us women getting half the pay of men for the same job.

We followed Matron into the first-class dining room, now converted into an intensive care ward. Here, the seriously wounded would stay. We presented our papers to the chief medical officer, along with our blood group card. I was O, the most common and the most needed. The transfusion procedure was a new and marvellous thing that saved many lives. The technique consisted of two glass tubes, one inserted into the donor, the other into the recipient, with a length of rubber hose between. The very idea of having to do this horrified me, and I was relieved when Matron assured us it was only on a voluntary basis.

The first-class staterooms accommodated the hospital elite: doctors, medical corps officers, the chaplain, and Matron herself, of course. We VADs, nurses and orderlies resided in third-class cabins at the front of F deck. My cabinmate, Nurse Josephine, and our neighbours – trainee nurses, Barbara, Joan and Patricia – were great fun. Together, the five of us settled in, sure we would become friends for life. F deck was a fine place to be, until they raised or lowered the anchor. Then, the ribs and girders of the *Britannic* transferred that peculiar cacophony through our accommodation.

A magnificent din also struck up when the stokers' shift changed. The spiral staircase leading down to the firemen's tunnel was right behind our cabin. The coalmen, in hobnailed boots, clomped up a racket at the change of each shift. Up and down the metal steps they clattered with no regard for the tremendous noise that rang in our ears.

When the stomping stopped, and I broke the silence with a sigh of relief, the monstrous watertight fire doors below us trundled to a close with a final thud that shook third class. As we worked twelve-hour shifts, we only suffered the stokers' racket once every twenty-four hours. Just to have a bed would be bliss, and sharing a bathroom hardly mattered.

Dinner was almost formal, and held in the grand dining room. Four hundred medical staff dined together. As we ate, I imagined how marvellous it would be to travel as a passenger on the ship. I felt homesick from time to time, and dreamed of Mother's delicious toad in the hole.

I discovered a great advantage to being on F deck. Just down the corridor was the glorious white-tiled swimming bath! With teak ladders at each end, entering the water was far easier than going into the sea at home. A row of changing rooms on the port side of the poolroom reminded me of beach huts in St Margaret's Bay, at home. The starboard side was lined with patterned marble, and luxuriously lit by gold sconces. I couldn't wait to swim in such sumptuous surroundings.

I had just unpacked when the steward delivered a parcel addressed in my mother's hand. What luxuries I discovered! A tin of Dundee cake, four tablets of coal tar soap, a precious slab of chocolate, and a carefully wrapped book. I imagined Mother thinking of me while she packed everything. She probably shed a tear for Sissy, too. Dear Mother. How I would miss her. I wanted to hug her right then.

The book was filled with pictures of women workers in factories, bronzing and soldering and making high-explosive shells, amongst other things. I could imagine Mother being shocked by what she saw. The author, Minister of Munitions, Mr Lloyd George, claimed: 'there were never such useful or dedicated workers as the women of the munitions' factories.'

My heart swelled knowing darling Sissy had worked in a place like this. Row upon row of missiles, thousands of them. Women, it was true, had their heads wrapped like puddings in a muslin cloth. I could never have imagined the scene just from Sissy's letters.

I turned another page and gasped with shock. There she was. My darling sister, an angel in heaven for almost a year and so badly missed, yet she stared up from the page smiling right into my eyes as if she knew this very moment would happen.

I was crying without realising and ignored a knock on the cabin door. I just wanting to absorb the brightness of my precious sister's smile.

CHAPTER 9
SHELLY

Dover, present day.

IN THE SPARE ROOM OF WHITE COTTAGE, Shelly kept her eyes closed and allowed memories of the first time she had met David and his dog to fill her mind.

* * *

I haven't been watching you at all,' he said with a slightly hurt tone and a faint blush. 'I'm a lifeguard, it's my job to watch the swimmers and you're good, you stand out. Why don't you join the swimmers' club? They coach people with potential. Anyway, that's your choice. Tell me, what should I do about my dog?'

'How long have you had her?'

'Since I was a boy.' Shelly tried to guess how old he was, but failed. A distant look came to his face. 'She cocks her head and stares at me when I speak to her, like she's saying, "Talk dog, will you, boss? I'm not a human, you know."' He laughed softly and scratched the top of her head. 'She's my companion, tripping hazard, hot water bottle, and the best friend a guy could have. If I'm not giving her enough attention, she pushes her head under my hand and peers up at me with her amazingly deep eyes telling me she wants to be fussed.' His face lit up as he spoke. 'And when I take my shoes and socks off, she licks my feet with her big, sandpaper tongue until I'm laughing out loud, then she steals a sock and races around with it. At least she used to.' He turned to the dog, his voice went quiet. 'What will I do when she's gone? I want to . . .' The rest of the sentence gave up trying to make it into the real world.

'How terrible. I've never had a dog, tell me more.'

He glanced up, but hesitated for a moment. 'We have an understanding, me and Pat. In the early days, she was a bundle of raw energy, but so was I. She ruined the furniture and woodwork. My poor mum . . .' He glanced up at the sky with gentle eyes, then down again. A simple gesture that told Shelly his mum had passed away too. 'My mum put up with a lot from the two of us. Yet she seemed to understand how important Pat became to me. In teaching the dog some discipline, I was teaching myself at the same time. Anyway, we helped each other along in those early days, and now, she's all the family I have.'

They sat in silence again until Shelly made a suggestion. 'I think you know what you must do if you really love her. Give her the best week of her life, then let her rest in peace.'

He stared at the paving slabs. 'Yeah, sure. I wish it was as easy to do as it is to say. I can't imagine life without my dog, she's just, well, an extension of me. I was an only child, going off the rails a bit. Almost got expelled from school but then my parents, well my mum, got me this cute, sweet puppy from the animal shelter for my birthday. I simply fell in love with her. She changed my life, gave me a reason to get up in the morning, and I couldn't wait to get back to her after school. She had six pups, they're all still going strong. Two of them are guide dogs.'

Shelly heard the pride in his voice. 'Then you should take her to see her children one last time.'

They sat in silence again, until he said, 'I think you're right, great idea, thanks.' Another pause. 'Why were you crying?'

She touched the bracelet and felt her sadness gather. 'I don't think I can talk about it.' She sighed. 'I know I should, but it's too difficult.' She gasped, tried to conjure up some energy to explain. 'I lost . . .' She couldn't quite get there. 'I mean, well . . .' Her mouth wouldn't form the words that were in her head. Everything was out of sync and the emotion overwhelmed her again in one great suffocating wave.

Fat tears brimmed and spilled over as she forced the two words that she sensed he would understand. 'My mother . . .'

'You lost your mother?' Shelly nodded. 'Oh . . . sorry. Perhaps we shouldn't have barged in on you the way we did. You need to be alone; I understand, really.'

She nodded again. A tear splashed onto the back of her hand. The dog made a sad little whimper and licked it away with one great swipe of its pink tongue. Shelly leaned forward and rested her cheek on the dog's broad head. 'Thank you,' she whispered. 'You've been a big help.'

'I have to go to work soon, but I can't leave you like this. Please, can I buy you a coffee, or a Coke? You'll feel better after a sugar hit, honestly. Grief is so exhausting. I've been there,' he said simply.

She thought about it, shrugged, and nodded.

They walked over to McDonald's where he ordered two cappuccinos. Giving all their attention to their drinks, they were silent for a moment, then, aware he was watching her she looked up. 'What?'

His kind smile started in his eyes, then lit up his face. She smiled back, then after an unknown length of time, when they must have looked ridiculous to fellow diners, she snapped back to reality. 'Hello?' she said.

He shook his head rapidly. 'Sorry, was I staring?'

She nodded, although his smile was still with her, like a tiny spark of warmth in her chest.

He said, 'I don't even know your name.'

Shelly realised she was batting her eyelashes, then felt the heat of a blush.

'I'm David,' he said, sticking his hand across the table. 'My grandad was a David, my dad was a David, and when I have a son, he'll be a David, too; or probably Dave. Most people use Dave these days, don't they? Firstborn son, family tradition; I come from a long line of Davids. How mad is that?'

She found herself laughing and stuck out her hand. 'How do you do, David? I'm Shelly. No long line of Shellys, but my mum just loved the name.' They grinned at each other and, for the first time since Christmas, Shelly felt a little joy at the mention of her mother. Under the table, her fingertips sought the bracelet and a secret smile directed at her mum bloomed in her heart. This David from a long line of Davids had broken the shackles of misery and set her free for a few minutes. She felt lightheaded, dizzy.

'That's a great idea of yours,' David said, breaking her thoughts. 'I'll take Pat to see her pups . . . well, they're not pups now, of course, but your children are always your children, I guess. What made you think of it?'

'I'm going to be a vet.' Shelly pulled up short of saying *when I grow up*. 'I have an affinity with animals, you know, I understand them and they understand me. Can't imagine life without them. I think it's because I'm an only child.'

'I'm the same about water. I only feel complete when I'm in it.'

'Swimming, you mean?'

He nodded. 'Diving's my biggest pleasure. I want to earn a living as a Tec diver, but it's not something you can just walk into and it's expensive to get the qualifications. That's why I do the websites and lifeguarding.'

'What's a Tec diver?'

'Basically, a deep diver that breathes mixed gas, and makes decompression stops on the way up.'

'Sounds complicated and dangerous.'

'It's another world. Do you snorkel?'

She shook her head. 'Never tried.'

'You should. It's amazing. Me and my mate Simon, we go whenever we can. I can't even begin to describe it. It makes you forget everything.'

'I don't want to forget my mum, not for a moment,' she said quietly. She looked into his face, and saw his awkwardness. 'I hope her memory never fades, ever; but I just want to say, you've helped me a lot, today. I've never been able to talk about her, before. Not at all. Thank you. It hurts so much, you can't imagine,' she whispered. 'Even so, this afternoon has helped.'

His shoulders dropped. 'That's cool. Pleased to hear I've been some use. You see, I lost my mum too. I know how you feel. Like it's never been so bad for anyone else. I guess it really is the most painful thing.'

She didn't want to give him the wrong idea. 'You've been really great, thank you, but actually I meant my mother's bracelet. I collected it this afternoon. I'll never take it off.'

He looked a little hurt and stared at the table. 'Of course, sorry.' Another awkward silence. 'I don't suppose you'd help me with Pat, you almost being a vet and all.'

'No, no!' She shook her head. His shoulders went up again and she remembered he was hurting too. 'I mean, yes, I really would like to help with your dog, but I'm not almost a vet. I haven't even started training yet.'

He let out a sigh. 'Great, thanks, that's really ace.'

* * *

'Shelly, tea!' Eve called from the back of the surgery. 'Shelly! Did you hear me? What's up with you today? You seem distracted.'

'Ah, sorry, daydreaming, didn't sleep too well.'

'Want to talk about it?'

'No thanks. It's just something I heard, playing on my mind. I'll buckle down to the lab results. Do you have anything special on?'

'Nothing I can't handle. Have you booked your holiday yet?' Shelly shook her head. 'Well, please *do* hurry up. I'm waiting to book mine but can't until you're sorted. If you can't decide which island to visit, why not book for Athens and you can simply go on from there?'

'I'll do it today, promise.' She thought about DJ and swore to herself. She'd phone him after work. No more putting it off. Her mouth dried just at the thought. What could he want after all this time?

Through Google, Shelly discovered the *Britannic* sank in 1916 and now lay just over a mile from the small Greek island of Kea. She wished she'd taken notes while listening to Gertie's cassette. What year did Gertie board the *Britannic*? She'd check the moment she got home.

Was it possible to dive the ship? Wouldn't that be amazing? She YouTubed the wreck, then Kea, and explored the island online. Wouldn't it be great to fulfil all her holiday requirements in one convenient location? Was there a dive outfit on the island? Yes! Now she longed to be there. However, it wasn't on the tourist trail and hadn't an airport. She'd have to fly to Athens, and take the fifty-minute ferry to Kea. She hesitated; it was the end of May, the start of the egg-laying season for turtles all over Greece. Before listening to Gran Gertie's tape, she had considered Zakynthos, turtle beach, to photograph them, but with patience and good luck, it was possible to capture this phenomenon on any quiet sandy beach around early June.

When Eve saw Shelly log off for the day, she eagerly turned towards her. 'So, have you booked?' she asked. 'Where're you going?'

'All done. Next weekend, the island of Kea, Greece.'

'Well done you! Kea? Never heard of it.' She picked up a pen and moved over to the calendar. 'Go on then, give me the dates and I'll mark them off.' Shelly did. 'Damn it, you'll be away for your birthday! We'll have to celebrate when you come back.'

* * *

At five thirty, Shelly let Eve out of the surgery's front door. 'Good job today, thanks, Eve. Sorry if I appeared a little distracted.'

'Don't worry about it, just get a good night's sleep. See you tomorrow.'

Shelly locked the front of the shop, then went into the back, checked her two overnight patients in their cat pens, set the alarm and security camera, and left.

Two minutes later, she was back. She punched in numbers to disable the alarm, then pulled DJ's letter out of her bag and reached for the phone. She could do this! She could . . .

She still didn't know what to say. It had been such a long long time.

Whatever you do, Shelly Summer, do not cry!

The ringtone stopped. *The person you are calling . . . after the tone . . .* and so on.

'Oh!' She hesitated, almost hung up, then decided to speak 'Hello, this is Shelly Summer. I received your letter saying you wanted to meet. I'm going away soon, so it would have to be this week, or in a few weeks' time. Please call this number to confirm a place and time. Thank you.' She pressed the hash to end the message, aware her voice had been cold and unemotional. Then all the sentiment she'd held back, all the pain, still so raw, burst forth and tears trickled down her cheeks. Why had life been so cruel to her? The ginger tom in its overnight crate curled its tail around its feet and watched her.

'You don't understand,' she said to the cat, a sob catching her by surprise. 'It's not what you think. I don't want him back, not after all this time. It's too complicated. Yet, I do . . . oh, how I do!'

Just as she reached for a paper towel, her mobile rang. Sods law, an emergency at the worst possible moment. She dried her face and picked up. 'Summer Veterinary, emergency service, state your name and phone number, please.'

'It's DJ. I was put through to this number.'

Shelly gasped. 'DJ? Look, DJ—' Then a sob escaped. She hoped he hadn't heard. 'I don't know what you want from me exactly.'

'Sorry, I realise this must be difficult after all this time. I just want to understand why you walked away. I don't have any ill will, but I need to know your reason for leaving.'

'DJ, let me explain, I was seventeen, my mother had just died and my father was having some kind of breakdown. I was trying to study and work at the same time to get myself into university. I simply couldn't cope with anything else. It was all too much.' She gasped, dangerously close to losing it. 'I'm sorry, really, but I can't talk now.'

'I can hear you're upset; I don't want that. Can I see you?'

'Yes, all right.' It might be best to meet somewhere, get it over with, or else he might turn up at the surgery, or stalk her, or call at White Cottage. 'Why don't you suggest something and let me know?'

'I will, thank you.'

CHAPTER 10
GERTIE

On HMHS Britannic, *1916.*

STARING AT THE WONDERFUL PICTURE of my sister in Lloyd George's book, I hardly heard the knock on my cabin door. It swung open and Matron stood there looking displeased. 'Did you not hear me knock, Miss Smith?'

Tears were rolling down my face. I sniffed hard and nodded. 'It's my sister, Matron. I just found it. Look, a photo of her before she became a VAD on Lemnos where she got the influenza and died.'

Matron stretched her neck and spoke down her nose. 'I can see it is not a good time, Miss Smith. I'll speak to you in the morning.' Then she turned away and disappeared down the corridor.

I never did discover what she came for. That book became one of my most treasured possessions and at this point, I still have it.

* * *

Our days were filled with scrubbing decks, making beds, and medical lessons, though we did have some time off each day until we reached our destination. This period was occupied by gymnastics, which were led by Sergeant Jones from Pontypridd in his white trousers and white vest. It's a wonder the dark haired, broad-chested soldier had the bravery to stand and raise his arms above his head before that many pairs of appreciative eyes each day.

The swimming bath was available to men in the mornings, and women in the evening. I swam every day, becoming faster and stronger with each session – keeping my promise to Father and writing how many laps I had done in my letters to Mother. I even joked that if the worst happened, I would be quite able to swim home from wherever I was. I loved the pool – loved competing with other nurses in impromptu races – and enjoyed the immensely clean feeling as I dried off. Sergeant Jones saw me punishing myself one evening and suggested that I train for the 1920 Olympic selection and even offered to coach me.

'Really! Do you think I would stand a chance? What would I have to do?'

'We would need to send off your best lap times, name, address, and date of birth.'

Date of birth? There I would come unstuck. My euphoria plummeted. 'Sir, I came here to tend the sick. This is a full-time occupation so I think it would be best to forgo the temptation of joining the Olympic team. But I thank you for offering to assist me.'

* * *

Time passed quickly. Besides our chores, we practised various forms of bandaging and endless sterilising. Such was my naïvety, during our first lifeboat drill, I thought we'd all be ordered into the lifeboats and lowered to the sea. I soon discovered the drill only consisted of fetching our lifesavers, which were twelve cumbersome cork blocks stitched inside a canvas tabard with tapes at the sides. We had to put them on properly, and gather at our designated muster stations. A simple procedure. What could possibly go wrong? The entire exercise was a waste of time in my opinion.

After passing through the Strait of Gibraltar, we entered the Mediterranean. The air grew warmer and we spent more free time on deck playing cricket and deck quoits. I continued to spend at least an hour each day improving my swimming.

The ship arrived at Naples on 17 November and embarked coal and water. The port seemed overwhelmed by battleships and troop carriers, both moored up and anchored off. These ships were served by barges that offloaded supplies. The vastness of the war started to enter my perception.

Amorous soldiers and sailors swarmed everywhere, and we enjoyed their wolf whistles when we were together. My heart pitter-pattered and my cheeks burned when they accosted us with this absurd flattery. However, if alone, I hated the raucous attention and flew back into the company of my colleagues. Of course, we all stuck our noses in the air and marched away; I admit to swinging my hips with a little more gusto than usual.

Our first patients boarded; six non-combatant soldiers destined to stay with us until they recovered or HMHS *Britannic* returned to England.

A storm whipped up mountainous seas, keeping the ship in port longer than planned, but on the Sunday afternoon, Captain Bartlett decided to take advantage of a break in the weather.

Matron Merriberry, who both inspired and terrified me, gathered a group of us to E deck as the ship prepared to leave port.

'Nurses!' she cried, her full bosom quivering. We stood to attention, matching her upright stance, chest out and head up. 'I selected the eight of you to attend our new patients.'

My heart pounded; how marvellous to be chosen. I would be exemplary, people would say so.

Matron glanced at each of us in turn. 'Look on it as an honour and an opportunity to gain as much experience as possible. Staff, or myself, will be available at all times. I want you to make the most of this unexpected chance to improve your skills.'

Fierce yet fair, they said of this woman with biceps like a man. She gave us instruction on each patient and ended with a booming, 'Any questions?'

Barbara, straightforward as ever, raised a hand. 'Is it possible to know where we're headed, Matron?'

Merriberry rolled her wide shoulders and frowned, pausing for a moment to consider. 'As we won't meet land again until we arrive at our destination, I don't see why you shouldn't know.' She drew herself up. I held my breath. 'We are heading for the port of Mudros, on the island of Lemnos. It's the largest hospital clearing station in Europe, thanks to the tragedy of Gallipoli last year.'

I gasped, clasped my hand over my mouth, and stared at Matron.

'Miss Smith, is there something you wish to say?'

'No, Matron, yes, Matron, my sister was there. I'm trying . . . in her footsteps . . . to help my parents get over their loss.'

Matron paused, unravelling my nervous words, and after staring at the floor for a second, she nodded and continued. 'The island is home to major medical facilities and supported by hundreds of Australian nurses in their own field hospital, as well as our British force and facilities. More than a hundred thousand casualties were transported out of Mudros last time I was there. Thousands of soldiers are receiving medical care there now, and waiting to be shipped back to Britain. Numbers are rising by the hour.'

There was a stunned silence, for who could imagine that many soldiers? I glanced at our six patients. One of them caught my eye and winked. I turned my attention back to Matron, but still felt a blush burn into my cheeks. I feared I had been naïve to hope the soldiers wouldn't give me trouble, but Matron was ahead of me. She turned towards our six patients and raised her voice.

'Gentlemen, welcome to our fine hospital ship, the *Britannic*. These excellent nurses will take good care of you until we reach Mudros. However, I warn you; we have a certain amount of ice on board and I'm eager to demonstrate the procedure for an ice bath. This painful technique is known to cure certain afflictions, sometimes permanently. The slightest misbehaviour, from any of you, will give me my first subject. Is that understood?' She glared at each in turn.

Their smiles fell.

* * *

HMHS *Britannic* left port, but the sea rose again tossing the great vessel from side to side. I hugged myself, head spinning, saliva rushing into my mouth. My first experience of *mal de mare*.

The promenade deck became unsafe. We secured everything that moved on E deck. Nevertheless, the area became an obstacle course. Patients threw up in their beds, and I discovered changing linen was impossible in a rolling vessel. The sea crashed across the deck from port to starboard as we pitched and tossed.

In one hazardous exercise, everything not welded to the floor was brought in and lashed down by the crew.

In the salon we squealed, clutching each other in horror when we saw one poor fellow outside lifted clean off his feet, somersaulting on the crest of a wave across the deck until he was dragged to a halt by his lifeline. Those brave men clung on as they worked in the most perilous conditions.

The next morning, at six thirty, I took my usual swift walk around deck after a hurried breakfast, before going on duty at seven. A brilliant blue sky reflected on a flat, millpond sea. At last, the Greece I had imagined! I sensed the magic of this amazing country that both Sissy and Arthur had described. The warm, silky air stroked my skin. I knew I'd be swimming in the turquoise Aegean sea at the first opportunity. Distant islands broke the horizon, the scene wonderfully calm and beautiful. One would never guess there was a war going on. Lost in the beauty of it all, I was brought back to now by the first of six tolls from the ship's bell. I peered up at the crow's nest from where the sounds rang, then I checked Sissy's beautiful silver watch; yes, it was just coming up to seven o'clock. I raced to the ward.

The vice-captain had completed the inspection and the night staff, gone for breakfast. The day shift, plus the doctors and surgeons, joined those tired nurses for an early morning meeting on the procedure once we arrived at Lemnos.

I, the least important person, found myself in charge of the ward for thirty minutes. Determined, I threw my shoulders back and proceeded to complete my chores. But my elation faded, as it always did. While training, I'd listened to the experiences of other nurses, afraid to think of what might lay ahead. I hadn't foreseen work that involved the basic, bodily functions end of nursing when I signed up as a VAD. Mopping brows and changing bandages, I'd thought. Smiles from grateful soldiers. 'Get used to it,' Barbara had said. 'It's only composted food after all.' That thought helped me a lot.

'Sluice duty, Smith,' Staff Nurse ordered. The stink of excrement raced up my nostrils like a slippery worm and made me shudder. 'Then irrigate Corporal Perkins's dressing.'

I glanced at the handsome Corporal and caught his mischievous wink.

'What if something happens while everyone's away?' I asked. 'Shall I come and get you?' Even I knew this was an imprudent thing to say, begging for catastrophe to pounce the moment I was left alone.

'No. Don't come interrupting the meeting. Use your initiative, Smith,' she replied brusquely. 'You'll be fine. What can possibly go wrong with six invalids who are hardly at death's door and half a dozen bedpans, in half an hour?'

My thoughts went to the island of Lemnos where, we'd been told, four thousand casualties awaited our arrival at the port of Mudros. We would arrive later today. I couldn't imagine that number of injured men. Where would Matron put them all? The *Britannic* only had three and a half thousand cots in her wards.

I would be up to my elbows in bedpans.

I called on our Sissy for strength, knowing my responsibilities were a test. In the back of my mind, I could hear her bold voice. *Come on, Gertie, you're my sister; dig deep and find your courage. Don't let the side down, for God's sake! How can we claim equal pay and equal respect as women if we can't even deal with a little stink or unpleasantness? There are plenty of eighteen-year-old soldiers suffering far more for their king and country!*

Then, I found myself alone with the six male patients. My heart thumped as though I was surrounded by a threatening gang. They would know, of course, that I was a fraud. I was no more a nurse than I was a twenty-three-year-old. I felt their eyes on me, like crows around a chicken carcass. *Don't look at them.* Sweat drenched my armpits. Their eyes scrutinised my body whichever way I turned.

I heard Sissy's voice: *Collect the bedpans and hide away in the sluice room, Gertie.*

The men made the most of my naïvety.

'Nurse, I have a terrific swelling, could you take a look?' one cried, which brought much laughter, but left me mortified. Every time I bent down to collect a pan, they clucked or whistled. I was desperate to get out of that ward. I'd just stacked the ward's porcelain pots by the door when Perkins called.

'Nurse, my dressing's drying up!' My face was already in flames, and I was in such a state by that point, it wouldn't have taken much to set my tears off. The sandy-haired engineer who'd called me over had suffered a damaged arm when a jack failed and a wheel hub crashed down on his humerus.

'Don't let them get to you, nurse,' he whispered. 'Just think of them as naughty children. You're doing fine and the other nurses will be back in fifteen minutes.' He smiled in such a lovely way. 'Now, open the screw at the base of that bottle of hypochlorite of soda, above the bed, and allow it to run down the tube and into my dressing. It's going to kill any germs that are still hanging around.'

'Thank you, it's my first time,' I said quietly. 'I'm a little nervous.'

He smiled, glancing around at the other soldiers. 'The best way to deal with the other patients is to be just as cocky back. Make sure they understand that you're in charge.'

'Thank you,' I said quietly, then in a louder voice, 'There, you'll be fine, Corporal.' He was an incorrigible flirt and had a wicked twinkle in his eye. The truth was, I found him to be quite adorable. According to his chart, the Corporal was twenty-three. A hint of freckles and boyish good looks made him appear much younger.

'Will you call me Johnny, nurse?' he said quietly, then winked. He glanced at my name badge. 'You're real pretty, Gertie Smith. Is there a boyfriend back home?'

'Behave, you're too bold, soldier. You'll get me into trouble.' My heart fluttered whenever our eyes met.

'Why, what will you do, chain me to the bed like one of them suffragettes? Oh dear, you're blushing again, nurse. We'll have to overcome that little weakness or the other patients will never give you any peace.' His gentle smile exposed even white teeth that showed no sign of him being a smoker. He frowned. 'Cor, miss, I'm not one to complain, but it ain't half stinky in here.'

'It's that lot,' I said, nodding at the white porcelain tower by the door. 'I was about to take care of them when you distracted me.'

A shudder rumbled through the ship with such violence, I had to grab a bedrail to stay upright. The bedpan tower toppled, their contents spilling onto the ward's floor.

'What on earth was that?' I cried. 'Good Lord, look at the mess. Matron will be furious!'

'Boilerhouse problems by the sound of it,' Perkins replied. 'Don't worry, the *Britannic*'s guaranteed unsinkable.'

'Didn't they say that about the *Titanic*? Look where that got them.' I stared at the floor, wondering what had rattled the ship with such violence.

Perkins's neighbour pleaded, 'What a pong! Can't you open the portholes?'

'No, it's forbidden. What if a big wave came in and soaked all the bedding? Where would we be then?'

Andrews, the ship's painter with a broken leg, piped up. 'Look outside, nurse. Flat as glass it is. Besides, they're twenty-five feet above the water line, I know, I was painting around the port-holes below us when the cradle tipped and dropped me onto the quayside.' He pointed to his leg strapped into one of our new Thomas splints.

'What's the point of portholes if not to ventilate the deck?' Perkins said. 'Just open them for ten minutes. Let in some fresh air.'

'Go on, nurse! Do us all a favour,' another patient cried. 'Ten minutes won't hurt. Worse than mustard gas, that stench is.'

They all joined in, bullying and teasing and doing their best to embarrass me.

'Stop it! All right, that's enough now! Just while I'm in the sluicing room.' I rushed the length of the ward, turning hefty bronze pivots and swinging the portholes open. For a moment I was Sissy: in control, in charge, doing the job and being competent . . . and it felt wonderful!

The men clapped and cheered. Still blushing, but soaking up the glory, I scurried off to the sluice room, returning with a mop, bucket, and hand shovel, when repeated short blasts followed by a long blast on the foghorn reverberated through the ward.

'Of all the times to have a muster-stations drill! Right, I'm going to give you all your lifesavers, try and get them on yourselves. I have to mop up this mess and close the portholes before Staff Nurse returns or I'll be for it!'

I had hardly started when the corridor filled with rushing nurses. Gloria, a fellow VAD, rushed into the ward first, skidded on the slurry, and with a loud squeal, landed on her bottom in the mess.

Staff Nurse followed. 'Heavens above!' she bellowed almost slipping over too. 'What bedlam is this?'

I tried to explain while, in a great flurry of activity, the other nurses helped patients into their lifesavers.

'It's not a drill, this is the real thing, Gertie,' Staff Nurse snapped. 'Hurry, fetch your lifesaver, papers and valuables and return to your muster station immediately. Quick as you can now!'

CHAPTER 11
SHELLY

Dover, present day.

SHELLY HAD MADE HERSELF LATE by dragging the trunk to the top of the stairs, but how would she get it down? She barged into the kitchen with the toothbrush sticking out of her mouth, stabbed the kettle switch to on, and was about to race back to the bathroom when she realised her father and the postman were sitting at the table. Relieved that she'd pulled her robe over her underwear, she bid them good morning.

'Malcolm's brought the post, Shelly, so I invited him in for a cuppa. Would you like to take the weight off your feet while I make you a brew?' Gordon said.

Shelly stared at him. 'What?' This was a first, Dad offering to make her a mug of tea! Then the penny dropped. He was trying to fix her up with Malcolm. As if she hadn't got enough to deal with. 'You're both very kind, but I'm running late.'

'Our Shelly's very conscientious, Malcolm; it's a wonder she hasn't got herself wed to some lucky fella by now.'

Shelly pointed her toothbrush at her father. 'Dad! Cut it out.' She turned to Malcolm. 'Sorry I don't have time this morning, Malcolm. Thanks for bringing the post, but you could have dropped it into the surgery, saved yourself the bike ride.'

'No trouble. Any time I can be of use, vet, just let me know.'

She nodded at him, glanced at the clock, hurried towards the stairs, then swung around. 'Actually, there is something, Malcolm. Would you come upstairs with me?'

Dad blew a raspberry into his tea, choking and spluttering.

'Dad! I'm warning you!' She turned to Malcolm. 'Take no notice of my father, clearly he's lost the plot. I'm about to have him certified. The thing is, Malcolm, I've got a trunk of my grandmother's things at the top of the stairs and it's too heavy for me or my father. Do you think you can manage to get it down?'

'Glad to help,' he said, squaring his shoulders. He hauled the dusty leather trunk down the stairs.

'How on earth did they manage a thing this size without wheels? It must weigh a ton.'

'I guess, if you could afford this much luggage, then you could afford a porter,' Malcolm said, dragging it into the kitchen.

'That's great, Malcolm, thanks.' She pulled on her coat and grabbed her bag. 'Bye, Dad!'

* * *

That evening, she mopped a thick covering of dust off the trunk. 'Goodness knows how long it's been up there, Dad. I wonder what's inside. It was always locked when I was a kid on a Christmas present search. I never did manage to find the key. Do you know where it is?'

He chuckled. 'Did you think we didn't know what you were up to? It's hanging on the back of the tallboy door in the loft.'

Shelly laughed. 'What? But how did you know?'

'Believe it or not, we were young ourselves once, and we both searched the house for presents whenever we had the chance, too.'

'I'm quite excited.' She dragged the case between two arm-chairs. 'I'll dish up the dinner first, then put the next cassette on. What do you say, Dad?'

'Fine by me. 'Ere, what do you think of that Malcolm? He's real sweet on you, told me so himself.'

'Dad, please. I don't need a matchmaker. What were you thinking asking him in without me knowing? What if I'd come down in my underwear, or just a towel? I'd have been mortified.'

He blinked at her, clearly confused. 'I was just thinking it's about time you got yourself a husband and a couple of kids, you're not getting any younger, and I won't be around forever, Shelly love. I'm afraid you'll be all by yourself here.'

'Aww, you're worried I'll end up a lonely old spinster? Dad, you're really sweet. But times have changed. There's nothing wrong with not marrying, or living alone. Us women are in con-trol of our lives and careers these days.'

'But what about . . .' He appeared to be struggling for the right word.

She smiled. 'If I want company, Dad, I can go into any pub and snap my fingers. Honestly, you don't have to worry about me.'

He stared at her, processing what he'd heard. 'I think you've done a wonderful job getting yourself through university, taking care of me and setting up the surgery. Your mother would be as proud as I am.' Then, he blurted as an afterthought, 'But what about me grandchildren? I'm not blind to the fact that time's running out.'

They stared at each other for a moment, both saddened and confused by the series of thoughts, words, and memories that lunged from the past. Shelly's anger rose and she had to turn away from him before she said something she knew she would

103

always regret. *How could he forget? It was his fault he didn't have grandchildren around!* She stared out of the window lost in her rising feelings. 'Dad . . .'

'No, wait, Shelly love, I've got to say this. I think about it every day and it's been too many years. But I could never get the words said. Help me out by keeping your back turned, and don't speak till I've finished.'

There was a sickening silence while she sensed his emotional struggle. She heard him sigh, then realised she could see his reflection quite clearly in the glass.

'Shelly, what I did after your mother died was wrong. I want to say, I'm really sorry, and I've regretted it for decades. My only excuse is that I think I had some kind of breakdown.'

She watched his reflection. He dragged a big white handker-chief from his pocket and dried his face before he continued. 'What I did, making you give DJ up after your mother died, well, I could have handled it better. I want to say how sorry I am for all the hurt I caused you . . . and I've been trying lately, you know, to be nicer.' He blew his nose noisily. 'That's it,' he said. 'I'm sorry.'

She couldn't speak. In some fairy-tale fantasy, she would hug him and forgive him, of course, and life would go on with his burden, and her burden, lightened. But this was the real world. The terrible pain he had inflicted on her almost twenty years ago, had been deliberate and vicious. She stared at his reflection, too numb to speak, and afraid that whatever she said would be wrong.

'I'll put another Gran Gertie tape on while we eat, OK?' she said.

He nodded glumly and she hoped the tape would contain a little humour. They both needed a smile.

In her mind, she heard her great-grandmother's voice whisper:

Forgive him, Shelly. Your father's just a lonely old man doing his best. He simply struggled along from day to day in those terrible days after your mother died, blaming the world and dealing with the injustice while trying to hide his confusion and pain. And being a man, he would never ask for help.

She had never thought about it like that before. *Poor devil.* But then again, she was little more than a child, desperate for the support of the only parent she had left.

The tape clicked and hissed and Gran Gertie's words filled the room, so sharp and shockingly clear that Shelly half expected to see her standing in the corner, smiling. Then came the after-shock. The grand old lady with a neat grey bun and pale blue eyes wasn't standing there with her arms loosely folded beneath her shapeless bosom. Her feet weren't planted a foot apart in pink, fur-trimmed Christmas slippers. However, that was how Shelly always saw her.

The voice that filled White Cottage was younger than Shelly remembered. Clearly, her great-grandmother's spirit had come to life in the room.

How I miss you, Gran Gertie.

Gordon was shovelling steak and kidney pie into his mouth like a condemned man. The emotional outpouring had given him an appetite. Then he looked up, and said, 'Your mum told me that when she was a toddler, Gran Gertie would stand at the back fence, shake a can of seed, and stare at the sky for ages.'

Shelly pressed pause. 'Why?'

'Waiting for Icarus, a carrier pigeon, with a message from someone special in Greece.'

'From Greece? Wouldn't that be too far for the poor little bird, unless it thumbed a lift off EasyJet?'

He blinked at her. 'No, a good bird can do it at a push.'

She resisted the urge to make a joke, Gordon took his birds very seriously and woe betide anyone who poked fun at them.

Shelly opened a beer and passed it to her father, then placed their plates in the sink.

'I'm shocked by Gertie's tapes, Dad. I had no idea she'd had such a life. Let's open the trunk, shall we? Did you pack it?'

'No, someone from the parish council, after the funeral. But if I recall, the trunk was practically full already.' He thought back. 'I was in no fit state for anything. Do you remember much from then, Shelly?'

She looked into his eyes and nodded.

'I do know you're still suffering, not just from your mother's death, but from all that followed too. I feel bad about that, Shelly love. I'm ashamed of myself.' He frowned, glanced at her, then the floor, then back to her. She had an odd feeling that she didn't want him to say what was on his lips.

'Don't go there, Dad.'

'I must, you see, I know it's my job as your father, to advise you no matter how old you are; but I'm no bloody expert, am I? So, I have to say this in my own clumsy way. Have you thought about going for some kind of help, treatment, grief counselling, like?'

Deeply moved, she smiled softly. 'I deal with it in my own way, Dad, don't worry. I keep busy . . . and of course, I dive. Every time I dive, it sort of dilutes what happened a little; do you know what I mean? It's a kind of therapy. Anyway, let's drop the subject and get back to the trunk. You say the church people packed it?'

He shrugged and sighed again. 'Not sure. It's all a bit blurred. I was always going to go through it, but the time never seemed right.'

The rusty key refused to turn until Gordon sprung the lock.

At the next attempt, it popped open and they both stared at the contents.

CHAPTER 12
GERTIE

Greece, 1916.

To be told to go and collect my valuables from the cabin was surprising and contradicted the drill we'd been taught. Although there was a strong sense of urgency, there was no panic. I glanced at the portholes, praying nobody would notice they were gaping open. I marched to my quarters and snatched at things, while wondering what was going on. Had a boiler exploded? I couldn't think of another reason. We were a hospital ship, therefore we wouldn't come under attack.

I spun around in my cabin. What was important? Mother's letters, documents, a lipstick, a clean uniform, my bible, my diary? They should have told us what's classed as invaluable. I stuffed things into my pillow-bag, then hurried up top.

At the muster, Matron checked everyone had their lifebelts tied properly. Some nurses were pulling their petticoats off, and I was about to join them when I remembered Sissy's book, under my pillow. Oh my! I could not leave it behind. I slipped back, through the doors, down the staircase to F deck. Without wasting a second, I stuffed the book into my pillow-bag and then returned. Such a big ship – such a long way to and from my cabin. I burst through the main doors onto the deck, red-faced and breathless.

To my horror, my companions and Lifeboat 1 had gone. All that remained were a few petticoats folded neatly on deck. Clearly, the owners believed they would return to claim their garments once the emergency was taken care of. I raced to the rail and saw the lifeboat and its seventy-five occupants dangling just above the water.

A sailor was also leaning over the rail, watching, then shouting instructions to the two men above us who were handling the lifeboat davits, great metal cranes that swung the lifeboats out and then lowered them. Towards the stern, two of the lifeboat davits were also starting to move, both appeared to be lifting full lifeboats over the side. I could see a great deal of activity in that area and thought I should go there immediately. To add to my panic, the deck was rapidly taking on a steep slope.

About to hurry along to the next muster station, something came sliding in front of me, tripping me and sending me sprawling to the floor. Pain shot up my leg as I scrambled to my feet. The deck was tilting and the first sparks of panic got the better of me. I cried for help.

A loud whistle sounded above the screeching mechanism of the davits. One of the men working the lifeboats above our muster station must have seen me fall. He yelled something that didn't reach me and pointed to his group. Now I think back, I must have been in shock because although I felt no fear, for a moment I was overwhelmed by hopelessness and couldn't move. Matron Merriberry came racing around the corner with a clipboard in hand.

'Good grief, Miss Smith! Why are you on the floor?' she cried. 'Where have you been! The captain's given the order to man the lifeboats, but we've missed ours now. Come along, let's hope the next one has room for us.'

The *Britannic* turned, headed towards a distant island, then the engines stopped. We hurried, I hobbled, pain in my ankle slowing me. Matron strode off in a walk that almost ran.

'Come along, Miss Smith!'

'My ankle, Matron. I fell, I can't . . .'

'For goodness' sake! Put your arm around my shoulder.' She supported me around the waist and ushered me towards the stack of lifeboats. 'Why haven't you got your lifesaver on?' She called over the noise of the screeching davit. 'Really, Miss Smith, you must learn to obey orders!'

Matron's remark gutted me. Wasn't I always doing my best? Hadn't I tackled every foul job with all my energy? I noticed she had abandoned her petticoat and thought perhaps I should do the same, but there was no time, and even as we arrived at the muster, I was still trying to deal with my ankle pain and clutch onto my bulging pillow-bag.

The last lifeboat at this muster appeared to be full, but the sergeant in charge ordered everyone to make room for two more. He thrust a lifesaver at me.

Matron was given a place in the bow, and the pale, silent occupants of the stern bench budged up for me, then my pillow-bag was thrown in. I struggled to try and get my lifesaver on. We were lifted, swung over the side, and part lowered. Terror filled me as we hung far above the water. One of the men called up, 'For God's sake, set us down on the water!'

I prayed to Sissy and Arthur to keep us safe!

Lifeboat 1 was ahead of us, almost meeting the sea. Our vessel continued to hang halfway down the side of the ship. Perhaps there was a problem with the lowering mechanism. I hoped we would not have to jump from this great height. Why didn't I take my petticoat off? At least I could swim; I guessed some of my companions could not. Could I rescue anyone from drowning? What terrible choices would I have to make? I tried to see Matron. Many lives would depend on her survival. If she ended up in the water, I'd try to save her first.

To start with, everything moved in a steady, comforting way. I assured myself, the King's Navy had trained for this unfortunate eventuality. Then the ship rocked and the lifeboat rim crashed against the *Britannic*'s side. Everyone cried out when the green glass stripe that ran around the hull shattered. Glass daggers flew into the boat and hit some of the crew. Thankfully, eyes and faces escaped serious damage and our sturdy lifesavers spared anybody from being decapitated.

The *Britannic*'s bows dipped further, tilting us, terrifying everyone as we swung precariously, only six feet above the Aegean. Thank God the sea was flat. Then we continued down. However, the moment we reached the water and ropes were released, the propellers started up again.

Overwhelmed by the scene, I could hardly draw breath. My fear was not at that minute for myself, but for the people in Lifeboat 1.

As *Britannic*'s bows sank, her stern lifted. The three giant propellers rose and were now half out of the water and continuing to rise. The further they came out of the sea, the faster they turned, looming like a giant bronze of Poseidon himself. I cowered, hands pressed against my chest, covering the red cross on my starched apron.

Above us, another lifeboat had paused on its way down, but they could not see what was happening immediately below them.

The propellers created a malevolent maelstrom, spray flying through the air to pepper us like holy water at benediction. Turbulence sucked Lifeboat 1 and its seventy-five terrified occupants – the wounded from my ward, the nurses who

111

tended them, my cabin mates – towards the exposed, spinning blades with inescapable force. Somewhere between them was my empty seat, and Matron's too. Some of those who were facing the propeller saw their doom approach, and started to jump out of the lifeboat like rats from a sinking ship. Thrashing and splashing, they tried to swim away. Everyone else scrambled towards the rear of the lifeboat, terrified by what was about to happen.

Realising the fate awaiting his companions, sea-scout George, the quick-witted errand boy, grabbed a line that dangled from the side of the ship and hung on. The fifteen-year-old raced from end to end of the nine-hundred-foot vessel with messages while good-natured sailors and medical staff called, 'Run, George, run!'

The lifeboat was pulled from beneath him.

'Hold on, George!' I shouted, doubting he could hear me for the roar of turbulence. Everyone clenched their fists. I waved frantically at my patients in that doomed boat. 'Corporal Perkins, look out! Get away from there! Jump! Swim away!' I screeched with such vigour my throat burned raw.

Perkins stared as his packed vessel drew nearer the fatal blades, the din of them filling the air until it drowned out the screams of terror. Less than an hour ago, Perkins had winked at me cheekily, enjoying my embarrassed blush. And now . . .

* * *

Above the Corporal's helpless craft, the ship's lights flickered once, then went out. HMHS *Britannic* bellowed and roared, the sounds rising from the liner's bowels and shuddering around us.

'*Though I walk through the valley of the shadow of death,*' the chaplain chanted, his voice timorous, two fingers making crosses in the air. *'I will fear no evil: for thou art with me; thy rod and thy staff they comfort me.'*

I gripped the side our lifeboat, my knuckles white, hysteria short-circuiting behind my eyes and all my attention fixed on the poor souls in the first lifeboat and those in the water, as the turbulence continued to pull everything towards the propeller blades.

Somebody, help them! God save them!

My body trembled, horror shaking me to the bones. Painfully helpless, I regretted lying about my age.

My knees were pressed against the priest's in the cramped boat. 'Please! Please, can't we throw them a rope?' I begged, aware that I should sit quietly like the others, snivelling and gasping and politely looking away. But I had no control of myself and knew it was wrong to pretend this was not pure horror. To turn away would be cowardly. I wanted to share their last moments, be with them in thought and spirit. All those poor, poor souls, about to suffer a horrible end. 'We have to stop the propellers!' I repeated faintly, knowing my pleas were futile.

The doomed oarsmen rowed with all ferocity, for what else could they do?

Choked by panic, and fury with my companions, I tried to stand and wave my arms. If only we could get away from the side of the ship, we could signal to those above, who were still filling lifeboats, what was happening. Nobody was *doing* anything! I was trying to run in a nightmare. I knew what was needed, but no matter what, I couldn't change the situation. My neighbour, the cook, yanked me back into my seat and delivered a fierce slap on my cheek. The shock and the outrage were appalling, then I found myself held tightly against his broad chest as my tears raged. I struggled free and fisted my eyes, unable to drag them away from the occupants of that ill-fated vessel.

The ship was long, nine-hundred-feet, there was still time – yet the wide propellers continued to turn dragging the relatively small craft towards them.

'No, please dear God, no!' I prayed.

The crammed lifeboat moved closer and closer to the destructive blades. Men heaved oars against the pull of water, still screaming for a rope to be thrown, reaching out, trying to clutch onto the *Britannic*'s slippery antifoul.

The din increased; deafening, whirring, people howling, and the roar of water turbulence. The blades spun faster and faster.

Another man jumped; I couldn't make out if it was Perkins. His head bobbed in the foam, arms thrashing in a futile attempt to escape the maelstrom, dragged feet-first towards the elegant bronze screw, then he disappeared. The foam spume turned red for a second, as did a mist in the air.

Moments later, the bow of the first lifeboat splintered. Oarsmen continued to row for all they were worth, to no avail. Bodies were tossed like jackstones from a child's hand. Nurses and patients threw themselves into the sea, but many suffered the same horrific fate. 'They're all going to die . . .' I whispered, my tears rising and my body turning cold to the core. The propeller claimed its victims. The water foaming red; dismembered bodies tossed into the air.

The young scout still dangled from the line, but how much longer could he hold on?

Another hollow moan from the dying vessel reverberated over the water like a death cry. I buried my face in my hands, not wanting to see more, then I realised our lifeboat was gaining speed. I stared at a sea that tossed and turned like a restless sleeper under a blanket of splintered lifeboat and chewed limbs. Bodies seduced by the false promise of safety. They had felt secure for a moment in that white-painted vessel, as I had.

Terrified, we ploughed through the carnage, headed for similar disaster.

We passed under the boy scout. 'I can't hold on any longer!' he yelled.

We had already travelled three-quarters of the way towards the propeller. The *Britannic* was such a length; the biggest translantic passenger ship in the world before the military got it. I locked eyes with the priest, for a moment thinking about my parents. They'd be devastated to get the news. I'd failed them.

Noise and chaos brought me back to now. 'Should we jump and make a swim for it, before we get any closer?' I cried above the din.

'Are you stronger than those monsters?' The priest nodded towards the churning propellers. 'I don't think so. What hope has a mere girl against blades powerful enough to pull God's oceans under a ship this size? Pray with me, Gertie. Pray for a miracle.' His voice was loud, but calm, a preacher's voice, but there was madness in his eyes. His words rose above the growing thrum of our destiny. '*Our Father, who art in heaven . . .*'

Everyone joined in, focusing on the priest as the turbulence almost capsized us.

'Mother!' I cried, seeing her sweet face as terror and turmoil crashed through my mind. If I could fill my thoughts with her, then death would not be as bad.

The water was now thick with the chaos of limbs and wreckage in a boiling soup of sea. I closed my eyes, overwhelmed by a need to be with my parents, many miles from this hellish situation. I yearned for my mother's arms around me in my final moments.

People at the front of our boat scrambled towards the back, dangerously close to upending us; but why should I worry? We were doomed.

CHAPTER 13
SHELLY

Dover/Greece, present day.

'Well done, Dad.' Shelly had thrown the lid of the trunk back and they both stared at a grey blanket that covered the contents.

'Looks like an army blanket,' Gordon said. 'What's on the label?'

'It's embroidered, *Johnathan Perkins*.' Shelly frowned. 'Does the name ring a bell?' She was relieved to be concentrating on Gran Gertie now. Shelly's past was just as big a monster as that ship's propeller, and she was just as terrified of being dragged towards it.

'Wasn't Perkins the engineer in the ward, and in the other lifeboat, the one that might have got chopped up on the last tape? 'Ere, rewind it a bit,' her father suggested.

'You might be right, Dad.' They listened again and realised it was the very same Corporal. 'What a wonderful historical record,' Shelly said. 'Imagine if this blanket could talk, it's over a hundred years old. Like new, too. I wonder why Gran Gertie kept it. Sentimental value, do you think? Perhaps, you know . . . who can imagine what went on underneath it? By the way, Gran Gertie's husband seems to have been a forbidden subject when I was younger. Do you know who he was – Corporal Perkins, or somebody else entirely?'

'Like I said, it's not my job to tell you.'

'She always used the name Smith. To be honest, I took it for granted it was her married name, but if her father was Dr Smith, it was her maiden name,' Shelly said.

'That was the name of her son too, your grandfather, Adam Smith. Let's hope your answers lay in one of those tapes. Anyway, my memory's going, Shelly.' Their eyes met. 'One of these days you'll have to sign me into The Gables, you know. Gertie was very happy there.'

'Are you worried, Dad?'

'Yes, of course. I'm eighty. But I'll tell you something, when I'm not worried, that's when I need to go and stay there.'

'We can visit the place if you like. Or there might be other solutions.'

'Nah, let's get back to the trunk and what's-his-name's blanket.'

Shelly lifted it out and gasped. 'Oh my, look! Christmas presents. Mum must have hidden them in here before she went shopping.' Her heart squeezed. 'Let's put them to one side.'

Gordon stared at the parcels. 'Perhaps we should have a Christmas dinner in your mother's memory this year. Maggie would love that. All she wanted was to give us a good time. Seems a shame to waste it. What do you think?'

'Oh, Dad, that's the loveliest thought. If it wouldn't be too painful, I'd love it.'

'Recently I've come to realise, she wouldn't want us to be so miserable every year. I know we've never celebrated Christmas since, because of me. But, I felt it just wouldn't work, trying to be happy and festive. It would all be a lie.'

Once again, Shelly recalled Gordon ripping the decorations down on Christmas morning, his face nasty with anger, his sobs loud. She had curled up in her mother's armchair, snuggling into the thick cardigan her mum had tossed over the chairback just before she left. It still smelled of her. The comforting, oaty smell of fresh porridge. Shelly had wrapped the sleeves around herself like a hug and cried until exhausted, yet nobody put real arms around her and said it would be all right.

She had longed for the father-figure she'd known and loved, her big, cheerful, Dad, always full of fun, but that person had died with her mother. Hardly surprising that she threw herself into the arms of the first man that showed any affection. She yawned into her hand. 'Sorry, Dad, but I'm beat. Perkins's story may have to wait until I'm back from holiday.'

*   *   *

Shelly fell asleep imagining all the pleasures of her upcoming trip. Packing, travelling, arriving – she loved it all and didn't really care where she was going, so long as she could dive, take amazing photographs, and lay on a sunbed with a good book. She woke early, with a smile. One day nearer. She should get some clothes organised. Half a dozen cotton tops, shorts, jeans to travel, capri pants and a skirt, a few luxury toiletries, sandals and walking shoes, swimwear, and her snorkel kit, of course.

Just to get away from everything familiar was an adventure.

*   *   *

Shelly slept on the plane and arrived, reasonably refreshed, at Athens international airport. Pleased to have packed all she needed into a cabin bag, there was no waiting around. She stepped out of the terminal at precisely midnight, that magical moment between yesterday and tomorrow. To her left, an enormous sign said, WELCOME TO ATHENS, to her right, the blue and white Greek flag, and the EU circle of gold stars fluttered side by side. The excitement of arriving thrilled her. The heat of the day, tucked away under the paving slabs for the night, still left the air around her snugly warm.

Guided by an information board that promised to lead her to the coach terminal, she moved between pools of golden streetlight. Twenty minutes later, she was riding the coach past an enormous sculpture of the Olympic rings.

'Madam ... madam? We are here, the ferry terminal. I get your bag,' the coach driver said.

She must have fallen asleep. The deserted port was a blaze of light, with several small ferryboats, but no people. The driver took her case from the hold. The wheels made an obscene noise on the concrete.

'You go to Kea? You have boat ticket?' the driver asked.

'Yes, yes,' she replied.

'I take the bag,' he said, taking it from her. 'Is this ferry here.' He nodded at a squat ferry, which it seemed had been waiting for the airport bus.

'Thank you, you're very kind. It's lovely to be taken care of.' She dropped a couple of euro into his hand. He beamed and put her bag on the ferry.

Fifteen minutes later, she was enjoying a coffee and doughnut and the wide smiles of a waiter who insisted on bringing it to her table. She watched mainland Greece recede into the distance, and half an hour later, caught sight of Kea lighthouse.

* * *

At Popi's Apartments, on the promenade, she turned her watch forward by two hours, and saw it was four in the morning, local time.

She dumped her suitcase in the room, made coffee, then sat on the balcony. The ferry had left, the place absolutely silent and pitch dark. Then her eyes and ears adjusted. She saw the dense, star-spangled sky broken only by a pulse from the distant lighthouse. The gentle *shush* of wavelets caressing the beach below reminded her she would swim later.

After some time, Shelly stuck a small bottle of water into her backpack and stepped out with camera and torch to photograph the sunrise. She walked along the water's edge and inhaled the ozone-rich sea air. In Britain, the sea had a pungent, fish-and-chips saltiness, but the Aegean air was so salted-caramel she licked her lips. She sat on the warm sand, hugged her knees, and remembered the first time she had come to a Greek island. She was sixteen, on an adventure with the man she loved. *Oh, David.* How could she have known that one, self-indulgent week, nearly twenty years ago, would destroy so many lives?

Shelly had dozed through the flight and now yawned and stretched, her head muzzy and eyes watering. The idea of staying up to capture the sunrise lost its appeal. There would be another dawn tomorrow. As she turned, her torchlight caught a row of deep, undulating paddle-tracks across the sand just ahead. Goosebumps rose on her arms and a rush of adrenalin wiped out her weariness.

What good luck was this! She backed up a few metres and dropped to her knees, the sand damp under her shins. Turning the torch off after switching the camera on, she flicked the ISO to its highest setting. The picture would be grainy, but using flash under the circumstances was unthinkable. Her heart pounded. She made a conscious effort to breathe quietly and stared into the shadow of the low tamarisk trees. Apart from the first soft sounds of the dawn chorus and the gentle clack of rolling pebbles on the waterline, silence surrounded her. She felt at one with nature, like a wild animal herself.

Perhaps the turtle had been and gone? She couldn't make out a returning trail in the sand. Ten minutes passed. She feared her camera battery would run flat. Then, gathering light illuminated movement to her left and she heard the scrape – scrape – scrape.

A magnificent loggerhead turtle, *Caretta caretta*, had finished laying and now shovelled sand over its hundred-plus eggs. Shelly stared in awe. Keeping her distance, she crawled up the beach a few metres, then stretched out on her belly, supporting the camera with her elbows in the sand.

Glorious creature!

The turtle, over a metre in length and weighing two hundred kilos or more, pushed mounds of sand into the nest-hole. Without looking back, and leaving nothing but a gentle dip to tell of her activity, the creature, which remained unchanged since prehistoric times, started her solemn pageant towards the sea. The shell, which at first appeared dull and crusty, caught the amber light of dawn and shone like burnished jewellery. Dragging her enormous weight, the loggerhead left a second, heavily scalloped track on its return to a life under the waves.

When the turtle drew level, she seemed to notice Shelly for the first time. In three laboured steps, she turned and lumbered straight towards the camera. Shelly didn't know what to do! To say she was breathless with excitement or fear sounded trite, but it was certainly true. She decided to keep photographing. The shutter clicked, obscenely loud in the silence. The closer the loggerhead came, the faster Shelly's heart beat. When the creature filled the frame, she took a last shot then raised her head a little to gaze over the camera.

The turtle appeared sad with its turned-down mouth and tears spilling like molten gold in the rising sunlight, but she knew they were only salt secretions, expelled from seawater it had swallowed. The loggerhead peered at Shelly with round, JET eyes. She feared it would snap at her hand or face. The hard, bony mouth had jaws capable of crushing lobsters, hefty crustaceans . . . or her precious camera. The turtle, much heavier than her, could do serious damage if it felt endangered.

I'm not a threat to you or your eggs. Return to the deep, amazing turtle. Go in peace.

She fancied the turtle heard her thoughts. After a moment, the creature turned her head towards the waterline and the gathering light on the horizon. Shelly smiled and for a moment, tears pricked the backs of her eyes. Exhaustion, or perhaps pleasure, made the turtle pause when the first wave touched her front flippers.

'Go, go!' Shelly whispered. 'Your work's done here. Goodbye, old girl. Stay safe.'

She swiped away a tear.

Torn between racing back to her room to study the pictures or staying on the empty beach to enjoy the peace, an enormous sense of miracle filled her chest. She glanced back towards the nest site. The gentle basin and ribbon-loop of tracks in the sand led from the waterline to the base of the low, cement promenade and back again. They were clearly visible in the morning light. An open invitation to curious kids and egg hunters.

She hefted several large stones and piled them against the cement behind the nest. After levelling the dip, she hurriedly kicked the flipper tracks flat and added her own footprints.

No evidence of the turtle remained. She sat on the edge o the cement and scrabbled in the detritus at the bottom of he rucksack for a pen or marker. She found a bottle of scarlet nai varnish that Eve had insisted she try. Perfect! After makin sure no one was paying attention, she daubed three large dot of polish onto the wall to mark the spot. She would return.

* * *

The town still slept, apart from some activity and subdued ligh coming from an alley that led off the quayside. Beach-side caf lights went on. The smell of fresh bread reached her and sh imagined the baker tipping racks of crusty cobs off oven tray Moments later, a door opened, and the baker, rotund an wrapped in an enormous white apron, hefted a wicker basket c bread into the street.

'*Ela, psomi!* Come, bread!' he yelled. On hearing the cr lights went on and women appeared, taking one or two loaves.

'*Kaliméra,*' they called to each other, their smiles as bright an sincere as their well wishes for a good day.

The scent of fresh bread made Shelly's mouth water and he brain cry out for strong, rich coffee. In the shade of a magnificer mulberry tree, Shelly drank from a bottle of water to soothe he throat.

Again, she recalled that first holiday on the island of Syro only remembering her childish delight of building sandcastle with her father. He had her running up and down the beac with buckets of water for the moat. There were ice creams, an warnings about not eating her dinner if she had one more! An of course, the sea. But if she really concentrated on taking he mind back, remembering how it was, then perhaps the hay feve that made Gertie sniffle and her eyes water was not hay fever at all. Did Gertie really go to her room every afternoon? Shelly suspected she would have to visit the island of Syros to find out the answers to her questions, or perhaps Gertie would reveal all on a later cassette.

Flat water in Kea's bay glinted with a web of refracted sunlight, like a giant turquoise dreamcatcher holding down nightmares. Shelly could imagine Gertie's terrible experience here, screams of terror and fear. In a blink the image disappeared, leaving nothing but peace and beauty.

The taverna owner's eyes shifted her way as he unlocked the restaurant door, clearly surprised to see a stranger at his table before eight in the morning.

'*Kaliméra!*' he called, which she knew meant good morning. 'One moment, I come.'

She nodded. The excitement of the last couple of hours still buzzed through her. She wanted to voice her experience, share the thrill, tell of the turtle, yet she knew the importance of discretion.

A ferry rounded the lighthouse. She watched it reverse skilfully up to the quayside by the harbour wall, the tailgate down long before it reached land. The minute the mooring lines were hefted over the stanchions, passengers and vehicles poured onto the island. Cars raced up from nowhere, parking randomly, dragging boxes from the ferry and cramming them into their cars and pick-ups. People kissed, hugged, hurried, and everyone shouted. Cafés filled, and suddenly Kea had come to life.

CHAPTER 14
GERTIE

Greece, 1916.

OUR LIFEBOAT ROCKED VIOLENTLY. The desperate call to Mother had hardly reached utterance when a deafening noise tore through the air. I slammed my hands over my ears. The propellers ground to a halt. Rebounding waves sent our rocking lifeboat scudding violently against the side of the long ship – away from that bloody finale.

Gasping and sobbing with disbelief, everyone stared at the bronze fins looming over us only yards ahead. Although they receded, I half expected them to resume turning with their murderous intent.

Delirious with relief, I started to laugh, and laugh, before tears raged down my face. How fine is the line between life and death? At any second, everything could change. Who held our fate in their hands? Our Captain, God, Satan, throwing dice on who would get our souls? We had to get away from there immediately.

'She's alive!' someone at the front yelled, breaking my erratic train of thought. Several men heaved a woman in nurse's uniform out of the water. Oh God, it was Josephine, my cabinmate Josephine, alive! The boy scout slid down the rope and swam on his back, away from the ship, legs frogging it, arms like windmills, the adult's lifesaver keeping him buoyant. Far above us we could see other lifeboats being lowered. Our boat drifted away from the propellers, towards the front of the vessel. Then I realised the current of water pouring into the front portholes, the ones I had opened, was pulling us along.

Someone shouted, 'The ship's gonna roll, pull hard, lads!'

Our skipper ordered, 'Take us clear of the funnels or we're damned for sure!'

I stood, placed my palms against the metal hull and pressed for all I was worth. The skipper pushed his oar against the ship's side too. Suddenly, the lifeboat seemed to break the suction. We lurched away with such abruptness I lost my balance. In an instant, I tumbled over the side, hit the water, and was going down. The cork lifesaver was no match for the weight of my long uniform.

Through my blurred, underwater vision, I could see the clinkered bottom of the white lifeboat, the red-brown antifoul below the *Britannic*, sunlight reflecting through flotsam and dis-membered bodies on the surface. Father's voice resonated in my head: *Promise you'll never give up, Gertie!*

The tapes of my lifesaver floated before my face and I real-ised I hadn't tied them properly. I grasped for them, feeling a sharp stab of pain in my wrist, then a wisp of blood before my eyes. I looked towards the seabed. In a shaft of refracted sunlight Sissy's watch glinted and flashed, beckoning me to follow as it spiralled down, out of reach. Down, into the unknown.

Dragged under by my blue serge dress, long apron, and pet-ticoat, I struck out in an effort to swim to the surface. Up, up, up towards air, a breath, a chance, but despite kicking hard, the skirt hindered my legs and the weight of my uniform was too much for my feeble arms to battle against. *I won't give up, Papa!* The lifesaver was under my chin. I struggled to pull it down, but it seemed determined to leave me. I remembered my father's hand over my face pushing me under the water and I kicked with all my might for he who had tried to teach me this lesson.

* * *

I believe I was still plunging downward, my eyes fixed on the blurred, glinting shape of Sissy's watch as it danced a zig-zag path into the depths. I recall thinking *I must keep trying,* or I would go past the point of no return. At that moment, I glimpsed a slick grey torpedo shape loom out of the darkness and race towards me. Now I was done for.

My thoughts went to my dead siblings, sure I was about to join them. The lifesaver passed over my face and headed for the surface. Hit hard in the belly, then pushed helplessly through the water at inescapable speed, I saw air bubbles, lifeboat wreckage and body parts fly by. Everything was so confused, I didn't know which direction I was going, up or down? How could I be travelling at this terrifying speed?

Shock hit me when I broke the water's surface in an explosion of foam, my arms and legs flailing and my scream finding voice in a most unladylike way. Shocked, I realised whatever thrust me through the sea with such alarming urgency was *a living thing.* How was that possible? The strength and speed by which I'd been forced upward, racing towards a life-saving breath, was impossible to comprehend; and by an animal . . . a creature that I sensed had exceptional power and intelligence.

They hauled me back into the lifeboat. Hands tugged at my clothes, people groaning under the weight of me, my ungainly clumsiness as nurses and crew manhandled me back to my seat

I shook violently, teeth chattering, another scream trapped in my chest while I tried to grasp what had happened. The priest yanked his jacket off, having had the forethought to put it on over his lifesaver. He kindly wrapped it around my shoulders.

'You're safe! Praise be to God! That was a glorious thing, to be sure,' he said. 'I've never seen anything like it!' He crossed himself and raised his voice. 'We prayed for a miracle, dear brethren, and Our Lord delivered. Trust in Him and thou *shall* be saved!' he cried over the boat, taking full credit for my rescue.

Sobbing and coughing up seawater, I curved myself into the strong, safe arms of the baker. 'What happened?' I gasped when I could finally speak. 'At first, I thought it was a torpedo. It hit me so hard in the belly and lifted me. I was drowning . . . going down . . . down.'

'A dolphin,' the priest cried over the racket now coming from the ship. 'Brought you clean out of the water. I never would have believed such a thing if I hadn't seen it with my own eyes.' He struggled to his feet and raised his hands. 'Glory be to God!' Then he wobbled a little and plopped back onto his bottom.

For a moment, everyone stared at the spot where the creature had disappeared. Somebody started clapping, then everyone joined in, whooping and hollering in a manic kind of joy. Yes, miracles do happen, and everyone on that lifeboat understood they had witnessed one.

Silence fell just as suddenly, faces turned away from the propeller. Someone wept. Everyone closed their eyes, or turned them towards the centre of our boat. Nobody wanted to look upon the carnage that floated around us. Most were shivering in spite of the bright sun. The groaning and complaining that resonated from the ship in its battle to stay afloat also changed its tune. A great whoosh came from the open portholes, as if the *Britannic* expelled her final breath. The gale-like draught was so strong it pushed us away from the vessel. Anything small enough to fly out through the eighteen-inch portholes did so, scattering gauze, bandages, paper dishes, gloves, caps, and cotton wool over the water like confetti.

'What's happening, another explosion?' I asked.

The priest shook his head. 'The air's being forced out as the ship fills with water – that air would have kept her afloat if only it had been trapped inside. Now she's doomed for sure.'

'You mean if the portholes weren't open, she would have stayed afloat?'

'Exactly. Didn't you notice that all the doors opened inward? Those heavy, watertight doors are built to keep not only the water from coming up through the ship but for keeping the air inside too. The air keeps her afloat.' He shook his head forlornly. 'Now, some fool has opened some of the portholes and all is lost. Countless lives wasted because the ship that was destined to save them, is sinking.' He crossed himself. 'God have mercy on our poor boys. Most will die, not because of our enemy, Kaiser Bill, but because of some incompetent on board who can't obey orders.' He peered at the water. 'If only HMHS Britannic could have stayed afloat long enough to reach land. She could have been repaired and returned to duty.' He shook his head forlornly.

'But, Father, those portholes are usually many feet above sea level, who would ever have imagined they'd end up on the waterline?' I said.

'That's why we have a captain, miss. A man capable of foreseeing every scenario, who gives orders for that reason. Like God, he must be obeyed, without question, under every circumstance. If he gave orders for the portholes to remain closed, and somebody who knew of his order still opened them, that person alone is guilty of this catastrophe, and the massive loss of life that will follow the ship's demise.'

It was me . . . me!

The horrible truth came home to haunt me for the rest of my life. *I* was responsible for the ship sinking. Me, showing off in front of six recuperating soldiers, had caused this great catastrophe. Now what would happen to the thousands of wounded soldiers, waiting for us to rescue them? I knew what would happen. They would die! All because of me and my stupid vanity!

Wave after wave of remorse ran through me, but remorse wouldn't save lives. Nor would it ease the pain of the dying, or those who writhed in agony while they waited for a ship that would never arrive.

Our men rowed furiously. 'Why don't we head for the island, instead of going around it?' I asked.

'We're trying, but the current is so strong in this channel, it's pulling us past,' the cook said.

'What is that place, the island?' I asked the priest.

'I believe it's the Greek island of Kea,' he replied.

Another lifeboat full of uniformed staff rowed away from the *Britannic*. Their boat rocked violently as sudden turbulence burst through the calm sea. The oarsmen heaved away, and I sensed their urgency. The *Britannic* was so low in the water now, I wondered how she was still afloat. The ship's bell clattered musically from the crow's nest, breaking a moment of unnatural silence, then two long blasts of the whistle sounded above the clamour. I remembered the drill, it meant abandon ship immediately. A final lifeboat pushed away.

My sadness ballooned inside me. Nobody spoke, silence reigned in our lifeboat. Everyone gazed at the final seconds of that most majestic ship, paying homage to her like the great goddess of the sea that she was. We all knew these moments would stay clear in our memory until the day we ourselves died. The air was heavy with the most wretched grief.

'Look! They're leaving,' I whispered, reluctant to break the silence. 'But somebody's still up there, on the bridge, look!' Wet, shaking, and clutching my bruised belly with one arm, I lifted the other and pointed.

'Your hand's bleeding,' the priest said. 'You must have caught some of that broken glass.'

I looked down and noticed the rip in my sodden apron bib. In a flash of clarity, I remembered the sharp stab as I had tried to grasp the lifesaver tapes. 'No, it was Sissy's watch pin,' I said while imagining my dear sister's silver timepiece descending through the turquoise Aegean. Only God could know how deep the water was at that point? Perhaps the watch was still spinning slowly towards the seabed. Perhaps it was the glint of silver that had attracted the dolphin's attention in the first place. Could my mother's gift have inadvertently saved my life? So overwhelmed by this glorious thought, I trembled and started to cry silently.

The baker put his arm around my shoulders. 'You're in shock,' he said. 'But try and stay calm, you're safe as can be, and we'll soon be on dry land.'

The sea had drawn level with the *Britannic*'s control centre. Staring at the vessel, the chaplain crossed himself again. 'Look, that's our brave captain, still in his pyjamas. May God save his soul. If he doesn't get away now, he'll be sucked under with the ship.'

The men, one in uniform, one in pyjamas, walked off the deck at the side of the bridge, straight into the water. They swam to a raft, we all watched, willing them on, as they pulled themselves to safety. The sinking ship groaned and gasped in its dying moments. A lifeboat picked up the two men and rowed clear, while HMHS *Britannic* seemed to hesitate for a moment.

A series of deafening detonations rose from below. I guessed the ship's boilers had exploded. Not that I knew anything except what I had read in the broadsheets about the *Titanic's* demise. I had found the personal accounts of surviving passengers fascinating, but never dreamed I would, one day, find myself in a similar situation.

The massive ship slowly rolled to one side and with a thunderous toll the four funnels snapped off in succession, each hitting the water in a great, metallic belly-flop that made our lifeboat bob violently. 'Hold tight, everyone!' one of the oarsmen yelled. The chimneys hissed and wheezed and their final breaths rose like steaming ghosts in a display of exhausted power.

Our mighty vessel slipped beneath obscenely calm water, its great bell tolling once, then silenced forever.

Moments later, the sea bubbled and heaved, agitated, as if trying to swallow something too big for its gullet. Cork-filled lifesavers belched to the surface and jets of seawater spumed into the air as Davy Jones made room in his locker for the damned ship.

Less than an hour had passed since I had been ordered to use my initiative – and the bedpans had toppled.

The sun beat down, blinding flashes bounced off undulating water, stinging my eyes. My face prickled with the salt from my weeping – or from the sea – I couldn't say. Perhaps they were one and the same. An ocean of tears wept for drowned sailors, sunken ships, and Sissy's lost watch. The balding priest knotted the corners of a large handkerchief. Somewhere, I had lost my uniform cap. I stared at the flotsam, hoping to spot it when, to my horror, I saw a body near us. A man floated on his back, limbs outstretch like a starfish.

'There's a person in the water!' I shouted, pointing at his white canvas lifesaver. The oarsmen rowed in the direction of my finger. 'I know him. It's Corporal Perkins!' I shouted.

As they dragged Perkins over the side, the boat rocked violently and took on a great wave. We found ourselves almost calf-deep in sloshing seawater. We hauled bags of valuables onto our knees and someone screeched. 'We're sinking!'

'There're bailers under the seats, use them!' our skipper ordered.

With some clumsiness, Perkins was manhandled into the back of the packed lifeboat and laid across our knees. The mechanic had a terrific gash across his forehead, so deep it exposed his skull. I pressed two fingers under the curve of his jawbone and barely felt the flutter of a pulse. 'He's alive, Matron, just! Hardly a pulse. What shall I do?' I shouted towards the front of the boat.

'Compress the wound to stop the bleeding!' she called back.

With the Corporal's head in my lap, I said, 'Excuse me,' to the priest, took the handkerchief off his head, and pressed it against the wound.

A male voice came up from the other end of the bench. 'His foot's gone!'

Horrified, I leaned forward to peer down the row. They were holding the soldier's limb up, the end of his trouser leg flapped for a moment, then concertinaed towards his knee exposing a mashed stump where his left ankle and foot should have been. I bit down on a scream before it escaped. It had started. The terrible injuries I would be expected to deal with, calmly, in my career as a nurse. Someone clutching a brown leather bag scrambled through the boat, which rocked violently again. When the man looked up, I recognised the surgeon.

134

'Give me your belt, sailor,' he said to one of the crew. 'Keep the limb elevated while I stop the bleeding.' He fastened the belt tightly around Perkins's thigh, then he scrambled up to sit next to the priest. He thrust his fingers under the Corporal's jaw and closed his eyes. After a moment, he shook his head. 'He's lost too much blood, I'm afraid he won't make it to shore.'

After all we had been through and given what I had done, I could not accept that my patient was going to die. Outraged, I yelled, 'No! Surely there's something we can do? We can't just let him die like this!'

'He needs blood, miss, and he needs it right this minute.'

Right now, I would do anything to save the life of our poor Corporal Perkins.

'Then give him my blood, I'm O, it does for everyone, doesn't it, sir?'

He shook his head. 'That's very noble, but I don't have the intravenous transfer equipment with me, miss.'

I remembered the two wide-bore needles, the glass tube and the rubber hose connecting everything together from my training days. 'Please, there must be another way. What's to stop you using a hypodermic syringe? Please try!' I started rolling my sleeve up. 'Please, sir, if he was your son ... he is somebody's son, we should at least try! My brother Arthur, if he'd had blood, perhaps he wouldn't have died, sir. Don't you see? Somebody could have saved him if only they had been brave enough. If only ... oh, sir, you don't know what that would have meant to my mother.'

He stared into my eyes for a moment, then he shouted, 'Stop rowing!'

CHAPTER 15
SHELLY

Greek island of Kea, present day.

THE TAVERNA OWNER BROKE INTO her thoughts. 'Hello, lady. What you want, *café*? Where you from?' He asked brusquely. His eyes swept over her dark hair, pale skin, and long legs.

'England.'

'Ah, is good, I am Makris. You like, frappé, Nes?'

'Greek coffee, sweet, please.' A strong coffee would set her up for a swim.

'*Kafé, glykó!*' Makris yelled towards a woman in the open kitchen. 'You alone? Married? Why you here? Holidays?'

'I'm tracing my family tree,' she said. 'Look, the ferry's leaving already.'

'Yes, is going to Syros. Is near here. Tree? What tree?' He glanced up at the heart-shaped mulberry leaves.

'No, no, I'm tracing my roots.' She stifled a giggle as his eyes travelled down to the base of the trunk. 'My great-grandmother was an English woman, Gertie Smith. She was on a boat and stayed here for a while after it sunk.'

'Ah, the *Britannic*?'

Surprised, Shelly nodded.

'My grandfather say it hit a mine, or it was torpedoed by a German U-boat. There is still much talk. Was it a ship for the sick, or a secret carrier of guns and soldiers to help the forces near Gallipoli?'

He crossed himself, then his eyes lit up.

'My cousin have the best dive school. If you like, I get you a good price, yes? You no have worries with Aries and his boys. The father of Aries helped the famous Jacques Cousteau, he found the ship, you know? He dived down to the *Britannic* many, many times. So, you want to dive?'

'Yes, I want to dive,' Shelly murmured, gazing out over the flat water, wondering just how far away the magnificent turtle was at that moment. She imagined it, buoyant in the blue Aegean, joyously rolling in ribbons of reflected light; frolicking, free of its eggs and weightless in the water. Could that crusty *Caretta* be cavorting over HMHS *Britannic*'s wreck? She peered past the lighthouse and tried to visualise how the hospital ship looked now, the oval shadow of *her* turtle sliding silently over the coral-encrusted hull.

* * *

Shelly approached the dive centre. A guy who looked as though he needed a good night's sleep was loading diving gear into a trailer.

'Anyone in there?' she asked, nodding at the open door of a square, stone building. 'I'm looking for Aries?'

'Oh, Harry. He's inside, but there's no snorkelling trips today, madam,' he said. 'Harry's just back from Athens.'

Shelly smiled. 'Thanks.' She headed into the shop. The thrum of a compressor filling dive tanks vibrated through the open doorway. A shaft of brilliant light pierced the room, illuminating a table cluttered with water and beer bottles and throwing everything else into deep shade. Two young men, both breathtakingly handsome, studied their iPhones at the table. The room smelled of damp clothes, sweat, and beer.

'Hi, who do I speak to about a dive?' she asked brightly.

They glanced at each other, then the older one said, 'Sorry, there's nothing available until next week. Where did you want to dive, *love*?'

'The *Britannic*.' She nodded over her shoulder towards the sea.

'Ha! Sorry, no chance. To start with, you have to be a very experienced diver, *love*. We don't just take anyone. Secondly, you need permissions.' He stood, at least six-two, fit, early twenties. 'Best to book an easier dive, or perhaps a snorkel trip.'

Condescending prick!

She dropped the smile and stared into his face.

'Have you dived before, *love*?' He took a step towards her.

'MS *Zenobia* – Cyprus, *Cirkewwa* – Malta, *Fortunal* – Croatia; *Thistlegorm* – the Red Sea, and,' she paused for effect, 'the *Lusitania*. Also, at least fifty more hundred-metre-plus wrecks . . . *love*.'

She narrowed her eyes, picked up a beer bottle and studied the alcohol content. 'Is this the only dive outfit on the island? I was hoping for something a little more professional, *love*.'

The smirk fell from his face. She glanced at the older guy and was surprised to see him grinning as she spun on her heels and stormed out.

* * *

On her walk back to the port, she kicked herself for being unfairly abrupt and judgemental with the diver. She sat on one of the benches that ran along the edge of the beach, closed her eyes and listened. The sea forged its own unique sounds, rich with dormant strength and whispers of endless secrets. She needed to go in, allow the harmonious murmuring of each gentle wave bathe her spirit and dilute her tension. If she allowed her imagination free rein, she could hear the echoing sounds of dolphins and whales, the plaintive mewl of high-flying seagulls drifting over the oceans, the laughter of children as they decorated sandcastles with cockleshells. The roar of an approaching motorbike shattered her musing.

She would never see the *Britannic* if she alienated herself from the dive outfit. Why couldn't she be as patient with men as she was with cats and dogs? The motorbike stopped behind her.

'Need a lift?' She turned and saw the older guy on a quadbike. 'I'm going round to the port,' he called.

She hesitated, wanting to sit a while and enjoy the peace, but here was a fresh opportunity to get on friendly terms with a diver. 'Great, thanks,' she called.

He was early-to-mid-forties; strong physique and deeply tanned. Tight curly hair with the first signs of grey, eyes hidden behind shades. She climbed onto the quadbike beside him.

He turned off the engine, used a forefinger to drag his glasses down the bridge of his nose, then gazed over them with piercing brown eyes. 'Can I say, I'm sorry about before? That was my son, Elias. It was his twenty-first yesterday and, well, everyone's a little hungover this morning. Perhaps we all sounded a little patronising.'

She shook her head, stared at the sea rushing towards them, then dashing away – like a dog chasing something that scared it. 'Yes, a bit, but to be fair I'm a little tense from lack of sleep. Let's forget it, shall we?'

He nodded and started the engine.

'Can I make amends ... buy you a coffee?' They pulled up outside a pavement café near the ferry terminal. 'Harry Dennis, owner of Dive-Den.' He thrust his hand towards her. 'The locals call me Aries.'

She shook it firmly. 'Shelly Summer.'

'Where're you from then, Shelly Summer?' he asked while they waited for their drinks.

'Near Dover, England. You? Dennis doesn't sound very Greek.'

'Born here, but my grandparents were English, from Portsmouth. My grandfather started the business just after the last war. Needless to say, I've been diving since I was a kid. You're clearly qualified, but there's a lot of rigmarole getting the permissions for that dive. It's listed as a British war grave. Also, the Greeks control the deep dives because of antiquities, even though the wreck's owned by an Englishman, Simon Mills. All in all, it's a paperwork nightmare.'

He stared out across the water, as people who love the sea always do. Calm, content, at peace with himself and the world. She smiled, understanding exactly where he was at.

He returned from his daydream and continued. 'On top of that, there has to be a remotely operated vehicle, and a Greek official watching and recording everything that goes on with regard to the wreck.'

'I see, sounds complicated. I should have done some research before I came over. To be honest, it was a last-minute trip.' She peered across the bay at a lighthouse on the rocky promontory that led into the harbour. He followed her eyes.

'One of the oldest lighthouses in Greece, takes its name from the little church next to it, *Agios Nikolaos*, St Nicholas. Built on the ruins of Poseidon's temple in 1831.'

'Poseidon's temple?' She smiled. 'Interesting.'

He nodded. 'It was in use when the *Britannic* went down, though not lit, of course, as the *Britannic* went down in daylight.'

'Did she sink far from here?'

'No, just over a mile, or three kilometres if you like, out from the lighthouse there, and a little to the right.' Diamond light glanced off the perpetual motion of the bay 'Why do you want to dive the *Britannic*?' he asked.

'My great-grandmother was a nurse on the ship.'

His eyebrows went up. 'That's interesting, did she survive?'

'Yes, she did.'

He turned his attention back to the open water. 'There's talk about it being made into a museum, did you know?'

She shook her head. 'Surely they're not going to try and lift part of it? That would be impossible. She's nine hundred feet long. Without a doubt she'd break up and a century-old ecosystem would be lost, all because some entrepreneur wants to make a few bob.' She caught his calming look and wondered how many panicked dive students he had settled with that steady gaze.

'No, they're considering taking submersibles down. We're trying to put a small museum dedicated to the Kea wrecks together. So far, it's just a few bits of memorabilia that the locals gathered in their nets over the century, or bits that washed up just after it happened. A couple of cork lifesavers with the name stencilled on. A lifeboat, complete with oars, though the plaque has gone to Liverpool's maritime museum; and some enlarged pictures of the *Britannic*'s construction in Belfast. There's a video too, sponsored by one of the dive-equipment manufacturers. I'll take you to have a look if you like. Tell me about your great-grandmother.'

'Nothing much to tell, yet. I'm just starting to look into her life. First World War and all that. She passed away in '98, a few days after her hundredth birthday.'

'A great age. Jacques Cousteau took one of the surviving nurses down in a submersible to see the wreck. Sheila MacBeth was in her eighties at that time. Those nurses were quite remarkable women by all accounts.'

When he smiled, the knots in her shoulders melted away. 'No, I didn't know. That was kind of him, and brave of her.'

'Your great-grandmother must have had some stories to tell.'

'I guess she did, but I was only thirteen when she died. My mother was heartbroken. You see, her mother died just after giving birth, so my great-grandmother stepped into my grandmother's role. She was quite wonderful.'

'You were lucky; most of us never get to meet our great-grandparents, or hear their experiences.'

'Gran Gertie was a strong woman. I loved her very much, but I didn't know about her being on the *Britannic* until recently. She was unbelievably brave. You see, you had to be a minimum of twenty-three to be accepted in the Voluntary Aid Detachment, but she was so determined to nurse the wounded soldiers, she lied about her age and got away with it.'

'She sounds cute.'

'Cute?'

He raised his hand as if to stop her words hitting him. 'Sorry, wrong word, perhaps. I didn't mean . . . she just sounded cool, that's all.' He stood.

'No, it's me who's sorry – ignore me, I'm just tired.' She smiled. 'I was travelling through the night and then I noticed a turtle nesting just before dawn so I stayed up to watch. Such an amazing thing . . .' Damn, she wasn't going to tell anyone. She blamed her loose tongue on lack of sleep. Lids heavy now, skin itchy, and her brain running on five per cent battery. 'Anyway, it was so magical, I sat on the beach for another hour and watched.'

She sighed. 'Must go for some shut-eye, Harry, I'm in danger of nodding off while I speak.'

'Poor you.' He laughed gently and sat down again. 'Just before you go, can I ask, was she tagged, the turtle, did you notice?'

'I didn't. It wasn't quite light, but I'll check the photos.'

'You took snaps in the dark? She'd be disorientated by the flash. Did you happen to see if she made it back to the sea?' He stared at the waterline.

She wanted to rest her head on his shoulder. 'No, once I'd taken some selfies of me catching a ride on her back, I left.' She forced her eyelids up and caught the shock on his face and would have laughed if she'd had the energy. Harry, she realised, was simply concerned for the turtle's welfare.

'Oh . . . you're joking, right?' He looked slightly embarrassed. 'Sorry. Sometimes, tourists, you know, have no idea.'

'I need to go. Thanks for the lift,' she said, pushing herself to her feet then headed towards her room, across the road.

Shelly stood on her balcony for a moment. Below, Harry swung the quadbike around and headed back to the dive centre. She peered out towards the distant lighthouse and imagined her great-grandmother sleeping in one of the nearby houses, exhausted from her ordeal, or looking out at the very same view.

Minutes later, she slid under a crisp white sheet, closed her eyes, and drifted into a dream that recalled scenes from the first Greek island she had ever visited, Paros.

In her mind, she was floating on her back, arms and legs spread. The sun, warm, on her face and belly, and the absolute bliss of being on holiday, alone, with her first, real, boyfriend. The glory of being in love, of sleeping in his arms, of knowing he loved her. The certainty that one day they would marry, have children, and live happily ever after.

Shelly slept with a smile on her lips, hugging her pillow. 'David . . .' she murmured in her dreams.

* * *

Sun streamed through the hotel's window. Shelly, disorientated for a moment, wondered where she could be and why she lay in bed when it was clearly daytime. She blinked at her suitcase, relaxed, and gathered her thoughts. The little fish-shaped clock on the wall told her it was mid-afternoon. She would check out the next beach, go for a snorkel, eat local food, and sleep with the balcony doors open and the sound of the sea drifting in. Perfect.

She phoned work, relieved to hear Eve was managing perfectly well without her. Then, she called her dad, he didn't answer. Right after dinner, she would find a frivolous gift for each of them. Now she felt better. A small task to complete would give her day a sense of purpose.

While peering into gift shops and cafés, Shelly became aware of local eyes following her, one of the first tourists of the season. Between a fish restaurant and a ticket office she discovered a rack of sepia postcards showing Kea as it was. Her excitement rose as she bought one of each, and a vague plan to further record her great-grandmother's life germinated.

A short stroll along the pale sand brought her to the simple little church on a promontory dividing the bay. Under a deep cobalt sky, the blinding white chapel, surrounded by a flourish of wild asphodels bursting from the rocks, made the perfect photograph. She would dedicate at least one day solely to photography, but for now, she needed to swim, to lay the ghost of David and that terrible day. Every holiday was the same. This first swim, a pilgrimage in memory to the day she lost David.

*   *   *

She hoped the rock that the chapel stood upon would continue just as steeply under the water. A sanctuary for myriad sea creatures. Small octopus, pipe worms with their colourful chrysanthemum-type heads; fat, coral-coloured starfish, sea urchins, young sea bream and striped, colourful wrasse. Picking her spot on the pristine sand, she dropped her sundress and beach bag, pulled on her snorkel gear, and walked into the sea.

Once the water reached her thighs, she slipped on the fins. It had been so long since her last holiday, she stood for a moment, savouring her surroundings. The sun, on its descent now, sparked off the water. She took a deep breath through her snorkel tube, testing it, then dived below the surface, scudding along the seabed. The thrust of water stroking her shoulders, back, and legs. A sensation of speed, weightlessness, and adventure surrounded her. A smile hovered in her chest, then spread through her body. This underwater world was so beautiful it made her want to laugh and cry at the same time.

Small boulders lay scattered over patches of pale sand, cross-hatched by silver lines of glinting light. The shadows of fish played across the seabed. She wondered how Mother Nature disguised them so well that they disappeared leaving only their telltale shadow on the sand below.

The bottom sloped away until she was two metres beneath the surface. She wanted to stay down, explore, but her chest tightened with the need for air. More fish appeared once she had the eye for them, picture-book perfect, congregating in shapeshifting murmurs. Swift and silent. Her heart thudded, her blood thickened, needing oxygen, she must go up, up, breathe. Half a metre of moray eel slid from under a rock. A body of pure muscle, thick as her forearm, wearing nature's warning livery of yellow and black. Lips turned in, cheeks hollow, like an old man without his dentures. Repugnant yet hypnotising. The fixed, smiling mouth showed a hint of razor teeth, while two satanic eyes drew her. The devil in the deep blue sea.

Her head buzzed; her chest exploded with the need to breathe now. Why couldn't she stay down longer? Feel his pain in the last moments of his life. Pay the price for her wrongdoing.

The water, so crystal clear, painfully reminded her of that terrible day when the man she loved was taken away from her, right before her eyes. Why did it happen? And why did she have to keep punishing herself like this? She had loved David so much . . . and it was *only* a bracelet that her mother had bought her for Christmas. In a cruel twist of fate, her mother was dead because of it. Just a piece of silver with a few poignant words engraved around the inside. Beautiful, sentimental words, but not worth the lives of all those people she loved.

Was this hateful hex destined to go on? Whose life would be destroyed next – DJ's? After that terrible year with so much pain and loss, Shelly had found it impossible to forgive herself again. For twenty years, she had feared what might happen to anyone who came close to her heart. Now, with no notion of the danger he might be inviting upon himself, DJ wanted to come back into her life. Her precious DJ. If he knew about her past, he would want to get as far away from her as possible.

At the root of all Shelly's heartache was that beautiful, silver bracelet.

Her memory returned to the island of Paros, and David. She recalled treading water, pulling the snorkel from her mouth and begging. 'David, please, if you love me, try and find my bangle.' Shelly remembered his grin – his last grin – ever. She'd slept with him for the first time, the night before. She was a grown-up now, and loving it. He was showing off too, winking at her, touching her at every opportunity – her hand, her neck, her cheek. Smiling with almost religious sincerity. David and his woman. His fins breaking the surface as his head went down. She, proud that he was doing this for her, feeling her power.

Shelly returned to now, with a flick of her fins she headed up, up . . . She'd left it too late! Her lungs screamed, her head buzzing louder and louder, her vision turning black in the corners. She broke the surface! Hauled in those first, desperate, breaths, her chest heaving painfully. Then, she floated on her back while her pulse returned to normal. Her eyes were closed as she pulled her steamed mask back, enabling hot tears to run straight into the sea – saltwater into saltwater. No matter how often she told herself *it wasn't her fault*, she always knew it was. Oh David.

A few months later, she met DJ.

CHAPTER 16
GERTIE

Greek island of Kea, 1916.

UNDER AN EVER-HOTTER SUN, on a sea as flat as glass, the bailers kept bailing, but the rowers raised their oars, and yard by sneaky yard we floated on the millpond sea, never closer nor more distant from the island but drifting in the invisible grip of the current. The surgeon rummaged in his bag and firstly used cotton wool to rub a little alcohol onto my wrist. Then he brought out a syringe. For a moment my bravery wavered. I shuddered at the size of the needle, which seemed to grow larger as it came closer to my flesh. He tapped my wrist and pushed the wide-bore needle against an artery. It resisted, then quite suddenly the needle popped through my skin and I heard someone gasp. The barrel of the syringe was glass and as the bright red blood filled it, my head began to swim.

'Deep breaths, nurse. Are you all right?' the surgeon asked.

'I'm only a VAD, sir. Yes, just a little lightheaded. It's a very odd sensation.'

'Press down on your artery while I withdraw the needle and insert it into the soldier's vein.' He turned to the priest. 'Please, help her. This needs to be done quickly, before the blood starts to clot. I can't see to them both at once.' He took the Corporal's arm and emptied the contents of the syringe into it. Turning back to me, he said, 'Do you think you can manage another one?'

I nodded. 'Yes, of course. I believe two pints are possible, are they not?'

'I think one more syringe should be enough to maintain a stronger pulse. Your sacrifice is admirable. Tell me your name, young lady.'

Before I could reply, someone rasped, 'Boats!' I looked up, glad to be distracted from the wide-bore needle. People were pointing and waving at the first of several small craft chugging out towards us.

The surgeon managed to complete his task and although I felt lightheaded, it was a relief to know Perkins stood a much better chance of survival now.

'What is that place?' I asked the chaplain, trying to distract myself from the shocking ache in my midriff, and the painful throb of my ankle. I also avoided looking at the sea in case I saw Perkins's missing foot floating in the flotsam. Was there no end to this nightmare?

'As I said earlier, I believe it's the Greek island of Kea,' the priest said, pressing on my wrist as the surgeon withdrew another syringe full of blood.

'But how on earth will we get home?' I whispered to myself.

I promise I'll never give up, Father!

If he hadn't insisted on that ridiculous thing! Me in my father's long johns, slumped over the dining-table protector cork, my father yelling orders at me. *Kick, Gertie, kick!*

The child inside me rose, needing the guidance of an adult. A child desperate to be told that everything would be all right, that it *wasn't* my fault. I glanced at the other end of Perkins, the concern on everyone's faces. He was maimed for life. There are penalties for wrongdoing and at that moment, I feared I should be hung for this.

No, no, don't even think such things!

I was going mad with the worry, but one wrong had led to another and somebody should pay. I shouldn't have lied about my age, that was the start of it all. One small, simple lie had led to this carnage, and I had a terrible feeling it wasn't over. 'I'm not fit to be left in charge – to use my initiative.'

The chaplain stared at me, trying to make sense of my jumbled words. 'I don't think you should give any more blood, child,' he said. 'You're in danger of becoming a little hysterical.'

I fought the temptation to tell him that I had opened the portholes. Perhaps all the Corporal's fellow patients had perished. I hung my head. I had to do everything I could to try and save his life.

Nobody must ever know I was responsible, but what if Perkins told, and what would his reaction be when he discovered he'd lost a foot? Yet what difference would the truth make to anyone now? I must take my secret to the grave, and along my journey through life, I swore I would do everything I could to atone for the terrible thing I'd done.

The Corporal's eyes fluttered and opened a little. 'I died,' he slurred. 'I find myself in the arms of an angel.'

I stroked his cheek. 'Behave, Corporal. Heaven's full enough after today, so you're on leave for a while.' A splash on his cheek confused me for a moment, then I realised it was one of my tears.

His eyes narrowed. 'My head feels pretty close to Heaven already, nurse.'

Realising the proximity of the soldier's head to my woman parts, I felt myself blushing again. 'I'm warning you, Corporal Perkins, any nonsense and you'll be over the side.'

He closed his eyes and smiled. 'Don't cry, nurse, I'll look after you. Do I have all my limbs?'

I looked at the surgeon. He put a finger to his lips and shook his head.

'As far as I can see,' I said. 'It's difficult to tell. But you'd better make sure you keep control of them, or you'll find yourself in a greater predicament.' I held his head to my chest to prevent him from looking down and seeing his elevated leg. He turned his head towards my breasts, smiled, and closed his eyes again. He became so still, I wondered if he was still conscious.

The surgeon took his pulse and smiled at me. 'That did it. Well done, nurse.'

Some distance away, I saw the Captain helped from the raft into a lifeboat, then he boomed orders through a megaphone. We were too far away to make out his instructions. On the horizon, the grey shapes of two battleships approached. Not knowing if they were friend or foe, we were all relieved when a small, brightly painted *caïque* came alongside with a rounded but rustic skipper at the prow and a younger man at the tiller.

I stared at the old fisherman. His loose, tanned skin folded over the bones of his face like warm toffee. Thick, wind-dried lips smiled from below a hedge of silver moustache. His teeth were mismatched, and tobacco-stained, and his elbows stuck through holes in his dishevelled jumper. When he beamed reassuringly, deep crow's feet around his eyes concertinaed like a brown paper fan.

Clearly pleased to rescue our lifeboat, the man boomed words in Greek that nobody understood, yet they were comforting as my mother's hug after a nightmare. He poked himself in the chest with his thumb. 'Yianni! Yianni!' Pointing at the younger sailor at the stern, he yelled, 'Manno! Manno!'

The powerful little fishing boat fixed a line and tugged our vessel to a natural harbour on Kea, just over a mile away. However, due to the strong current and overladen boat, it took us two hours to cover the short distance to safety.

We soon learned the fishermen were father and son. They helped everyone onto the quayside. Stretchers were brought for Corporal Perkins and Josephine, who had regained consciousness and refused to be treated like an invalid. Manno reached out and took my hands – his big brown eyes comforting, yet at the same time, mischievous. Under his gaze I felt safe, yet flustered. The moment I stood on firm ground a stab of pain rose from my ankle. Everything swayed and my knees buckled. Manno swept me up against his wide chest and then set me down on an old trunk that stood against the harbour wall.

'I'll come back for you, *koukla*,' he said. 'Sit here.'

Relieved that he spoke English, I watched him take command of shaken men and distraught women with his steady, reassuring manner.

I had not experienced shock before. One moment I felt in control, capable of helping others – the next, my head was in my hands and I wept bitterly. Someone touched my shoulder.

'Stiff upper lip, Miss Smith. We have to set an example,' Matron Merriberry said.

'Sorry, Matron.' I sniffed hard and wiped my eyes.

'Stay out here until your propriety's restored, then come inside. The mayor of the island is on his way. We're having a meeting in half an hour and I want to see you setting an example.' Her voice softened. 'It's been a shocking day, but remember to thank the Lord we weren't in that first lifeboat. If you hadn't taken so long, we might not be here now – isn't that a fact? What held you up?'

'It was my sister's book, Matron. I'd forgotten it and couldn't bear to leave it behind. They said collect your valuables, you see, and that is the most valuable thing I own. In an odd way, I do believe Sissy saved our lives with her picture in that book.'

Matron rushed away as if she herself couldn't stand the thought.

* * *

I kept thinking about the dolphin and its incredible strength. Why had it done such a thing to save me? But even before that, there was a chain of exceptional events that led to me escaping death.

If Mrs Pankhurst hadn't made Sissy such a feminist, she would not have longed to work. She would not have been in the munitions factory when the photographer came around, or have had her photograph in that book. If I had not gone back for it, Matron and I might not be alive now, because we would have been in the first lifeboat. Perhaps this was all an act of God? Was there a greater reason behind my survival? This thought – that I might be part of a greater plan – was even more terrifying. Of all the people on that ship, I was the one that deserved to die. If I hadn't lied about my age I wouldn't have been on the ship. If I hadn't disobeyed orders – hadn't opened the portholes – the *Britannic* would have gone the extra mile and made it to port. Perhaps dying was too easy. Was I destined to live out my atonement on earth? With this in mind, I dreaded to think what punishment lay in store for me.

At that moment, I swore to God that, for the rest of my life, I'd sacrifice whatever was most valuable to me to compensate for my wrongdoing, in the hope that nobody else would get hurt.

Manno came to my side again. He placed a finger under my chin and lifted it. 'Are you well now?'

'I'm sorry.' I turned away and took a deep breath, appreciating the value of air. 'I don't know what came over me. I mean . . . it's all so incredible. It was the dolphin. Why did it save me like that? In all my life, I've never heard of such a thing.' I searched his face for the answer, but how would he know? 'The priest said it was a miracle.'

'Be calm, I will take care of you. You are safe with me, *koukla*, no worries,' he said, patting my hand. 'What do you mean? What dolphin?'

I stuttered the events of the past hour. Confused and exhausted, not sure what I actually said and what was simply a vision in my head. I pressed my belly, the tight ache confirming my rescue, confirming the dolphin and the reality of the moment.

'Ah, you met Delphi.' He peered into my face again, then turned and stared over the sea. 'Stay here, I will come back to you.' Then he said, 'You are so beautiful the flowers on my island will wilt in your presence.' Thrown off balance by this nonsense, I felt a spark of anger at his frivolity in the circumstances, then I found myself defeated and gawping after him. He left to help the other survivors, occasionally glancing my way. He threw a smile, setting my face aflame. I blushed again, caught watching him, my heart fluttering every time our eyes met. What was this damned foolishness? I cursed him, cursed myself, cursed my belly that became more swollen and painful by the minute. My day was already too eventful.

* * *

The quayside thronged with Rubenesque women wearing long, dark skirts; embroidered aprons, and white petticoats. They bustled everyone into the harbour *kafenio* where honey-sweetened herb tea and homemade biscuits were handed out. Names were taken, papers looked at, and lists drawn up. The locals made a general fuss of their visitors, shouting, patting cheeks reassuringly, and nudging people into chairs that lined the room.

'They seem very organised and not shaken at all by this,' I said to my cabin mate, Josephine, who seemed fully recovered as she passed me a cup of the strange tasting tea.

'Haven't you heard?' She lifted her chin towards the window. 'The very same thing happened here last week. The SS *Burdigala* sank in almost the same spot.'

I made no sense of it and stood alone in the midst of my friends, fellow VADs, and orderlies. My uniform soon dried on the outside, yet garments that lay next to my body were damp and heavy, mouldering against my skin. How I longed to remove them, and how delicious it would be to swim in the pale, iridescent water of the bay – but my marvellous swimming costume had gone down with the *Britannic*.

Who could I speak to about what had happened? I wished for my father. The sudden urge to tell all rose inside me again. I should confess that my actions had caused who knew how many deaths. I searched for the priest but when I found him, the awful words wouldn't come. I trembled and kept my mouth shut.

In the end, who would be receptive to my story, and would I be able to stand their disparaging air when they all knew the truth?

The room became stuffy as more people came inside for the meeting. After a loud clanging, a man in a crumpled suit spoke in Greek. He stared at me for a second and not understanding his words, I felt accused. Manno translated. 'The mayor would like to welcome everyone to the town of Korissa on the island of Kea.'

A uniformed ship's officer that I had not seen before addressed the room telling us of the current situation.

'HMS *Scourge* and HMS *Heroic*, the two ships that came to assist, had no more deck space for us. They are taking our good fellows and countrymen, survivors that they picked up at sea, to Piraeus, which is the port for Athens. If you haven't already put your name down on the register, please do it now; one hundred and fifty of us await collection here on the island. The ships have signalled our presence to the admiralty and we await transportation. There are several casualties and they are being treated in the school room at the back of this building, which has been transformed into a temporary hospital. Any questions?'

One of the men stuck up his hand. 'What happened to the *Britannic*, sir?'

'We don't know yet, and I'd suggest you don't speculate.'

Feeling trapped and restless in that crowded room, I drifted outside again and stared over mounds of yellow fishing net and lobster pots. Beyond the lighthouse, the two grey ships that had stopped where the *Britannic* went down were sailing away. I guessed they had finished collecting bodies and survivors. A chill ran through me. Could I really be hung for going against orders and causing all those deaths? I gripped the only lamppost, clutched my throat, and imagined the ground opening under my feet, falling, falling, waiting for that final, neck-snapping moment.

I should have drowned while I had the chance.

CHAPTER 17
SHELLY

Greece, present day.

SHELLY WANDERED ALONG THE EMPTY beach uplifted and glad of the solitude. She came upon the site of the turtle nest, sat by the daubs of red nail polish and placed her hand flat on the sand. With her eyes closed, she imagined a hundred beating hearts below her palm and felt her chest expand with the glorious miracle of nature.

Stay safe, little turtles.

The rich blue sky faded to pale mauve, then streaks of red and wisps of pink; colours and patterns mirrored in the perfectly flat water, giving the illusion that the lighthouse promontory hovered above the sea's surface. She reminded herself why she had come: Gran Gertie's story of tragedy, and she supposed, triumph. There must have been triumph, because she remembered her great-grandmother as a happy, and more importantly, a contented person. If Gertie had planned to spend the rest of her life atoning for her sins . . . had she done that? What happened to ease her conscience? Now, Shelly regretted not listening to all the tapes before her arrival, but there hadn't been time. How had Gertie restored balance to her life after such a catastrophe? Shelly wondered what price had she paid?

* * *

Could there be any record of Gertie having been in Kea? It was so long ago. Still, didn't she remember Gertie saying the ship had some connection with the *Titanic*? Lost in her thoughts, she continued along the soft sand, crossed the narrow road, and sat at a pavement café.

According to the old postcards, the port had been little more than a *kafenion*, a general store, and a school when a half-drowned Gertie first arrived. Shelly spread the pictures across the table and studied them. They showed simple, square buildings with flat roofs, surrounded by houses that belonged, according to the shopkeeper, to fishermen, sponge divers, tradesmen and a shepherd.

Suddenly, Shelly realised she wasn't alone. A waiter peered over her shoulder at the postcards. 'You must go up the mountain tomorrow, far from the pirates, to see our beautiful city, madam,' she said.

'Pirates? City?' Shelly blinked at her. The fish-shaped island of Kea was less than twelve miles across.

'Christos will take you on the bus. There,' she pointed across the road, towards a bend in the bay, near where her turtle's eggs nestled half a metre below the sand. 'Next to the taxis. Nine o'clock in the morning.'

Shelly peered at the harbour wall, wondered where the chest had stood, and planned to walk along there in the morning. She tried to imagine Manno. What did he look like? He had to be handsome and rugged, of course, because he was the lifesaving fisherman in young Gertie's story. Did she fall in love with him? Shelly smiled to herself, recalling her own first love, the lifeguard, David, and remembering her overwhelming emotions.

'*Yiasas*, Shelly Summer, we meet again!' She jumped violently. 'Sorry, I didn't mean to frighten you,' Harry said.

Shelly placed a hand on her thumping heart. 'I was day-dreaming. Hello, Harry the diver, where're you off to?' His smile appeared wide and warm and she felt none of her earlier irritation. 'Will you join me for a coffee?' she asked, hoping to make amends for her abrasiveness.

He lifted one finger to the waitress, then sat opposite her. 'Did you have a good day?'

'Wonderful, I'm about to find somewhere to eat, any recommendations?'

'Meat, fish, or vegetarian?'

'I'm easy.'

He smiled widely again and raised his eyebrows a little. 'Well, that's good to know, but what about the food?'

She tutted, rolled her eyes and turned her head away to hide a smile.

'There's an excellent fish taverna in the next bay, I can take you,' he said.

What did he mean . . . he would take her for dinner, or he would give her a lift? Unsure of herself, she glanced into his eyes, then turned away quickly when she felt a blush rising. What the hell? She never blushed!

'Thanks, but I'd like an early night after all the travelling. I've a lot planned for tomorrow. Is there anywhere special closer to home?'

'Here is as good as anywhere.'

'I don't see anyone eating.'

'Too early, we're not a tourist island. The locals don't eat until after nine thirty.'

'I see. I'd like to ask you some questions about diving around Kea, if I may?'

With an amused look, he nodded, down and sideways, the Greek way. 'Anything you want.'

'Will you join me for dinner, or is there somebody cooking for you at home?' she asked.

'No, there's no one at home. I like your photographs.' He nodded at the postcards.

Was that a deliberate change of subject? 'Ah, I'm trying to understand my great-grandmother's time here.'

'You take pictures too?' he asked, keeping his eyes on the postcards. 'I noticed you had a professional camera when we met.'

'It's only a hobby. I do several things, mostly I'm a vet. Do you take pictures?'

'Just underwater, for the website. Though I haven't taken any for a while.'

'Sounds like fun.'

'I wonder if you'd like to look at the *Britannic* museum tomorrow? Well, it's not exactly a museum yet, just a few bits and pieces and a film.'

'Tomorrow?' She smiled. 'That would be a nice birthday treat.' Perhaps she was moving things along a little too quickly, but she only had a week.

'It's your birthday?' he asked, of course he did, she knew he would. He peered into her eyes. There was a promise, a question, a secret, and laughter. 'Then I must present you with something memorable, if you'll allow me?'

'Really, Harry, I came away this week because I didn't want a fuss. It's just a birthday, a day in which I spoil myself a little and remember my childhood.' Despite the words, parts of her tingled slightly, and judging by his smile, her eyes gave her away. She couldn't remember the last time she had flirted, or felt so hot. It was a good feeling. Exciting and silly and frivolous all at the same time. Although she was only playing with him, it made her heart race and her body sing with romance.

He laughed joyfully, and she wondered if he felt the same, that thrill, an unspoken question.

'Sounds intriguing. I wonder what you have in mind?' she said, narrowing her eyes slightly, sending the message, she was interested.

'Somewhere special to eat; then we have a festival in the next bay, Vourkari, tomorrow night. It's the name day of my very good friend, Ipomoni.' She frowned. 'Ee-pom-on-ee,' he explained. 'It means patience. It's his name day so we all celebrate with him, all his family and friends, and all the other people named Ipomoni, all over Greece ... Greeks all over the world, actually. It's like everyone's united in one big birthday party.'

'I like the concept of everyone celebrating together.' But was Harry inviting her to more than a festival? His eyes were treacle-toffee brown and just as warm. Suddenly, Shelly realised she would like to know him better.

They ate at the shore taverna, drank wine and watched the sunset. The lighthouse caught her attention. The light was on now, hazy in the dusk miasma. His hand touched hers while they were talking. She didn't pull away but looked deep into his eyes.

'I hope you're having a good time,' he said. 'Tell me about your favourite dive.'

'That's a tough one.' She closed her eyes for a moment, then recalled a moment of utter bliss, clear water, and shocking beauty. 'The Red Sea, perhaps. Both the reef and the wrecks were exceptional.'

'Never been, though I've always wanted to. Work gets in the way, you know?'

'I know. The reefs are shallow enough to snorkel, and that's what I prefer to do there. It's the greatest wonderland.' She narrowed her eyes, seeing the spectacular underwater seascape all over again. 'Lots of sea horses, don't you love them? It's breathtaking, you must go.'

He nodded. 'Yes, I think I must.'

* * *

The next morning, he met her for breakfast. 'Happy birthday! I've managed to get the key for the *Britannic* museum,' he said. 'Or at least the beginnings of it, we hope. I thought you'd be interested to see what we've gathered so far. The work's spasmodic, funded by small change left from the annual Tourist Development Grant for the Cyclades islands.'

'It's relying on tax-payers' money?'

'No, it comes from the European Union, but Kia's bottom of the list. Santorini and Mykonos top, and almost every other Cyclades island lay in between.' He shrugged. 'We need a sponsor if we're ever going to get it opened to the public.'

'What about crowdfunding? Surely there are enough fanatical First World War navy aficionados that would be interested in chipping in a few bob. Have you thought about opening a web page? After all, it can't need that much money once it's set up – can it? A building, a couple of part-time staff in the season. I don't know.'

'Me neither. There's an abandoned enamel factory just off the port road, it would be perfect for the museum. But what we really need is something from the wreck that people would come halfway around the world to see, or perhaps interact with.' His eyes narrowed as he spoke and she could see he was passionate about it.

'Most things can be seen online these days. You mean, like the ship's wheel?'

'Perfect, or the prize of finds . . . how about the ship's bell, the big one that was over the crow's nest?'

'Wow, that would be something!'

He grinned, enjoying her enthusiasm. 'But it's all up in the air, as they say. The dive centre takes up every minute of my day. Never found the time to look up how we'd fund a museum. You can't imagine the hours I work.'

'Ha, really! I set up my own veterinary surgery, don't forget.' She smiled at him. 'I know how difficult these things are. Never enough hours in the day, are there?'

He laughed. 'You've got that right!'

'You work so hard to maintain a dive school, but when was the last time you dived for pleasure?'

He scratched the back of his head and squinted sideways. 'Mm, two months back we had a client and nobody available to take him. But diving just for fun – for me – perhaps two years ago.'

She grinned at him, in their shared understanding. 'About the museum, brainstorming's pretty good, at least you get to see who's really interested and enthusiastic.' She took a breath. 'I could give you a hand when I get back home. I mean, I don't have to be here to help set up a website and I've just finished my latest online study. You could have it up and running by the time I come back.'

'You're coming back?'

An intense moment passed between them. 'Possibly, for the turtles.' She saw a question in his eyes as they met hers.

And maybe for you, she mused, but didn't say. Her eyes narrowed as a soft smile dusted his mouth. He knew – and she was glad, they were on the same level.

* * *

Word spread that Shelly was the great-granddaughter of one of the surviving nurses from HMHS *Britannic*. Everyone treated her like a celebrity. The dive video was fascinating. She longed to go down and see the enormous wreck for herself, but the preparation made it impossible for the moment. Perhaps next time. However, Harry did have a surprise for her.

He took her for dinner at the highest point of the island, the village of Ioulis. 'Ee-oo-lees!' he said, pronouncing it for her. The small town was pedestrianised. Square houses with small windows and red-tiled roofs clustered over two hilltops, these were also sprinkled with belltowers and churches. 'So pretty,' she murmured as they wandered along narrow streets marked with little painted arrows on the cobbles to guide the visitors. The ground floor of some houses had been converted into shops and all manner of handcrafted gifts were on sale. She bought a beautiful silk scarf hand-painted with magnolia flowers and local birds for Eve, knowing she'd love it.

'I paint this,' the woman said while patting her chest.

'You did it?' Shelly was astonished. Harry took a photo of Shelly and the woman, Despina, with the scarf held up between them. Then Despina led them to a café across the road where her sister served them with coffee and a type of shortbread smothered in icing sugar.

After, they wandered down arched passageways lined with more interesting shops, and bought a jar of honey in one

164

emporium simply to stop the owner almost force feeding them various bee products, including several tots of honey rum.

They turned their attention towards the churches and the view out across the Kea channel towards mainland Greece.

'It's all so pretty,' Shelly exclaimed as they came out of the church of Agios Spyridon.

Harry beamed, proud of his island. They wandered down narrow streets with brightly painted shutters, under arches, and up and down steps.

'I'd never have found all these special places by myself,' Shelly said, pointing her camera at another bright pink door flanked by urns of fiery orange nasturtiums with leaves of shamrock green.

'This is so perfect,' Shelly muttered. 'I'm drunk on the glorious colours.'

'Ah, nothing to do with three tots of honey rum then?' Harry joked.

As evening fell, he slipped his hand around her waist and ushered her through a doorway. She found herself in a charming taverna where the host led them to a small, jasmine entwined, balcony with a view down the mountain.

'Smell that perfume.' She gazed at the tiny, white flowers that dripped from the trellises around them. 'Such dainty flowers, but the scent's intoxicating, it's so powerful!'

He plucked a sprig and placed it behind her ear, his fingertips lingering on her neck. 'Happy birthday,' he said.

She gazed down the mountain, towards the darkening, cobalt sea, and watched occasional headlights snake up the road from the port. Delicious aromas drifted from the taverna kitchen, making her realise how hungry she was. To the sound of tinkling bouzouki music, they ate local food. Starting with a mezze, bite-size pieces of local sausage and a variety of cheeses, before lazily moving on to the main course. Shelly ordered lobster spaghetti, one of Kea's most popular dishes, according to Harry. He had rooster in wine sauce. They fed each other forkfuls to try, both claiming they had the better dish.

'Absolutely delicious,' she said, placing her knife and fork together. 'Who'd think there would be such a gastronomic delight at the top of a mountain on a tiny island?'

'Tell me about the *Lusitania*. I'd have given my right arm.'

'Ha, yes, I have a few extra qualifications and they got me onto the team.'

'Like what?'

'You'll find this painfully boring. Zoology was part of my six-year veterinary degree. Once I'd qualified, I did a one-year Open University course in Marine Biology. I started to study for my Ship's Safety Officer certificate because, sometimes, I found myself concerned by the relaxed attitude on dive boats. Afterwards, I completed a paramedic science course, which took a year. I've just finished the last stage of the follow-on, which qualifies me as a paramedic. It's really fascinating and I love it. Plus, of course, I have a fair number of deep dives under my belt.'

'What's next, pilot's licence?' he said in a sarcastic tone.

Her head snapped up, ready for a rebuff but he was grinning, and she laughed. 'I'm a bit sad, aren't I? It's just, well, it's only a couple of hours study each evening, then I end up with a real qualification. I've done it since uni. Prefer a challenge to nights of monotonous TV and social media. I mean . . .' She shrugged.

'What was the *Lusitania* like?' he asked again.

She hesitated.

'It was the most dangerous dive I've done, and not that wonderful. So many missiles down there, and the visibility poor.' She turned her mouth down. 'How about you? What's your favourite so far?'

'I plan to show you one of my favourite dives tomorrow.'

'Oh, my goodness, you're spoiling me!' She had wondered why he ordered water with the meal, now she understood.

'I hoped to dive while I was here, so this is too good to be true, thank you, Harry.'

'Well, it's me that should thank you. You made me think when you said we end up working for the wrong reasons. I haven't had a recreational dive for a long time. It's always business, you know?'

She nodded. 'Where are you taking me? I must confess; I only know a little information about the *Britannic*. I didn't have time to research.' She felt overwhelmed. 'I'm so excited! Please tell me where, and all the details.'

'It's the *Burdigala*. Three kilometres out, seventy metres down, upright, on her keel. She sank just seven days before the *Britannic,* and there's only two miles between them. Also, and you'll love this, she was the second largest ship in Greek seas, only the *Britannic* being larger.'

'What a lot of coincidences.' They both stared out into the dark, their eyes drawn to the distant beam of the lighthouse. 'Was there . . . I mean, did anyone die?'

He nodded. 'A young engineer, French, killed by a broken steam pipe.'

'Poor kid.'

He nodded. 'Awful. But the same questions remain. Did the *Burdigala* hit a mine or was she torpedoed?' He shook his head. 'It's a mystery, and for that reason, my favourite dive.' He grinned. 'You'll love it.'

The excitement in his voice, matching her own thrill, sent shivers through her. 'I'm sure I will, thank you so much. I can't wait. Where was she destined, Lemnos?'

'No, the other way. Heading for France to take on troops. At 10.45 a.m., same time as the *Britannic*, a midships, starboard explosion, identical to the *Britannic*, and like the *Britannic*, sank within the hour.'

'Good heavens, surely that's too many coincidences to be a coincidence? What do you think? You must be intrigued by it all?'

'I think we should consider a pudding.'

'A man after my own heart.'

'I am.' Her head snapped up. *What was he saying?* 'Intrigued by it all,' he said, seeing her fluster and laughing. 'Let's get the dessert menu.' He raised a hand.

'According to the report, a periscope was spotted,' he said, then turned to the waiter and waved the menu away. 'Baklava and ice cream.'

Shelly glanced down the menu. 'Yogurt and honey with local walnuts, please.' She returned her attention to Harry. 'Go on.'

'Even though the ship was sinking, the Captain ordered the *Burdigala*'s gunner to fire at the periscope. Fifteen cannon rounds were deployed, but who knows if they were successful? We've never discovered a submarine wreck.'

'But that same submarine may have sunk the *Britannic* a week later?'

'Possibly.'

'Was the channel known to be mined?'

He shrugged, held his hands out, palms up. 'How could they know? It was a busy sea lane, but the other ships were smaller, therefore not so low in the water.'

Shelly thought for a moment. 'I'm guessing mines would be held by a cable or chain to an anchor, yes.' He nodded. 'Even if the depth was two hundred metres, it would be a difficult and time-consuming operation for a German ship to lay a series of mines at that depth, unseen, in a busy channel. Anyway, there seems little point in such a risky operation for one or two mines.'

'Good thinking, Shelly.' Harry grinned.

'Elementary, my dear Harry.' Shelly laughed. 'Your English is very good.'

'British education. Bristol uni.'

She was silent for a moment. 'Harry, if both sides were eager to brag about their destructions, well, we know why Germany wouldn't want to say they torpedoed the *Britannic* – because it was a hospital ship – and there was an international agreement. But, why wouldn't they want to say they torpedoed the *Burdigala*? Unless . . . it wasn't the Germans?'

Harry raised his eyebrows and smiled quizzically.

'No . . . you're not saying . . . that someone was after the submarine and inadvertently torpedoed our own ship?' She shook her head. 'Twice? I don't think so. Or . . .' She sighed, sensing she was on to something, but didn't know what. 'I'll give up on that for the moment. Are there any other mysteries connected to the wreck? Any First World War nurses walk the Kea beaches on the night of a full moon, for example?'

Harry laughed. 'No, but there is the ship's bell. The prize of all bounty divers. A huge thing, situated up the radio mast. Reached by a spiral staircase inside the mast. Would have sounded the distress signal. Every dive has a look for it, but no luck so far. It's my quest, my passion, to find that bell. It's all so fascinating, don't you think?'

'I won't be able to sleep now, thanks very much!' she admonished him playfully.

On the dark balcony, the night-flowering jasmine opened fully, surrounding them with small white stars. The scent increased, heady and intoxicating. Twinkling village lights illuminated the town's cluster of red-tiled roofs and domed churches. Couples strolled along the cobbled streets below. When the breeze changed direction, she caught the aroma of barbecued lamb being turned on a spit, or warm honey, basil, or cinnamon. Far away, she could see the lights of great container ships and crude-oil tankers slipping through the Kea channel. She wondered if the taverna had existed when the *Britannic* went down, because the event would have been clearly visible from such a vantage point.

'What are you thinking?' Harry asked.

'I'm trying to decide if this is the best birthday I've ever had.'

He smiled right into her eyes. 'Don't decide yet. The night is still young. What would you like to do next?'

CHAPTER 18
GERTIE

Kea, 1916.

THE SCHOOL ROOM THRONGED WITH nursing staff and crew, yet I could only see two men in coal-blackened vests. I remembered the firemen's change of shift. That endless tramping of feet on the spiral staircase behind my cabin, down into the belly of the ship. There must have been many stokers to fuel such an enormous vessel. Were they drowned in the bowels of the boiler room, trapped inside as she went down, or picked up by the rescuing battleships?

I remembered the trundling racket of the watertight fire doors opening for the change of shift, but I don't recall hearing them again. Perhaps in the panic, I'd missed it. Please God don't let all those poor, coal covered men still be in the boiler room at the bottom of the sea.

I rushed around, searching for Matron to ask. My heart was thumping and my tears queuing up, waiting for the first chance of release. I saw Nurse Josephine across the room and squeezed through the crowd.

'Please, Nurse Josephine,' I called.

She stopped and turned around. 'Gertie, thank goodness you're safe, I was concerned.'

'Can you tell me if all the firemen got away safely? It seems there are only two here.'

She shrugged. 'I think they all escaped. They got into trou ble for lowering a boat and rowing away from the ship withou orders. The Sergeant ordered them back and made them pick up drowning people. Why do you ask?'

'Oh, I was worried they might be trapped. What happened to the poor engineer who lost his foot, the patient we hauled out o the water? Did he die? I gave him some of my blood.'

'It was you? Everyone's talking about it. Why are you crying?

'Oh, I don't know, Josephine . . . I really don't know. I want to go home.'

I kept myself busy with the other VADs, as we became accustomed to this strange place. We tore a sheet into strip for bandages, helped local women cut up bread and cheese and washed cups and jars as they became empty. Several o the survivors needed medical attention, like the boy scou who had deep rope-burns on his hands. The surgeon, pale and tired, his long, sensitive fingers scrubbed to within an inch o their lives, was talking to Matron. The local doctor, short and round and brown-skinned, was attending to Perkins, clearl unconscious and stretched across three café tables.

* * *

By late afternoon, word passed around that we would be col lected in a day or two. The local schoolmaster, Mr Pantalies spoke English. He took charge of the situation, billeting the *Britannic*'s medical staff and crew with various local families.

I found myself in the care of an elderly woman, wizened yet spritely, with dancing eyes paled by cataracts. Her house standing directly on the harbour, consisted of a single room a spacious white cube with small shuttered windows and on

172

door that opened onto the quayside. Leaning against the front of the cottage were an upturned row-boat, heaps of yellow fishing net, and a single chair with a sagging, rush-mat seat. A tall iron anchor stood rusting by the window and, next to that, a donkey with a rope connecting one front leg to a hind leg. A chipped enamel bucket of water stood next to the beast and a hammock of greens hung from a nail in the wall of the house.

The blue front door was in two parts, the top hooked open. The woman in black led me inside, and I was surprised to see the room had a compacted earthen floor, a quarter of which was taken up by the largest raised mezzanine bed I had ever seen. Three wide wooden steps, flanked by polished cupboards and drawers, led up to the sleeping platform. The small space on either side was filled by rough-plank shelves stacked with neatly folded linen.

Two feet below the beamed ceiling, another rough shelf fringed the room crammed with bric-a-brac. Gaudy painted plates, exotic flowers made of starched linen, feathers, and pine cones; china figurines, Jesus pictures complete with bleeding hearts and crowns of thorns, a silver crucifix, and ornate oil lamps that I doubted had ever been lit.

On crocheted doilies that hung, limp as Dali's clocks, over the edge of the shelf, stood the most bizarre collection of fishing memorabilia. A spider crab, open claws raised towards the ceiling as if waiting to hug God, and a giant clamshell, pale as a dead circus clown, grinned lifelessly towards the door.

Below the shelf, even more out of sync with everything, hung a metre-wide tapestry of a Swiss scene depicting swans on a lake surrounded by snowy mountain peaks. Next to the tapestry, the contents of a dark-wood frame drew my attention. Outlined in chalk and charcoal, on heavy grey paper, was a simple, classical drawing of a naked young man with what appeared to be a pair of real white bird's wings outstretched from his shoulders.

'*Icarus!*' the old woman yelled in a squeaky voice when she noticed my interest. '*Icarus!*' She wagged a crooked finger at the picture. I recalled my father and his pigeons at home and longed to hear him yelling at me in his loud, bombastic way.

The room smelled of mothballs, bees wax, and basil.

The petite woman, clearly proud of her home, banged a fist against her heart. '*Yiayá!*' she cried.

I nodded, made a little bow, and mimicked her, thumping myself in the chest. 'Gertie!'

She pulled in her chin and frowned. '*Tee?*'

I smiled and nodded, pleased to connect with the grand lady. 'Tee . . . yes, all right, that'll do.'

*　*　*

Night fell quickly, as if God had his fill of this terrible day and drew the drapes. I ventured onto the quayside and sat on the old chest. Moments later, Manno appeared.

'Are you OK now?' He dropped his head to one side and thrust his hands into his pockets.

I glanced into his eyes and then looked away. 'Yes, thank you.' I wanted to be bold, in control, yet in his company my insides quaked. He reduced me to something fragile and slightly frightened.

'Come, walk with me around the harbour,' he said.

Flustered, I hesitated. In my medical training, I learned that patients came with instruction labels pinned to their chest, telling the nurse what to do. Also, we were told how to behave in certain situations. At that moment, I thought *all* men should come with an instruction book. Young women of a certain age and class would benefit from hints on how to handle unpredictable behaviour. How to deal with the forward ones, the men who took liberties, and those who melted a girl's heart. Life was difficult enough without having to analyse every word uttered by exuberant young men. Was Manno asking me to walk out with him in a formal manner, or simply being friendly? 'Um . . . I . . .'

'Ah, you are tired, no worries. I go home now. Perhaps I will see you tomorrow?'

I heard the question in his voice. 'Where's home? Do you live here in the town?'

He sat beside me and stared out to sea. 'No, we live on another island over the horizon, Syros. My father and me, we are the mail boat. We trawl for fish from here to there, sell the catch on the quayside, deliver the mail, and sleep a few hours. Then we return, fish until we arrive here, sell the fish, deliver the mail, and start back again. We were just on our way to Syros when your ship sank. What's your name?'

'Gertie, Gertie Smith. Mrs *Yiayá* calls me Tee.'

He laughed, confusing me.

'*Tee* means "what?" in Greek,' he explained, 'and, *Yiayá* means grandmother.'

I blinked at him, still trying to make sense of things. 'It's been a terrible day,' I said. 'Thank you for rescuing us.'

Manno shrugged. 'Nothing. I will see you tomorrow, Gertie-Gertie, yes?'

'No, it's just one Gertie. My name is Gertie Smith.'

'Why you tell me two?'

I shrugged. 'My mistake, sorry.' Then I dared another glance into his brown eyes. 'Yes, I'll see you tomorrow.'

175

'I will walk you back to *Yiayá*,' he said.

'Really, there's no need.'

'But there is, I must protect the flowers . . .'

'Oh, stop it!' I cried, holding my belly and laughing.

At the cottage, he entered with me, and *Yiayá* exchanged a knowing smile with him, then said something that I didn't understand.

Manno turned to me and said, 'My grandmother says you must take all your clothes off immediately so she can dry them, or else you will become very sick. I will help you.'

'What?' I spluttered.

Although I was very sure *Yiayá* didn't understand English, she seemed to know exactly what Manno had said. She snatched her knobbly walking stick and started swiping at him and poking him with all the force she could muster. She yelled at him in her high squeaky voice something that sounded like, 'Fidget! Fidget!'

Manno backed towards the door with his arms curled over his head. *Yiayá* gave him a hefty poke in the stomach that winded him and as he brought his arms down, she walloped him over the head. He backed out, but lost his balance and ended up on his bottom in the dirt, outside.

Still yelling at him, *Yiayá* closed both door partitions and bolted them. As she turned towards me, all the anger left her face. She made a firm nod: *that showed him not to mess with me*, then she grinned with merriment.

The dear lady gave me a nightgown and indicated I should remove my damp clothes and hang them on a clothes maiden that she zig-zagged before the wood-burner. She clucked and huffed and shook her head when she saw the purple bruise that spread across my middle. After leading me to the bed, she indicated I should lay down. The next thing I knew, dawn light filtered through the window. The old woman was snoring softly in the only armchair.

* * *

I dressed quickly, delved in my pillow-bag for a letter, wanting a connection with home, then I slipped outside.

The sun pierced the horizon, sending golden shafts of light across the firmament, I stood on the shore, which connected with the curve of the port, and thought about my parents. I must put my name on the list, so they learn that I survived. So much had happened, I must write to them and tell them about being saved by the dolphin. I pressed below my ribs, feeling the heavy ache of my bruised abdomen. Perhaps I had a cracked rib. The creature had hit me with such force.

My flashbacks were gaining strength. Split seconds would ticker-tape through my brain. I must have glimpsed the dolphin's eye because later, I recalled being drawn into that mysterious sphere of innocence and extreme intelligence. An instant of understanding had flashed between us. A contact of minds chorused by rapid clicking, reminiscent of swallows on a telegraph wire in autumn. Then I noticed there were no telegraph wires in Kea.

The water, flat and golden as honey, mirrored the surrounding harbour, houses, and hills. The scene so lovely after all that had happened, for a moment I wanted to weep. My soul was torn by the loss of life, and the loss of that great ship that would have saved the lives of so many of our boys. The tragedy would follow me through life, silently, like a shadow. A nightmare to endure for the rest of my life.

CHAPTER 19
SHELLY

Greece, present day.

SHELLY AND HARRY ENJOYED THE perfect setting. A balmy Mediterranean night, a jasmine-scented balcony, two compatible adults attracted to each other, and a view over the prettiest little Greek island. Were they in each other's arms, whispering words of love? No. They were debating the First World War with great excitement.

Harry rested his chin on his fists and peered into her eyes.

Shelly shook her head, trying to unravel the facts. 'Tell me again, Harry. I want to make sure I've got this straight.'

'The facts are: the Germans had a substantial submarine fleet, twenty-three different classes, commissioned for mine laying. The U73 submarine laid Minefield 23, down there.' He nodded into the darkness.

'A mile or two out from St Nicholas lighthouse?'

'Exactly, only days before the SS *Burdigala* sank, and then the *Britannic* sank, of course.'

'So why did the *Britannic* sail straight into that same minefield? As it's such a busy sea lane, why didn't a minesweeper pass through first?'

'Because the skipper of the *Burdigala* was certain his ship had been struck by a torpedo. Several of the men had seen the periscope and the missile trail quite clearly. Fifteen rounds were fired before they abandoned ship, but no evidence of a submarine wreck has ever been found. Also, those waters were deemed too deep to mine.'

She realised her hand was in his. 'I'm so enjoying this!'

'Me too.' He grinned. 'Take into account the maximum length of mooring rope used with UC-47 mines was a hundred metres. The *Britannic* sank in a hundred and twenty-one metres, but the explosion happened where the Kia Channel is much deeper.'

'Oh wow! So how could it have been a mine? That's the bottom line, isn't it?'

'But more interestingly, why would people want to claim it was?'

'Can we calculate how far Captain Bartlett managed to bring the *Britannic* towards the shore after the hit? Has anyone discovered the depth of the Kea Channel on the ship's route? And is there a map of the minefield in the German war records? It all sounds a bit fishy to me.'

Harry grinned, his eyes shining brightly. 'You're not just a pretty face then.' He reached over the table and took her other hand. 'I feel as though I've known you all my life. May I ask you a personal question?'

She blinked at him. 'You can, but I can't promise to answer it.'

'What's such a beautiful and intelligent woman like you doing here all on her own?'

'That's a simple one. I'm getting away from it all.'

'Family?'

'No. Only my elderly father. You?'

'Two boys. You saw them at the dive centre.'

'Nobody else?'

He shook his head. 'I'm divorced. My ex returned to Norway after the legalities, ten years ago.'

'Ah, I see. Sorry to be blunt. Just, best to know . . . you know?' she said.

'Are you?'

'Not at all. I did fall in love a long time ago.' She hesitated. 'I was very young, sixteen. It broke my heart. I promised myself I'd never go through that pain again.'

'And now, do you still feel the same way?'

'I . . . I don't know.' Something seemed to have changed. She wanted to be honest, but couldn't find the right words.

Harry drove her back to the port. 'Thank you for a wonderful evening. I haven't enjoyed myself so much in, I don't know, twenty years,' she said.

'I would invite you for a nightcap, but with your birthday dive tomorrow morning, it wouldn't be sensible. So, I'll walk you to your room, and leave you to get a good night's sleep.'

Outside her room, he asked, 'You do have your key?'

'Yes,' she said, lifting it from her pocket.

'Then I will kiss you goodnight, if I may.'

With her back against the door, she tilted her face up and closed her eyes. She felt vulnerable, yet at the same time, totally safe in his embrace. His lips brushed hers, lightly at first, then she felt his hands slide behind her back, and he gently pulled her closer as he kissed her again. As passion gathered, their chemistry strengthened and melded to become an ever-brighter flame. A fiery spark ignited a blaze of passion and suddenly she longed for him to stay the night, and she understood that was his desire too.

'I want you to stay,' she whispered.

'You know I want to. With all my heart, I want you.' He kissed her again and his body hardened against her. 'But the dive, we need to conserve our energy and get a good night's sleep.

Tomorrow is the only chance you'll get and I know you'll regret missing it. So, let's make a date for tomorrow evening, shall we?'

She melted against him, ached for his body. His lips came down on hers once more. She wanted him so badly she was almost trembling.

'If I stay another moment, I won't have the strength or will power to leave,' he said, kissing her lightly on the mouth. He turned and started walking away and she willed herself from calling him back. She let herself into the room, went straight to the balcony, and watched him drive away.

* * *

At the ferry port, two other divers waited, all grins and testosterone, in an open RIB dive-boat. Harry introduced his sons, Elias, in charge of the boat, and Petros who would set a dive-line to the *Burdigala*. Two good-looking boys, although their personalities appeared quite opposite. Petros, the fun-loving younger brother, was clearly having a good time. Elias, wearing a constant frown, didn't hide the fact that he disapproved of his father bringing her aboard. Her own fault, she thought, after all, she had put him in his place the first time they met. Perhaps he held a grudge. The two guys moved to the bow while Harry guided Shelly to a seat beside the wheel at the stern and handed her a life jacket. After motoring respectfully out of the harbour, he opened the throttle. They crashed up and over the waves, sending spray rocketing into the air. *It's a guy thing*, she thought. What's the point of a speedboat if not speed? She clung on and clenched her jaw, not wanting a chipped tooth as a holiday memento. The three men grinned as they hurtled towards the dive site.

Kitting up and testing gear was the only tedious part of diving, but as Shelly confidently went through her mental list, anticipation thrilled her. Harry went off the side first and waited while she finished her methodical preparation. Finally, she sat on the tyre, smeared a little demister in her mask and wet her face. Ready, she pulled on the mask and stuck the regulator in her mouth. Holding them both in place, she rolled back into the water.

On surfacing, she gave him the OK sign and let a little air into her BCD, which she always thought looked more like a life jacket than a buoyancy control device. She descended beside him. The water, glass clear, and the magic of her surroundings, that feeling of flying, thrilled her as they started to descend seventy metres to the wreck; intoxicated by the freedom of being able to move in any direction, or simply hang, motionless and weightless in surroundings as blue as the sky above. Even birds could not do that. Using a rebreather, instead of an open-circuit breathing system, meant there were no air bubbles to break the silence and frighten the fish.

The deliciously warm water cooled as they descended making her grateful for the dry suit that seemed unnecessary up top. The freshness cooled her second skin, but it was more autumn than winter, and quite welcome, calming her excitement and slowing her down. She glanced up; the glow of the surface dimmed as it became more distant. She could stay all day in this endless, sapphire space, this weightless world restricted only by oxygen reserves.

The gentle shape of the ship crept towards her from the darker blue below. The image came into focus the way a dream starts, from nothing to an epic, yet without beginning or end. The *Burdigala* revealed herself and Shelly introduced her spirit to the ship in an intimate moment that she would never be able to describe to another. Intoxicated by the silence of this other world, she drank in the beauty of it all.

She tried to control her excitement, once again concentrating on breathing calmly, slowing her heartrate, saving oxygen. Although it was darker now, and everything turned a deeper blue, some sunlight still filtered down thanks to the clear water. She relied on her headlamp to see into the depths of the wreck as she approached.

The *Burdigala* sat on her keel, like a sleeping fish on the bottom, upright, ready to sail away at its first disturbance. Then she saw why it couldn't. The hull was cleanly cut into two, almost exactly across the centre.

The similarities between the *Burdigala* and the *Britannic* fascinated her. By studying this wreck, would some vital piece of information come to light as to why these two magnificent ships were destroyed? Harry had dived the *Britannic* and the *Burdigala* several times, was he looking for information too? Something didn't add up, but she couldn't put her finger on what it was.

She took a few seconds to enjoy the thrill of the moment; her body, weightless and free. What really caused the *Burdigala* to sink? She glanced across to Harry, three metres to her right. Did he know? Was it in his best interest to keep the mystery alive? He made the OK sign with his thumb and forefinger, which she mirrored. Her only regret was that she had not had the opportunity to read about the ship before this visit. She knew almost nothing, but she consoled herself; she would be back.

The place was a wonderland festooned with delicate vegetation and coral-like structures that rose to resemble gothic, yet lacy architecture. Fat hats of sulphur-yellow sponges, barnacles, anemones and crustaceans in every shade of pink and orange, all spread before her. Saddle oysters, like pale blue discs of delicate flaky pastry, nestled between fan-like vegetation. Rigging turned into furred pipe cleaners by microscopic organisms that grew on the ropes. Fifty metres of fishing net hung like swags and drapes in a curtain shop window. Shelly had to remind herself the *Burdigala* went down in 1916. The ship had slept in the very same spot on the seabed for over a hundred years, yet it seemed so fresh, so alive!

Gliding over the top deck beside Harry, she was careful to use her fins as little as possible so as not to kick up silt and reduce visibility. He headed towards the bow. The wooden decking had long gone, but the iron framework remained in place like a giant waffle iron covered in a multitude of crustaceans that made the ship's skeleton a classic wreck reef, teeming with wildlife.

She aimed her lamp through the structure, to the lower deck. The light bleached away colour at the centre of the beam, changing the pink icing-sugar formations into delicate antique lace. She longed to venture inside and turned to look for Harry. He investigated an enormous cannon that seemed perfectly preserved on the foredeck. She was tempted to venture inside the ship alone, but common sense stopped her. Somehow Shelly knew she would come again.

Harry turned, peered through his mask, searching for her, his lamp shining through the fishnet, her headlamp catching his face, blinding him. She caught his squint, the spotlight giving his face a ghoulish appearance. In one horrendous moment, her twenty-year-old nightmare returned with stark reality. Her scream, dulled by the rubber of her breathing tube, was hardly audible to Harry, yet it exploded in her chest as the past roared up before her.

Suddenly, she was sixteen again. She'd never snorkelled before. The young man she adored was teaching her . . . but things went wrong, so terribly wrong.

'My mother's bracelet,' she had pleaded. 'Please, please, try and find it. Dad will go crazy if I lose it.'

Then she was floating on her back, shaking, screaming, screaming, 'Help! Help me!'

An age before anyone reached her. Splashes as men jumped into the sea. Shouting. People pulling her away. Ambulance sirens. The smell of bleach. Doctors, nurses, policewomen, foreign language, forms. Newspapermen with their cameras. *Look this way! Flash!* Medication that made her drowsy, numb. Days of battling with a fogged mind, tears, questions. Asking for forgiveness. Her father's arrival in Greece, his anger because she'd lied to him about a school trip. Going home to England. Her father furious, impossible to talk to.

She felt the shaking of her shoulder and in an instant, she was back in the present with Harry beside her, his eyes questioning. He held out a hand, wiggled and tilted it from side to side, asking if something was wrong. Shelly shook her head, then nodded, made the OK sign, and realised she was holding her breath. She made a conscious effort to calm herself and concentrate on her breathing.

God, oh, God! Would it ever go away? The past . . . the nightmare.

Suddenly, she didn't want to see DJ. To explain why she'd left him was too much to live through once again. She had almost buried her awful history. Every year, every dive, the nightmare faded a little more. Now DJ would want her to dig it all up again, and re-live the pain, just when she felt ready to move on.

She could still feel Harry's eyes on her. He tapped his watch. Time to ascend. She felt the tightness of sobs trapped in her chest, tears stinging, steaming her mask. Then her lamp caught the drape of fishnet again. The fabric of her nightmares. It jerked and shivered as if alive in their perfectly still surroundings. She nodded towards the vast curtain of yellow nylon. He followed her gaze, then they moved together towards it, to investigate.

CHAPTER 20
GERTIE

Greece, 1916.

'Ah, there you are, Miss Smith,' Matron said. 'I haven't had a chance to voice my pride in you. Very commendable action in the boat, you certainly saved the young soldier's life with your transfusion of blood.' She had a way of rolling her shoulders and pulling in her chin before she gave an order, as if rising to her own authority. 'As you know, there are a hundred and fifty of us, here on the island. Everyone else was taken to the port of Piraeus. We'll be collected shortly but that Corporal you helped to save needs immediate medical attention. I want you to observe the amputation of his lower leg this afternoon.'

I had never attended an operation before and I found myself both thrilled and horrified to be invited.

'How is he, Matron?'

'We've packed the wound in salt to prevent infection, but this causes the patient unbearable pain. Better to remove the shattered bone and prepare a good stump ready for a prosthetic. The sooner it heals, the sooner we can fit him with an artificial limb. Come now, help scrub out the school room ready for the surgeon.'

I hugged my abdomen as I stood.

'Are you all right?'

'Just a little bruising where the dolphin hit me,' I said. 'I'll be fine when the swelling goes down.'

'Come inside, let me take a look.'

* * *

Matron removed my apron and helped me onto two tables pushed together. I undid my button-fronted dress, and she opened my corset and combinations, and examined my abdomen. 'Have you any pain in your left shoulder?'

'No, Matron, it's just where the bruise is.'

'I'm concerned you might have suffered some internal damage. The surgeon will come and look at you. Stay on the table.' She spread a modesty sheet over my unbuttoned dress.

The surgeon, Dr Raymond, pressed and pummelled from sternum to pelvis, concentration rigid on his face as he mapped my innards in his mind.

He turned to Matron. 'Her bruising is consistent with a severe blow. To make sure it's nothing more serious, she must lay quietly on her back with no movement if she can help it. Keep her corset on for support, but not too tight. That garment probably saved her from a ruptured spleen. I'll take another look tomorrow.'

'Right, let's get you into the other school room with the patients,' Matron said, before calling over a couple of the *Britannic*'s crew who were seconded as stretcher-bearers.

In the temporary hospital, my bed was next to Corporal Perkins. Poor Perkins moaned and whimpered, rolling his head from side to side. The patient to my left, with the head injury, was heavily bandaged and hardly conscious. There were four other casualties.

188

'Perkins!' I called over. 'It's me, Gertie.'

'The nurse?' He continued to display his awful pain.

'Yes. Listen, they're going to operate on you soon. You'll feel better when they've sorted you out and cleaned the wound.'

'I've lost my foot, so why's it such absolute agony? I'm going mad here – mad – I wish I'd died!'

'You'll be fine. It's the salt, that's all. It's saving you from gangrene. Try and tell yourself that. Just the salt, Perkins.'

'Just the salt. Just the salt.' Then he let out a bone-crunching holler. 'Put me to sleep! You wouldn't let a dog suffer like this. Why me?'

'Think about the future when you've got your new foot. They say you can hardly tell these days. Also, you're out of the war. Isn't that grand, Perkins? You'll be down at the Pally dancing the tango with beautiful women before you know it.' I stared across at him, conscious of his intense discomfort, my eyes aching with unshed tears. My punishment for allowing myself to be bullied, wanting to look important and in control of my patients. If only I hadn't opened the portholes! At that moment, I'd have done anything to take away the Corporal's awful pain.

I had mixed feelings about missing his operation. Although this would have been my first real procedure, I didn't think I could watch the bone-saw being used on him because of my actions.

*   *   *

The next day, I felt wretched. 'What's happening out there?' I asked as Nurse Josephine administered the Corporal's medication.

'There's a ship in the bay, minesweeping.' She stuck a ther-mometer in Perkins's mouth. 'When they're sure there's no

189

danger, the vessel will tie up, then they'll ship us to Athens. Matron said you're to stay here until the surgeon's seen you. How do you feel, Gertie?' She placed a hand on my forehead. 'You appear a little flushed.'

Josephine would have been in her late thirties. Mature for a nurse as only unmarried women were accepted into the medical corps. She was not exactly homely, in fact her features were quite faultless, but they always seemed drawn into a knot. A person couldn't relax in her company. Josephine was generous with her atmosphere of tension and one squint from those eyes would halt so much as a wince when a hypodermic went into a vein.

'Gracious me, I'm so hot after two days in this corset, even my arms and legs ache,' I said. 'It's so uncomfortable to sleep in, nurse.' I noticed the bed at the end of the row was now empty. 'What happened there?'

'Ah, another sad case. The gallant officer died of his injuries. Nothing we could do but ease his pain and hold his hand at the end.'

'How sad, he seemed such a nice man. Were there many fatalities?'

'We don't know, of course. Most of the survivors, casualties, and bodies were picked up by the other two ships. I guess there'll be an inquiry. Everyone wants to know how such a thing could happen.' She sighed. 'The ship was supposed to be unsinkable, wasn't it? It's a disgrace, if you ask me.'

Inquiry! My heart stopped for a moment, and I understood the term, *sick with fear*.

Nurse took the thermometer from Perkins and stared at it. 'He's got a temperature. Let's check yours.'

Twenty-minutes later, Matron Merriberry, the surgeon, and Nurse Josephine, all wearing masks, filed into the school room.

The other invalids were examined first, and then removed from the room.

'Put a QUARANTINE notice on the door,' the surgeon said. 'The last thing we need is an epidemic on the island. The influenza's already costing us more soldiers than the war itself. See if anyone's had influenza in the past twelve months – if so, there's a chance they have some immunity. They can stay behind to take care of these two.'

I thought about dear Sissy and knew I had to do all I could to get better. If I died of the influenza after all this . . . oh, my poor parents! They would be completely heartbroken. I *had* to get better!

The surgeon continued. 'Reduce the Corporal's morphine in doses, the amputation site's healing nicely. I want everyone checked before they board HMS *Foxhound*. Anyone with a dry cough, temperature, severe headache or muscle aches must be moved into here. It's our duty to protect the people of this island, and to contain the outbreak. The VAD seems to be suffering from bruising only, but her temperature's up and she's already showing influenza symptoms.'

'Please can I take the corset off, Matron?' I asked.

Merriberry gave an enquiring look to the surgeon. 'I don't see why not,' he said.

When they'd left the room, I asked nurse, 'What did he mean about the *Foxhound*?'

'That's the name of the ship commissioned to take us all away, back to Piraeus, the port of Athens, I think, though nobody's very sure. Anyway, they're all hoping to leave this afternoon.'

'What? You mean they might not let me go on board! I'll be stuck here?' My heart plummeted.

191

'He's afraid you and Perkins might spread the influenza. He's quarantined you with the Corporal and left me in charge.'

'But that's not fair!'

She nodded, her mouth a tight line. 'You're right, but there's nothing I can do.'

Then I thought perhaps it was justice. After what I'd caused, I'd probably get pneumonia and die like half of those who caught the dreaded illness, and that would be the end of it. Poor Perkins. Sooner or later he'd realise what had caused the *Britannic* to sink, and he'd hate me enough to tell the authorities. My parents would be ashamed.

Perhaps Perkins would develop pneumonia and die, then nobody would know the truth. I stared across at the next bed. How could I think such a thing! The poor man had lost his foot and been in absolute agony. It wasn't something that could be undone. Then again, if he hadn't bullied me . . . but that was no excuse for me breaking orders!

Such terrible thoughts . . . what was I turning into? Had these monsters and demons always been inside me, waiting like dragon's teeth to spring into life?

Tears gathered in the corners of my eyes and trickled into my hair. Everything was so awful, so unforgivable. If only Sissy had lived, none of this would have happened. Why was I saved – for my parents' sake? A miracle, the priest said, but I knew the truth. It was so I could live out my punishment.

'Nurse Gertie, why are you crying? What's wrong?' Perkins asked. Even though his words were drowsy from medication, there was concern in his voice.

I glanced across at him, lying on his back, eyes closed. He was usually a confident man, a decision maker, a man who cared. Good-looking with a square jaw and straight nose. As I studied him, a warm feeling gathered inside me. I was so glad he didn't suffer the terrible fate of his fellow passengers in Lifeboat 1. I sniffed. 'Nothing, really, I'm just being silly. How do you feel, Corporal?'

'Good, a little lightheaded, muzzy, but no pain.' He reached across the gap. 'Will you hold my hand for a moment, nurse?'

I reached over and took it. Was this fate showing me how I should live out my penance, doing whatever Corporal Perkins wanted for the rest of my life? Would that be such a bad reparation? I imagined children, chickens, the smell of freshly baked bread, wildflowers on the table, me serving Corporal Perkins his dinner.

'You feel hot,' I said.

His eyes didn't open, but he smiled widely. 'It's you, nurse, sending my temperature up.'

'Soldier! I hope you're not going to give me any trouble.' I tried to sound stern, but honestly, I wished he could put his arms around me for a few minutes. Quite an outrageous thing, yet I needed to absorb some strength of spirit, because mine was well and truly depleted.

* * *

A groan woke me in the night. I turned my head in its direction and looked into Perkins's pale face. His eyelids fluttered, then he was returning my stare.

'How do you feel after the operation?' I asked.

'I don't know . . . my ankle hurts, but not as bad as it did,' he slurred as if drunk.

I pushed myself upright and sat on the edge of the bed, but then gasped and had to slap my hand over my mouth to avoid crying out. Perkins's sheet had slipped to the floor. His leg was off at the knee. I hadn't realised the extent of his amputation, and I felt sure he hadn't either. Oh, the poor man!

'What's wrong?' he muttered urgently, screwing his eyes as the pain kicked in.

'Nurse, please! Corporal Perkins is conscious,' I called towards the desk.

The nurse came over. I lay down and watched my neighbour receive a morphine injection. In minutes, Perkins's face relaxed and he gave me a slow wink. 'Promise you won't leave me, nurse, promise.'

I melted under his gaze and wanted nothing more than to comfort him. The man was a cripple for the rest of his life – because of me.

*　*　*

I dozed in the makeshift hospital, losing myself to the heat and the boredom, when a knock woke me. 'Food!' somebody called.

Nurse Josephine waited a moment before opening the door to find three trays on the floor. She brought them into the school room, slipped a mask on and then brought one over to my bed.

'I'm really not hungry, nurse. It seems I've lost my appetite,' I told her. 'It's the disappointment of not being allowed on the ship.'

'No, it's because you're coming down with the influenza. It's important you keep your strength up, Gertie, so do try to eat something. Come and sit with me for a while.' She placed the tray on the teacher's desk, alongside hers. 'Egg lemon soup and fresh bread. A most delicious meal.' She glanced at Perkins. 'I'll let him sleep while we eat.' Her spoon was halfway to her mouth when she became aware of her mask. She hesitated.

194

'Look, it's foolish to put yourself at risk. I'll go and eat at my bedside,' I told her, and stood up.

The soup had no taste, and I had no appetite. Just getting out of bed had made me feel weak and shivery. I was coming down with the dreaded influenza. Reminding myself this illness had killed my sister, I ate most of my meal, then returned to my cot. When Nurse Josephine came to collect the tray, I asked for an extra blanket.

She accommodated me, then turned her attention to Perkins who, by this time, was awake.

'I'm just going to prop you up with some extra pillows, Corporal,' she said. 'You've been on your back long enough, and we don't want bed sores, do we? Then I'll feed you.'

'I can feed myself, nurse. I've lost my foot, it's not that big a deal.'

Josephine took pillows from the empty beds and brought them over. 'Right, put your arms around my neck and I'll pull you up.' She heaved and he came halfway up into a sitting position, then Perkins let out the most bone-chilling screech.

'Where's my leg?!'

CHAPTER 21
SHELLY

Greek island of Kea, present day.

HARRY TAPPED HIS WATCH AGAIN and signalled they only had another two minutes on the wreck. Now running out of air, they had to start their long ascent. Around the other side of the fishnet, they saw the problem. A turtle weighing more than two hundred pounds struggled in the net, caught by its back flipper. Harry moved forward to deal with it, but Shelly nudged him aside and withdrew her dive knife.

The net had cut deep into the flesh. Shelly didn't know how long the poor turtle had been trapped. She knew it needed to surface and breathe at least every four hours. Maybe it was heading towards land to lay its eggs. She pulled off her dive gloves, knowing the operation needed a delicate touch and, even with her veterinary skills, the operation would take some time.

Harry shook Shelly's shoulder, tapped his watch, and made the sign to ascend. Shelly shook her head. She could not leave the turtle to die. She pointed to Harry's dive knife, then tugged at the net above the turtle. He got the message and started cutting through the strands of nylon.

Shelly slashed at the net below the turtle, terrified that one of them would become entangled and the nightmare of her past repeat itself. The turtle stopped struggling, whether dying from lack of oxygen or sensing they were helping it, she couldn't know. Seconds ticked by, their tanks becoming more depleted. Shelly willed herself to stay calm, to slow her heartbeat, to save oxygen. They had to have enough air to rise slowly. Finally, the last strands of polymer broke away and keeping hold of the turtle, they hauled it between them as they started their slow ascent.

Keeping one eye on the time she clipped herself to a loop in the shot line and hung there for her decompression. Harry came alongside, and they both worked on cutting away more of the punishing net from the turtle's flipper. All the time, she hoped the turtle had enough air to hold on a while longer. Harry clung on to the front of the shell. Everything depended on the turtle not making a race for the surface to breathe. If it did, they would have to let it go or suffer the fatal bends.

Her blood boiled. How could fishermen be so careless? Why couldn't manufacturers go back to using cotton, hemp, or wool nets? At least those materials would eventually rot away. The net they were cutting off the turtle may have been hanging off that shipwreck for over half a century, and killed countless marine mammals in the most horrible way.

The dive apparatus impeded an urge to scream angrily, as loud and hard as she could. She diverted her thoughts and concentrated on drawing the last nylon filaments from the creature's wounded flipper. After swapping places with Harry, she started freeing its head. Cautiously, she looked into the turtle's eye. One snap from that powerful beak could cut through her airpipe, which would certainly kill her.

As the last clump of net came away, Shelly gave the turtle one last look deep into its eye, made the OK sign to Harry, and gave the enormous carapace a gentle shove towards the surface. Great joy blossomed in her chest. Harry reached for her hand and together they watched the turtle's silhouette rise through the lighter water above, pale turquoise light bouncing off the dark amber shell. Shelly was overcome by euphoria, made more intense because she couldn't smile with an air-hose gripped between her teeth. Her elation was not just because the pressure against her dive suit had lessened, or because the turtle now swam free, but because she had realised the truth of the situation and come to terms with her nightmare.

The details of what happened that awful day were there all along, but they always hid behind Shelly's self-blame. Uppermost in Shelly's memory of her holiday with David and Simon, was that she had caused a string of events that led to a tragedy. The suppressed reason why she absolutely had to dive *now* was to prove to herself that if she had been able to dive *then*, she would have saved him.

However, in truth, if she had managed to dive, she may well have also become entangled in that same net and it could have been a double tragedy. Even if she hadn't gone on that holiday with David, he would still, most probably, have investigated what was in the bottom of that old sunken boat, and the tragic outcome would have been the same.

All this time, subconsciously, Shelly had been searching for a way to prove that if she could, she would have rescued David, she would have cut the fishing net away from him, as she had with the turtle, and he would have escaped his awful fate. But she simply didn't have the skill to dive. What happened to David was not her fault! It had nothing to do with her precious bangle, or her obsession with her mother's death. It was an accident that may well have happened whether she had gone on holiday with him, or not.

Her sense of relief was so intense, she almost floated to the surface without the essential decompression stop.

She squeezed Harry's hand. He couldn't know what this dive meant, that something so significant had happened.

They pulled themselves up the boat ladder, feeling the force of gravity dragging at every muscle and limb, and the weight of their equipment making their emergence from the sea almost impossible. Harry's sons stood either side of the dive ladder and hauled them up until they eventually plopped onto the bench, feeling almost unbearably heavy now that they were out of the water. The boys relieved them of diving gear and then they wriggled out of their dry suits, too exhausted to speak.

Sometime later, partly recovered, they sat side by side as Harry's sons dealt with the chores to close the dive. 'That was magical, thank you,' Shelly said, hardly able to raise her voice above a murmur. Harry nodded and smiled.

* * *

'Are you going to tell me what happened down there?' Harry asked over dinner that evening.

'Ah, on the *Burdigala*?'

He nodded.

'Hm, yes, sorry about that.' She hesitated; she never spoke to anybody about David, but somehow she found herself longing to open up to Harry. 'Something catastrophic took place when I was sixteen, before I'd learned to dive, and it all came back in a similar scene.'

'You seemed traumatised.'

'Traumatised? No, it was just a recall. I was only sixteen, my first boyfriend, David. Someone I loved . . .' She battled to keep calm. 'Well, he got into trouble, tangled in a fishing net. I saw it all but couldn't help.' She had to stop and take a breath in order to say the essential words that she knew would help her to heal.

'It ended in tragedy. So, you see, when your face lit up behind that net, it gave me quite a start.'

'Must have been awful. You were sixteen?'

She nodded, suddenly realising she had no appetite. 'Please, it was such a wonderful day today, I'd rather not spoil it by recalling that nightmare. If you don't mind, Harry, I'll tell you about it another time.' He nodded. 'Thank you,' she said softly, feeling the memory of David take a respectful step back.

Harry reached across the table and touched her wrist. Shelly offered her hand and he took it, silent for a moment. 'I lost *my* friend, too,' he said simply. 'Narcosis. It was many years ago, yet sometimes it's like yesterday. I always remember him and use extra caution when I'm organising my tanks for a dive.'

She nodded again. 'Like yesterday, yes, I understand that. Was it on a dive?'

'It was, just a week after his wedding. I was in the boat,' Harry said. We were very young; I was only eighteen. Though he was three years older than me, we'd been friends all our lives, through school, everything. He was my hero. That day, we high-fived then Spiro went down. I never saw him alive again.' He stared at his plate. 'Two and a half years later, I married his widow, Anita. It was such a mistake. Grief and love are not the same thing. Our break-up was a mutual decision. We're still friends and see each other because of the boys. You must meet her when she comes over, she's a great woman and you'd get on very well, I'm sure.'

'I'm sorry, Harry. What a tragedy. You never quite get over it, do you?'

He shook his head. 'He simply had a heart attack brought on by the narcosis. You prepare so carefully, it seems impossible, but when a man gets dive-drunk, it's difficult to get some sense into him. His dive buddy thought he was filming something close up and wasn't concerned when he didn't move for a few minutes. When they were due to start their ascent, he realised something was wrong . . . but it was too late.'

'Until now, I've found that I must keep diving, like I'm doing it for David,' Shelly explained. 'It's like every experience under the water, every sensation, I'm sharing with him. Does that sound crazy?'

Harry shook his head.

'But diving with you has been different, Harry. Something's changed, and I'm not sure why?'

He shook his head again. 'There comes a time to let go of grief, I learned that much. It doesn't mean you no longer care, but in a way, you owe the person you're grieving for a life of your own. Does that make any sense?'

Shelly thought about it. Harry had put it so simply: *You owe the person you're grieving for a life of your own.* It was a profound statement; one that she knew instantly would change her life. She recalled the start of Gran Gertie's tape: *The most difficult thing we have to learn in life, is to let go of those we love, my darlings.*

They sat in silence for a while, both occupied by their memories until Harry spoke again. 'These days have been very special for me, Shelly. I do hope you come back.'

'Thank you, that's a kind thing to say. You've given me such a marvellous time, and though I haven't learned much about my great-grandmother, I feel there's a special story waiting to be uncovered.'

He pushed his plate away. 'One last pudding?'

She grinned. 'What do you suggest?'

He bobbed his eyebrows and they both laughed. '*Kadaifi* and frozen yoghurt?'

'Oh, it sounds perfect.' When it arrived, she glanced at her handbag. 'I know this is really naff, but would you mind if I recorded the moment?'

He looked at the camera, smiled unselfconsciously and shook his head. 'I don't mind what you do.'

Shelly focused on her pudding, pressed live view, and started recording. She lifted the camera to take in his smiling face. 'I've had a wonderful time with you,' she said, knowing the camera was picking up her voice.

'You're very special,' he said, the charismatic smile returning and his gaze penetrating her eyes in a way that transfixed her. She ended the video, knowing she would enjoy watching the moment again and again.

Shelly wanted to kiss him right there and then, but noticed the taverna owner watching. She smiled to herself, then threw him a slow and deliberate wink.

He flinched, startled, and turned away. Harry had seen her action. 'What?' he said, looking over his shoulder.

She giggled. 'He's been staring at us for an hour straight. I just thought I'd see what would happen.'

'You are very . . . *átaktos*. I don't know the English word.'

'A-tak-tos?' She got her phone out and pulled up Google Translate. 'Ah . . . mischievous. Yes, I do my best.'

They laughed, warmed by the wine and the day. 'It's been lovely, more than that, very special. Thank you, Harry.'

Hand in hand, they walked along the promenade, towards her room. 'Promise me you'll come back.'

'I'm only on day three.'

'I don't want to spend the rest of the week wondering if I'll ever see you again.'

'I will,' she said, her attention caught by the flash of the light-house. Did Gran Gertie walk along the same path, and in whose company: Corporal Perkins, or Manno the mailman?

CHAPTER 22
GERTIE

Greece, 1916.

'Where's my leg? Where's my bloody leg?' Perkins screamed. 'They've cut my damn leg off! Where is it? I want to see it, *now!*' The startled nurse let go. He fell back onto the bed, then hauled himself onto his elbows. 'Where's the surgeon who butchered me?'

'He's away on the ship, Corporal, heading for Piraeus.' Nurse Josephine backed away. 'He saved your life.'

'Johnny,' I said, remembering his name. 'You need your medication. You're having a panic attack. Try and breathe steadily. Come on, give me your hand and we'll do it together. Breathe in, hold it, let it go slowly.' From the corner of my eye, I could see Josephine filling a syringe. She swabbed his other wrist and stabbed him with the hypodermic.

'Come on now, Johnny,' I said. 'Breathe in, hold it, let it go slowly.'

He stared at me, his eyes glazed, wide with the horror of his discovery. 'There's a part of me out there, somewhere, and I don't even know where it is. Now, I'm not whole, not complete . . .' His voice became heavy, dull, and more slurred as the seconds ticked by. 'I'll never sleep again . . . God knows what they will do to me next time.'

I kept talking to him, distracting him from the facts. 'Come on, Johnny, give me your hand. Let's breathe together,' I encouraged him again. 'I'm here for you. I'll always be here for you, don't forget, you have my blood flowing around in your veins. We can get through this together, Johnny . . . together.'

* * *

This is the start of it, I thought in the middle of the night. Perspiration trickled off my forehead. Another punishment for causing so much misery. My throat burned, limbs deadweight, head throbbing. I stared at Perkins. He appeared to be in the same state, flushed, sweating, eyes wide and unblinking, staring at the ceiling.

Perhaps he's died.

'Nurse Josephine,' I croaked, the words hurting my throat. 'Some water, please.' She came over with a glass. 'No, Perkins first. He's overheating, look.'

'He's just had his morphine. I'm trying to reduce his dose, but he gets so distressed. Poor man. I hadn't realised that he didn't know the extent of his amputation,' she said hurriedly, sighing and holding her hand over her mask for a moment. 'I guess he was so heavily sedated, it simply didn't register when they told him.' She stuck a thermometer in my mouth. 'I have to report on your condition in five days. If your temperature goes down, they'll probably pick you up in a week or so.' She read the thermometer. 'It's over a hundred. You'll be feeling pretty rotten.'

'I am, but at least I still have two legs.' We both looked at Perkins. His eyes had closed. 'Will they send us back to England?' I asked.

'I don't know, to be honest. You might be picked up by a ship on its way to Lemnos. I've heard they're awfully short of nurses. I'll probably go there too. I've been meaning to ask, are you the woman who gave him blood in the lifeboat?'

I nodded. 'I want to train to be a proper nurse, as soon as I can.'

'Have you told anyone?' she asked.

I shook my head. 'I wasn't sure I could do it, but I am now.'

* * *

At sunrise, eight days later, I walked out of the school room. Weak, but deliriously happy to be back on my feet, I took myself to the old chest on the quayside and sat in peace, enjoying the wonderful view of the harbour and surrounding village. Although it was the first day of December, the air had a spring-like quality. The windows in square white buildings flashed gold, reflecting the rising sun. The day was fresh and still and made me feel oddly weightless. The bay, mirror flat and crystalline, and on the rocky seabed, hundreds of silver fish darting in and out of the green-brown sea grass. I moved to the edge and gazed into the water.

Instantly, my mind flashed back to the bay at home and the Sunday afternoons of my childhood, kneeling at the edge of the water with Sissy beside me. Mother's voice calling, 'Don't let her fall in, Sissy! I don't want her to get wet stockings.' The sound of cork on willow as Father played cricket on the sand with Arthur. Mother spreading a table cloth and unwrapping paper parcels of sandwiches and pouring homemade lemonade. Later, Father and Arthur skimming stones and arguing about the number of bounces. Big white fluffy clouds. My wonderful childhood.

I looked up. There were no clouds here, and the sky was ten times bluer. How I wished dear Sissy could be with me.

The fishing boat's thudding engine drifted over the sea, louder as I put my ear nearer the water, drawing my attention towards the horizon. The red and blue boat rounded the lighthouse. My heart skipped. Without even thinking about it, I primped my hair and smoothed my uniform, which the kindly *Yiayá* had washed, starched, and ironed while I lay on my bed. Even the rip where Sissy's watch had been was neatly stitched.

My thoughts went to my parents; they must have heard about the ship going down. I should send them a message right away. Let them know I'm safe. The fishing boat didn't seem to be moving, so I walked around the harbour to the *kafenion*.

'I want to send a telegram to England,' I said very slowly to the *kafenzies*. 'Tel-e-gram.'

He lifted his chin, showed his palms to the ceiling, and shrugged.

I poked the table several times, mimicking a telegraph operator. 'Dot, dot, dot, dash, dot, dash . . .'

'Ah!' the old man said. '*Tilegrafo?*'

'Yes, yes, *tilegrafo*!' I cried excitedly.

He shook his head. 'We no have.'

'How do you send urgent messages?'

His eyebrows puckered as he unravelled the foreign words, then pulled his hands into his shoulders and wiggled his fingers. '*Poula! Poula! Áthina!*'

'I don't understand,' I said, shaking my head.

He repeated the episode only this time shouting at the top of his voice.

A teenage boy raced into the *kafenion* and a boisterous conversation took place before the lad turned to me and said, 'You have urgent message for England?' I nodded. 'I am Pavlo, my father is the mayor of the island.' He did a head waggle. 'We can send a pigeon to Athens with few words. They send a ticker tape to England. Arrive tomorrow.'

'Good! Thank you, young man. Who do I see?'

'Come, come, we go to the mayor, my father.' Another head waggle. 'He plays the *tavli*.'

I followed him, away from the harbour. We tramped up compact earthen streets, so narrow they'd barely take the width of a robust donkey, never mind a coach and four. The mayor was involved in a game of backgammon outside a small house. A number of villagers sat in a semi-circle around the two competitors, eyes riveted on the game. I squinted at the mayor. The man had a very relaxed mode of clothing but a perfectly waxed and curled moustache of some grandeur.

This was 1916. The world was at war and people were fighting and dying for their country. Yet here, in this little pocket of Greece, the head of the island played a board game in the street. A small pocket of normality in the chaos that was the world today. The scene gave me hope that one day all of Europe would return to normal. It reminded me what we were fighting for. The simple freedom of village life, tradition, and family values.

I introduced myself and offered my hand. He shook it so vigorously I felt my knuckles pop.

The pleasant-looking youth with bare feet and unruly dark hair spoke to the mayor, his father. The men got to their feet and stared at me with embarrassing frankness. After a moment, the mayor said, '*Ela*, come.'

We walked back to the harbour, the rest of the men, about ten, followed in a procession behind us. I noticed Manno was mooring up. 'Nurse!' he yelled across the quay, waving an arm. I suppressed a grin. 'Look, I have something for you!' he yelled, raising a pair of crutches.

I beckoned him to come over. Manno strode around the curve of the harbour and thrust the crutches at me.

'The doctor of Syros sent these for the sailor.' He glanced at the crowd then back to me. 'What's your problem?' He stared right into my eyes which, honestly, made me tingle.

Oddly breathless, yet also embarrassed, I couldn't speak. I turned away to break the intimate look between us and noticed our bystanders nodding and smiling at each other.

Self-conscious and confused, I pulled myself together.

'My parents will think I was killed on the *Britannic*, Manno. I need to send them an urgent message to say I'm all right. You see, my brother died in battle, and my sister, a nurse, has died recently too. I'm all they have left. They'll be dreadfully anxious and heartbroken. I must inform them that I am unharmed as soon as possible.'

'Virgin Mary! They must be crazy with the worry. If I have to glue wings of Icarus onto my own shoulders and fly to England myself, I will make sure they get your message, *koukla mou*.'

I recalled the picture on *Yiayá*'s wall and did my best to blank out certain bits of the drawing. Manno could not fly into England in such a blatant state of undress.

What? Oh, my goodness. Was I losing my mind – thinking such ridiculous things?

Yianni came scuttling over to Manno, waving his arms at his son, and then thrusting his hands towards the boat and its fish. A heated conversation took place until Manno held a hand towards me.

Yianni's face softened. 'Ahhh,' he sighed knowingly.

The onlookers grinned and nodded at each other again.

I seemed to be centre stage of a Shakespearean play that I didn't understand, and my cheeks burned with embarrassment. 'What's going on?' I asked quietly.

'No worries,' Manno replied, lifting my chin and smiling into my eyes again. 'Let's go and prepare your message.'

I walked around to the back of the school with Manno. Although the village was a somewhat ramshackle affair – created with no apparent sense of planning, order, or even straight lines – the pigeon loft was a complete contradiction. The coop was a marvellous, symmetrical, construction on stilts. The wooden building had a red-tiled, A-frame, roof and a platform that ran around the outside with a stout wooden ladder for access.

'What a beautiful loft, Manno,' I said.

'All the small islands have them.' He stuck out his chest in such a way I almost expected him to start strutting around me, cooing and bobbing and dragging his tail feathers. The thought brought heat to my cheeks and I wished I could find a way to stop blushing.

Manno spoke to the mayor for a moment, then he turned to me. 'We're going to return Aphrodite to Athens. Aphrodite, she is the goddess of love; you know this?' He bobbed his eyebrows.

The damn blush! I bit my lip and nodded.

'Athens will send a telegraph to England, so now, we go to write your message in not many words,' he said.

Back in the *kafenion*, I constructed my letter to Father. I had to reduce it to as few letters as possible, which was difficult. Eventually, I settled on: *Dr Smith. White Cot. Lighthouse Ln. Dover. UK. I am unharmed. Safe in Greece. Love Gertie.*

Mama would be in tears. Papa's stern face would hide his emotion. My parents would embrace, silently, unable to voice their relief.

* * *

I watched as the boy wrote in tiny letters on a cigarette paper. Manno rolled the fragile note so gently with his big fisherman hands, then slid it into a small tube, and fastened it to Aphrodite's leg. There was a sense of ceremony in the air as they released the pigeon. The sturdy bird flew in a low circle over the houses, orientating herself, then she set off, gaining height until she disappeared into the deep blue sky. For a moment, silence fell over the village as everyone's eyes followed her.

I told Manno, 'My father's a doctor, but he keeps pigeons too. He used to race them, but now he works for the government.'

'Your father works for the British government?' He frowned and pulled in his chin.

'Yes, his pigeons are taken overseas and return with messages for the military. Last year, one of his pigeons, Geronimo, saved the lives of fifty soldiers.' I smiled, proud of my father and pleased to relate the story.

'Holy Mother!' Manno crossed himself again. 'Tell me how a little bird could save so many men.'

As I told the story of Geronimo, Manno translated it for the bystanders. 'A platoon had advanced in France, pushing the enemy back faster than anyone expected, but they lost their radio equipment. Due to lack of contact, another detachment mistook the platoon for an enemy force. They set about firing on them with heavy guns.' The villagers stared, wide eyed, at Manno while he spoke. I continued, 'The platoon had no form of communication apart from a couple of my father's pigeons. At dusk, they released Geronimo with the necessary information about their position.

'By dawn, the attacking force had been informed of the situation by radio. Eventually the two sections came together and they organised a successful, unified attack on the enemy.'

Manno's audience applauded and patted me heartily about the shoulders calling, '*Bravo! Bravo!*'

'Very good! I like it. Walk with me,' Manno said.

Flustered again, I had to admit I needed guidance on these things. I'd never walked out with a boy before. 'I have to take the crutches to the school first,' I said. 'Thank you for the help.' I rushed away and barged into the quarantine room.

'Nurse Josephine, please, can you help me? There's a fisherman, the one who saved us, who wants me to walk out with him. I don't know what to do. I've never walked out with anyone before, and there's no chaperone. It's not correct, is it?'

Josephine laughed and stared at me for a second. 'Gertie, it's war-time. The rules have changed. If you like him, and you trust him, then there's no harm in walking out together, alone. But stay close to the village.'

'I don't suppose you know what *koukla mou* means?'

The nurse laughed again. 'Yes, get used to it. *Koukla mou* means *my doll*.'

'Don't go!' Perkins called melodramatically from his bed. 'You belong to me, Nurse Gertie. You can't go walking out with some Greek fisherman who calls you his doll. Not when your own blood pumps around my veins! You have no idea of his intentions, and anyway, you'll break my heart. Haven't I suffered enough by your hand?'

Did he know the portholes had caused the sinking? Would he tell them it was me who went against orders and opened the portholes?

'That's not fair, Corporal Perkins,' I said. 'Your words cut me deeply. You know very well that I saved your life on two accounts! First, when I got them to pull you out of the water, and second, when I gave my own blood to keep you alive.' I rushed to his bedside. 'So you must shush now! You seem to be doing so well. Look. I've brought you a pair of modern crutches which the fisherman brought all the way from the island of Syros, just for you. How are you feeling?'

He gave me a sulky look. 'I'm getting better. Nurse says I can get up for a while tomorrow. Promise you'll come and visit, help me to walk with one leg. Don't leave me to lie in an empty room wondering where you are, and who you're with.'

'I will, of course I will. We've been through a lot together, haven't we, you and I?' I had to make him think well of me, not blame me for his loss of limb. 'Really, Corporal Perkins, I couldn't believe it when I saw you in the sea and got them to pull you into our boat. You were almost gone at that point, you know? If I hadn't insisted on your rescue, you wouldn't have lasted another two minutes in the sea.'

'It really was you?'

I nodded. 'You'd lost too much blood already. It's quite remarkable the way you've recovered, despite the influenza and everything. You're a very lucky man.' Desperate to change the subject and not talk about the ship, or make any mention of his leg, I went on. 'I've just sent a carrier pigeon home; well, not all the way to England exactly, but to Athens, so my parents will know I'm all right. The mayor attached a little note to its . . . um, wing.'

'Wing?' Josephine cried. 'That's unusual. They usually fix it to the . . . erm.' We exchanged a startled glance.

'Would you like a cup of tea, Corporal?' the nurse asked. 'I'm just about to make one.'

Perkins nodded and I continued hurriedly. 'Anyway, the bird's flown off and my parents will receive the message tomorrow. Isn't that amazing? What about you, Corporal Perkins, do you want to send a message to your family?'

'No, I don't want them to know anything, not yet. I'll be out of the army soon. My arm's healed, and the stitches come out of my head wound later today. Almost as good as new, aren't I?' he said cynically, before glancing down the bed. 'When I arrive home, I want to walk through the door on two legs. They didn't even know I was on the *Britannic*. My mother and father think I'm still at the barracks fixing army vehicles. Who knows, perhaps I'll get that job back, I mean, you don't need two good legs to be a mechanic, do you?' He frowned as if thinking about it.

'You're right, of course,' I said, realising the irony. He would free up another able-bodied soldier for the front line, too.

CHAPTER 23
SHELLY

Greek island of Kea, present day.

ALTHOUGH IT WAS HER LAST night in Kea, Shelly had decided to sleep alone. There were so many things she wanted to think about before she headed home.

The turtle trapped in the fishing net had shaken her badly and brought the incident of her bracelet back with so much clarity she felt the tears run into her hair and then her pillow.

Was she doomed to this punishment for the rest of her life? She couldn't dive without the memory of that day, when everything went wrong. It crushed her heart; a lifetime of regret returning each time she went into the sea. Yet she had to dive, to understand why David was so addicted to it. In a way, she also did it for him. She told him about every dive, talking quietly, sometimes aloud – sometimes only in her mind – she recounted every sensation, not that he could possibly understand. It was far too late for that, and of course that was the very thing that broke her heart.

She thought of her mother's Christmas gift. If Mum hadn't bought her the bracelet, she would not have been sitting at the bus stop that day. Mum would not have been killed. Shelly would not have gone to the jeweller's that day and met David. If Shelly had not treasured the bracelet so much, she would not have kept it on all the time. It would not have slipped off in the sea. David would not have dived for it. So much had happened because of that one thing, the bracelet.

These thoughts went around in her head, making sleep impossible. She reached out and turned the bedside light on, dazzled for a moment. The unsettled feeling simmered away inside her, then she remembered her final video of Harry. Oh, Harry. She was falling in love, and knew it. She had to look upon his face. In a moment, she was out of bed and turning on her camera. There he was in the pudding video, smiling at her. Alone in her rented room, she smiled back at the camera, melting, wishing she wasn't alone after all.

Moving her thoughts along to Gran Gertie, she must have been devastated when Sissy's fob watch went spiralling down not two miles from where Shelly had just dived. But Gran Gertie was saved by the dolphin, a miracle in itself. If the dolphin hadn't saved Gran Gertie, Shelly would not have been born. Shelly had gone on to save the lives of many animals, and as a stand-in paramedic, a few people too. As a nurse, she guessed her great-grandmother had also saved soldier's lives.

Rather odd, the way everything worked out, she thought. Feeling calmer, she relaxed in her hotel bed and allowed her thoughts to drift.

*   *   *

'Could you come here for a moment?' Shelly whispered when Harry came to her room, the next morning. 'I've had such a wonderful time, the best.' She slipped her arms around his waist and kissed him. 'Thank you, Harry. Now I'm going to take you for a wonderful breakfast.'

At their usual café, they ate eggs and fresh bread at the water's edge, and dropped crumbs into the sea for jostling fish. He touched the tips of her fingers. She peered into his eyes and sighed.

'You will come back?' he said.

She nodded. 'Definitely. You will let me know if an opportunity for a dive to the *Britannic* arises in the future, won't you?'

'Actually, there's a dive scheduled for the end of August, organised for the Directorate-General for the European Environment.'

'I don't understand.'

'It's the European Commission's department responsible for EU policy on the environment,' he explained, making it no clearer. 'There are a couple of TV companies bidding for the film rights too. We've been involved in the organisation over the past two years and now we're almost ready to go.'

'Oh, wow. I'll be here then, to see my turtles hatch.' She raised her brows and stared at him hopefully.

He shook his head. 'Sorry, two years in the planning – it's all booked up, Shelly, even the reserve divers. Still, with your pedigree, if you're here and there's a last-minute drop-out, who knows, there might be room on the boat if you'd like to second-assist? But don't get your hopes up. It's highly unlikely.'

'Thank you.' She realised Harry wouldn't have time for her that week with such a huge responsibility on his shoulders. Still, it would be great to help kit-up the divers and hear their first impressions when they emerged after.

'Possibly dive marshal, second assistant at an outside chance. A *very* outside chance. Logging diver returns, checking equipment, assisting with emergency cylinders on the drop and shot lines. Though you're dreaming. It's highly unlikely to happen.'

'How many actual divers?' she asked.

'Four.'

'How many on the team?'

'Twenty in total, plus the boat crew and the antiquities dive marshal. Thirty-two including me,' he said.

'Antiquities dive marshal?'

'As if our expenses aren't high enough, we have to pay for a Greek dive inspector and a remotely operated vehicle. The ROV operator's job is to record that we don't steal priceless antiquities. Jack Cousteau has a lot to answer for,' he said flippantly.

'He dived here, didn't he?'

Harry nodded. 'Found the wreck in '75 and dived it in '76, long before there were any restrictions. He and his team made sixty-eight dives to the *Britannic* and rumour is he brought up some artefacts.' He shrugged. 'There's been much speculation about those treasures, not least the ship's bell. The main bell's so special, it's the heart of the ship. It would have rung out the alarm in the first place. Unfortunately, that makes it the highest prize for fortune divers, a real crown jewel to be hunted for.'

'So you don't think it's still down there?'

He shrugged again. 'After almost a hundred dives, and everyone looking out for it, I doubt it.'

'For a moment, I was thinking of that film . . . what was it? Ah, *Raiders of the Lost Ark*. You know?'

Harry laughed. 'I understand what you're saying, but Cousteau was an amazing guy. A pioneer of scuba, or aqua-lung as it was called then; also sea-scooters, the diving bell, shark cages, and many things connected with deep-sea diving. Yes, an adventurer, but he was a brave and clever man who brought the underwater world into the home. The general public lost themselves in his TV documentaries about sea life. Cousteau said something like this: *Once the sea casts its spell of wonder over a man, it holds him in those nets forever.*'

Shelly gasped, emotion exploding in her chest.

'Are you all right?' He lifted her chin. 'You look upset.'

She nodded. 'I'm fine. It just took me back, you know, the fishing net? I'll tell you more next time, promise.'

He nodded and smiled. 'Whenever you're comfortable. No worries. Just come back soon, will you? By the way, what time's your flight from Athens?'

'Eight this evening.'

He blinked at her. 'That's in twelve hours. What are you going to do until then?'

She tapped her camera, which was slung around her neck. 'I'm going to photograph the city. Never had time before.'

He stuck his thumb and forefinger into his mouth and made the most enormous whistle. 'Right then, I am going to show you the Athens you wouldn't otherwise see, all right?'

It was her turn to appear shocked. 'You mean you're coming with me?'

'I certainly am. If you like? I'll show you an Athens that isn't in the tourist guide, then get you to the airport and stay on the bus to meet the ferry back to Kea. What do you think? If you are comfortable with the plan, I'll just nip over there and get a ticket.'

'That sounds amazing, actually. I would love it.'

Harry entered the ticket office just as Elias raced up on a scooter. 'Did I hear my dad whistle?'

'Yes, actually. He's just gone to buy a ticket. He's coming with me to Athens,' she said, beaming with happiness.

'What! I don't believe it. Where is he?' He glared around. 'The ticket office, you said?'

'Look, Elias, I don't want any trouble, OK? It was his idea. Why are you so angry?' Surely he wasn't still hungover from his twenty-first celebration?

'Why? I've got a basketball match; he was supposed to come – he always comes.' He stormed over to the ticket office and barged inside.

Bugger!

Two minutes later, he reappeared and raced away on his Vespa. Harry came out of the office, stood for a moment, following Elias with his eyes and grinning. 'My son needs to grow up, I'm afraid,' he said with a chuckle in his voice. 'He's had everything he's wanted all his life, my fault. Consequently, he considers nobody but himself.'

'Look, Harry, I really don't want to come between father and son.'

'Tough. I have wishes too. Come on, it's an adventure! I'm really looking forward to it.' He grinned, hooked my arm, and marched me onto the ferry. 'Quick, up to the top deck so you can get some pictures of the lighthouse as we pass. Then, we almost go over the *Britannic*. You need to imagine how it was. Well, no you don't because the lighthouse and little church next to it were exactly the same, just the port itself was sparse in those days, but you have the old postcards, yes?'

She nodded, looking out over the sea. 'I'm trying to imagine the *Britannic*, on the bottom. The sheer size of her is mind-blowing. I mean, nine hundred feet long! I can't get my head around it.'

'OK, try to imagine ten of these ferry boats end to end, heading for this island while it's bow ploughed ever deeper into the Aegean. The captain, Captain Bartlett, must have felt sure she would make it, and perhaps he would have, if the portholes hadn't been open.'

Shelly's thoughts snapped to her great-grandmother with an urgent wish to change the subject. 'Tell me, how come your English father ended up here?' she asked.

'Ah, that's quite a story. I'll tell you shortly, but take a note of all the windmills on the island as we pass.'

They stared at the landscape as Kea disappeared into the distance. In the lounge, Harry ordered eggs on toast and fresh orange juice.

'It all started just after the Second World War,' he said. 'My grandfather, Gerrard Dennis, was working for the British government.'

Shelly's eyes widened. 'He was a spy?'

Harry laughed. 'Nothing so dramatic. Britain feared they would run out of coal, even then, and were searching for alternative energy. Kea had the largest windmill complex in the Cyclades.'

'So your grandfather came to work on a project and fell in love with the island?'

'He did, but it was more than that. He fell in love with my mother and married her. He became good friends with another man who was half English and helped him with the language. Then, one day when they were working on a windmill, tragedy struck.'

'What happened?'

'A massive beam fell from the roof, my father's friend ran forward and pushed him out of the way, but unfortunately, his friend caught the end of the beam on his head and was badly hurt with a fractured skull. He was in a coma for a long time, everyone thought he would die, but eventually he made it.' Harry stared at the window. 'My parents sort of adopted him. I forget his real name, but we called him Theio, which is Greek for uncle. The blow left him with poor vision, and not a lot of sense.' Harry smiled fondly. 'He was a simple soul, always fun, and good-humoured too. We all loved him.'

'What happened to him?'

'When my parents got older and couldn't look after him, they paid the monks at the convent, on Syros, to take care of him. Theio loved the churches. Sometimes we'd take him to one and he'd just sit there, smiling and gazing at the candles and the gold chandeliers, but most of all he loved the icons, especially the virgin and child. He would kneel before it and gaze up with the most adoring expression.'

'What a moving story. Did they find his family?'

'Theio wouldn't allow it, he would rather they believed him dead than burden them. We should go to Syros one day and lay some flowers on his grave.'

'He died?'

'I'd think so. I haven't seen him since I was a boy, and he was an old man then. I guess he'd be near a hundred now. My parents and grandparents are long gone. I mean, there are lots of hundred-year-old Greeks, believe me. You just have to go into any village *kafenio* to see them sipping their morning coffee – but come on, what are the odds?'

* * *

Before long, they left the bus in the centre of Athens. Harry's excitement was contagious. In a taxi to the foot of the Acropolis, he muttered statements like: 'The cradle of Western civilisation,' and 'The birthplace of democracy.' On top of the great flat rock, Shelly stood in awe under the magnificent columns that skirted the Parthenon. She photographed everything. Harry led her around the walls where they looked down on the city and pointed out landmarks. She zoomed in, knowing the enjoyment she would get from her pictures later.

222

Harry studied his watch. 'Eleven thirty, quick, we're running late! We have to get back to Syntagma Square for something very special!'

They raced down to the street, jumped on a packed bus without a ticket and hoped an inspector didn't get on. When he did, they squeezed through the other passengers and got off from the middle doors, laughing like naughty children. A short taxi ride took them to the houses of parliament.

'You'll have to jump out at the lights, is not allowed to stop now because the *Evzones* are changing guard,' the taxi driver said.

Harry paid the driver. He pulled up sharply and they both leapt from the taxi, the door nearly taking out an enraged scooter rider. The square was crammed with locals and tourists.

'Let's see if we can get a better view. Put your biggest lens on the camera,' Harry suggested. 'Right, now come on!' He took her hand and tugged her around the tourists to a policeman on crowd control and Harry spoke to him in Greek. As a result, the officer directed them to a spot with a good view.

'This is amazing, thank you,' Shelly said. 'I've never seen so many soldiers. Just look at the uniforms, and they're all so tall and handsome.'

'It's part of the requirement.' Harry was beaming with pride. They watched the changing of the presidential guard until Harry said, 'Come on, it's almost over, let's get away before the crowd starts to move.'

'Where are we going now?'

'The best museum in Greece, you'll love it! Come on, keep up.'

CHAPTER 24
GERTIE

Greece, 1916.

MY HEART WENT OUT TO Perkins. He put on a brave front, but inside I guessed he was struggling to retain his sanity. I tried to imagine how it must feel to suddenly discover part of your body is elsewhere, missing in action. He frowned a lot now, especially when he thought nobody was watching. But when he caught me looking at him, his cheeky grin that touched me so deeply returned.

'No nonsense now, Corporal. You must get some sleep,' I ordered, trying to hide the affection in my voice. 'You'll need all the strength you can get if you're going to be out and about tomorrow.' I kissed two fingers and placed them on his forehead.

'Now I really will have sweet dreams,' he said, closing his eyes, his face expressionless without the pain. For a moment, I saw a different person, a young man who laughed with the boys, who hugged his mother and shook hands with his father. A man who wanted to play football, and dance with pretty girls. A man who loved his job, took pride in whatever he did, and in his appearance. As I looked down on him, I sensed his alternating euphoria and depression and the confusion that his mood swings caused.

Josephine had told me many things about amputees and what they went through. Phantom-limb pain, jumpy-stump, acute depression. When I became a qualified nurse, I wanted to specialise in this field, to try to make amends.

'Be careful,' Josephine said quietly from her desk. 'Your job is to take care of his body's healing, nothing more.'

* * *

Later, I walked around the harbour and sat on the chest with one of my letters.

'What are you reading?' Manno asked, sitting beside me, a little too close for comfort.

I moved to the edge. It wasn't correct for a man to sit in such close proximity without so much as an invitation. 'It's private,' I said. 'From my mother.'

He moved closer again.

Annoyed, and determined to hold my claim on the chest, I got up, walked around him, and sat at the opposite end. Manno frowned at me.

I bit my lip to stop myself grinning. 'Stay over there, please.' I pointed at his end of the chest.

'I like you,' he said, his words stoking the heat already smouldering in my cheeks. 'Is no problem. You don't want to talk with me.' He shrugged and put on a dejected look, which I understood was play-acting. 'I was thinking to take you to see your dolphin, but if you no want, is all right.' He turned away from me and stared across the sea.

'What? You know where he is?' I sat down.

'But of course . . . We are very big friends, me and Delphi.'

'I can't go anywhere without a chaperone.' I stretched my neck and looked away.

'I understand, you do not trust yourself alone with me? This is perfectly normal. I have the same problem with many girls.'

'You are too bold, Mr Manno, I suspect you've been told that before too. I would love to see the dolphin again, but I have a certain responsibility here. Poor Corporal Perkins has lost his foot.'

'Then he will never marry, poor man.'

'Of course he'll marry. Why shouldn't he take a wife once he has a new foot and is back at work?'

Manno pulled in his chin. 'Bah! You think so? In Greece, only perfect men take a wife. If there is something wrong with a man, like only one foot, then the family hide him away.'

Yianni, who sat patiently in his boat, shouted towards us. 'Manno, *ela!*'

'I will leave you to your work, and get on with my own,' Manno said. He stuck his arm out. 'It is the custom here, if someone saves your life, you shake hands with them each time you meet.'

This seemed such a charming custom, and I had noticed a lot of handshaking went on between the islanders. I reached out and took his hand. 'Then I must say: thank you for saving my life.'

'Manno!' his father called.

Manno lifted my hand and quickly kissed the back of it, then turned and leapt into the boat.

'Manno! You are *so* bad!' I called.

He grinned, released the mooring ropes then pushed the vessel away from the quayside. 'Until tomorrow!' he shouted. 'I will give your good wishes to Delphi!'

Yianni cranked the engine and it spluttered into life. The boat turned away from the town and motored down the centre of the harbour. I watched until the fishing boat disappeared past the lighthouse of St Nicholas.

* * *

'Goodnight, Gertie,' Josephine called that evening as I walked out of the school room.

'Goodnight, nurse,' I called back absently, my head full of Corporal Perkins. I could not get Manno's words out of my head. Just because Perkins had lost half of his leg, didn't mean he wouldn't make a perfectly fine husband. Yet, knowing that some people would think like Manno filled me with sadness. It made me want to hold Perkins to me and tell him things would work out; that I would always care deeply for him.

I gazed out over the darkening sea, following the path that Manno had taken. My heart filled with romantic thoughts of the fisherman. The evening was heavy with heat even though it was December. My pigeon would be flying through the colourful sky towards Athens. How wonderful it must be, I pondered, to soar through a sunset.

Tomorrow, my parents would know their daughter had survived. Mother would cry and I could hear Father's voice as he patted the back of her hand and said, 'There, there, no need for tears, dear. Our daughter's safe.'

A flourish of red light swept over the firmament, dramatically silhouetting Kea's iconic lighthouse. Manno would soon return from Syros with his fishing nets and sack of mail. Would he be thinking of me at that same moment? I turned towards the schoolhouse. Tomorrow I'd help Perkins to walk with the aid of crutches.

I returned to *Yiayá*'s cottage where she pulled me to the table and served me a thick pancake filled with mild cheese, covered with a ladle of golden honey. I can honestly say it was wonderful. I discovered the word for delicious in Greek when I rubbed my belly and gave her an enquiring look.

'*Nostimo!*' she squeaked with clear delight. 'Nos-tee-mo!'

I fell asleep thinking about dear Perkins, yet it was Manno who appeared in my dreams. Manno came to my bed, in my imagination. I felt myself drawn into the fisherman's arms, imagined his kiss heavy on my lips, and felt his arms around my waist pulling me against his body. In my dreams, I would yield to his exploring hands, and I would boldly whisper loving words into his ear.

Sensations I had never experienced before raced through me, not quite pleasure – not quite pain – something far more delicious exploded in the secret depths of me as sleep carried me away. I longed to feel his hands slip inside my bodice, or under my skirt. But, oh dear, I forget myself . . . yet my feelings for Manno were growing so strong that it seemed I had no control over my thoughts.

* * *

The next morning, I woke, lonely and withdrawn, continually turning over my memories of the awful sinking. With no confidante, I kept everyone at a distance in case, in a moment of self-pity, I dared to confess what I was responsible for. Why did I open the portholes and cause all those people to die such a horrible death? I was so upset, my insides trembled violently. No matter what I did, no matter how hard I tried, I could never give Corporal Perkins his leg back, or give those poor unfortunates their lives back. I was condemned to suffer for them all, and then burn in hell.

The compensation was mine to give, and I could start to even up the scale by making Corporal Perkins as happy as possible.

This wasn't difficult. He kept telling me he was sweet on me. In truth, this gave me a thrill because I liked him too. If Manno hadn't come along, complicating things, I could have liked Corporal Perkins above all others. Yes, I could even have loved him.

But I feared Manno had stolen my heart. Perhaps this was my punishment, to relinquish the man I loved for the man I was indebted to.

Outside, on the quayside, the sun sparkled on the water. A black and white cat romped with its kittens. A seagull strutted across a boat canopy. Women rushed to and from the bakery calling their greetings to each other, loudly, with determined merriment.

In the bakery, the intoxicating smell of fresh bread made my mouth water. I greeted everyone, as was the thing to do, and bought three loaves. Villagers patted me like a child, touched my uniform and my hair. Their happiness rubbed off, and I gave a loaf to *Yiayá*, and the other two to Josephine.

Breakfast, which I ate with Nurse Josephine and Corporal Perkins, consisted of warm, creamy milk over a brown rusk, and strong, bitter-sweet coffee.

Josephine said, 'Your pigeon will have arrived in Athens, and they're probably sending a tickertape to England right now. It will arrive at your home town any minute, Gertie. I'm sure your parents will be relieved to hear you're in good health.' She spoke quietly, without her usual smile.

'Thanks to you and your care, Josephine. I am beyond grateful.'

'Just doing my job.'

'What about your parents, do they know you're safe? Where are you from?'

'Tipton, north of Birmingham.' She lowered her eyes for a moment. 'My parents were killed in their beds by a Zeppelin bomb, in January this year.'

229

'Gosh, how awful. I'm terribly sorry. I can hardly imagine what you've been going through.'

'The raid was meant for Liverpool,' she went on. 'High winds blew the Zeppelin off track. My parents and sixty other village people perished that night.' She lifted a napkin and revealed three apples on a dish.

'A dolphin saved me,' I said, the words coming uninvited, surprising me as much as Josephine. 'I don't know why I said that. It was the apple skin, it reminded me.' I ran my thumb over the fruit. 'Sometimes those terrifying moments come back so fiercely I want to cry. They are like . . . sobbing around my heart.' I sighed. 'That sounds awfully mad.'

'Some doctors are talking about a thing called delayed shock. It's a real condition,' Josephine said. 'When your brain tries to deal with something that is too awful, or too illogical for it to cope with. The anguish will fade with time.'

I looked into her eyes and saw she was talking about herself as much as me. 'How much time?'

Josephine shrugged. 'It's different for everyone.'

Perkins interrupted. 'Can we try the crutches yet?'

Josephine gathered herself with a stretch of her neck. 'It's early days, Corporal. We'll adjust them for you after lunch. They have to fit perfectly, and we have to check your arm too, then we'll move on to your mobility.'

'Blimey, talk about the walking wounded, eh, nurse.' The joke on his lips wasn't reflected in his eyes.

The door banged open. The hall was full of people peering into our room. Pavlo rushed in with no regard for the quarantine sign. 'Nurse Gertie, a pigeon has come! There is a message for you in English. The mayor, is coming to read it. A ship comes for you.'

'Thank God. At last,' Josephine muttered.

'Let's hope they're taking us back to civilisation,' Perkins said. 'I'll go crazy if I have to stay in this damn room much longer.'

'No point speculating,' Josephine said. 'I'm hoping to get to Lemnos, my sister's nursing there. There's been no news for months. Every day I wonder how she is. I don't even know if she's heard our parents have died.'

She sighed so deeply I wanted to put my arms around her.

Poor Josephine, I'd been so wrapped up in myself, I hadn't considered her.

'They'll probably want us back home,' Perkins insisted. 'There's bound to be an inquiry.'

I sensed a hint of malice about him and with a jolt of fear, I turned and rushed out of the room, straight into the mayor. Panicked – I feared they had discovered the truth and were about to handcuff me. I tried to sidestep him but the teacher caught my arm. 'Wait, we have news for you,' he said, keeping a firm grip. Pointing at the QUARANTINE sign, he asked, 'Is it safe to go in there?'

I nodded, my mouth too dry to speak. The teacher steered me back into the classroom. The three Greek men stared at us, unsure how to proceed with such important information. The mayor cleared his throat, squared his shoulders, and made what sounded like a formal announcement. Pavlo started to translate but the schoolteacher placed a hand on the boy's shoulder before giving us the news himself.

'*Ladies and gentlemen, HMS* Redemption *has arrived in Syros to embark the remaining British survivors. You will go to Syros with the mail boat in the morning.*'

This is it; I'll be in prison by Christmas, hated by those who lost loved ones, and my dear family shamed.

231

CHAPTER 25
SHELLY

Dover, present day.

THE TAXI PULLED UP OUTSIDE White Cottage. Shelly, lost in thoughts of Harry and her amazing holiday, stared at the house. The driver cleared his throat.

'Oh, sorry,' she said, pushing the fare and a tip into his hand. 'Daydreaming.'

'I'll get your suitcase. Good holiday, was it?'

'Brilliant, but it's always nice to get home.'

'It is, indeed. Goodnight now,' he said, after hefting her case to the gate. 'Or should I say, 'morning as it's near on two o'clock.'

After a dreamless sleep that left her fully refreshed, Shelly entered the kitchen. The room smelled of beer, BO, and bacon. Her father and Bill Grundy were laughing and cooking a fry-up.

'Morning, Dad, morning, Bill!'

'How was the trip?' Gordon asked.

'I'll tell you about it tonight, but I'm late for work – see you later,' she cried, grabbing her bag and keys.

''Ere, Shelly love, don't you want some breakfast?'

'No time, Dad.' She kissed him on the cheek. 'Must run. I'll bring fish and chips in this evening, OK? Is everything all right? No problems?'

They both nodded and shook their heads in a way that told her everything was fine.

'See you later then. Try not to get into trouble!'

* * *

Shelly arrived at the surgery at the same time as Eve. 'You look well,' Eve said. 'Did you have a good break? How was the diving, photography – and did you meet anyone outrageously sexy?' She narrowed her eyes with a look of mischief.

Shelly laughed. 'Actually, yes, brilliant on all three counts. What have we here?' She pointed to the doorstep where a dead goldfish lay belly up in a glass bowl. 'Oh dear, not again.' She opened a letter taped to the side.

Deer Vet Shelly, can you make Bob bettor agane. I will come after skool with my mum. Thank you, Ann Jones, age six.

Eve rolled her eyes. 'Another poorly goldfish?'

'Poorly as can be; Bob the third, deceased. Nip down to the pet shop when you get a mo', would you?'

'Only if you promise to tell me every detail of your holiday. It's been so quiet while you've been away.'

While they went about their work, Shelly recounted the basics, avoiding the subject of Harry, and dwelling on the laying turtle. At one point, she closed her eyes and could see Harry smiling across the restaurant table at her, which reminded her to go through the photos that evening.

Eve, who knew her better than anyone, laughed. 'Come on, no holding back now. I know you're not telling me everything!' Eve grinned. '*Was* there anyone special?'

'Maybe . . .' Shelly purposefully turned her eyes back to the appointment book. 'I see we've got Mrs Jackson's Dobermann in for a teeth clean this morning.'

Eve nodded.

'Can you prep, make sure we're OK for Telazol, and that the anaesthetic machine's set up and ready to go? Check the monitors and get the oxygen feed ready. They're bringing him in just before we close for lunch so we can get on with the job right away. He's so big, and has a real nasty streak when he gets anxious, I don't want him hanging around.'

'Sure, leave me to it. I've asked Mrs Jackson to muzzle the dog, after last time.' Eve paused. 'So, go on then, was he really gorgeous?' she persisted, pushing her dark hair behind her ear and turning towards Shelly.

'Absolutely none of your business.' Shelly studied the appointment book.

'I know. But was he?'

Shelly kept her head down, but nodded rapidly and both women chuckled.

'Come on then, at least tell me when you're going back?' Eve prodded.

'I might go back when the turtle eggs hatch – if it's all right with you, of course. I'd love to see the adorable little flappers scuttling down to the sea.'

'What's his name, then?' Eve said, refusing to be side-tracked.

'What? Honestly, is that all you think about?'

'Pretty much, yes.'

'Harry.'

'You going to tell me everything?'

'Nope.'

The surgery buzzer went. 'I'll go,' Eve said. She returned two minutes later. 'There's a first. Gerbil in a whisky bottle. Mr Rider wants to know if we can get it out before his boy comes home from school.'

'Was the bottle empty when it went in?' Shelly asked, peering at the sleeping rodent. 'I fear it'll have one hell of a hangover.'

'When are you going back then?'

'You're driving me crazy now! I said, when the eggs are ready to hatch.'

Eve giggled.

* * *

At ten to one, Shelly heard the front door open, she guessed it was Mrs Jackson with the Dobermann. Eve called from the front, 'Shelly, it's for you!'

Shelly went through and was surprised to see her father standing at the counter.

'I hope you don't mind me calling, Shelly, but Malcolm brought this for you, after you'd left this morning. I thought it might be important.' He thrust a letter towards her.

DJ's handwriting was on the envelope. She'd been pushing thoughts of him to the back of her mind, but couldn't quite forget him. 'Thanks, that's kind of you to bring it, Dad. Would you like a look around while you're here?'

'Me? Well, yes, I would. Often wondered what you do all day.'

Just then, everyone's attention was taken by a kerfuffle in the doorway. Mrs Jackson was hanging on to the window bar with one hand, and the Dobermann's leash with the other. Shelly opened the door.

'Can I help?'

Mrs Jackson was sweating and red in the face. 'I'm afraid he remembers when I last brought him here – to have his nuts off – I don't think he'll ever forgive you, vet.'

'Poor sod! Neither would I,' Gordon muttered.

'I see you had his ears cropped, against my advice.' Shelly tried to keep her tone even, despite her anger.

'Not me. My son. I was furious.' She uttered, with forty-five kilos of unhappy muscle pulling her out of the door.

'Let me help,' said Eve, reaching for the lead.

In a second, everything changed. The Dobermann's hackles went up, along with its lip. The whites of his eyes flashed and the snarl that came from him made it terrifyingly clear it was on the verge of a savage attack. Despite the muzzle, it could do some serious damage.

'Everyone look at the floor, immediately,' Shelly said flatly though her heart raced. 'Mrs Jackson, can you wrap the lead around the window bar and tie it off?' She did. 'Now everyone step backwards without turning away from the dog. 'Don't look at him, don't speak, don't show your teeth even in a smile.'

Shelly made a humming noise which immediately caught the dog's attention. The snarling stopped and he dropped his head to one side, then peered at her curiously. Shelly mirrored his behaviour, then she spoke softly, turned slightly sideways and moved a little closer. She made a fist with her hand and slowly raised the back of it towards the dog's muzzle. All the time, she talked quietly until it lowered its head and dipped towards her. She scratched under his collar and he sat.

'Good boy,' she said softly.

* * *

An hour later, with the dog anaesthetised, Shelly cleaned below its gumline. 'There it is, the reason for his bad temper. It looks like a bee sting inside his mouth,' she said. 'Must have driven him crazy, especially when Mrs Jackson put the muzzle on.'

'Your dad was amazing, wasn't he? I mean, even I was a bit rattled, but he just stood there, calm as you like.'

Shelly straightened and stretched her back. 'Yes, he was, even I was surprised. That's the plaque removed. Now a quick de-scale and polish for a brighter, whiter, smile.'

'And a more kissable mouth . . .' Eve interrupted, then giggled. 'Come on, now. I need to know all the details about Mr Fantastic.'

They laughed and joked until Shelly started to feel a little disloyal, because in fact, she missed Harry terribly and couldn't wait to finish work and give him a call. She would just thank him for a wonderful week, and wasn't naïve enough to think he would be missing her already. She'd seen *Shirley Valentine* and suddenly realised Harry bore a strong resemblance to Tom Conti when that film was made, decades ago. She closed her eyes and imagined his smiling face.

'Excuse me,' Eve said. 'You're doing far too much grinning, vet. It's a little scary after all these years.'

They laughed again and got on with the day until Ann Jones collected a miraculously recovered Bob at half past three.

'I've got a little present for you, Ann,' Shelly said. 'It's a booklet on how to take care of Bob. It's for grown-ups really, so do you think you could get Mummy to read it to you?'

Ann nodded seriously and passed it to Mrs Jones.

* * *

On the way home, Shelly pulled over and opened DJ's letter. She had to see him, or risk regretting it for the rest of her life. Why was all this happening to her now? It couldn't have come at a worse time. He sent a date, time, and place. A small snack bar, The Honeypot Café, not far from the practice. Agreeing to see him was one thing, but she hardly dared think about the effect he would have on her.

*   *   *

'You had a good time then, Shelly love?' Gordon asked halfway through their meal that evening. 'You going to tell me about it?'

'I had a wonderful time.' She told him about the egg-laying turtle, and diving the *Burdigala* wreck. 'The island's so close to mainland Greece, yet it's almost a wildlife sanctuary.'

'Will you be going back any time soon?'

Shelly nodded, watching her father's face. 'In about two months, I think. I'd like to see the baby turtles return to the sea.' She thought about Harry. Eight weeks seemed a long and lonely time before she'd see him again. There was so much she didn't know about him, silly stuff, trivia. If she could, she would go back tomorrow. She closed her eyes and imagined being in his arms.

'That's good,' her dad said, pulling her back to reality. ''Cause next time I might come with you.'

Shelly looked up, her mind racing through several scenarios of what that might entail. With a tight feeling in her chest, she threw all her effort into sounding delighted. 'Oh, Dad! How lovely. What brought this on?'

'Well, Bill got the hang of taking care of me birds. And that was the biggest reason for me not going with you.' He peered at her, rubbing the bridge of his nose as he contemplated. 'And I have to tell you, Shelly love. I'm not as young as I was. Don't be fooled by the pomade and Pond's cream—'

'Dad!'

'No, really. Today, I realised how hard you work. In fact, I realised that I don't know that much about you, my own daughter. And I was dead proud of the way you handled that rabid dog. I thought you just took money off cat people and puppy lovers.'

'Dad!' she cried again, trying to stop herself laughing. 'It wasn't a rabid dog, it had a bee sting in its mouth. Can you imagine how that felt?'

'Well, anyway, the long and short of it is, I'm coming to Greece with you, next time.' His eyes narrowed in a scheming way. 'Would you mind if I brought Malcolm along?'

So that was what this was about. 'Dad! No, you can't bring Malcolm. I hope you haven't said anything to him.'

'He really likes you, Shelly.'

'I've met someone!' she blurted. His face lit up, and she almost said something she might have regretted later, so she just thought it: *Oh, for fuck's sake!*

'Really? Was that—'

'Stop right now, Dad! I'll tell you about it when I'm ready. Now let's drop the subject before I get angry. It would be lovely if you came to Greece with me, but I'm just as happy for you to have Bill or Malcolm round here for the week. Now, I'm going to play another one of Gran Gertie's tapes because I'm hoping to know the whole story before I return to Kea. So, you can listen with me or go and watch the telly.'

Gordon decided the football was more important.

CHAPTER 26
GERTIE

Greece, 1916.

AFTER A HURRIED LESSON ON the crutches, Perkins hopped up and down while Josephine and I folded the bedlinen and tried to restore the school room fit for purpose.

'I must say farewell to *Yiayá*,' I said. 'I'll see you on the quayside in a few minutes.' I rushed around to the matriarch's home and found the cutest white goat tied to the donkey loop in the wall. I knocked on the door while the goat nibbled on my apron bow.

'*Ela! Yiayá*,' I called.

'*Agapití mou!*' My lovely!' she cried reaching up and tapping my cheek.

I stepped inside and the old lady's face lit in such a lovely way that I knew I would miss her terribly. 'Me,' I pointed at my chest, then out towards the horizon, 'Syros!'

Yiayá's eyes widened as she understood, then with an alarmed voice, she shook her head and cried, '*Allá o engonós mou se agapáei!*' She thumped her heart with alarming ferocity.

With no clue as to what she was saying, I pointed at my chest then out to sea and shouted, as shouting seemed to be the thing to do in a serious situation, 'Me, *Gertie*, go with *Manno*, to *Syros*!'

The lovely old lady blinked for a moment, pointed at me, slid her two forefingers against each other and cried, '*Tee, Manno, Syros?*' in a questioning way.

'Yes, yes!' I replied, happy to be understood, though confused by the finger sliding. 'With Manno.' Then *Yiayá* did an odd thing. She placed one hand on my head and made the sign of the cross three times with the other.

Yiayá was so lovely and kind, on impulse, I enfolded the little woman in my arms and kissed her cheeks. Then to my alarm, I realised the old lady was weeping. 'No, no, *Yiayá*,' I said, wiping her tears away. 'Me . . .' I drew a circle in the air then pointed at the ground, 'Kea!' It was the only way I could think of to say I'd come back.

'O *engonós mou se agapáei*,' *Yiayá* said again, and I made an effort to memorise the words as they seemed so important to the old dear.

'Gertie!' The cry came from outside.

'I must go, *Yiayá*.' I lifted the woman's hand and kissed it, then hurried out of the cottage and headed for Manno's mooring where Josephine and Perkins waited with my pillow-bag.

Manno's boat approached. My heart fluttered, but then I stared in disbelief at the contents of his *caïque*. A basket of fish, a pile of yellow net, his father Yianni, and a huge, curl-horned ram whose goatish stench overpowered everything. The creature was clearly unhappy with his mode of transport.

'Holy Moses, what the blazes is that?' Perkins cried. 'Just take a look at the business end of that ram! He's got gonads down to his knees!'

Josephine and I blushed at Perkins's choice of language.

'Magnificent, yes?' Manno beamed as if it was a personal compliment. He leapt onto the quayside, tugging on the goat's rope halter. '*Ela! Ela! Malaka!*' he yelled, telling the ram to come, then swearing at it.

The ram, nimble despite its robust size, hurled itself at solid ground. Manno thrust the rope into Josephine's hand. 'Hold on to him, nurse, while I get the post.'

Josephine pulled in her chin, reluctant to breathe the acrid goat-stench that encircled her. Startled to the point of speech-lessness, she wrapped the rope twice around her fist and gripped tightly.

The ram, clearly uninterested in its human audience, sniffed the air. Manno steered the wooden wheelbarrow towards the boat and his father passed the mail sack up. Before anyone could react, the ram caught the scent of *Yiayá*'s pretty goat. It hurtled towards the cottage, its physical attributes making its intentions very clear, dragging a yelping Nurse Josephine with it.

The ram was not a romancer. The creature mounted the goat without so much as a 'hello'.

Josephine, her face aflame, turned her back on the beasts but kept a grip on the rope.

Manno strode over, took the rope from Josephine's fist, and with a grin said, 'Very good, nurse. Maybe you marry a shepherd, yes?' He tied the ram's halter to the metal ring while Josephine scurried back to me.

Manno thrust the air with an open hand, in the direction of the ram's behind in a slightly lewd manner, and grinned at Per-kins.

'Is one happy boy, yes!' he cried.

Josephine and I stared at the fisherman, then at each other. After a moment of shocked silence, we grasped one another to save falling over while trying to contain our laughter. 'This will not do,' Nurse Josephine squeaked, trying to apply a sombre face while smoothing my apron. 'Not the correct conduct for upstanding nurses in public.'

'More's the pity,' Perkins muttered, glancing at the goats

* * *

An hour later, Josephine, Perkins, and I were in the fishing boat with Manno and Yianni. I peered back at Kea as we sailed out of the bay and past the lighthouse. So much had happened on that island, and at that moment, somewhere below us, HMHS *Britannic* lay on the sea bed, along with Sissy's watch. I glanced at Corporal Perkins's foot, and wondered what he was thinking. He looked up, straight into my eyes, and I saw such sadness. I wished I could hold his hand for a moment.

Then Manno caught my eye and winked. My spine tingled as I tried to hide the thrill I felt when he looked my way. 'You no worry, *koukla*. My boat, she is unsinkable.'

'Isn't that what they all say?' I remembered *Yiayá*'s words. 'Manno, what does: *O engonós mou se agapáei,* mean?'

His face darkened and his brow furrowed. 'Who says these things to you?'

Alarmed by his attitude, I shook my head, 'It doesn't matter.'

'No, you must tell me. Who said this, *koukla mou*?'

'*Yiayá.*'

The aggravation left his face and he tilted his head back to laugh heartily. 'Ah, this is good.'

'But what does it mean?'

I glanced over to Josephine, but as I did, the nurse turned away, smiling. I returned my attention to Manno. 'Tell me.'

243

He let go of the tiller, cupped my chin and peered into my eyes. '*O engonós mou se agapáei* means: my grandson loves you.'

'Oh!' Heat rose in my cheeks. 'And this?' I slid my forefingers side by side.

Manno grabbed the tiller, stared at his fist, then, threw a challenging glance at Perkins, who seemed to understand more Greek than me.

'Manno?'

'Ah, it means – well, you saw the goats, yes?'

Horrified to realise why the old woman had blessed me. I returned my stare to Josephine who wore a sympathetic smile. 'Don't worry about it,' she said.

I clasped my hands between my knees and stared at my feet.

Outside the bay, the little boat rolled and bobbed on the blue water.

'Don't you put the nets out?' I asked Manno.

'Not here, there are bombs down there. Is not safe.'

'Bombs? My God, we'll all be blown to bits!'

'No worries, you're safe with me, *koukla*, they're fixed to the bottom with a long rope, but they're for the bigger ships which are deeper in the water.'

The boat bobbed about as we chugged over the waves. Manno said something to his father who then pulled a box from under the seat. He emptied the contents into our laps, replaced the lid, and then set the top as a table. He laid fresh bread, a beautiful pink dip with a strong scent of fish, plump black olives, and lemon wedges, before us. Josephine clamped a hand over her mouth and shook her head. She shuffled to the front of the boat, a look of utter despair on her face.

The food was wonderful! 'What was the pink dip, Mr Yianni?' I asked. 'It's really delicious.'

'Is *taramasalata*; is made from the raw eggs of the mullet fish and stale bread, all whipped up with lots of extra virgin olive oil.'

The information was too much for Josephine. Her face turned grey and she hung over the side. Yianni guided her to the back of the boat, which he said was a much better place for her to be, under the circumstances.

Soon, the little fishing boat approached a hilly, barren island. 'What is this place, Syros?' I asked.

'No, it's the cursed island of Giaros,' Manno replied. 'Nobody lives there. Giaros no have the water. They say if you step on the island, you will die a terrible death. In the old days, the Mediterranean pirates buried their treasure there, but then they all got sick and died because the well they dug was filled with seawater.'

'Did anyone find the treasure?' Perkins asked.

Manno lifted his chin. 'How can we know? They would keep it secret, yes?'

'It appears quite forebidding,' Nurse Josephine said, staring with puffy eyes at the high cliffs. 'A difficult place to get on or off.'

'Are you feeling better, Nurse Josephine?' I asked, noticing a little colour had returned to her cheeks. She nodded.

As we skirted the landmass, I saw a great splash in the water. At first, I thought it was someone swimming, but we were a mile from the shore. I squinted with my hand shading my eyes and realised I must have been mistaken.

'What are you looking at, Gertie?' Josephine asked.

'I thought I saw splashing, over there, but it's stopped. Perhaps my imagination.'

'Or fish,' Josephine said. 'I've seen them leap out of the water on a calm day.'

The sun glinted off the sea, then suddenly there was another great splash further to the right.

'Oh! There it was again. Did anyone see it?'

'That will be a dolphin, nurse,' Manno called over the throb of the engine.

'A dolphin ... could it be my dolphin? The one that saved me – Delphi?'

'Who knows,' Manno said. 'There are many dolphins in these parts. Listen to me. You must think good thoughts and send them to the dolphins. If you are true enough, they will hear you and come.'

He steered the boat a little closer to the cliffs. We all scanned the water as we travelled on, praying to the dolphins, hoping they would appear.

'This is nonsense,' Perkins said. 'How can they hear our thoughts?'

'I don't know all the answers, I just know what they do,' Manno said. 'There is something so magnificent and powerful in nature, but we humans are not capable of understanding. Not since we turned away from these natural things, and started to worship money. Let me ask you something, my friend, of all the bodies in the water – and I am told there were plenty – how did Delphi know that Nurse Gertie was the one who should be saved? If the dolphin had not saved Nurse Gertie, then Nurse Gertie could not have saved you.'

We were silent with his words, disbelieving, then wondering, could he be right? We were still engrossed with our thoughts when – with an exclamation of shock from us all – a dolphin leapt up behind the boat. I believe I squealed. The dolphin bobbed in and out of the water alongside us, reminding me of one of our Arthur's skimming stones. Then I realised there were several of them, impossible to count because they were dipping up and down through the water like crotchets in a lively tune. They raced to the front of the *caïque*, ducking under the prow and coming up on the other side. Laughing at us with their upturned mouths and wise, round eyes. I almost cried with joy.

I scrambled down the centre of the boat to the bow, in a most unladylike way, not caring what I looked like, only wanting to get closer to the dolphins. Josephine held her hand out and guided me to squeeze onto the bench between her and Perkins. I twisted on the seat so that I could hang over the prow.

Goodness, they came so close! For a moment I was back in the water, descending through the detritus and carnage, following Sissy's watch to the bottom. I had thought it was a torpedo rushing towards me, because I had seen them, hundreds of them, lined up in Sissy's book. I had never seen a live dolphin before and had no notion they were so intelligent. I felt blessed.

Perkins rocked back and forth, rubbing his thigh.

'Are you in pain, soldier?' I asked, reluctant to turn away from the water.

He nodded; lips a thin line, face ashen.

'Oh, please, Nurse Josephine, can we help him?' Suddenly, my heart ached for poor Corporal Perkins.

Josephine felt his forehead and took his pulse. 'Too much activity all at once.' She turned to Manno. 'Is it much further?'

'Another two hours, maybe. We are halfway. You want I make a bed with the nets so he can lay down in the bottom of the boat?' She nodded. Yianni took the tiller and they all gripped the sides as Manno manoeuvred the mail sack to the back of the boat. He gathered the great pile of nets into the centre. Josephine's face stiffened. She focused on her patient, and struggled to get Perkins prostrate on the fishing gear.

'I'm going to give you a shot to ease your pain, Perkins,' she said, kneeling at his side and producing a hypodermic from her medical bag. She turned to Manno who was standing firmly with his hands on his hips as if on dry land.

'Can you stop the boat for a moment? I need to be accurate with the needle.'

Manno spoke to his father, and Yianni turned off the engine. The silence was wonderful. The little boat lifted and dropped gently on the swell. Perkins groaned as Josephine injected the morphine.

'You'll feel better in a few moments, Corporal. Relax now,' she said.

'Look,' Perkins whispered, staring at the sky. 'Vultures, up there, waiting for the end of me.'

We all turned our faces up. A large bird hovered above us, its body perfectly still, wings shivering so fast they appeared to hardly move.

CHAPTER 27
SHELLY

Dover, present day.

On Shelly's day off, a letter came in the post; this time for Gordon. Shelly's curiosity rose when she heard him chuckle.

'Everything OK, Dad?'

'Um, yes, why shouldn't it be?' Gordon said, squirrelling the letter back into the envelope, stuffing it into his pocket. 'Just a race entry form. How about you?' He nodded at her tablet.

She stared at the email from Harry, then read through it again with her hand over her mouth. Her dad couldn't possibly know how she felt about Harry, yet he stared at her with an all-knowing look.

'There's a dive to the *Britannic*, Dad. I did actually know about it, but there was no chance of getting on it. Now, a reserve diver's not too well. If he's not a hundred per cent in time, Harry's going to try and get me on standby. Gosh, I'm so excited! I won't be able to go down with the divers, you understand, but just to be there, on the dive boat, well . . .'

'The *Britannic*?' Gordon frowned. 'Sounds familiar. Wasn't that the ship Gertie was on, you know, the one she sank? Near that place we went on holiday.'

'Yes, you knew about it sinking, then?' Shelly's jaw dropped.

He nodded at the cassette player. 'Me and your mum listened to the tapes after she died. Gertie made them for your mum and you. Didn't I tell you? Guess I forgot. I forget a lot, these days,

Shelly. You got to the bit where she was in prison . . .? Poor kid must have been terrified.'

'What?' Shelly cried, startled by his words.

'I guess not then. Well, there you go – yer don't listen – I think yer've got wax, Shelly love. I told you she 'ad a rich and varied life. Now I'm goin' up to me loft to fill this form in. Don't be getting up to mischief.'

Shelly blinked at him. 'You're getting too cheeky, Dad! Anyway, don't be all day up there, Welsh rarebit for lunch, followed by a big fresh fruit trifle. That OK for you?'

His eyes widened. 'You mean proper trifle with jelly? Not that shop stuff.'

'Absolutely!' Shelly said, then realised she was giggling. Once he'd gone, she opened her tablet and read through Harry's email again.

How's my favourite diver? I have some news for you, and a form to print off, fill in, sign and send back ASAP. I told you about the TV company dive, in August. Well, they asked if I could have an all-rounder on hand in case of illness, unforeseen circumstances, et cetera. Get this back to me pronto with a list of dives done, and any references you can muster. I'll do my best for you. I miss you, hurry back here whatever happens.

I can't get you, or your body, out of my head. Roll on August.

Lots of love and long, long kisses,

Harry XXX

Oh, Harry!

She told herself to calm down. It was unlikely she would be part of the team, but still, there was a slight chance. Past experience would work in her favour. Despite his advice, her hopes were up about as high as they could be. She called Simon Ludgate, the proprietor of Dover Divers and explained the situation.

Apart from Gordon, Simon was the only other person who knew of the tragedy in Shelly's life. Close friend and dive enthusiasts, Simon and Shelly had met bi-monthly since the accident, for the past twenty years. They always discussed David, of course. It was David who'd brought Simon and Shelly together.

'Happy to give you a diving reference, Shelly,' Simon said brightly. 'What about the *Lusitania* team – would you like me to have a word, what can you offer to make it worth their while?' he continued.

Her excitement bubbled up, even Simon realised there was a slight chance. 'If I get on the dive, I'll go up to their club and do a talk on the *Britannic*, how's that?'

'Sounds great, what about us, can we get some unique video footage for our website, or photos, if we supply the gizmo?'

'You know I'll do anything for you, Simon.'

'Can I ask, what made you choose the *Britannic*? I don't remember you mentioning it before.'

'It's amazing, Simon, listen to this, my great-grandmother was on the *Britannic* when it went down. Well, not exactly *on* the ship . . . she got to a lifeboat.'

'Blimey, that's incredible!'

'I found a box of cassettes where she'd recorded her life story. Honestly, I was blown away! It's clear she blames herself for the sinking. She survived and when she was in her nineties, she recorded the whole story. I haven't heard it all yet, in fact I'm about to play another tape. Meanwhile, thanks. I owe you, Simon. I'll see you next month, as usual, of course.'

* * *

251

Once Shelly had her dive application prepared, she made trave arrangements for Kea. Peak season on such a small island coul be a problem, so she would book her accommodation ASAP.

She had learned so much, researching most evenings sinc her return from Greece. Now, she was eager to take another loo at the contents. She slipped her hands into her pocket and stoo watching the cassette. Her fingertips touched DJ's letter. With sigh so heavy it seemed her heart deflated a little she pressed th off button.

It was no good, she had to deal with the letter before she coul concentrate on everything else. Besides, what harm could it d to meet DJ, just the once? He could be revengeful, might war to get things off his chest that had festered there for years. Ho could she know? He might have been holding a grudge sinc that dreadful day when she walked away from him. The awf thing was, she had to admit, although she hadn't seen DJ fo nineteen years, and here was the truth, she knew she still love him. She knew that for sure.

So where did that leave her and Harry? There was such distance between them. And then there was her father.

She took a deep breath, picked up the phone, and dialled DJ number again. The moment someone picked up, her dad walke in. She dropped the receiver into its cradle, folded the letter, an slipped it back into her pocket.

That evening, Shelly returned from an emergency. The kitche was empty, no sign of supper. She peered out of the window Dad had set up a deckchair at the bottom of the garden, a crat of pigeons at his side. He sat with a can of bird food in his fis With his eyes turned up to the sky and his face full of hope, h reminded her of the sad icons that hung in Greek churches.

'Come home, pigeon, make an old man happy,' she prayed, deciding to make him a mug of sweet tea. She plugged the kettle in and pulled DJ's letter out of her pocket.

'Are you all right?' Dad asked, coming through the doorway. 'You look pale.' He nodded at the letter. 'Not bad news, I hope.'

'No, no, just from someone . . . not important.' She shoved the letter back into her pocket, but her hand stayed there, fingers curled gently around the paper.

'I'm going to the club, will yer drive me, Shelly? I 'avent got time for the taxi.'

'Yes, of course, Dad.'

'Two hundred and thirty-five miles, at seventy miles an hour – how amazing is that?'

'What? Which club are you going to, Dad?' Shelly said, alarmed.

'Not you, daft girl, the bird. She's flown 235 miles, what a cracker!'

Shelly laughed. 'Yes, of course, silly me. Do you think you'll get a prize?'

'She's clocked in already, from the chip on 'er leg, but I won't know how the others have done until I gets to the club.'

'Well, good luck, Dad.' She kissed his cheek. 'Come on, let's go.'

CHAPTER 28
GERTIE

Greece, 1916.

MANNO WAS TRYING TO PACIFY Perkins. 'No worries, my friend. Is not a vulture up there, is Eleonora's falcon. He catches the little birds that head for the island. There are many falcons here, nesting on the cliffs.'

The wooden fishing boat had seemed a sturdy vessel in the harbour of Kea. Now, I stared around at the vast sea and wondered how Manno knew which way to steer. As we progressed, towards Syros, my fear of what awaited us continued. Another landmass loomed on the horizon.

Manno cried, 'Now you see her! That is my island, the capital of all the Cyclades.'

Our progression seemed painfully slow, but eventually we chugged close to the undulating landmass.

'She is beautiful, yes?' He didn't wait for an answer. 'My family has lived on this island since before Christ!'

Perkins opened one eye, glared at Manno, then shut it again. I hoped the morphine would keep him down a little longer.

Manno continued. 'The Persians, the Romans, the Franks, the *malaka* Turks, and even the French have tried to take her away from us, but they fail. Syros, she belongs to us, and she will always come back to us, the Greeks!'

Silence settled over us, each sensing the other's disappointment as our little boat chugged through gentle waves. The scenery was nothing but bushland and boulders, dull as the island of Yaros, but without the dolphins and falcons and stories of buccaneers. Manno peered at our disillusioned faces, then back at the landscape.

'Ah, no worries, you must wait to see our city, she is coming now, you wait . . . We, the Greeks, we build our city so beautiful that we had to hide her away from the pirates. Still they came, so we build another city on the top of the hill over the first, and from there, we fire our big cannons at the invaders until they leave us in peace.'

We rounded a promontory. 'Oh, my goodness!' I gasped as we continued towards the picturesque harbour. 'How very beautiful.'

A steeply sloping natural amphitheatre rose from the port giving us a unique view of all the buildings.

'Here, we have the best schools, theatres and libraries in all Greece, and we trade with every one of the other islands. They all admire us.'

Grand Venetian dwellings stood proud, dwarfing the smaller, white, flat-roofed Cyclades houses with tiny square windows. Neoclassical villas, perhaps built by rich and flamboyant sea captains at a time when Venetians ruled the country. Painted in a multitude of pastel colours, the houses appeared crisp and clean, rinsed by sunlight and staring solidly out to sea. Balconies with ornate spindles, jutted like open drawers from the smooth, plastered walls of peach, ochre, or pale blue. Elegant folding louvres and fancy fascias framed tall windows. All this, displayed below ridged, terracotta tiles on an apex pointing to heaven.

'Oh, it's so beautiful!' I gazed at the eclectic buildings delivered from the dull topography with all the colour and excitement of a surprise gift. As we drew close, I felt myself change too. One could never be sure of what lay ahead, but the view was so uplifting, I felt hope for the first time since the sinking. Perhaps everything would turn out well in the end.

Our boat entered the harbour. Moored at the quayside was a grey naval vessel, daunting as a prison. They've come for me. I had cost our country many thousands, when they needed it most. Now I must rise up and accept the consequences. If I pretended to be twenty-three, I also had to act as if I were twenty-three.

From now on, I'd stop cowering and face the future. A noble speech to myself, yet, my insides wilted. What might happen? Would they hang me when they discovered all the facts?

Perkins stirred. I moved to kneel at his side. 'Could I have a little water, please, Manno?' Our skipper half-filled an enamel beaker from a tank under his seat. I cradled Perkins head and helped him to drink, then dipped the corner of my apron into it and dabbed his forehead.

He stared at me. 'Tell me this is not a recurring nightmare, and that I still have at least one complete leg, nurse?'

'Don't talk nonsense, Corporal, of course you do.' I continued to cool his red face. 'I must say, this scar on your forehead has healed nicely. The surgeon did an excellent job stitching you up.'

The humour left his eyes. 'I'd like to get hold of the person responsible for all this.'

My heart banged. Was it really possible that he had no recollection of what happened in the ward? I turned my eyes away and stared at the water just outside the boat, remembering the flotsam and human debris, and that terrible time in the lifeboat. Realising I was holding my breath, I exhaled slowly, my breath feeling hot in my nostrils.

'I'm quite sure it was not down to one person, Corporal Perkins; and I think you realise it too.'

'They must pay,' he said, his face hard as he looked into my eyes. 'Whoever caused the *Britannic* to sink – they must pay.'

'I'm quite sure they will, Corporal,' I whispered. For a moment, I wished we were alone together and I could hold him to my breast, and kiss him tenderly. His mood swings were due to his injuries, I understood that; everything would be all right because I intended take good care of him, for always if he wanted. I was close to telling him he would always be perfect to me. Knowing those words would mean everything to him. But that was me, Gertie Smith, the hypocrite who had caused those very injuries by her own self-centred vanity in the first place. I reminded myself how much I had wanted to appear in control, superior to those poor patients in the ward.

* * *

I shifted my attention to the two-funnelled battleship that lay alongside the quay.

'You see? That's SS *Athena*,' Manno said as we motored past. 'She came in last night. She will take you away after dark.'

'Where are they taking us, Manno?' Perkins demanded.

'They tell us nothing.'

'So how can you know we are leaving tonight?' Perkins scoffed.

'Because yesterday, they ordered fresh meat to go on board this evening. Is logic, yes. If they were leaving tomorrow, they would order fresh meat tomorrow. *Logic* is a Greek word, so you see, we understand these things.'

Perkins pulled his mouth around to one side. 'The sooner we get back to England and civilisation, the better.' He slid his hand up and down his thigh and narrowed his eyes. I guessed he was still in pain, though he never complained.

Insulted, Manno stuck his chin out and glowered at Perkins. With the two of them staring at each other, I was reminded of the time my mother placed a couple of cockerels in the hen pen.

'You forget where your civilisation came from, my friend. While you lived in caves and wore animal skins, we were building our great temples in Greece and wore robes of the finest silk. While your weapon was a lump of wood, we had the Olympic games.'

'Is that what they tell you? Well, your teachers are off the mark!'

I felt a surge of panic. Their irritation was in close to exploding into something dangerous.

'You insult my country and my people!' Manno glared. ' should throw you out of my boat!' He boomed so loudly cowered. 'Yes! Get out!' Manno continued. 'Into the sea with you! When you are crying to come back into my magnificent boat, this beautiful *koukla* here will see you for the big *malaka* you are!' He held his hand towards me.

Josephine and I exchanged an alarmed glance.

'Manno, the Corporal doesn't know what he's saying, it's the morphine,' Josephine said. 'Take no notice. He's had a really bad time lately, and don't forget, he came to your country to defend it. If he hadn't been fighting for Greece's territory, he wouldn't have lost half his leg. He's on your side, Manno – and he's made a great sacrifice. You should be thanking him.'

Manno's father spoke quietly to his son in Greek.

'Look, there are people on the quayside waving at us,' Josephine said.

To my relief, Manno's tone softened. He studied the port and then explained his theory.

'You see, sport? They are loading mules. So, you are going to Lemnos. This is for sure. They bring tired mules back from Lemnos – they take fresh ones to Lemnos – this is how you say; a fact. You understand now, my friend, your word: logic, it comes from the Greek word, *logiki*. You are leaving tonight, going to the island of Lemnos where the wounded of the world wait for nurses like this *koukla* and her friend.'

Josephine rolled her eyes again, a trait to which she seemed prone in Manno's presence.

CHAPTER 29
SHELLY

Dover, present day.

SINCE UNIVERSITY, AND SETTING UP the veterinary practice, Shelly had spent neither time nor money on herself, never feeling the inclination to make the most of her looks. She ignored glamorous Eve's constant invitations to accompany her to the hairdresser's or nail salon. What was the point? She was thirty-seven, why pretend to be younger?

'What you're not realising,' Eve said, 'is that you're a very attractive woman, if you would only . . .'

'Only what? Come on, spit it out.'

'Well, take a little pride in your appearance. If you're going to meet this Harry again, don't you think you should at least get used to wearing a little mascara and lipstick; and get a professional haircut instead of hacking at it when it's getting on your nerves?'

'Why?' Shelly said, shaking her head.

'It's just par for the course. At least give it a go, please? Humour me.' She studied her nails and then polished them on her thigh. 'You can come with me after work on Wednesday for a manicure.'

Shelly huffed and squinted at Eve. Perhaps it wasn't such a bad idea. At least it would distract her from DJ's letter. She planned to phone him again, but it never seemed to be the right moment.

'Now if you'll excuse me,' Eve said with her bossy-triumphant look that always made Shelly laugh. 'While it's quiet, I'm slipping down to The Beauty Beyond to book us both in. What's your budget?'

Shelly thought she might as well push the boat out as this was a one-off occasion. She certainly wasn't going to turn it into a regular occurrence. 'Fifty quid?'

'Right then, a hundred and fifty quid to knock you into shape. Wednesday straight after lunch as it's your half day.' She ripped off her surgical gloves and tossed them. 'I'm off to book.'

'What? I'm not paying out all that for a haircut and nail job. Are you mad?'

'Don't worry, I'll take it out of the petty cash. That's how I usually pay for mine.'

Shelly nearly choked. 'What! You're kidding me!'

'Yes, I am.' She laughed. 'But I had you for one tincy, juicy second, didn't I? Anyway, you're worth it, Shelly. So no more nonsense.' Shelly stood there stunned while Eve headed for the high street. 'Back in thirty with Pot Noodles and doughnuts, all right?' She was gone before Shelly could protest.

* * *

With Eve out of the way, and the practice closed for lunch, Shelly saw an opportunity to speak to DJ with no interruptions. She had to deal with it. She snatched her handbag, hurried over to the phone, and before a minute had passed, she had punched in the numbers and heard the ringtone.

'Hello?' he said.

Time and distance contracted. Her heart squeezed and she felt slightly spongy inside. She hesitated, took a breath, then lunged on. 'Hello, it's . . . erm, Shelly. I got your letter, DJ.' She heard him exhale and a little spark of fear went off in her gut.

'Good. So, will you come to the café? Or is there somewhere else you'd rather go?' His voice was distant, not giving anything away. For the first time, she wondered if he was as nervous as her.

'No, the café's fine. Look, this is difficult for me. It's been nineteen years, and, well . . .'

'I see, I did wonder . . . I realise it's been a long time since, you know, and I wondered if I'd been replaced,' he asked.

'No.' She swallowed hard. 'Not at all. Look, I don't know how much you know . . . about what happened.' She drew in a shaky breath and tried to hold it, to calm down as her past loomed up. 'I understand you want to see me, but please, I don't want any trouble. I was only seventeen when . . .' She sighed. 'If it's some kind of revenge you want, then you'll be pleased to know I've been through hell for the past twenty years.' Her emotions rose and she realised she wouldn't be able to talk for much longer. 'I'll meet you at that café at four o'clock on Wednesday. Goodbye.' She ended the call abruptly, but didn't seem to be able to terminate her emotions. Her heart was breaking and she simply couldn't hold back the tears. Why was this happening now, after all this time?

* * *

'Don't tell me you're coming down with a cold,' Eve said when she noticed her red eyes.

Shelly tried to dismiss it. 'No, they're just protesting to the very idea of wearing mascara every day.'

'You can do it. Come on, woman up.'

Shelly forced a laugh.

Eve came and sat on the corner of Shelly's desk. 'Listen, I can't help but notice something's been bothering you lately. If I can help in any way, you just have to say, you know that, don't you?'

'Oh God . . . Is it that obvious?'

Eve nodded. 'I don't like to see you upset. It's worrying, and although I'm not going to pry, just tell me if it involves money or health, please, because I can help with at least one of those things?'

Shelly felt her heart swell. 'You're so kind, Eve, thank you, but you don't have to worry. My finances and health are both under control. I'm meeting someone from my past on Wednesday, to sort out a few things, then I'll be fine, promise.'

'Don't forget we've got our hair and nails at half one.'

'No problem, I'm meeting him at four. I guess we'll be finished at the salon by then.'

'And you know what, there's nothing like a pamper for giving a girl confidence. Not that you're lacking . . . right?'

Shelly smiled. 'Eve, thank you.'

* * *

Finally, Wednesday arrived. With two cat neuters and a batch of paperwork for pet insurance claims, Shelly didn't have time to think. Someone had left a box of puppies on the doorstep, and an Alsatian with an ear infection was a tricky customer. By one o'clock, both Shelly and Eve were looking forward to the salon. As the clock ticked towards one-thirty, Eve stared at the phone and muttered, 'Don't ring, don't ring!' On the dot, Shelly locked up and they scooted six doors down to the salon.

Bella, hairdresser extraordinaire with impossible nails and plumped lips, ooh-ed and ahh-ed, pushing her hands firmly through Shelly's lustrous brunette hair, scrunching, smoothing, stepping back and studying,

'Don't be nervous, darling, you won't feel a thing.' She pulled Shelly's locks back into a ponytail and with one executioner's swipe, chopped it off.

Eve squealed. Bella said, 'Oops, darling,' and Shelly stared at the clump of hair that lay next to her chair like a dead cat in the road. She felt the urge to gather it gently into a posh shoe box and give it a decent burial.

Two hours later, Shelly and Eve left the salon. 'You look, a-maz-ing!' Eve said. 'At least ten years younger, and hot!' She grinned. 'I don't know why you've never had a posh-bob before? It *really* suits you.'

'Thanks. You look wonderful yourself,' Shelly said. 'I don't know that I'll ever get used to these nails though.'

'Tell you something, he's a lucky man, whoever he is.'

Shelly shook her head in alarm. 'No, it's not like that at all.'

'Yeah, right, whatever.'

'No really. Anyway, I don't want to be late. Thanks for organising all this, Eve. I'd never have done it alone.'

'You have a nice night,' Eve called turning away. 'I'll expect a full report tomorrow, OK?'

Shelly laughed. 'Sure. Bye for now, and thanks again!'

She strode through town, her copper-streaked, chestnut hair bouncing with each step. Catching her reflection in a shop window, she saw a new woman. Feeling empowered, invigorated, she admitted to herself, she wanted DJ to . . . what? Forgive her?

Love her? OK, she would settle for *like*, if it was the best she could get. She turned into the next street and saw the café ahead. She stopped and stared, owning the moment in her mind. Building herself up, convincing herself, she was in control and could walk away at any time; but where would that leave her heart?

The door of the Honeypot Café seemed to grow as she approached. An *Alice* moment. She was ten minutes early, took a window seat, ordered tea – milk, no sugar. There was nobody about. The day seemed to darken, like a storm was rolling in. Her hair would be ruined by the time she got back to her car. A waste of money. God! She was turning into her father.

The tea came. 'Looks like rain,' the woman said as she placed it on the table.

Shelly nodded, smiled weakly, she didn't want a conversation. She got DJ's letter out of her bag and studied the writing again. There was nothing sharp or jagged about it, not that she knew anything about analysing a person's handwriting. Not many people actually wrote letters these days, did they? She couldn't believe he'd found her after all these years.

Four o'clock, he'd written, then confirmed when she'd phoned him. Shelly glanced at the fly-speckled clock: three fifty-five. Would she recognise him after so long? She was holding her breath. 'Breathe!' she told herself. Nice and steady. Calm thoughts.

She stared out at the street. A sudden spatter of rain, then the storm clouds parted and shafts of sunlight speared through the trees and glinted off the wet pavement. Her eyes darted up the empty street, then at the clock. Two minutes to four – yes, she would leave! She jumped to her feet. Her thigh caught the table, her teacup rocked, then toppled. Tea splashed over DJ's letter. His handwriting blurred. In a desperate effort to rescue it, she pulled a tissue from her pocket and dabbed the paper.

The waitress rushed over. 'Aye, don't worry, love. I'll see to it.'

'Sorry, sorry,' she said. 'It's from someone important, very important . . . all I have are his letters!' She heard hysteria in her own voice, and with those final words her tears raced for release and the clarity she'd sought smacked her hard in the heart.

Of course she had to see him!

In a time-stopping moment that would stay with her forever, DJ was at her side.

Recognising those wide blue eyes immediately, a knot in her throat became so painful she couldn't speak. Her pulse raced and tears pricked the backs of her eyes. She shoved the damp letter into her pocket. DJ cupped her elbow and led her to a clean table. He sat opposite her and reached for her hand.

She stared at the big fist that covered hers and remembered the baby that had gripped her little finger, before they took him away.

From under his mop of sandy hair, DJ peered at her and hesitated. She recognised the tension in his eyes, and perhaps anger. She hoped not. Then, finally, she saw tenderness.

He leaned slightly towards her, squeezing her hand gently, his voice little more than a whisper.

'Hello, Mum.'

Shelly gasped. 'Oh, DJ.' She placed her hand over her mouth for a moment. 'You're the absolute double of your father. If only David could be here too.'

CHAPTER 30
GERTIE

Syros, Greece, 1916.

As we entered the port of Syros, bobbing about in our little wooden *caïque*, several dull grey warships loomed over us like ominous ghosts. The water flattened and the engine calmed as we slid towards the quayside, where our ship awaited. Yianni and Manno seemed to be arguing, arms in motion and voices raised. Noticing the alarmed look on my face, Manno explained.

'Do not look so afraid, little one. We must decide if we should drop an anchor or not. We are afraid the big ship will catch it and drag us away in the night. This will kill us both and destroy our boat . . . Now, we think it is best to not use the anchor.' He turned off the engine and drifted toward the quayside. People stood by to catch a rope that Manno threw. With no anchor to act as a brake, Yianni fell to his knees in the bow and stuck his arms out to prevent the boat crashing into the concrete quayside. I watched the process with great attention, feeling the correct procedure may come in useful one day. Eventually we moored up.

Amid back-slapping and hand-shaking, Yianni and Manno were treated like long-lost heroes. '*Ela!* Come and eat my friends!' and 'We play backgammon this afternoon!' and 'I wait you in the *kafenio*, sport,' showing off their English for the sake of those aboard. Women sashayed past, swinging their hips and batting their long dark lashes at both father and son. A bystander could suppose the fishermen were heroes returning after many years – not days.

Two soldiers and a Red Cross nurse transferred Perkins onto a stretcher and hefted him along the wharf towards the warship. I carried his crutches while Josephine and Manno brought the bags.

People lined the quayside selling their wares; live hens, cockerels, and rabbits in bamboo crates. Josephine and I bought oranges, stuffed them in our pillow-bags, then we stood on the harbour edge and ate one between us. We stood there in the late-afternoon sunshine, our eyes narrow with pleasure as we enjoyed that fruit, and even now, when I think about it, my mouth waters. That orange was so sweet, juicy and fresh, and our fingers were shiny and delicately perfumed from the oil in its thick skin.

The air buzzed with clatter and chatter. Excited locals had an opinion on everything and voiced it loudly. I guessed it was a big thing for the Syros people to have warships in port and so many strangers on the quayside. A stall holder shouted to Josephine and I. 'Ela! Ela, koukla!'

We went over to his table of produce, at the edge of the bustle. Odd-looking fruit and vegetables were on display. Among them were giant pumpkins, all kinds of dried beans, herbs of every description, mounds of lemons, buckets of what I thought were damsons but I learned later were olives, and many things that were new to us. He gave us a handful of the biggest brown dates I'd ever seen, something neither of us had tasted before. They were wonderful, sticky and so sweet, like gigantic caramel raisins. Some medical staff had left the ship to buy cigarettes from pedlars that gathered at the end of the gangway.

The crowd parted for a youth wearing a red *tarboosh* with a long black tassel on his head. He also wore baggy striped trousers that gathered around his ankles. The boy had a tambourine hanging from his back and pulled a brown bear on a chain. He tied the chain onto one of the mooring rings, then started playing the tambourine and singing. The bear immediately stood on its hind legs and started dancing, nimbly hopping from one foot to the other.

I was thrilled to see such a thing and knew I would be telling my father all about it when I got home. 'Look, Josephine, the bear's dancing so nicely! I'm going to give the boy a little money.'

'Don't you dare!' she cried vehemently. 'They burned the bottoms of that poor bear's feet when she was only a cub, baby, in order to make her do that. Look at her face, she's terrified, poor girl!'

'They burned her?' I looked into the bear's eyes and yes, clearly, she was in torment.

'When she was very young, every time the boy beat the tambourine, they would stand her on hot charcoal, giving her terrible burns under her feet. Now, with every beat of the instrument, she expects that same pain again, so in pure terror she hops onto the other foot. Sometimes, a bear will go mad from the dreadful horror, so they tie her down and rip out her teeth and claws so she can't hurt anyone. It's obscene.'

'That's made me feel quite sick,' I said. 'Shall we go on board?' She nodded and we moved towards the gangway.

'Wait, *koukla mou*. Come back!' Manno cried as I started up the runway.

My heart skipped at the sound of his voice and I realised I didn't want to be parted from him. I turned and saw him striding towards me. *Oh!* I wanted him to whisk me up into his arms and carry me away. Confused by my foolishness, whic] unsettled my quest to become a nurse, a great feeling of happi ness raced through me. I rushed towards him.

He grabbed my hand, his words almost tumbling over eacl other. 'When will I see you again? I don't want you to go. W are never alone together and there's so much I want to sa} and more than that. I like you a lot. A lot!' He leaned forwarc slid his cheek against mine until his mouth was over my ea. 'I want you,' he growled. The words were so unexpected, the overwhelmed me. I stared at him like an idiot as he withdre\ to a respectable distance and continued. 'You must come an see my house. When will you return?' Then he got so excite(he was speaking to me in Greek but didn't seem to realise. Hi eyes narrowed as he spoke, and there was such passion in hi tone that I thought perhaps it was just as well that I did no understand him.

People seemed to move in closer and I wondered if they wer eavesdropping. Aware that my cheeks were blazing, I glance(around hurriedly, hoping nobody heard or understood what ever he was muttering.

Josephine rolled her eyes. 'I'll wait for you at the top.' Sh nodded at the ramp.

Unabashed, Manno returned to speaking English and con tinued. 'I am not happy that you leave me. I am even more no happy that you are leaving with the English.' I knew he mean Corporal Perkins. 'Give me one kiss, just one, to remembe you by.'

'Certainly not. How bold of you!'

The people hovering nearby gave up pretending and gathere(around. Unsure of myself, I tried to imagine what Sissy woul(do. Life was difficult without a role model and, in truth, I reall wanted to kiss him – oh dear – I really did. But, not there on the quayside in front of all the gawping strangers.

He grinned. 'I made you angry? You become more beautiful when you are a crazy woman. I am in love with you, *koukla mou*. My nurse.'

I glanced up into a blue sky that seemed to be twinkling with mischief. 'What a ridiculous thing to say, Manno, stop it! People are watching us. You don't even know me, and you're causing me untold embarrassment.' Yet I was thrilled to be called a woman, and a nurse. However, my future was dedicated to atoning for the deaths of my companions on the *Britannic*. I would tend the sick, fulfil Sissy's dream, and save some poor mother's son as I had cost so many theirs. I felt myself grow, right there on the quayside. Yes, Manno made my heart race. I could even convince myself that I was falling in love with him; and longed to feel his lips pressed against mine. Nevertheless, my only experience of love came from the writings of Victor Hugo and a DH Lawrence book that belonged to Sissy, which I was sworn to keep away from my parents' eyes.

Despite the tingling dramas that made me narrow my eyes and squeeze my knees together, I was determined not to be swept away by the fickle and flimsy chords of my heart. I had a greater calling, and by God, I would fulfil it!

'Write to me? My heart is breaking, is bleeding all over the port!' Manno cried, then he snatched a red rose out of the flower-seller's bucket and went down on one knee. 'Swear you'll come back to me, *koukla*!'

Aware that people had stopped whatever they were discussing in order to watch us, and one man appeared to be taking a little money from some of them, it occurred to me that the

271

scoundrel might be taking bets! I could cheerfully have killed the mailman.

'Manno. Get up! You're making a spectacle!'

'I will, but only when you promise to return. I should have given you a pigeon in Kea. Forgive me. Swear you will send me letters. Say you will come back to Syros.'

'Perhaps; I'll think about it, but who shall I write to?'

'Me, of course.'

I smiled despite my embarrassment. 'No, I mean how shall I address the letter, if by some faint chance I do decide to write to you?'

'Ah, I understand. Manno Psaras, Syros, Cycladese Islands, Greece. *Psaras* – it means fisherman in Greek.' He reached into his pocket and produced a small curled seashell on a ribbon which he slipped over my head. 'Here; is for you. Every time you press it against your heart, I will be with you. I swear to the Gods of Olympus, I will think about you every day until we meet again, *koukla mou*.' He lifted my hand, kissed my palm, then curled my fingers as if I were holding the kiss.

My breath wouldn't come, such was my longing . . . I had a need for him. I was afraid of him in an odd sort of way, yet also fascinated . . . like a moth near a candle flame. There was danger and captivation in equal measure.

Overwhelmed, I forgot about our audience and stood there blinking like a kohl-eyed actress on the silver screen, unable to deal with his words or our parting. Perhaps I would never see him again. At that moment I wondered if my feelings for him were love. They were different from anything I experienced with our courteous and suave Corporal Perkins. There was no rational explanation for the increase of my heartrate, or my fluttery breath, or the way I felt my body tingle, and arch towards him. My body was drawn to him as a thirsty animal is drawn to water. Inside, I was burning, pure as fire, yet at the same time my feet were rooted to the spot and I was afraid.

He placed his hands on my shoulders, his eyes sparkling. Conscious of another new sensation that startled me, I folded my arms over my tingling nipples and wondered if that was normal. I must ask Josephine, she seemed to know everything. Manno's face became intensely serious. 'I have no more words for you,' he said. 'Just this . . .' He lifted my chin and brushed my lips with his.

I stepped back and gasped, shocked by his lack of manners. To behave in such a bold way, and in public too! Somebody shouted, '*Bravo!*' and started clapping, and I hopped it had nothing to do with me. I felt everyone's eyes boring into me. I should slap him! Such effrontery, my parents would expect me to retaliate, defend my reputation. How dare he kiss me . . . without asking . . . and on the lips . . . this was too shocking!

With a huff, I lifted my chin, spun on my heel, and headed for the ship.

'Goodbye, *koukla mou!*' he cried. 'I love you! Until we meet again!'

The blaze in my cheeks would have lit a bonfire. Yet still, I turned and glanced back one last time before entering the vessel that would lead me to my destiny.

Oh, Manno!

* * *

On board the *Athena*, I shared a cabin with Nurse Josephine. We divided the cabin space, and set about arranging our meagre belongings. No sooner had we organised ourselves, a knock sounded on the door and an orderly presented us with instructions to report to the medical station.

'Right, here we go,' Josephine said, smoothing down her apron. 'Let's find out what they have in mind for us. Where are we headed?'

We hurried along behind the orderly, a frowning man who avoided our eyes, clearly uncomfortable in the presence of women. The ship had a confining atmosphere, nothing like the spacious *Britannic*. Corridors were narrow and dim, and two sailors walking in the opposite direction had to flatten themselves against the wall so we could pass. The floors, walls, and even the low ceilings were metal, giving a great feeling of strength, but also noisy and oppressive. We arrived at the medical station.

The surgeon was a tall, pale man with little hair and a neat, black moustache on a perfectly round face. Archibald Fitzgibbons reminded me of the peg dolls I made as a child. He offered Nurse Josephine and I a stiff little bow.

'You'll be pleased to know we shall arrive at the port of Mudros, which is the naval port of Lemnos, at 0500 hours, but you won't be able to leave until 0700 hours. We have a ship full of medical supplies to disembark there and we don't want you in the way.'

So Manno was right, we were leaving for Lemnos, not Britain.

Fitzgibbons continued. 'A good night's sleep would be in order, as it may be your last for some months. Trust me when I say the living conditions at the hospital clearing station are appalling.' He indicated for us to sit at his desk. 'The hospital staff are crying out for our cargo, particularly chloroform and morphine. I warn you, the medical situation on the island is grim. More than half of those who were due to be transported back to Blighty on the *Britannic* have perished already, or are on the brink of doing so.'

I felt my skin shrink at the mention of this fact. More deaths due to my own incompetence.

'Trench foot, gangrene, shrapnel wounds, dysentery, typhoid, and also a fresh outbreak of Spanish influenza are the main problems. On top of that, venereal diseases. Syphilis and gonorrhoea have reached epidemic proportions. The station is under-manned, short of everything, unhygienic, and most of the patients are kept under canvas. Due to the shortage of beds, the majority of the injured sleep on the ground, and as the winter rains reach their peak in February, things will only get worse. Food, like everything else, is in short supply, so eat everything you're given; and beware of the moles.'

Nurse Josephine and I exchanged a despairing glance, trying to keep the horror out of our expressions.

'Moles?' Josephine asked quietly.

'Yes, moles. Disgusting flea-ridden creatures, blind, with long claws. They dig their way up into the tents at night, then run like rats over everything and everyone. Most unhygienic. Screaming nurses will not be tolerated in a town of hospital tents where too many men are dying in terrible pain. Any questions?'

'Were the medical staff from the *Britannic* taken to Mudros?' Josephine asked.

'They were offered the statutory two weeks leave after such a sad event, but many who survived uninjured volunteered to work in local hospitals, and some went on to Lemnos and are working in Mudros now.' He folded his arms and stared into the distance. 'However, I believe they'll all return to England for another inquiry the moment they can be relieved – which

275

won't be for some time the way things are going. The ones that returned to the UK attended an unofficial inquiry on board the flagship, *Duncan*, on 24 November.'

'I see. Are there at least enough splints and morphine for the casualties now?' Nurse Josephine continued.

'There isn't enough of anything. Priority is given to those with over a fifty per cent chance of survival.'

'And the progression of the war? We had no news while on Kea.'

'I can't say. There is a plan, but I'm not at liberty to divulge it. You must be ready to relocate at all times.'

'How many patients are at the clearing station?'

'Can't be sure. Perhaps forty thousand wounded, sick, and dying.'

'And medical staff?'

'The answer to that is simply nowhere near enough – perhaps a thousand.' He paused to let the number sink in while appearing totally defeated. 'Yes, it's impossible, and most of the nurses have had no experience and hardly any training before arriving in Mudros, though they're full of good intention. What greets them is shocking – beyond their, or your, imagination. Most nurses cannot cope with the horror. Hats off to each one for trying but men with their guts hanging out, or arms and legs blown off . . . screaming with pain, well, it's not what they imagined when they signed up.' His eyes flicked to Gertie. 'Half of them leave in the first month. The situation is impossible; but we have a consignment of ANZACs due in from Australia and New Zealand any day now, mostly practised nurses, though I doubt any of them have experienced war wounds. We shall see.'

Nurse Josephine was silent for a moment and the surgeon took that opportunity to terminate the conversation. 'Now if you'll excuse me, ladies, I have to examine your Corporal before dinner as he's staying on board until we return to Athens, Malta, or Alexandria. I'm awaiting orders. We sail at 0900 hours. Be on board by 0800 hours sharp.'

CHAPTER 31
SHELLY

Dover, present day.

DJ ORDERED COFFEES WHILE SHELLY dried her eyes. Sunshine bounced in from the wet pavements outside.

'DJ,' Shelly said, looking into his eyes. 'You've no idea how long I prayed for this moment.'

'So why didn't you instigate it?' he asked, and although it could have been an aggressive question, there was no animosity in his voice.

'Because your father was my first and last true love. You see, I met David when I was sixteen. He chose your name, by the way. On the day I first met him, he introduced himself: "I'm David," he said. "My father was David, my grandfather was David, and when I have a son, I've no doubt he'll be a David too. Or more likely a Dave these days, it's more modern, isn't it?"' Shelly sat there smiling. 'I was crying in the town centre. He was trying to cheer me up. "I come from a long line of Davids," he said. I ended up laughing, it sounded so ridiculous. Your father's middle name was John, so you were named David John, DJ.' Remembering the moment, Shelly smiled, then she filled up and placed a hand over her mouth for a moment to stop herself sobbing. 'My mother had just been killed, you see . . . in the most tragic accident on Christmas Eve. I was depressed like you can't imagine. Your father was incredible. The kindest, most understanding person I'd ever met. I was so alone it hurt, but when

I was with him, he took all my pain away. At the most difficult time in my life, your father, David John Evans, gave me hope and determination.'

'David John Evans,' he whispered as if testing the words.

Shelly nodded. 'I asked the people who adopted you if they would keep your name, it was important to me, and they agreed on David John. Although I hadn't known your father long, he really made me feel I was worth something. I passed my exams, got through university, and built myself a successful business, all because of him.'

'Sounds like an amazing story. I don't know anything about him. On my birth certificate it says, *father unknown*.'

'That was my choice. I wanted to keep you. I wanted you to have my name. Of course, that was impossible. I had no support. My father was having a breakdown after my mother's death. Then his sixteen-year-old daughter tells him she's pregnant. Can you imagine? Anyway, despite my objections, he insisted you would be better off growing up with a family desperate for a child. One that could afford all the things that would give you a good life.' Shelly sighed and sat back. 'It was a difficult time. Did you have a good childhood?'

'I did. My parents had a daughter, my sister April, quite unexpectedly when I was eight. Six months later, we emigrated to Australia. I came back to study at Cambridge and as I was here, I thought I'd try and find you.'

'Cambridge! Goodness. What are you reading?'

'Marine biology.' He stared at Shelly. 'What's wrong, you look startled?'

Shelly struggled. She needed more time with her son before she told him about his father. But her feelings were bubbling to the surface, she had no choice.

'Your father would have wanted that. He was a recreational diver when I met him, but he planned to go on to greater things.'

'Please, tell me about him. Where is he now?'

She glanced around the café. Another couple had come in and were drinking coffee, and three giggling girls were at the counter. Shelly smiled sadly. 'Look, it seems impossible now, but I was about their age when I fell in love with your father.' She nodded at the laughing teenagers. 'We went on holiday together. Me, your dad, and his friend Simon.' She paused and took a deep breath. 'There was a diving accident . . . I didn't even know I was pregnant with you at that point.' Shelly had to stop and calm herself, as she always did when this subject arose. 'Sorry, but do you think we could save that for our next meeting? This is such a huge occasion for me. I don't want to rush it, or let it overwhelm me.' She tried to smile, but a tic caught the corner of her mouth so she covered it with her hand. He nodded but stared gloomily at the table. Shelly continued. 'Just let me tell you this, DJ. If things had been different, your father would have loved you like no other. He was the sweetest, kindest man imaginable and, oh, *how* I loved him.'

* * *

By the time Shelly got home, it was almost eight o'clock.

'I'm sorry to be so late, Dad. I've had the most amazing experience.'

'What have you done to your hair?'

'Oh – I'd forgotten – had a haircut. Eve talked me into it. She's trying to glam me up before I return to Greece. It's so expensive though! She doesn't realise I have commitments.'

'You have commitments?'

Shelly turned away quickly. Had he really forgotten? He seemed to be forgetting so much lately. 'Well, you know, the business and everything. Anyway, enough of that. How's your day been?'

'Good. Bill's daughter ran him over this afternoon and we've been discussing race strategy. We've eaten; fish pie and baked beans. Shall I ding a portion for you?'

Shelly laughed. 'Honestly, I'll bet it's delicious, but I've got so much to tell you, Dad, I'd rather do it over a bottle of wine as you've eaten already.'

'You'd better open a packet of crisps then, or you'll be hungover tomorrow. So why are you late, Shelly love. Is everything all right?'

She stared at him, trying to decide, and then she knew, it was time for the secrets to end. 'Sit down a minute, Dad. I've got something to tell you. But first, we're having a drink, can I get you a beer?'

'That'll do nicely. I hope it's not bad news.' He pulled out a chair.

'No, it's the most wonderful news. But please don't be hard on me. It's been a difficult day, a difficult month, to tell the truth, and I can't describe how relieved I am now that it's over.'

Her father looked horrified. 'Have I missed something? Just tell me it's got nothing to do with your health?'

'No,' she said again, patting the back of his hand. 'In fact, I've never been better.' She passed him a beer, sat opposite him and poured herself a glass of wine. 'You remember what happened just after Mum died, Dad?'

He stared at her, clearly not wanting to bring up the past. ''Ere, Shelly, let's not go over all that. What's past is past.'

'No, Dad, I need to say it. A year after Mum died, I had a baby.' Her father's face stiffened. 'A little boy, DJ, David John. He was David's son and I gave him up for adoption.' Shelly nodded. 'His father, David, was my first boyfriend. My only real boyfriend and I loved him very much. DJ was our baby. A beautiful, blue-eyed baby that I have never stopped loving. But David never saw our child, did he? DJ was born after the accident, remember.'

Gordon stood and went over to the kitchen cupboard, pushed the sugar and flour aside and pulled out an old bottle of whisky. 'I need a proper drink,' he said. He poured a good measure, took it over to the window. Standing with his back to the room, he stared out at the dusk.

'I need to go over it, Dad. I know it's difficult, but will you please listen? It's important to me, and I'm not sure exactly how much you remember.

'It was the week before school went back from the holidays. There was nothing much to do, I had good exam results and you agreed that I should go back to school and take my A levels, then go to university and train to be a vet. I was passionate about it. My boyfriend, David, and his friends, Simon and Roger, were going scuba diving to Paros in Greece for a week. Roger came down with shingles . . . or mumps, I can't remember. Anyway, he couldn't go. He said if I paid to change the name on the ticket, I could have it.' She looked over at her father. 'I told you there was a trip to Greece for the sixth formers and you said I could I go.'

She closed her eyes and recalled how horrible he'd been. He'd said her mother had just died and all she cared about was having a good time. He'd said she was a disgrace to her mother's memory. She'd cried herself to sleep every night with no notion of how badly her father was hurting, or how badly he needed a pair of arms around him, especially from his sixteen-year-old daughter.

'Anyway, you kindly came up with the hundred pounds and I went to Greece with David.' Silence fell over the cottage, each of them lost in their heartbreak.

'I borrowed it off Bill,' her father said quietly, breaking the hush with his hurt. 'I'd just been laid off because of me lungs, but the pension wasn't enough for all the extras of yer mum's funeral. They just about cleared me out.' He sighed as his shoulders slumped. 'Someone must have informed social services that I was finding it hard, cos they came a-knockin', wantin' to come in and see how we lived.' He swiped his hand across his face and stood straighter, proud, his voice harder. 'I didn't want their charity! I wasn't going to be beholden to anyone so I told them to piss right off. Then Father O'Donnell came to visit so I told him he could piss right off too. They didn't bother me after that.'

Shelly stared at him. Her father never swore. She had no idea he'd struggled with his finances until he told her about her mum asking for the taxi money on Christmas Eve. It simply never crossed her mind. Knowing how proud her dad was, she could just imagine the scene at the door. Poor social workers. Poor priest. Poor Dad.

'Anyway, to shorten the story, everything went wrong on that holiday, didn't it? What a tragedy. Then, nine months later I had a baby boy, DJ, who went straight to his adoptive parents. Broke my heart. I never forgot him, my baby, my child, but I never saw him again – until today.'

Gordon turned from the window and stared at her but she couldn't read his expression, and she desperately hoped she wasn't making another mistake.

'He's nineteen, of course, studying marine biology at Cambridge. It's got nothing to do with me, but I can tell you I'm so proud, Dad. Do you think I could invite him for Sunday lunch?'

Gordon made a short gurgling noise, a hiccough of sorrow that drew her attention. His hands came up to cover his face and his shoulders shook.

'Dad, oh, Dad!' Shelly jumped up and went to place an arm around his shoulders. 'I'm so sorry, honestly, I didn't mean to upset you.'

He shrugged her off, scurried across the room with his face turned away from her, then left for his loft. Shelly started to go after him, but then decided he needed space to deal with his demons.

* * *

An hour later, Gordon came back into the kitchen and slumped into the dining chair.

Shelly sighed. 'I'm sorry, Dad. I didn't want to upset you, I wanted . . . hoped, you know, that we could all come together as a family, at least once.' It was her turn to get emotional. 'I've been so lonely.' She studied her hands.

'I wish it was gone, all this pain,' he said.

'Mum wouldn't want us hurting like this either.' She looked up. 'It's incredible that my son, your grandson, has found us. Let's make the most of it, please.'

Gordon was silent for a while, then he spoke gently. 'I genuinely thought I was doing the right thing, Shelly. You do understand that, don't you? I had so much pain, and I was at war with the world for the injustice of Maggie's death. Then you, my little girl

284

up the duff. Of course it was my fault. I knew I'd driven you away when I should have been there to support you. But I'm human too. We'll never know if I made the right decision, because we can't know how things would have turned out for you both if you'd kept the baby. It's just . . . you were so young, Shelly.'

Shelly recalled the giggling girls in the café. That's how she must have appeared to her father and in that moment, she understood him completely. She got up, placed her arms around him, and kissed the top of his head. 'You made the right decision, Dad. In your position, I'd have done exactly the same.'

He sighed and hung his head for a moment. 'You don't know what that means to me, Shelly love. All right. Invite him here on Sunday for a roast.'

'I'm on call next weekend, so the Sunday after, will that be all right for you, Dad?'

He stared at his knees silent for a moment. 'Well, I'm not sure about that. I'll have to consult me social calendar, won't I?' Then he looked up. Smiling sadly. 'Of course it's all right, daft girl.'

CHAPTER 32
GERTIE

Syros, 1916.

Wanting to see a little more of Syros, we hurried down the gangplank and discovered the town had an energy that we had not experienced before. The place was very different from the sleepy island of Kea.

The town appeared to be a steep hill that ran down into the dark, blue sea. This hill was topped by an imposing, angular building which covered the entire peak. Strong, straight, unembellished walls of sun-bleached yellow were pierced by rows of small rectangular windows, and before it, the largest of many ornate bell-towers.

'What is that place at the top of the hill, it looks like a prison?'

Josephine looked up and laughed. 'No, it's the Catholic monastery of St George. You can walk up there if you want, it's beautiful inside.'

'Quite a climb, though, perhaps I'll save it for next time.'

The rest of the town displayed intense architectural contradictions. Majestic Venetian captains' houses, and Cyclades white cube dwellings complemented each other. A town of cathedrals, churches, and chapels of every size and colour from baroque to byzantine, neoclassical to modern. Yet between these painted walls of blue, yellow and white, there existed an air of harmony. Styles of great splendour or simplicity, stood side by side dominating an occasional scramble of vermilion bougainvillea. Each building appeared to have a unique view of the harbour and simply slotted into its own comfortable place.

Josephine and I hurried up and down the steep roads that were mostly steps. We admired the splendour and robust colours of Orthodox churches, and lit candles in ornately carved sand-troughs next to stout oak doors. At the entrance of the sombre Catholic church, we felt minute in the solemn vastness of the building. With no time to explore further, we hurried back down the perilous steps that led to the port and our ship.

* * *

From the stern railings, we took a last view of Syros. The ship pulled out of the harbour as the sun neared the horizon. From the high deck, we could see the entire amphitheatre that was the town. Now, from a distance, it became clear that the buildings were on two hills, each topped by the largest church in that area with the monastery being the crown.

'What an enchanting place,' I said. 'One day I'm going to return and investigate Syros properly. Just this short glimpse has made me want to come back.'

'Ah, nothing to do with Manno the mailman then?' Josephine asked kindly, tilting her head to one side and, as I'd come to realise was her trait, narrowing her eyes mischievously.

* * *

Dinner was a simple affair: bully beef, boiled potatoes, and large, sweet processed peas. It smelled and tasted wonderful. I sat next to Nurse Josephine, on a table reserved for the medical staff. The surgeon and a relief doctor joined us and asked about the *Britannic*'s sinking. I remained quiet, my heart fluttering as Josephine filled them in with all she knew. There was no mention of portholes. To my enormous relief, everyone's concern seemed to be whether a torpedo or mine sunk the ship that, like the *Titanic*, was deemed to be unsinkable.

Before retiring for the night, Josephine got on her knees at her bedside and prayed. I wrote a letter to Manno. He had been such a big part of my journey so far that I decided to tell him about the portholes. I had to tell somebody; it was eating me up. I needed to discuss it with an older, wiser person before it slipped out by accident. I thanked him for the way he had cared for us all, and told him I was sorry we parted, and that I would come back one day, if I could. I sealed the letter and placed it in my apron pocket. The post was censored, so the last thing I wanted was for someone to read it. I would post it from whichever port we called into next.

Then I slipped out to search for Perkins and found him on a bed in the medical centre. 'Ah, here we are. How are you doing, Corporal?'

'For a soldier with his head sliced open by a twenty-four-foot propeller, arm shattered by the back axle of a three-ton jeep, and leg chopped off by an overzealous surgeon, I can safely say I'm as well as can be expected. Kiss me.'

'Behave, Corporal! You're exaggerating, and the man I've come to care for is bigger than that.'

'Do you really care for this wreck of a man, nurse?' He peered at me with forlorn eyes, a man lost in his situation with no idea how to handle it, and wondering where he will end up. 'I feel so completely alone. Sometimes, I wish you hadn't saved me.'

Oh, poor man. 'Don't you dare talk like that, Corporal. You have my blood flowing through you, and let me tell you; *I* am courageous, and *I* come from a long line of courageous people! So you just gather up all that courageous blood of mine and keep a grip on it, do you understand me, soldier?'

'*He* kissed you, I saw. They were taking me on board.'

'He took a liberty and admittedly I should have slapped him, but I was too shocked, Corporal. Now, no more nonsense. I'll thank you not to mention it again. Did they feed you?'

'I think they forgot; but it's not food I'm hungering after, Nurse Gertie.'

I ignored his boldness. 'I'll go and see if I can get you something from the galley.'

'I love you,' he said.

'Don't talk such nonsense! You hardly know me.'

I dared to glance into his eyes and caught a sudden flash of the truth.

Behind his foolery crouched debilitating fear. I hadn't considered his situation until that moment but if anything happened in the night, what chance would he have? Even with the aid of crutches, could Perkins traverse the sloping decks of a sinking ship to a lifeboat? Or even get off his bed in time? And could the Corporal swim with only one complete leg? All these things, I realised, must have gone through his mind. The horror of being trapped and alone. In the case of a torpedo hit, watertight doors would be closed before he could get through. He would drown; all alone in the grey hulk.

'To tell the truth, Corporal, I'm a little afraid after all that happened on the *Britannic*,' I said. 'What are the chances of it happening again?' I reached for his hand and squeezed it. 'Do you think the Hun know we're here? Perhaps they're following us in one of their U-boats, just waiting for the right moment. What do you think?'

'I think you really ought to kiss me.'

'I think you know perfectly well I am not that sort of girl.'

'That's why I've fallen in love with you.'

'Stop it, now, or I'll leave.'

Perkins hitched himself clumsily up onto his elbows, a grimace of pain distorting his handsome face. 'You're perfectly lovely; do you know that?' he said.

When I placed my hand on his cheek to test his temperature, he took hold of my wrist and held it there, pressing his face against my hand.

'Is it hurting a lot?' I asked, searching his features, hoping my attention would work the magic of healing him. 'You must be very tired, pain is so wearing and although you're very brave, I see through your act, Corporal.'

His smile was slightly mocking, yet his eyes were so feverishly bright, I prayed he was not falling foul of gangrene or sepsis.

'Call me "darling" and mean it – give me just one kiss to take with me – then if I die in this damned war, at least I can take that to heaven with me.'

I peered into his eyes and saw the truth; his fear, his tenderness, and there was love in the way he gazed at me too. My heart beat hard for all the young soldiers, and for what this war might do to them. The injustice of it. The pain they would endure, and the tears of their families who would never see their boys again.

Without realising, I moved my face towards him and found my lips on his and his hand on the back of my head. His breathing became laboured and instinctively, I realised I should move away. My face was on fire, and my heart almost bursting from my chest.

'I love you, nurse. Promise you'll find me when you come back to Blighty?'

'Oh goodness,' I whispered, pulling away from him, feeling his kiss still on my lips. 'That's enough of that now.' His eyes were sparkling. I'd never seen him looking quite so happy and it made me glad ... Glad, and powerful, and generous, and in control. 'Now, you must tell me how we will avoid Kaiser Bill's torpedoes,' I said in little more than a whisper. 'For my heart's very afraid of what might happen.'

'You can give your heart to me, Gertie Smith, I will take good care of it, I give you my word.'

Oh, I felt myself melting away with his lovely words, but did he mean them? I was not sure. His injuries were bound to change his mood, Nurse Josephine had already told me this. He only meant half the things he said. 'Dear Corporal Perkins, I'm sure you have many fine ladies awaiting your return to Blighty.'

'Don't try and change the subject, nurse. You must kiss me again. That was the best medicine and must be administered every three hours for a speedy recovery.'

'Behave, Corporal. You must be delirious. Perhaps I should use my initiative and get the orderlies to prepare an ice bath.'

'Ice? Where would they get that on a ship in the Mediterranean? I think I'm safe.' He winced again.

'What is it?' I took his hand.

'It's my foot, my right foot. Strange as I haven't got one.' Suddenly he was angry. 'The pain goes on throbbing, though they cut it off a month ago.' He reached down towards the missing limb. 'Damn queer when you reason. I feel it's still there, sometimes it even itches.' He glowered at me for a moment. 'Do you think my foot believes it's still attached to me, down there on the bottom of the sea? No, of course not, it will be long gone, won't it. Eaten by crabs and scavenging fish. Perhaps that's what I'm feeling! What do you think? Is my old foot playing this cruel game, or is it my brain making fun of the poor cripple? How many times do I feel a twinge, a twitch, a little pain, then I look down and realise, I've been fooled again.' His bitter laughter would have curdled cream. 'How do you scratch the itch of a phantom limb?'

'You're just tired, Corporal. You need all the rest you can get in order to heal properly.'

'Tired!' he yelled angrily.

'Shush now,' I said, startled. 'I'm not supposed to be here. You'll get me into trouble.'

He lowered his voice and seemed to calm down a little. 'What will become of us, Nurse Gertie? What chance have we got together? You're young and healthy and very beautiful and if I close my eyes and dream, I see you with our child on your hip.'

'A child . . . Oh my.' I humoured him. 'Is it a boy, or a girl?'

'We will have a boy and a girl, I guess, so take your pick. First, I will marry you, naturally, and build you a fine house, the best, admired by everyone. You'll be so incredibly happy you'll be laughing all the time.'

'Aren't we going a little fast here? I came in to check your dressing and five minutes later I'm married with a child on my hip!' I smiled. 'Anyway, I think you have a fine imagination for someone who's never even heard me laugh.'

'Of course I've heard you laugh, let me think now . . .' He screwed his face up. 'Ah, yes, it was on the *Britannic*. Wait, it's coming back . . .' He lifted a finger and closed his eyes for a second. 'You were left in charge of us by boss woman. You were being too hoity-toity by far, then the bedpans toppled and there was poop everywhere and we laughed so much.' He stopped and chuckled. 'I've never seen anyone go so red in all my life before, your face was scarlet.' He paused, squinting at

292

nothing. 'I'd forgotten all that . . .' He frowned, clearly trying to remember the incident more clearly.

Horrified, the last thing I wanted was him dwelling on his last morning aboard the *Britannic*. I had to change the subject. 'Seriously now, tell me how we'll avoid the Hun's torpedoes? I'm a little anxious, to tell the truth, afraid after all that's happened.'

He returned to now. 'I think the admiralty ask themselves that same question every time a vessel leaves port, Nurse Gertie. They'll be zig-zagging to avoid enemy torpedoes, don't you worry.'

I heard the bravado in his voice. The very idea that he should protect me made him feel stronger.

'We could sleep on deck. What do you think?' I asked.

'We're probably safer here, below. You can stay if you're afraid.'

The tension in his voice made my heart squeeze. 'Thank you, I'd feel safer. I'll get the lifesavers, just in case, and pull two chairs together to fix myself a bed.'

'My blanket's in that kit bag in the corner, make yourself comfortable.'

I found the lifesaver locker and took two cork and canvas belts out, then pulled the grey army issue blanket from Perkins's duffel. Once I was settled beside his bed, he reached for my hand again.

He stared at the ceiling. 'I don't remember much from the *Britannic*,' he said. 'I'd forgotten how we teased you. Was that the same morning?' he said casually. 'I don't remember any-thing much from before the lifeboat. That was the nightmare. Everyone screaming, panicked, climbing over each other to get to the back. I can see their faces, mouths and eyes open wide, hysterical, but the only noise was the ear-bursting racket from the propellers . . . then nothing until I woke in your arms.'

My intense relief to hear him admit this made me feel faint. He didn't know I'd opened the portholes. Did he remember it was me on duty that morning, though? Would he say as much under questioning at an inquiry? Should I tell him. And if I did, what would his reaction be?

'I was saved by a dolphin,' I said, the words shocking me as much as him. 'It pushed me up to the surface and saved my life.'

'You were hallucinating.'

'No, really. They all saw it, the priest said it was a miracle. I was going down, almost giving up. When I asked the priest why I'd been saved, later, he said it was because God had a plan for me, and I wonder if that plan was to save you, dear Corporal. To give you my blood. The surgeon said you were going to die and there was nothing we could do. I had your head in my lap, and I could not stand the thought of you dying in my arms, so I insisted he took some of my blood and put it into you. You know the rest.'

'You're very brave. I will always be in your debt.'

Those few kind words made me want to cry. It was as if bravery and cowardice, truth and lies, all melted together and leaked out of me as tears. How would I ever be able to put everything right?

'When the dolphin came towards me, I thought it was a torpedo, Corporal. You see, I'd never seen a dolphin before. It hit me with such force, the surgeon said if it hadn't been for my corset, I'd have suffered a ruptured spleen.' I was glad he could not see me blushing at the mention of my undergarments. Overcome by tiredness, I closed my eyes.

'I don't even know where my spleen is. Have I got one, or is it a woman thing?' he asked.

'It's just under your ribs, around here . . .' I reached over and touched his bottom rib then quickly withdrew my hand, but he caught hold of it, and pressed it against his chest.

'Do you think you could ever come to love somebody like me, nurse?' He was silent and as I looked, his eyes closed and his face finally relaxed.

'Of course, soldier. There isn't a girl in the world who wouldn't be swept away by a kind, handsome man such as yourself. Now get some sleep. Goodnight, Corporal Perkins,' I murmured, and in the back of my mind, I whispered, 'Goodnight,' to Sissy and Arthur too.

* * *

I woke in bright sunlight as the clatter of the anchor chain vibrated through the ship. The vessel had ceased bucking and rolling so I guessed we had moored in the port of Mudros. Although aching from my uncomfortable cot, my spirits soared to have arrived at my destination at last. I had a good feeling about the day.

'I'm going to get you some food, Corporal. I'll be back soon,' I said. Shivering, I wrapped the blanket around my shoulders and hurried to my cabin. Nurse Josephine was about to leave for breakfast. The two of us rushed to the dining room and just scraped in before it closed. The meal consisted of Huntley & Palmers hardtack biscuits with warm, diluted, condensed milk. I begged another two portions and took them to Perkins.

'I need to wash and shave first,' he said. 'Can you help me, nurse?'

'Me? I'm not sure I should. You must try and do things for yourself.'

I hooked him under the arm and over his shoulder and pulled. The gasp of his breath on my face, and a low groan as I heaved his body into an upright position, gave me a sense of power. 'There, swing your leg to the ground and I'll bring your crutches. Best if you manage independently as much as possible. I'll fetch water and soap if I can find it, so you can wash.'

'You're an angel. You know that I've fallen in love with you?' he said in a jokey, flirty way.

I smiled right into his eyes, pleased to see him free of the awful depression that could strike an amputee at any moment.

The door opened and the surgeon entered. 'Excellent, nurse. I see you've used your initiative.'

I remembered the last time I used my initiative; the world's largest liner sank and God knew how many people suffered the most horrible death because of it.

The surgeon turned to Perkins. 'Corporal, I've received new orders to drop you at Malta. You'll be picked up there by another ship and returned to Portsmouth.'

I trembled. Was this for the tribunal? Had the surgeon received orders that I was destined to go there too?

As if Perkins heard my fears, he asked, 'Will the nurse accompany me, sir?'

'No, you'll be in my charge. No need for concern, young man, I'll take good care of you, though I dare say I won't be as pleasing on the eye. Nurse Smith has orders to report for duty at Mudros clearing station, which is where we are at this very moment.'

My knees almost buckled with relief.

The surgeon turned to me. 'Thank you, nurse. Your work's done here. Disembark and report to your Chief Medical Officer on the quayside. They're treating as many casualties as possible, changing dressings and so on, before bringing them aboard.'

'Very good, sir.' I longed to bid Perkins a proper farewell, perhaps even gather him up in a hug, and plant a farewell kiss on his handsome face, but the first rule of nursing was not to get involved with a patient. I turned to him, threw my shoulders back and lifted my chin. 'Goodbye, Corporal. Safe journey and good luck with the new leg.' I left the room in a few quick steps.

* * *

I hurried to collect my belongings and disembark. Looking out from the deck, I studied the layout of Mudros. Long promontories on either side of the port made the harbour seem more like a wide river. As far as I could see, there were at least six battleships moored up in the bay and twice as many barges, loading goods onto the ships. Further along the quayside, cranes lowered barrels and equipment onto more barges. The distant horizon of Lemnos was broken by an arid mountain range that, in the morning light, took on the shape of a man's head.

The valley of Mudros was a town of white tents that filled the port and continued into the distant foothills. Barrels and bulging sacks lined the road towards the mountains as far as I could see. Stretchers bearing wounded soldiers covered the quayside below our ship.

I hurried down the ramp, past orderlies who supported limping, sagging men with grey faces. Nurse Josephine hefted her bag onto land, then attended injured men who were about to be stretchered aboard. The quayside rang with shouted orders, ambulance engines, and some plaintive cries from the badly wounded. The stench of cigarette smoke, engine fumes and body odour accompanied the general racket and bedlam.

Stretcher-bearers could not shift the patients as quickly as they arrived at the dock by ambulance.

Consequently, everything backed up with rows of wounded, some unconscious, some dully bemoaning their missing limbs. One soldier extended half an arm towards me, 'Please ... please ...' he whimpered. I saw pale faces, pleading eyes. Dull, red-brown stains of old blood. That stale stink of death lay damp and heavy as morning mist, in the still air hanging over Mudros harbour.

I understood this was the start of my penance. An atonement that I feared would last my whole life long.

CHAPTER 33
SHELLY

Dover, present day.

After Sunday breakfast, Gordon looked up from his racing magazine. 'Are you packing already? I thought you weren't going for another few weeks?'

'You're right, I'm not. I just wanted to get some things in the case, Dad.'

'Shelly love, do yer really think you'll need that old blanket in Greece. It is summer, you know?'

Shelly laughed. 'I hope not, Dad. No, it's for the museum in Kea. They're looking for things to do with the *Britannic*. And this belonged to a soldier who was on the ship. They'll love it!'

'In that case, yer should look in me big chair in the loft. Lots of old stuff from Gertie in there. She said it was 'er mother's sewing room before the war. The pigeon loft was outside in them days.'

'You are kidding me!' Shelly rushed upstairs, lighter, quicker, than she ever had before. Only weeks ago she had travelled to Greece, dull, depressed and desperate for a break. This time, she felt herself on the verge of a real adventure.

The loft chair was once an ottoman but, using a couple of pallets, Gordon had fixed armrests and a back to it. She often found him having an afternoon nap there.

Shelly flicked the light on and had to praise her father, the place was spotless as always. The loft ran the length of the cottage and was divided into two by a grille with a mesh door in the centre.

This kept the birds contained in one half of the attic, and left the other half to Gordon and his pigeon paraphernalia.

She heard her dad's footsteps on the stairs.

'I can't remember if I screwed the lid down,' he called. 'There's a tool box in the tallboy.'

A few minutes later she was unscrewing the lid of the ottoman and found it had been carefully lined with oilcloth and was crammed to the top with fabric. The top half was curtains, table linen, and bedding, including an enormous candlewick bedspread which she laid out on the floor and organised everything else in neat piles on top of it.

''Ere, yer look like you should be on the market, Shelly,' Gordon said with a chuckle.

'Buy your bedding here! The best price, best quality!' Shelly cried, playing up to his humour, sensing a little miracle had taken place with his recently uplifted mood.

'Aye, wait a minute. I remember that thing,' her father said, his face softening.

'What, the candlewick?'

He nodded. 'In them days – when me and your mum got married – you'd hand out a gift list to the guests a few weeks before the do and folk just got something off it. Yer mum put bedding and kitchen. Seems everyone got the same idea. We got no bedding except for five candlewick bedspreads, so we rolled one up for pillows, then used another one for a sheet, and had three atop of us. In the mornings we had candlewick fluff in our ears, noses, eyes, mouth and everywhere unmentionable. Then, we went downstairs and had breakfast: toast served up in one of our four stainless-steel toast racks.' He was staring at nothing, face aglow with happiness, eyes sparkling. Shelly nearly wept for him.

'When you were born, you had this fuzzy hair on yer head and I remember your mum said to the midwife, "It's probably not hair at all, it is probably candlewick fluff. It gets everywhere!" And we all laughed so much . . . She had a crackin' sense of humour, you know.'

Shelly struggled. She didn't want to discourage him from talking about her mother by being emotional. In all these years, she'd never once heard him speak of her, his pain was too great.

'That's everything,' she said, slightly disappointed after a final rummage in the bottom of the trunk. 'The rest is just three lumpy old pillows. Might as well turf them while we're here.' She hauled one out. 'Hang on a minute, they're not pillows at all, Dad. There's a drawstring at one end. I wonder if these are the pillow-bags Gran Gertie talked about on the tape?' She tugged at the slip-knot that fastened one and gently tipped out the contents.

'Oh my goodness,' Shelly muttered, putting down the ottoman lid and taking a seat. Her father sat beside her. They both stared. 'It's Gertie's bag, isn't it? The one she packed when the . . . the one that made her miss the first lifeboat . . . the one that saved her life. Jees, this makes it all very real, doesn't it, Dad?'

She picked up her phone and sent Harry a text.

I've found Gran Gertie's bag from when she was on the *Britannic*. Will bring contents for the museum. XX.

Shelly turned and saw her father slumped forward with his elbows on his knees. He stared at the pile of stuff. 'You know what, love, I think you should show this lot to . . .' he gulped, 'your son, next weekend.'

Shelly slipped her arm around his shoulders. 'I do appreciate that all this is very hard for you, Dad. I want you to know that

301

I understand. You never meant any harm, did you? I realised a long time ago; you were only thinking of my best interests when you insisted DJ went for adoption. I was too young, and perhaps I shouldn't have kept my pregnancy a secret for so long. I said things . . . terrible things, well, I'm sorry.' She could hear herself, crying, screaming.

I wish you were dead! I wish you were dead! I hate you!

His weathered old hands went up to cover his face for a moment. He drew in a long breath and said, 'I've regretted insisting on his adoption every day since, Shelly love. It hurt so much, I couldn't even speak about it. I tried a few times since, really I did, but it's embarrassin' to see a grown man cry. In the end I just gave up and tried to forget about the entire incident.'

'It's all in the past, Dad, but thanks. I really appreciate you telling me these things. I was pretty awful to you too. God, the things I said . . .'

'The difference is, you were a kid. I should have pulled myself together and known how to behave. You really loved him, didn't you, that David fella?'

'I did, with all my heart. What a terrible tragedy.'

'And DJ, he's my only grandson, and for my punishment, I missed every moment of him growing up. I used to imagine building model aeroplanes with him, teaching 'im stuff about me pigeons. I've sat up 'ere all these lonely years thinking about him while you was in college or at work, telling myself it was my own fault.' He sighed and shook his head. 'I can't believe he's actually coming here to meet me.' He hiccupped, then sniffed. After a moment with his thoughts, he said, 'Yer mum would have loved him, too. It's odd, but I've felt very close to her lately.' He looked up. 'Can't remember what I did two minutes ago, these days, but my early days with your mum have come back

302

with such clarity, like yesterday. Egh, Shelly love, we had some grand times I can tell you.'

Shelly couldn't meet his eyes. She got onto her knees on the candlewick and had a look at what had come out of the pillow-bag.

'For goodness' sake, Dad, look, Gran Gertie's uniform! How old must this stuff be . . . more than a hundred years?'

'Open the other cupboard door on the tallboy, Shelly.'

She did, and there, taped inside was an old 1997 calendar from the pigeon club with all the race dates ringed. 'See if you can get that calendar off without too much damage, will yer. It's got me first big race win on it.'

She managed to peel the corner tapes off and remove the calendar. Behind it, taped to the tallboy, was an original VAD poster with three volunteers in their uniforms. 'Look at that! Where did you get it, Dad?'

'It was in with Gertie's stuff. I wanted to hold on to it, for a keepsake. She was good to me, was our Gertie. Mothers-in-law can be tricky creatures, and though technically she wasn't mine, I respected her like she was.' He shrugged. 'So I wanted a souvenir when she passed in '98. Yer mum said I could have the poster.'

'You old softy!' She grinned at him affectionately.

* * *

As lunchtime neared the following weekend, Shelly showered and changed into a new pair of jeans and a white shirt. She applied a little make-up and sprayed her hair with something the hairdresser convinced her was essential for a healthy shine.

303

Her reflection in the mirror stared back anxiously. She would show DJ around the house . . . after all, one day it would be his. She glanced around the room and saw dust everywhere. Why hadn't she noticed it before? Realising she had an hour, she lunged into the old wire supermarket basket at the bottom of the broom cupboard and grabbed one of the cotton rags. With the remnants of a can of Mr Sheen, which she shook obscenely, she raced around the house attacking every flat surface. The phone rang. She balanced the can and rag on the back of the sofa and picked up.

'Hi, erm, it's me, DJ . . .' There was a pause. 'I'll be a little late, sorry, bad traffic. One thirty, will that be all right?'

'Of course it will. I hope you're hungry.'

'Starving student, remember?' They both laughed rather self-consciously. 'See you later.'

She stood there, smiling, her heart full of joy. Her own child, *oh*, it seemed impossible after all this time. She placed her hand on her stomach and recalled the weight of him in her belly. So much time had passed, it seemed impossible that this was the same little being.

'All right? How you coping?' Dad asked. 'Do you want me to set the table?'

'To be honest, I'm madly, stupidly, nervous right now. Look at those windows, I'll just give them a bit of a spray and wipe.'

'Calm down. Everything will be fine. He won't care if the glass is clean or not. He just wants assuring that we love him. So put some beers in the fridge and try to imagine how nervous he is. At least you're on home ground, Shelly love.'

'You're right . . . of course you're right, you always are. How do you do it?'

Gordon frowned. 'Truth is, I'm finding this hard too. Especially as it was me that made it clear he wasn't wanted.'

'Aw, come here, you old softy. What you did was hard, but it was in everyone's interest. We all know that.' She gave him a bear hug.

Ridiculous as it was, Shelly needed her father's support. If he hadn't been there, she would have gone to pieces and may not have responded to DJ's letter in the first place. She'd have fretted and pined, but not had the guts to face him. How could a woman give her own baby away? Seventeen or not, the thought was awful. Something she never got over, and now of course, she suspected her child never got over it either.

The doorbell rang. Her heart banged. 'I feel sick,' she muttered.

'Nonsense, off you go, you're his mum, don't forget,' Gordon said. 'Have a moment in private, perhaps show him the garden first. Don't forget, he's nervous too.'

'Thanks, Dad.' Shelly was already on the brink of tears.

CHAPTER 34
GERTIE

Greek Island of Lemnos, 1916.

THE RED CROSS VADS AND nurses rushed from patient to patient, doing their best for each in turn, reluctant to dwell on what they were dealing with. One soldier started screaming and thrashing with such violence it took four orderlies to hold him down. The surgeon rushed down the ramp with a pad and a bottle which he shoved at Josephine.

'Chloroform him!' he ordered abruptly before moving on to another invalid.

Eager to learn the technique, I stood at Josephine's side. She sensed what was going through my mind. 'Hold the pad near his mouth and nose, and be careful not to breathe any fumes.' I did as she said and watched as she dripped the sedating liquid onto the pad. As the fumes doped the soldier, he shuddered and the violence left him. The procedure took two or three minutes. The four orderlies sighed, sweating from the exertion of restraining the patient. They moved on without a word.

'Look at them all! Where are they coming from?' I asked Josephine.

'It's called triage. Soldiers, sorted into categories. Those not expected to survive are delivered last, the ones needing urgent attention, first; and various stages in between.' She turned to the chloroformed soldier before us. 'Poor lad,' she muttered, fixing the pad to his face and adding the doping drops. 'Call me if he stirs. Clean the wound while he's unconscious, Gertie. Cover it with a gauze pad, then find me. There's a trolley with all you need over there.'

'Yes, nurse.' I fetched the dressings trolley, sucked in a breath and lifted the sheet. Shrapnel had taken a sideswipe at him and cut away the front of his abdomen. His internal organs were throbbing in clear view and, horror of horrors, part lifted with the sheet that had stuck to them.

I was a VAD, not a nurse. My job was the tedium, the chores not worthy of detaining a skilled nurse, yet here I was dealing with living body parts that could have come straight out of my father's anatomy books. Stale saliva rushed into my mouth. I dropped the sheet, ran to the edge of the dock, and hurled my breakfast into the water. Shallow breathing and a thudding heart told me I was in shock . . . no use to anyone in that state. After pulling myself together, I got a grip on the situation and returned to the soldier.

I could do this! I was twice the person that had boarded the *Britannic* a few weeks ago. I owed my parents, for all the love and faith and support they had sent my way, and I would show them it wasn't wasted. I used forceps to take pieces of shrapnel out of his abdomen. I would have done this for our Arthur, if only I had been given the chance. Now, I did it for every wounded soldier who had a fretting sister or weeping mother at home. My tears dripped onto him, but apart from that, there was no sign that I wept as I worked. When I could do no more, the orderlies transported him onto the ship.

'All finished, what's next?' I asked Josephine, disappointed to hear the smallness of my own voice.

'Well done. You'll make a nurse yet,' she said. 'Go four stretchers back along the row, there's an ear missing. You've practised a head bandage, yes?' I nodded. 'Then clean the wound and do your best bandage. We have to keep the flies off it.'

The hours ran into each other with cleaning wounds, wafting away flies, and applying dressings. Six hours later, my thoughts went back to the soldier whose belly I had attended. I wondered if he would live and wished I had taken his name. We continued until the light started to fade, then we got a lift to the hospital in one of the returning ambulances. I think I learned more in that one day – when seven hundred men boarded the *Athena*, bound for Alexandria – than forever after. I ended the day ten times the person I'd been when I woke that morning. I would remember none of the injured, except for the first, he would stay with me forever . . . like my first kiss.

Soon, we peered from the back of the ambulance, which was little more than a covered wagon. The December landscape was lush with wild flowers. Local farmers were collecting the last of the day's olives from laden trees. Lemon and orange groves, heavy with their bright fruit, flanked the road to the field hospital and perfumed the air with delicate citrus scents. A wide, green valley ran from the port of Mudros, up to the distant mountains. Along the centre of the dale, like a great canvas dressing on a wound in the countryside, were many dozens of tents. These made up the wards of the clearing hospital.

We were allocated beds in the dorm tent, then, in the mess tent, ate something that seemed to be mostly rice with a few herbs. However, a tin mug of strong sweet tea saved the day. The best drink of my life.

They quickly showed us around before it became too dark. So much had happened, I was desperate to write it down in the form of a letter to my parents before I forgot. I wanted my correspondence to be a record of my life helping in the Great War.

Dearest Mother and Father,

I wish I could tell you where I am, but I can't. Only to say I am safe, in Greece, far from the front line, so no need to worry. The hospital is on an island, and here, it appears to be spring already. We passed many olive trees on our way and saw local people gathered around one. They beat the tree with long sticks to knock the olives down onto sheets or fine fishing nets. The ground is covered in the first wildflowers, mostly pink and lilac anemones. So pretty!

Our hospital looks like a circus, Mother. Rows of canvas tents, each holding fourteen beds. Also, huts of canvas and paper. Long, single-storey sheds of thin wood and roofed with tarred paper are divided into cubicles for eighteen patients. The nurses' corner is adequate. Two hundred yards away are scores of tents filled with the wounded. They've informed us that every night more are brought, and others taken away.

Every hour, troops pass by, whistling their marching tunes as they go down to the port. There are many hospitals like ours. The French are here. The port road is lined with hundreds of barrels of wine that belong to the French army. Then there are the ANZACs, the Australian and New Zealand troops. They have their own hospitals too.

I promise to write as often as possible.

Your loving daughter,

Gertie X

*   *   *

The next morning, after a cold wash and a quick breakfast, we were taken to our ward. The marquee was not ready. Yet the ambulances still came and unloaded their cargo of pain-ridden soldiers onto the duckboards.

Inside, orderlies, expert at laying wooden floors, competed against each other. They threw floors down and beds together as if it were an Olympic sport.

A sharp-faced doctor followed by several nurses, examined and labelled patients. Some simply bore a cross. These were removed and a patient on the floor moved into the vacant bed. By midday, heat in the marquee had built to an unbearable level, flaps were tied back and mosquito nets dropped over the entrances. Yet, flies still intruded, attracted by the rancid blood of open wounds. My first order was to clean and disinfect those wounds and limb stumps.

I was afraid of hurting the young men who had signed up with such bravery and enthusiasm. Close to tears, I found myself dabbing at a stump that was once an arm, promising all kinds of miracles, then Josephine stormed up.

'You're not helping him, Gertie!' She snatched the swab from my hand. 'Remember, there are a million microbes trying to enter this wound and kill our gallant soldier. *We* must destroy them! If our soldier suffers some discomfort, reassure him you're saving his life. Sepsis and gangrene kill more than any of Kaiser Bill's bullets. Do you understand?' she shouted, scrubbing vigorously at the wound.

'Yes, nurse. Sorry, nurse.' I glanced at the soldier's face. For a moment, his pain had gone and he winked.

Josephine's voice softened a little. 'Now go back to saving lives, and take no nonsense from these men.' She faced the soldier.

'Young man, if I catch you staring at this VAD's chest once more, I'll find the biggest ogre on the camp to give you a cold bed-bath, do you understand?' Weak laughter came from neighbouring beds.

310

The soldier's eyes flicked to my breasts and his face lit with a grin that dimmed the pallor of his pain.

Josephine winked, and I understood a part of nursing that would never be seen in the medical manuals. Pain relief was a state of mind, as well as opiates in a syringe.

Dear Mother and Father,

I hope this letter finds you well. Father will be pleased to hear I am learning so much.

I put on a brave face, but the truth is I have at times been overwhelmed by it all. However, every day is less shocking.

Today we were introduced to the doctors and surgeons and we visited the other military hospitals, to observe how they were run.

The first hospital, wards of tents, housed almost two thousand men with arms, legs, or faces blown off. The face wounds are the worst! Then, we had elevenses – bread, blackcurrant jam and strong tea. Next, the blinded soldiers. Five hundred of them learning to accept their future. The cripples will get new limbs, but the blinded?

The tents overflow, with hardly walking space between bodies. Wards are divided into ailments, dysentery being the largest with thirty thousand cases! Also, six thousand frostbites from who knows where. Add rheumatic fever, shrapnel injuries, and bullet wounds, and the figures become impossible.

Apart from this, I am fine and strive to excel in memory of our Arthur and Sissy.

Do not be alarmed if the letters are sparse once I start work in earnest.

Your loving daughter,

Gertie X

* * *

CHAPTER 35
SHELLY

Dover, present day.

SHELLY OPENED THE DOOR. DJ thrust a bunch of flowers at her. They both said 'Hi,' in the first breath, laughed awkwardly in the second breath, swallowed hard and gazed at each other.

'Are you going to ask me in?' he said gently.

'Actually, shall we go to the pub? We've got half an hour before dinner.'

He let out a gust of air, his shoulders dropped. 'Great plan, thanks.'

She nodded at the flowers. 'I'll just pop these in the sink, you can get in the car.' She lifted the car keys off the coat hooks by the door and tossed them to him. Two minutes later, she was beside him, pulling off towards The Rose and Crown.

They found a quiet corner, and DJ bought them each a pint of shandy. She watched him at the bar, he could have been his father. She wanted to weep.

'There must be so many things you want to know, and I promise I'll answer all your questions. But this is very hard, for me too, because ... well ... first I lost my mother, then your father. Then, I lost you. In a way, I also lost my own father at that time too, you see?'

He shook his head. 'I don't understand.'

'I didn't want to give you up. It was terrible. I was too young to stand up for myself with everyone pressuring me. And all these things happened in one tragic year that started when I was sixteen and my mother was killed in an accident. I never fully recovered. So please, I hope you'll forgive me if I sound bitter, or selfish, I'm not . . . not really; it's just that I am still hurting. There's so much love and loss and pain involved, DJ, I'll probably embarrass you on more than one occasion by bursting into tears.' She gazed at him, her son. 'But now, oh my God, I can't believe this – I just can't – I'm overwhelmed.' She pulled in a ragged breath.

He lowered his eyes from her face to the table, digested her words and nodded. 'You've had a hard time. I've often tried to imagine why you gave me up . . . why you didn't want me . . .'

'Please stop right there. There has never been one single moment when I didn't want you. I let you go to a new family, parents who I understood loved you as much as I did. They did, didn't they?' Shelly peered at him with a worried frown.

He nodded and smiled gently, but she sensed his unease.

'It was the right thing to do, for your sake. My father said, if I loved you, I would want you to have a better life than any seventeen-year-old single mother without an income could give you.'

'So, it was your father that forced you to give me up.'

Shelly nodded. 'It took many years before I stopped hating him for it. In the end, I realised he was right. I gave you up because I loved you so much. Not because I didn't want you.' She realised tears were trickling down her cheeks and dabbed them away with a tissue. 'Sorry,' she said with a smile. 'I did warn you. Please tell me – you have had a good life, haven't you?'

'Yes, very much so, but I grew up knowing I was adopted, and I often wondered about you, of course. My parents said you were very young, but they didn't know anything about my father. Can you tell me about him?'

Shelly sipped her drink, then blew through pursed lips. 'I'll tell you as much as I can about David each time we meet, but you must be patient, you're not going to hear the whole story straight off.' He nodded again. 'There will be times when I won't be able to talk about him at all, but rest assured, you will come to know and understand him.'

'Can I ask you some questions?'

She thought for a moment. 'Yes, of course. I realise you need answers. I was in that position myself once. The pain's intense, isn't it? And the bitterness, I was bitter for years.' He nodded. The old distress rose and she battled against it. 'It's so unfair,' she whispered. 'And it hurts so bad. But that pain made me determined to be my own boss and rule my own life. *Nobody* was ever going to tell me what to do again. Perhaps I overreacted.'

'How do you mean?'

'Well, the world and his wife said I couldn't look after you by myself, with no family support. So I spent the next nineteen years proving them wrong. I'm desperate for you to understand that I didn't simply cast you aside for the sake of convenience.

'The loss of my mother, then David, and then you, and in a way my dad too, was too much pain for any young girl to take. Soon, severe depression set in. Although I was little more than a child when you were taken from me, I had one consolation – you were in the safe care of a loving family.

'They said I had post-natal depression, but they never really understood. Slowly but surely, I came back from that dark pit and made a success of my life. I'm proud of that. However, losing you and your father has never quite left me. Twenty years later, and I'm still dealing with it and I know, for the moment, this isn't making any sense to you, but I promise it will.'

'I'm just realising how brave you've been to tackle this. Do you mind if I call you Mum? It feels a little odd, and of course I do have another Mum, in Australia, but nothing else would feel right. Better to get used to it from the start, I think.'

'I'd like that very much. So long as you don't mind my tears now and again.'

'Look, at any time, please, you can just tell me to shut up and go away, so long as you let me know when you're feeling stronger and I can come back. And if you ever want to talk, I'll always be here for you.'

'I think that's the kindest thing anyone's ever said to me. I don't want you to think I'm a wimp: I did get myself through college and university, and set up my own successful veterinary practice. I've got balls, DJ.'

He laughed. 'I believe it.'

'So, ask me a question.'

'Can you tell me something about my father. Just something?'

Shelly took a shuddering breath and, once again, ballooned her cheeks as she let it out. The action calmed her and she found herself dreamily thinking of the young man she had loved so passionately. 'David was the most amazing guy. A few years older than me, which was exactly what I needed. However, that was what my father objected to. I was sixteen and he was twenty-four. We were so compatible, so happy together.' She told him how they met outside the jeweller's shop. How David had been balm to her wounds. 'He was the sweetest, kindest man on earth, and incredibly handsome, like you. He told me later that he fell in love with me from that first moment in the high street. It was a moment in my life when I most needed love.'

'It sounds as though he was a romantic.'

She closed her eyes and nodded. 'David was a softy with a huge heart, and so grateful to me for helping him with his dog.'

'His dog?'

'A golden retriever, Pat . . . Pat the dog, get it?' They smiled at each other. 'That was so typical, your father had a great sense of humour. He'd had Pat for thirteen years, but she became poorly and he had to have her put to sleep.' She remembered how upset he was. 'It broke his heart. We took her to see all her pups before that final trip to the vet's. Years later, I wondered if it was all a plan of David's to get me to put my own grief aside. "Will you really help me take Pat to say goodbye to her puppies?" he asked as if it was a mammoth feat, when really it was just a kindness.' She took a sip of her shandy, remembering that day of sadness and incredible closeness.

'We spent the following Saturday and Sunday traipsing from house to home, watching Pat nuzzle and sniff her offspring. When the day was over, I went back to David's ground-floor flat and we talked until ten o'clock. I knew I'd be in terrible trouble with my father for being out so late, especially as he had no idea where I was. David sensed this. He said he'd go home with me and talk to my dad, tell him how marvellous I'd been. Terribly brave of him. I mean, my dad could have been a gorilla waving a baseball bat for all he knew.'

When DJ laughed, Shelly's heart melted. He sounded just like his father. 'Did he go home with you?'

'No, I persuaded him I'd be better on my own. David saw me into the bus and asked if I'd meet him at the vet's the next weekend.' Shelly smiled, then glanced at her watch. 'I think we ought to head home,' she said. 'I've been cooking all morning in your honour; shame if it spoiled.'

*   *   *

'About my father, your grandfather,' Shelly said in the car as they headed down Lighthouse Lane. 'Be gentle with him, will you? He's very nervous about meeting you, and he can get a little . . . grumpy.'

'He made you give me up. He didn't want me around. Do you know how that feels?'

Shelly sighed. 'He did, and that must make you feel unwanted, I understand that.' She pulled over and turned in her seat. 'But I want you to understand, *he* was having a breakdown, going through real mental torture with nobody to support him. He wanted to do the best thing for both of us – for you and me. I know he only ever meant well.'

DJ nodded. 'Perhaps I should have brought him of bottle of whisky, or something. Does he smoke?'

Shelly shook her head. 'No. He gave up cigarettes for New Year. He uses a vape, though. Claimed it helps him get over smoking tobacco but now he's addicted to the vape and gets frantic if he mislays it.'

'We have something in common, then.' DJ smiled out of the car window.

'There's one other thing. Last weekend, we discovered a bag of stuff that belonged to my great-grandmother. She went off to nurse in the First World War, just after the Battle of Gallipoli around 1916.'

'Nineteen sixteen, that's cool. What did you find?'

'Apart from a nurse's uniform, we don't know what's in there, we thought we'd wait until you arrived and then have a look together.' They pulled up outside the cottage.

'Thank you.' He turned towards her, still smiling. 'It's very peaceful around here, isn't it?'

*　*　*

After the introductions, Shelly was aware of tension building between DJ and Gordon. She showed DJ around the cottage, before returning to the dining table. They sat in silence as she dished out the food.

'What do you think of White Cottage then, DJ?' Gordon tried.

'Nice place, a good size family home.' Then, appearing slightly startled by his own words, he went on. 'Love the beams, really cool, Mr Summer.'

'You can't call me Mr Summer, lad. You're family, after all.'

Clearly, DJ went through a number of responses in his mind, but then gave up.

Shelly glanced at her father's glum face, wishing he would cheer up. Then they all glared miserably at the joint of beef in the centre of the table, dumping their woe on it. DJ was jigging his knee. The tap dripped into the sink. Shelly chewed her lip. This wasn't what she had envisaged.

'Wait, I forgot the mustard,' she cried, glad of the excuse to speak, feeling the hot accompaniment would somehow warm up the atmosphere.

They tucked into the veg, roasties and Yorkshires with only her father helping himself to a huge portion of beef, while DJ took a frugal slice, glancing around the table guiltily as he did so.

Shelly tried to make conversation, but the strained atmosphere prevailed until eventually, she jumped up and started shifting plates.

'I've made an amazing apple pie with real custard, who's up for a slice?'

Hands went up. 'I'll clear the table,' Shelly said, placing a blanket of tinfoil over the remainder of the joint and shoving it into the fridge.

DJ stood. 'Can I help?'

'Certainly not,' Shelly said. 'Dad, get DJ a beer, please.'

Gordon was clearly uncomfortable, and DJ noticed it too. 'Don't worry, I'm fine.'

In an awkward moment both DJ and her father moved towards the sofa and almost bumped into each other. DJ, aware of the tension, glanced at Shelly. Gordon suddenly threw his arms around the boy as if in a rugby tackle.

Startled, everyone froze.

''Ere, lad, I want to say I'm right sorry. Really. Can you ever forgive me? Not a bloomin' day's passed that I 'aven't regretted my decision all those years ago, and I ain't never forgot you, an' neither has our Shelly. You're me only grandson, lad, and I'm glad you're 'ere.' Then, he sniffed loudly and everyone realised how upset he was. 'I've been a right grumpy bastard since the day you left us, ask yer mother; and I'm good 'n' proud of the way you've turned out.' He let go of DJ, turned away and blew his nose with gusto.

Shelly exchanged an '*Awww*' look with DJ, then passed two bottles of beer over. 'Why don't you two take to the sofa so we can put the table back against the wall and have some room in here. We'll have the pudding on our knees, OK?'

Both men nodded and the tension broke as they pushed the table back to the wall and then flopped onto the sofa.

'Ouch, sorry, sat on something,' DJ said, pulling the scatter cushion out from behind his back, then holding up a huge pair of holey, pale-blue Y-fronts.

Gordon's eyes widened. ''Ere, I've been looking for them. They's me most comfy ones. Shelly, you 'aven't been using them as a duster?'

DJ's shoulders were shaking.

'For goodness' sake, Dad. There's no backside in them,' Shelly cried.

'I admits they's a bit thin in the seat, but the front's still good, and who's ever goin' to see my behind?'

Laughter exploded from DJ. 'You crack me up, Gramps!' he cried between gasps.

'You leave my crack out of this!' Gordon said, which made Shelly laugh helplessly too. In a few silly words, all the strain between them was blown away. Shelly took a surreptitious glance at her father and wondered if he had somehow orchestrated the whole fiasco just to break the tension.

* * *

The pudding was a great success with everyone having seconds. They talked for a while, Gordon telling DJ about his pigeons, then explaining about the steam engine he'd kept for him for the past twenty years.

Shelly smiled to herself, delighted to hear the ease with which they made arrangements for the following week. DJ, her son, fitted into the family, and wasn't that wonderful? More than she had hoped for.

'Come up to the loft, lad, have a look at me birds while Shelly gets on with the dishes, then we'll bring Gran Gertie's bag down and see what's in there, right?'

Shelly continued to clear up, smiling when she thought about her father apologising to DJ the way he did. Clearly, he'd been dreading the day he'd face his grandson. Half an hour passed and Shelly was finishing her coffee when the men returned from the attic with Gran Gertie's pillow-bag.

'Here, Gramps, shall we put it on the table?'

'Sounds like a plan, lad.'

They hefted the bulging pillow-bag onto the empty dining table. 'Right, here we go,' DJ said. 'Who's going to do the honours? I think it should be you, Mum. What do you think, Gramps?' He looked at them both, his head slightly to one side. 'It feels a little odd saying Mum and Gramps, you know?'

'Aye, course it does, but we'll all get used to it, lad. I remember when our Shelly was born. At first, it seemed right weird to call that little baby Michelle . . . Must admit, I called her a few other names at night, when she was teething. They came quite natural, believe me, but honestly, you don't want to hear them now.'

Shelly and DJ laughed.

Shelly's chest tightened every time DJ called her Mum, and she could see her father was quite overwhelmed by his new role too. She went right up to DJ and said, 'Look, we're all family here, do you think you could just . . .' She had to stop and gulp back tears. 'Give me a hug? I've waited a lifetime.'

DJ, who was six inches taller than her, pulled her to his chest and wrapped his arms around her. 'You can't understand what this day means to me,' he said quietly. 'Thank you.'

* * *

'That went all right, don't you think?' Shelly said, putting the last of the dishes away.

Gordon nodded at the window, towards the old oak tree where DJ was sitting on the bench reading some of Gertie's letters that they'd found in an oilcloth envelope in the pillow-bag. 'He seems like a nice boy; kind, good-looking, with a sense of humour. Of course, he'd get all that from his grandad. Runs in the family, don't it?'

Shelly laughed and marvelled at how her father's wit had returned. Her own joy was so great she felt an urge to pull on her ballet pumps and pirouette across the table, but she hadn't worn them since she was six years old.

'I'm just going to pack the contents of the pillow-bag into my suitcase to take with me next week. Is there anything you'd like to keep, Dad?'

'Well, I don't know, we didn't really have a good look, did we? Too busy yakkin'. Let's go through it together shall we?'

'Might as well finish going through the trunk too,' she said. 'I put the Christmas presents in my bedroom. I thought . . . well, about having a proper Christmas this year . . .'

'I know,' he said, way ahead of her. 'It's time we celebrated Christmas. I'll do it in honour of my wife, and you do it in honour of your son, OK?'

CHAPTER 36
GERTIE

Lemnos, Greece, 1917.

By chance, I came to see some of Lemnos. The beauty of that island brought all of Greece into my heart forever. Neither the magnificent architecture of Syros nor the rural simplicity of Kea, Lemnos was Constable's English pastures. Rolling hills dotted with sheep, groves of fruit trees, neat rows of beehives. Corn fields, wheat threshing circles and hay stacks. When I turned my back on those rural scenes and faced the coast, there were beaches of white sand and turquoise water like nothing I had seen before. The deep port of Mudros was another story. Frigates lined up, embarking coal and water unloaded by supply ships. A motley array of barges sidled up to the great frigates and destroyers, flogging their wares like gypsies in the market place.

One day, one of our orderlies came off his motorised bicycle and broke his leg outside our tent.

'Take care of my bike, nurse,' he muttered between gasps of pain. 'If you learn to ride it, you'll get a few tips when you deliver stuff, and you'll keep my job open for me. Say you'll do it?'

William carried messages from one end of the camp to the other. After a tentative start, I found the motorised cycle manageable and took the messenger's place, hurrying through the camp three times a day. I loved that vehicle and fetched supplies from the stores whenever we ran out of something crucial. I wished

Sissy could have seen me flying along the duckboards between the marquees.

Matron Merriberry approached Josephine and I as we came off duty one week before Christmas. 'Nurse Jones,' she said to Josephine. 'I want you and Smith to start in theatre, tomorrow morning, seven o'clock, understood?'

I could hardly speak, and only managed to squeak, 'Yes, Matron.'

'There'll be no Christmas celebrations, ladies,' Matron continued. 'The usual three-day ceasefire over the holiday has been cancelled this year. The murder will go on.' She stood taller and shook her shoulders defiantly. 'However, everyone's name is into a pillow-bag, and every Monday at dinner, I'll draw six out. Those nurses will be taken for a day out at the beach or the mud-baths with a picnic, weather permitting. Any questions?'

'Excuse me, Matron. I just want to thank you for putting me in theatre. I won't let you down, and my father will be very proud.'

She lifted her chins, huffed, and continued on her way, but as she turned, I saw the flicker of a smile, though it probably had nothing to do with me.

* * *

I managed to write to my parents every Sunday. Once a month I received a small parcel with things I had requested, plus a few treats from Mother; her Dundee or parkin cake, or a bar of prized chocolate. She told me, Father was proud to read I was training as a scrub nurse in the theatre.

I found the position much more rewarding than being in the tent ward.

'You wanted to rise through the ranks, Gertie,' Josephine said. 'Now, we're so short-staffed there are no restrictions on how far you may go. Just work hard and be eager.'

The operations were fascinating. My first theatre experience was a leg amputation, which reminded me of handsome Corporal Perkins, and the operation I'd missed on the island of Kea.

Josephine was the anaesthetist, and her being there took away some of my nerves.

The surgeon, Rumley, was a highly respected Australian. 'Ready?' he called as he entered the stone-built theatre with two orderlies and a poor wretch on a stretcher.

'Yes, sir,' we all replied.

'You, new girl,' he said to me. 'Stand next to the anaesthetist and do whatever I or she says, and don't speak. I can't abide chattering nurses.'

The patient writhed vigorously, his eyes staring in unashamed terror as he struggled against the orderlies.

Josephine spoke calmly over his whining. 'You'll be fine in a moment, soldier. Count ten for me. Come on now, let me hear you. One, two . . .'

She handed me a bottle with a glass stopper. 'Open when I say and close immediately after I've filled the dropper – and don't inhale the fumes.' I nodded. She had what looked like a miniature bullhorn, with a pad of cotton inside. 'Open.' I did. She took a dropper of liquid and said, 'Close.' Josephine emptied the chloroform dropper into the contraption and held it over the patient's mouth and nose. The hypnotising smell wafted around us like oriental silk. The patient continued to writhe while Josephine talked soothingly, but soon he became dopey. The red-faced orderlies let go of his limbs. Josephine continued until he lay still, then she pulled his eyelid back to check his pupil.

'Ready to go, sir,' she said, adding more drops to the mask.

'When nurse says so, open a window,' Rumley ordered, nodding at me.

'Right, give me the bottle and open the window,' Josephine said moments later. Then she instructed me to apply a blood pressure cuff and tell her the reading.

The surgeon and the theatre nurse cut away the filthy bandages that tied the leg to a length of wood. Then they cut away what remained of the shredded uniform trousers.

'There's a mess,' Rumley said, examining the two ragged wounds where shattered bones protruded. 'Hit in the back of the knee. Blown off his entire knee and the ends of the tibia, fibula, and femur. We can't repair what isn't there. Let's get on with it and amputate at the lower femur as close to the knee as possible.' He prodded and peered. 'No sepsis. Right, let's have a belt tourniquet on the thigh and get started. How are you doing, nurses?'

I'll never forget that; to be addressed as 'nurse' by a surgeon for the first time. How I wished Father had been there.

The operation was nothing like the line drawings in Father's medical book. Once the leg was in two separate parts, he lifted the lower half and dumped it in my arms. 'Stand it in the corner, nurse.'

Oh!

The limb was unexpectedly heavy, and I was shocked! Really shocked! I caught a glance from Josephine and understood this was a test.

'Yes, sir,' I said strongly, ignoring the foul-tasting saliva that rushed into my mouth. I propped the limb on its blackened, swollen foot in the corner; stuck my head out of the window and hauled in a fierce breath, then returned to the table. Rumley trimmed the muscle so that there was a good flap to sew over the end of the stump. Then he stitched the wound around a rubber drainage tube.

'Pay attention, nurses. I spend too much time on external sutures when any of you could relieve me of the task.' Without looking up, he said, 'New girl, how's your bandaging?'

'I'm the best, sir,' I said boldly, wishing I had the courage to tell him I could have done the stitches.

'Then get on with this and be snappy, there'll be another chloroform job in ten minutes.'

I am proud to say I applied my finest dressing to that limb. I thought of Corporal Perkins as I worked and I wondered if his wound had healed cleanly. Was he measured for a prosthetic, and could he go back to being a mechanic? Now, I realised the surgeon was right to take away a little more leg than appeared necessary. Better safe than sorry was the general consensus.

I missed Perkins and wished I had his address so that I could write to him.

* * *

'Good job, today,' Josephine said in our room. We had five hours to wash, eat, and sleep, so there was no time to deliver post or discuss the operation. What praise: *good job*! Despite my tiredness, I was proud and ambitious, and content with the day. I saw myself on the bottom rung of a ladder that I didn't know I could climb, or to what heights it would take me.

When back on duty, I tackled everything offered, and did my best. Despite the bone-aching tiredness, the thrill of my latest accomplishments spurred me on towards any new challenge.

* * *

After a month on Lemnos, my name had not come out in the draw. Josephine and I longed for a day off, a swim in the crystal-clear sea, time to chatter, laugh, sing and splash, most of all to bathe in the saltwater and sleep all day on the warm sand. The names of people who won didn't go back into the draw, so I consoled myself; Josephine and I were bound to win a day off eventually, even if we were the last two left in the sack.

My work continued in the theatre, assisting the anaesthetist, sometimes doing the final stitching, and dressing wounds. There was no part of a man that I had not worked on. February came and we saw the casualties change with the weather. Added to the shrapnel and gunshot wounds came severe frostbite. Feet blackened and stinking with gangrene were amputated. After assisting with the removal of both feet, a young cherubic soldier lost his battle and died on the table. He reminded me so much of our Arthur that I was shaken to the core.

I said, 'Excuse me,' left my post at the surgeon's side and rushed out into the evening air. The tears of helplessness raged for a few seconds, then I dried my face and returned to my post.

'We've only lost ten per cent of patients this week, nurse. A new record, I think. Excellent!' surgeon Rumley said without emotion and not looking my way.

By the end of February, I hoped to be able to deal with a drainage tube and stitch down a flap. I scrutinised every move of Rumley's hands with the utmost interest.

'Nurse!' he bellowed one afternoon, making me jump. 'Why is your head between me and my patient?'

'Sorry, sir,' I said, pulling back. 'I got carried away, sir. It's my target to learn the tube and flap procedure by the end of the month, sir.'

'Get out of my way!' he yelled furiously. 'Who do you think you are?'

'Gertie Smith, sir.'

I guess he hadn't expected an answer because he guffawed. 'Damned audacious girl, if you ask me.'

From that moment, Rumley took every opportunity to give me the most awful jobs and there were moments when I hated him, but as the challenges grew, so did my determination. It was mid-March before he took twenty minutes to talk me through the procedure. When the next leg amputation was completed that afternoon, he stood back and said, 'Go on then, now's your chance, nurse.'

I felt nothing but intense concentration as I forged on with a steady hand. Once I'd cut that final thread, I wanted to leap in the air! Both thrilled and obscurely terrified, I whispered, 'I did it!' as I met the surgeon's smiling eyes.

*　　*　　*

At night, tiredness, pressure, and fear of failing as a nurse, dampened my anxiety and shame over what had happened on HMHS *Britannic*. Sometimes, I would forget that I had opened the portholes and caused the great ship to sink before it reached land. Yet those darkest memories often surfaced in the early hours, when sleep was too precious to waste on things that would not change. Those bodies tossed in the air, only to be dismembered by propeller blades on their inevitable return. The screaming, my drowning, the dolphin, Sissy's precious watch, they all jostled against each other, pushing back sleep and claiming space in my mind.

During the daytime, my handsome Corporal Perkins often came to mind. I imagined the Corporal learning to dance on his prothesis. Never complaining, but always trying to do better.

Memories of Manno were a different story. They roared with tumbling, tantalising passion until my spine arched and my body tingled in the most delicious way. I wrote to him several times, but never received a reply. When he entered my thoughts, I longed for him, and wished so many things I could never say aloud or even put down on paper. I recalled the way he peered at me from under those long, dark, lashes – and the tender fullness of his mouth against mine when he kissed me. *Oh!* How I longed to kiss him again . . . longer, harder, deeper. There was no doubt in my mind, I was in love with Manno.

* * *

The following week, we were overloaded with work. Josephine and I often missed our evening meal and made do with dry bread and chicken soup, followed by strong cocoa provided by an understanding orderly who cared a lot for Josephine. However, we made sure we got to the dining room on the Monday, when Matron made the draw. That Monday, we were a little late for dinner and heard our names called as we entered the mess. A great thrill raced through me. At last, I believed, we had won a day away. We turned sharply and headed for the top table, both of us trying to reduce our grins to ladylike smiles.

'Eat, pack your belongings, and report to HMHS *Gabriel* on the port at precisely nineteen hundred hours,' Matron ordered. 'You're going home.'

CHAPTER 37
SHELLY

Dover, present day.

'So, DJ, YOU HAVE TO know something about Gran Gertie,' Shelly said. 'She was a rebel. Fought for the vote and women's rights with the suffragettes. Lied about her age so she could go and do nursing work in troubled countries she'd never heard of. As we understand so far, she was involved with events that unfortunately led to the sinking of the greatest passenger liner in the world, HMHS *Britannic*, though we won't have all the facts until we've listened to the rest of her memoirs. She's got us on the edge of our seats at the moment though.

'She recorded her own life story? That takes some courage, you know, she sounds like a real tough woman. Makes me feel proud.'

It was Shelly who felt proud, her heart melting to hear her son speak like that. 'Well, not brutally tough in the way we imagine. It seems she was always afraid of one thing or another, and as she was only eighteen when she went to war, she was unbelievably naïve, especially when it came to young men.'

Shelly told DJ about the cassette and tapes. 'We'll make you a copy too, if you're interested.'

His smile was slightly mocking in a mischievous way. 'No, you don't need to do all that, just upload them to the Cloud. You only do it the once, then we'll all be able to access them at any time.'

Shelly and Gordon stared at him, then at each other.

'The Cloud, Dad,' Shelly said with mock seriousness. 'Get onto it, will you?'

'Right, our Shelly. I'll just give Bill Gates a call, an' tell him I need a hand, all right?'

DJ grinned at them, strong, white, even teeth like his father, Shelly thought.

'I can come and do it next weekend if you like.'

'I'll be away in Greece next weekend, near where your great-great-grandmother's ship went down.'

'But you must still come for Sunday lunch,' Gordon cut in. 'I'll be here with Bill, and we could fire up the old steam engine. Anyway, why don't you come for the weekend? Yer mother's convinced we'll be up to no good, or that we'll burn the house down.'

DJ glanced at Shelly.

'Nothing would please me more,' she said. 'You can have my room, keep an eye on this old rogue.'

'Aye! Watch who you're calling old!'

DJ laughed and glanced from one to the other. 'I'd love to, why not? I can cook for you, if you like, Gramps.'

Gordon grinned. 'I'd like that.'

Shelly rolled her eyes. 'I can see you two are going to be trouble!'

DJ threw her a grin. 'Look, why don't I come early and run you to the airport? Meanwhile, let's upload a cassette right now? The longest part is playing a tape. We can all listen to a cassette, then you can continue uploading more after I've gone, or tomorrow. Whatever.'

'A wonderful idea, if it's not too much trouble,' Shelly said. 'Let me make tea or coffee while we listen to Gran Gertie for half an hour.'

'No, I'll make the drinks while you two see what's inside the pillow-bag,' Gordon said.

* * *

The room fell silent as the three stared at the contents of Gertie's bag. Shelly pulled her uniform onto a hanger and hooked it onto the picture rail. Gordon studied an enamel plate, bowl, and mug, knife, fork and spoon. Shelly ran her hand over the beautifully embroidered underwear. Under this lay another uniform and a bundle of letters that they were all curious to read, but decided to save for another Sunday. There would be many more such Sunday lunches, and the knowledge brought each of them a peculiar warmth.

Shelly stepped back in order to take in the bigger picture. Her father and son were united for the first time – a most amazing moment. She reached for her phone and took a quick snap before anyone noticed. She slipped her arm around Gordon's shoulders and gave him a little squeeze.

Gordon and DJ were in deep conversation.

''Ere, it happened like this,' Gordon said, lifting Gertie's mug. 'Each mornin' before I went off to the docks on me bike, yer grandmother, Margarete her name was but she was always Maggie to me, she'd make me tea in an enamel mug just like this one, to take with me.'

'How did that work, Gramps? You couldn't take a mug of tea on your bike.' DJ glanced up, caught Shelly's eye and winked.

'No, we used a twist, everyone did. Wasn't any teabags then, see. Hadn't been invented. Maggie ripped a square off the bread bag, they was waxed paper in them days. In the middle of the square she'd put a big spoon of tea leaves, three spoons of sugar, and a tablespoon of sweetened, condensed milk. She twisted the top round tightly and tucked it into me mug. At break time I just untwisted it, poured boiling water on, then fished out the paper.'

'Ingenious! Did you have anything with it?'

'Scones with a lovely great wedge of best butter. A great baker of scones was your grandmother.' He stared at his slippers for a moment. 'She was a wonderful woman, my Maggie.'

'Don't be sad, Gramps. I want to hear everything about you and my grandmother. I'm sure she was lovely. But you know what? I'd better put the tape on if I'm going to get the first one saved this afternoon. Is everyone ready? Right, check the lead's plugged in, OK. Right, this is what you do. Start the tape . . .'

* * *

'Sounds like she was quite a girl, our Gertie,' DJ said. 'If I'm descended from her, I'd like to trace my family tree. Who did she marry?'

Shelly shrugged. 'I'm hoping to learn that from the tapes. What do you know, Dad?'

'Now that would be telling. Gertie wanted you to hear the facts from her, so you have to wait.'

DJ grinned, loving Gordon's mischief. He turned to Shelly. 'Tell me about your holiday, Mum.' His eyes flicked to hers, testing the word again.

'Wreck diving, wildlife and travel photography, and chill. Diving's my passion. The Greek seabed's littered with ships, and I've visited quite a few – but I only discovered the wrecks of Kea recently. To tell the truth, I was going to cancel. Worried about Dad, you know?'

334

'Sounds exciting. Look, if it makes you feel better, I'll keep an eye on Gordon.'

'Aye, don't talk about me like I'm not here!'

'Sorry, Gramps.' DJ's smile turned to a frown and a distant look came to his eyes. 'Don't I remember you saying my dad wanted to be a diver?'

''Ere, he doesn't know what happened, does he, Shelly?'

Shelly shook her head. The room tilted. She struggled to speak. 'Yes. David was teaching me to snorkel,' she muttered closing her eyes. In an instant, she could see him through her mask, her scream weird in the snorkel tube, then she realised she was holding her breath. Startled, she filled her lungs and then groaned as the past flooded through her. 'It was a long time ago, DJ. A year in my life that I'd rather forget.' She went over to the window and stared into the darkness so her father and son could not see the lie, or the tears. With the tips of her fingers, she blotted the tears that had gathered in the corners of her eyes. She felt them watching, and the silence behind her said they'd caught the quiver in her voice.

* * *

The next weekend, Shelly gazed through the windscreen, her thoughts miles away. She had a small suitcase of holiday clothes and a large suitcase of Gran Gertie's memorabilia in the boot. She had worked hard to get Gertie's nurse's uniforms washed and ironed in time for the trip. Was she making a mistake, giving the family history away? After all, if things went south with Harry . . .

She turned to touch the arm of her driver. 'DJ, it was really good of you to stay the night, and run me to the airport on your way home. She tapped her forehead and shook her head. 'It's all happened so fast, I'm still reeling. Amazing that you had the courage to track me down. I thought hearts only broke with sadness, but my heart's completely shattered by happiness. Thank you.'

She sat in the passenger seat of DJ's battered Beetle. Next to her feet was an odd sock that clearly needed a wash, and scattered around that, some small change, one and two pence coins mostly. Between the seats, a burger box stuffed with rubbish told her he had hurriedly tidied the car in her honour. She smiled, recalling her student days, then glanced at the fuel gauge.

'Call in the next petrol station and let me fill her up.'

After a gentle argument and the rationale that a taxi would have cost more, they arrived at the airport with almost a full tank. Shelly persuaded DJ to stay and have breakfast with her before she went through passport control and he continued to Cambridge.

'I understand that you want to know about your father,' she said. 'It's only natural. The thing is, I find it very difficult to talk about him. Although I was terribly young, I loved him very much. I still do in a way. He took away all my anger and self-blame about my mother's death. I would certainly not have made it through to university if he hadn't guided me back on track.' She lowered her eyes and smiled. 'We adored each other.' She paused and quietly reminisced.

'What happened?' he asked.

Shelly swallowed hard. 'There was an accident. A terrible accident that happened abroad. I lied to my dad, he thought I was on a school trip. We went to a Greek island called Paros. David was going to teach me to dive. I hadn't even used a snorkel before. I

336

was so excited, mostly because I felt I'd grown up and that some-body loved me. You know how it is? I thought I was invincible. I guess it's the same for all teenagers.'

DJ nodded. 'I've been there.'

'Where, Paros?'

'No, believing I'm invincible. Just growing out of it; realising I don't know everything and if I don't swot like hell, I won't get my degree.'

Shelly smiled sympathetically. 'God, it's so hard, isn't it? Everyone reaches that point when it's tempting to throw the towel in, DJ, but believe me, it's worth the slog in the end.'

'Sometimes, the pressure's astronomical, and I'm convinced I'll fail my finals. It's easy to understand why people drop out. I mean, it sounds so wimpy, but hell, nobody knows . . .'

'*I* know. I did it, and you're my son. I'm damned sure you can do it too. I'm sure you'll be fine come exam time. But you know what? If you fail, it's no big deal. You can do it again. Don't beat yourself up over it, just do your best.'

'Thanks.'

Her thoughts spooled back to that Greek holiday. 'I told you about the bracelet, didn't I? The one my mother was going to collect when she was hit by the car.'

He nodded. 'You did.'

'Well, your dad, his friend Simon, and I stayed in the most beautiful little village in the world, Naoussa, on the island of Paros.' She realised she was holding her wrist. 'Although that bracelet had taken my mother from me, it sort of brought your father to me as well. How could I know it would take him away too?'

The dangerous point of the story loomed. She strengthened herself by breathing steadily, staring at the table. Everything seemed to be linked in a way that she didn't understand. Sometimes, she felt if she could only comprehend why it all happened to her, then the pain would go away. After a moment she found she could speak again.

'I never took the bracelet off, even slept and bathed with it on. It was a solid hoop and a real struggle to get over my hand. I don't know if it was the tanning oil I'd slathered on or the cool water, or a combination of both, but the bracelet slipped off while your father was teaching me to snorkel, on that first day.' With her hand on her chest, she took a deep breath and let it out slowly. 'Sorry, it's hard to say, even after twenty years.'

'Take your time. We can leave it for now if it's too difficult.'

'No, I want to tell you before I go. I was floating on the surface with my face in the water, proud of myself for learning to breathe with the snorkel. It was a bit scary at first, but I guess that's the same for everyone.' DJ nodded. She smiled, uplifted that he understood. 'Anyway, your father dived to the seabed and picked a little white seashell off the bottom. He held it up. I stretched my arm down to take it, but as I did, the bracelet slipped off and fell right in front of his face. He tried to grab it but missed. I couldn't believe my precious bracelet had come off. We were snorkelling over a sunken rowboat. The water was unbelievably clear, and the boat must have recently gone down because it still had a great bundle of fishing net in it, and I could see the oars in the bottom. It's difficult to judge, but I guess the water was only around two and a half or three metres deep there, but I hadn't learned to dive yet. I saw where the bracelet went and begged David to get it for me. I was wearing my mask, so I could see him clearly. He was showing off, and I was laughing inside.' She paused, felt the danger of tears pricking again. This was the first time she had recounted those events for almost twenty years and she remembered how difficult it was then. The police, the vice-consulate, her father, the social workers, they had all insisted she go over the tragedy again and again. Saying the words was like ripping open old injuries.

'That was our last joyous moment together. Our very final spark of happiness, locked in my chest forever.' She didn't have to close her eyes to see him, his face turned up towards her, laughter in his eyes.

She put her elbow on the table and her hand over her mouth. 'As he reached for the bracelet, it seemed to scud along just out of his reach. He kicked his fins hard and made a grab for it, but his forward momentum disturbed the fishing net and it mushroomed up like an atomic explosion. His eyes were fixed on the bottom, looking for my bracelet, so he didn't realise and . . . swam . . . right under it.' She gasped. 'Sorry.' She held her hand up in a halting gesture – to stop DJ speaking – then she took some deep breaths. 'When he turned to swim up, he got tangled in it. I could see . . .' She had to stop again. 'Sorry, do you think you could get us another coffee?'

He nodded and without speaking, took their mugs for a refill. By the time he came back she had composed herself.

'He was tangled in the net and couldn't come to the surface for air because, they discovered later, there was also an anchor and chain in the bottom of the boat. I tried to dive down to him but I didn't know how and kept bobbing up. I just . . . touched . . . his fingertips.' She sobbed, stiffened her jaw, and struggled again to steady. 'Excuse me.' After a gulp of coffee, she bit her knuckle until it hurt so much she feared she would draw blood. 'I spat out my snorkel and screamed and screamed for help.

'Your father's friend, Simon, and two water-sports guys were on the quayside. They jumped on a couple of jet skis but by the time they got to us, cut David free and got him back to land . . . Oh, God.' Shelly hiccuped with grief. 'Sorry,' she said. 'Difficult to . . . you know.' She took a shuddering breath. 'I was only sixteen, and two months later, I discovered I was pregnant with you.' She reached forward and touched his hand, smiling into his face. 'It was only the night before the accident that we, you know, for the first time. David was my only boyfriend, you understand?' She managed to flatten a rising sob, relieved now that the ordeal of telling him was over. 'You're his double.'

They sat in silence for a while, then DJ said, 'What about my father's parents?'

'David told me his mother had lost a battle against breast cancer ten years earlier, and his father had worked on the oil rigs. He was living in Scotland somewhere but I never met him and had no way to contact him. David and his father weren't the best of friends. Both parents liked a drink by all accounts, and he'd had a rough childhood. Anyway, he'd left home and they'd lost touch. The British Consulate in Greece took care of everything; getting David back to Britain and making all the arrangements . . . you know. Wonderful people!'

She glanced at her lap where the napkin that came with her coffee was in shreds. 'Tsk! Silly me.'

'Thanks for telling me all this. I can understand why you were reluctant. It can't have been easy.'

'There's more, but time's going by and I ought to go through to Departures. Give my love to Dad. Feel free to take my room. Have a nice time.'

'You too.'

They both stood, then Shelly slung her arms around him and hugged. 'Thanks for bringing me in.'

'Safe journey, Mum.' They smiled at each other, hiding the heartache of lost years, and still enjoying the novelty of their new-found relationship.

CHAPTER 38
GERTIE

Greece, 1917.

THIS WAS IT. THE ONLY reason they would want us *both* back in England would be to take part in an inquiry related to the sinking of the *Britannic*.

Walking along the main road towards HMS *Gabriel*, it occurred to me that, as far as I knew, the only person who survived Lifeboat 1, and therefore knew it was I that opened the portholes, was Corporal Perkins. Before we left for the port, I hurried to the mail room and explained I wouldn't be distributing the letters and parcels anymore.

There were letters from home for me and Josephine, so I gathered them and hurried to catch up. With our pillow-bags slung over our shoulders, we marched boldly towards the port. Several battleships were moored to the quayside, and many more were anchored out in the bay. We were ten minutes early arriving at the ship, so we sat on the quayside and read our post before boarding. My letter was from Victoria Pimlet, a fellow VAD I'd met while training. I hadn't seen her since the evening before the sinking and feared she had gone down with the first lifeboat. Therefore I was shocked to get a letter from her, which told me of events that affected the *Britannic* survivors.

Dear Gertie,

I hope this letter reaches you, as nobody seems to know where you are. All the medical staff, and the wounded, picked up by the battleships stayed in Athens until 27 November. We were ordered to write an account of the sinking. I was lucky to survive Lifeboat 1 after being pulled under by the propeller and hit on my head. The doctor said my long hair saved me, because it was braided and piled up, then pinned down by my veil. I came up in the turbulence, and some firemen rescued me. I still get headaches, but I am alive. Athens was amazing. We saw all the ancient sites then we worked in the Russian hospital in Piraeus. Eventually, they shipped us home. We docked at Southampton on Boxing Day. How happy we were to get off that ship!

I went to see your mother to see if they had heard from you. They made me terrifically welcome. They thought you had drowned and were pleased to get your telegram.

I met the very dapper Corporal Perkins from our ward. He's here now, walking very well with his new leg and flirting with everyone in his gentlemanly way.

An investigation into the loss of the Britannic took place on the flagship, Duncan, on 24 November, just before we left for Malta. Apparently, they couldn't get all the survivors together for the inquiry. More than thirty people died, but God knows how many were injured, at least twice as many. They say the Britannic hit a mine, but sank before reaching land because someone went against orders and opened the portholes on E deck. Can you believe that? Our own ward, Gertie!

I'm shocked, but I can't remember who was on duty when we went to our breakfast meeting, can you? There's talk they should *be hanged, not only because of the thirty killed, and the many injured, but also for the thousands that will die on Lemnos for lack of transport back home.*

I could not get my breath, and leaned against the harbour wall.

'Trouble?' Josephine asked. 'Your parents?'

I shook my head, unable to speak.

'It can't be that bad, Gertie, tell me,' she said quite matter-of-factly. 'Do you have bad news from home?'

'Swear you'll never tell?'

She nodded.

'It was me that opened the portholes!'

'You! Dear Jesus in Heaven, you?' She stared at me. 'You shouldn't have told me. Now what am I supposed to do? If they ask me questions, I can't lie.'

'Do you think they'll hang me? Perkins and the other patients bullied me – over and over – to open them for ten minutes, to let the bedpan stink out. Ward sister told me to use my initiative, you see; so in the end I did.' I tumbled on. 'I should never have lied about my age, but with my poor sister and brother both dead because of the war, I wanted to fight for England on their behalf, do you understand? Now I'm so terribly sorry and I don't know which way to turn.'

'Stop! You lied about your age, and nobody checked? Shame on them.'

I shook my head. 'I'd done really well in training, Matron said so. How was I to know we'd hit a mine or a torpedo a few minutes after I'd opened the portholes?'

'So how old are you?'

'Eighteen. Nearly nineteen.'

'Eighteen, and you've had people's lives in your hands, and taken part in the surgery? Oh, my dear lord!'

'The only people that know it was me, as far as I can guess, are you and Perkins, and I believe he's forgotten. I think he lost part of his memory when he was hit on the head.'

Now I'd made matters worse. How could I stop Josephine telling the inquiry panel it was me?

*　*　*

We boarded the *Gabriel* and proceeded to our quarters, a small cabin with four bunks, but thankfully we had the place to ourselves.

Josephine was silent, clearly deep in thought, while we organised our belongings. An orderly arrived with two fresh nurse's uniforms.

'Leave your clothes on the floor and I'll collect them while you eat and get them laundered for morning,' he said, avoiding our eyes. 'The Captain requests your company at dinner. I'll be here to escort you just before twenty hundred hours, ladies.'

'For goodness' sake, don't mention the portholes, the *Britannic*, or anything,' Josephine said with a tremble of panic in her voice. 'In fact, make yourself forget everything that happened before the dolphin, all right? Then you have a solid answer when you're interrogated. From this moment, I am also going to forget you ever told me. Do you understand?'

'Interrogated? Do you think they'll apply the thumbscrews or give me electric shock treatment to make me talk?' Sweat prickled my forehead. 'I am *not* a brave person, Josephine. Just the suggestion of pain and I'll be a quivering idiot with a mouth that won't shut.'

345

'Just stop that nonsense right now! You, Gertie, are a very brave person, one of the bravest I know! You have dealt with trauma and terrible injuries. You've stitched up horrific wounds, walked across a room with an amputated leg in your arms, soothed dying men, and calmed the hysterical. Don't tell me you can't cope with this! The past can't be changed. Now let's get on with our lives and try to make the world a better place for the future.'

I threw my arms around her neck as if she were my very own Sissy. 'Thank you, Josephine. I'm sorry I told you, but it's been terribly lonely keeping it inside. I would confess, but my poor parents, my father's a doctor, they would have a terrible time of it. I'm filled with remorse, I deserve to be punished . . . but my parents don't. This is not their fault.'

'Like I said, we can't change the past, so let's forget it now, and promise me you'll *never* mention it again.'

'I'll try my best.'

'That's not good enough. I repeat myself: promise me you'll *never* mention it again.'

'I promise.'

'Good. Let's see what our captain says this evening. You could practise looking gay and carefree because you're going home and have nothing to worry about. That's what they would expect from us mere women.'

*   *   *

There was nothing remarkable about eating at the Captain's table, except we had slightly better food, and a wonderful jam suet pudding. We learned that the ship would call at Syros to fill her water tanks. When Josephine and I retired, we enjoyed

346

simple pleasures; to lie on clean sheets, and to wear clean undergarments.

I wondered again about what might happen in England. How could I answer questions convincingly without lying? I had done a terrible wrong, too terrible to contemplate, and because of it, many people had died. Should I confess, lie, run away? Or claim amnesia as Josephine insisted.

My thoughts went to the island of Syros. Would Manno arrive with the mail boat from Kea while we were there? I closed my eyes and pressed my hand against my chest, how I longed to be in his arms. All my worries disappeared when I thought about Manno and the tenderness of his kiss.

I woke in my cabin at dawn, contented, having fallen asleep with a full belly for a change. Low sunlight streamed through our porthole and I heard much louder clangs and the clattering of sailors going about their jobs. This made me want to investigate on deck. We washed and dressed quickly, enjoying the luxury of warm water and clean clothes. Up top, we discovered the ship was approaching Ermoupoli, the capital of Syros, and I remembered Manno and my first kiss on the quayside.

A pale sun, huge on the horizon, floated above the mist-covered sea filling the sky with shades of orange and pink, then every colour of the rainbow mingled and merged, radiating the hope and fresh start that came with a new day. Great cathedrals topped the hills of Syros, overcrowded with colourful, cubed buildings that appeared like a jigsaw tipped onto a table. Yet, as the light increased, parts of the vista made sense and fell into place, gathering its surroundings, until the scene was a complete picture. Just as I remembered it. The mountains behind the island's capital were last to reveal themselves from the grey dawn. In a rising glow of tangerine light, the barren mastiffs made a perfect backdrop for the resplendent city. The sky had poured her tints and hues onto the buildings, and became herself nothing but a sheet of bright blue above the kaleidoscope of coloured dwellings and churches. Soon, all was as flamboyant as it should be in a proper Greek landscape.

'We're waiting for the next water tanker,' our orderly, who had introduced himself as 'Michael but Mike's fine so it is', in an Irish accent. 'These Greeks have a terrible water shortage, so they do. The tankers'll come and fill the ships with drinking water, so they will.'

Josephine and I proceeded to the mess for an amazing breakfast that consisted of great wedges of nutty brown bread sprinkled with rich, dark green olive oil and crunchy sea salt, then plain biscuits and solid blackcurrant jam. Strong, sweet tea and a glass of watered-down lime juice accompanied the meal.

'That was so good,' I said, rubbing my full stomach.

'So it was,' Josephine added, and we both laughed.

The ship's Matron, was a stick-insect with gaunt features, a whispery voice, and hair pulled into a long, grey-streaked bunch more reminiscent of an *old nag* than a *pony* tail. She found us in the dining room. 'Ah, here you are. As you're both experienced, from tomorrow you'll work on wards two and three – that's intensive care – until we dock in Southampton.'

We both nodded. 'Thank you, Matron.'

'However, the ship won't be leaving until after dark, nurses, so you're permitted to go ashore. Make the most of a last day of freedom, but be sure you're back on board by eight hundred hours.' She walked away, but then turned sharply. 'Oh, and if you find any *loukoumi*, I'm very partial.' She flashed long, narrow tobacco-stained teeth in the semblance of a smile, then disappeared in a flurry of nurses.

I blinked at Josephine, she shrugged. 'What's *loukoumi*?' I asked.

'Turkish delight,' she said quietly.

'Why don't they just say "Turkish delight"?'

'Shhh. Keep your voice down! You're not allowed to use the word' – at that point she resorted to miming *Turkish* – 'in this country unless you want your throat cut. They're arch enemies.'

'But that seems completely mad when they're neighbours; why?'

Josephine looked over each shoulder dramatically. 'I'm not saying. Not too sure, perhaps because they're on opposite sides. There's even an issue around who invented "Turkish" delight. Apparently, it should be called Greek delight. Anyway, if we see some *loukoumi* we should buy it for Rapunzel there. Get on her good side so we're not allocated dysentery duty or the syphilis ward.' She nodded towards the group of nurses that had surrounded Matron.

'Syphilis ward?'

Josephine glanced at me and rolled her eyes. 'Not now, Gertie.'

* * *

The cassette tape is nearly at its end, dear listener, but I want you to know that I'm telling you these things in the hope you're hearing them long after my death. I pray you'll appreciate my feelings, not judge me, and know that through all my adventures I was always doing my best for my departed siblings, my beloved parents, and my country. However, love has a mind of its own, and I am going to be frank. Cupid may or may not have pierced your heart with his mischievous arrow by the time you listen to these meanderings. I want to be completely honest, and will leave nothing out. So, listen on if you dare, and perhaps you'll understand.

CHAPTER 39
SHELLY

Greece, present day.

FOUR HOURS LATER, SHELLY STEPPED outside Athens airport into the warm sunny day. So much had happened since the last time she'd stood outside this airport. 'I'm here, Harry,' she spoke softly into her phone. 'I'll be leaving for Kea on the seven o'clock ferry; can't wait to see you.'

'The same here,' he said. A pause while they both enjoyed the moment. 'How do you feel about going straight to the Beach Taverna for a light dinner?' Harry asked, his heavy accent almost growled the words.

'Gorgeous man with hungry woman, sunny Greek island, good food at the edge of the sea, amazing sunset?' She almost giggled, intoxicated by happiness. 'Now let me think . . . mmm, yes, it sounds quite perfect.'

There was a pause and she knew he was grinning too. 'Then I'll meet you off the ferry, we'll go to Popi's to eat, drop your cases off, then take it from there.' The warmth of all he promised, and everything that was left unsaid, resonated in his voice.

'Lovely, I can't wait.' She sighed into the phone. 'See you later.' She ended the call, turned her face towards the sun and closed her eyes.

When she arrived on the quayside, he was there, and slipped his arm around her waist. She wanted to kiss him, but knew such public behaviour was frowned upon in Greece, and the restriction only heightened her excitement. He turned his face to hers as they walked.

'You didn't forget me then?' he asked.

'How could I, silly?' They stopped for a moment, peering into each other's eyes, the moment so intense she held her breath.

'Let's drop your bag off on the way to the taverna ... and perhaps you want to freshen up before we eat?'

'Dropping the bags off sounds good. I managed to freshen up in Athens airport. There's a shower and such in the priority lounge.' There was an urgency between them, trying to remain polite, both desperate to be in each other's arms.

'May I?' he said, the moment they stepped inside her room. He kissed her, leaning his body towards hers, the moment heavy with building passion.

'Stop now,' she whispered. 'We must go and eat.' She wanted him so badly.

At the taverna table, his leg pressed against hers. Her hand slid across the table, the tip of her middle finger connecting with his.

His mouth fell open slightly as he smiled. 'Wine?' he asked.

'Oh, yes.'

They ate, hardly looking at the food, their eyes meeting in a sensual dance. Dawn would come too soon.

*　*　*

She woke before daylight, lying curled against his body in the dark, listening to the sound of the sea. Now she was exactly where she wanted to be. Later, he would introduce her to the *Britannic*'s dive team. Although there was no chance of diving

352

ith them, he had secured her a place on the dive boat. Shelly would assist Elias, Harry's son. Harry's phone-alarm beeped. He stirred, slung an arm across and turned it off without opening his eyes. 'Come on,' he mumbled. 'Pull some clothes on, your turtles are hatching.'

'You're kidding?'

'No, chop-chop.'

From the sound of his voice, she feared he would go back to sleep. She leapt out of bed and turned the big light on.

Harry's face scrunched. 'Evil woman.'

She laughed, pure joy exploding inside her chest as she slung her camera around her neck. Five minutes later, they bustled out of the door and headed for the beach across the road. Harry handed her a torch. 'It's infrared. No need to worry about it disorientating the turtles. They won't see it.'

She smiled at him, resisting the urge to say, *I know*.

'I don't want to walk along the sand in case we step on other nests. Let's walk along the water's edge,' she suggested. They slipped their shoes off, left them on the pavement, then strolled, side by side in the shallows until they came to the right spot. 'It's here, Harry,' she whispered.

They stopped and shone their red torchlight onto the sand. 'I don't see any movement, perhaps it's still too warm.'

'Ah, you know everything about them, yes?' Harry said.

'I know they'll only emerge when the sand's cool enough down there. The heat was still coming up from the tarmac when I got off the ferry, so it must have been a very hot day. Let's go further along, perhaps there are others.'

He nodded, his hand taking hold of hers.

Apart from an irregular row of tamarisk trees and a couple of varnished council benches, the beach was empty and the

port completely quiet. Only the sound of wavelets lapping th
shoreline interrupted the silence. Their eyes had adjusted t
the dark. She looked up towards the horizon, but avoided star
ing at the lighthouse that pulsed, two flashes every six seconds
She didn't want to lose her night-vision. They saw no othe
sign of an emerging clutch and turned back. Then he stopped
pulled her against him, her camera hard between their chests
A cockerel, sensing the approach of dawn, crowed somewher
behind the village.

'Excuse me,' she whispered, moving her camera around t
the side. He pulled her back into his arms and she felt his bod
harden against her.

'I'm so glad you're here,' he whispered. 'I feel as though I'v
been waiting for you all my life. Does that sound crazy?'

She smiled, staring into the darkness, positively fizzing wit
happiness. Being wanted was so uplifting, and at the same tim
empowering.

Movement near their feet caught her attention. 'Harry, th
ground's boiling. Look,' she whispered urgently, breaking awa
from his embrace.

They both stared as a creature, resembling a tiny piecrust wit
flippers, broke through the sand. Flapping fins that seemed
little oversized, it trundled and bumped towards the waterlin
like a clockwork toy. Seconds later, dozens of miniature turtle
scrabbled up through the sand, setting their sights on the Aegea
waterline.

'Oh, isn't that the most magical thing you've ever seen?' Shell
stared at the scene. 'Excuse me. I have to video this,' she whis
pered while ramping up her camera's setting and turning th
program to video. 'Let's get behind them, in case any head fo
the street.' Seeing the event through the camera made it eve

more exciting because later, she could share the moment with the special people in her life.

* * *

Back at her room, she curled her body around Harry's. Although content, she could not sleep. Too much had happened in the last twenty-four hours. She lay in the dark, eyes wide open, remembering DJ at the airport, Harry at the port, the turtles on the beach, then Gran Gertie came to mind. This was how she must have felt sitting on the old chest against the harbour wall; simply overwhelmed by it all.

After breakfast, Shelly went out with several of the dive team, including Harry and his eldest son, Elias, in the sea research boat.

'What are we doing today?' Shelly asked as they rounded the lighthouse.

'We'll detect and mark the wreck,' Harry replied.

She stood next to him and studied the SONAR screen. Soon, the echo-sounder displayed a steady depth of a hundred and seventeen metres. 'It's very consistent now, what are we picking up?'

'The sandy bottom. We should be about ... ah, yes! Here we are now, a reading of eighty-six metres. We're over HMHS *Britannic* right at this moment.'

Shelly's heart skipped. 'How thrilling!' She imagined a frightened, eighteen-year-old Gertie in her drenched nurse's uniform with the torn apron, and Corporal Perkins's head resting in her lap as they bobbed about in the overcrowded lifeboat.

'We'll drop a line to read the strength of the current at various depths,' Harry was saying as Shelly pulled herself back to now.

'When that's established, we'll drop an anchor line to the actual wreck and mark it with a buoy to warn passing shipping we have divers down. The Kea Channel's a busy enough shipping lane. We must work with the local fishermen too. It's their main fishing territory and they've had to abandon it for less prolific fisheries while we prepare for tomorrow. We'll employ as many of them as we can while the dive's on.'

'What can they do to help?'

'Supply us with over-priced fish to start with.'

Shelly laughed. 'Public relations, hey? It's odd to think my great-grandmother almost drowned, and was pulled back into a lifeboat right here, over a hundred years ago. And the ship she worked on is below us right now.'

He read the excitement in her eyes. 'For the decompression stops on the divers' return, we're going to anchor a shot line with several large buoys that will hold vertically in the strong current.'

'This is back-up for the diving bell?' He nodded. She went on. 'The boat's extraordinarily well equipped, is it yours?'

Harry made a 'tsk' and raised his chin, the Greek expression for 'No'. 'It belongs to Oxford University. A couple of their graduates are on the team. Familiarise yourself with everything aboard, Elias gets impatient when things aren't going his way.'

Shelly nodded. 'Will do.' Her body was almost levitating with happiness. 'I'll be meticulous. Certified safety officer, remember.'

He nodded, eyes dark, narrowed, hot.

'You're so bad, Harry. Don't look at me like that. I need to concentrate.'

'Me too.' He grinned, leaned in and kissed her neck. 'But you make it hard.'

'Get a room, you two,' Elias muttered, scowling at them as he approached the console. 'We need to be single-minded today. Can't afford mistakes, right?'

* * *

Harry was busy with one of the technicians, so Shelly started working through her safety checklist.

'What are you doing?' Elias demanded. 'Please, I've asked you not to touch the equipment!'

She blinked at him, shocked by his aggression. 'I'm just checking battery life on the sea-scooters.'

'They were checked yesterday.'

'Well, I'm sorry to tell you, this one's almost empty.'

'What?' Elias stormed over.

Harry was alerted by his son's raised voice. 'Must be faulty. Well done, Shelly.'

She held her breath and counted five. 'Can't have too much checking when people's lives are at stake. Also, one of the rebreather batteries has a fully-charged tag, but appears to be almost flat this morning.'

'This is serious.' Harry glanced at Elias this time. 'Could you go over everything?'

'Of course! Don't I always, Papa?'

Shelly put in, 'There's possibly a simple explanation. Shall I check the cylinders?'

'Yes, let's double check everything,' Harry answered.

Shelly considered a change of subject. 'Can I ask, what's the dive for?'

'Ah, it's quite straightforward. Eco-science research, concerning pollution; and due to the latest equipment, they're

357

allowed to go inside and investigate the cause of the sinking for the first time.'

'After so long! That's exciting. Look, I know there's a meeting with the team this evening, but I'd like an idea of the dive procedure in advance, if possible, Harry. They've been here for a week already, going through the process. I want to make sure I'm up to the plate, so to speak.'

Harry turned to his son. 'Elias, go through tomorrow with Shelly, will you?'

'Me? I've got enough to do. Where's Petros, still in bed?'

'Really,' Shelly said in a calming voice. 'If it's inconvenient, there's no need. I'll be at the meeting tonight anyway, and I did read the entire Standard Operating Procedure online, all seventy pages of it. Sorry I asked, it was thoughtless of me considering the pressure you're under.'

Elias glared at her. 'Why don't you just concentrate on your own job, and also – as you've got your SSO certificate, you can also assist the meet's safety procedure officer, Brian Blake, make sure he's on the ball tomorrow. OK? Is that important enough for you?'

'Elias, that's out of order!' Harry said.

'Well, you should take care of your own girlfriends, Papa!'

'Enough!' Harry shouted.

Shelly understood. Elias feared he was losing his father to a woman and, to be loyal to his mother, he had to object.

'Look, I'm assisting you, Elias. Just tell me what you want me to do. I'm not here to score points or start a fight between you and your father, all right? I'm sorry I seem to have offended you in some way.'

Petulant little bastard.

CHAPTER 40
GERTIE

Returning to Syros, 1917.

LIKE ANY EIGHTEEN-YEAR-OLD, my heart roared for romance, and I longed for love. How I had longed for Manno in those dark hours on Lemnos.

I had written to him so many times, but he never answered. Nevertheless, his silence did nothing to dampen my ardour. This tormenting desire grew stronger each night! My love for Manno never wavered, but passion kept it company now and I knew I would not be able to resist the fisherman's amorous advances. In fact, I ached for them. My longing to lay in his arms became almost unbearable. After all, once I got back to England they might throw me into jail, or worse.

When I left Josephine to saunter along the quayside, enjoying the tranquillity and the safety of solid ground, I was not thinking of the beauty of Syros or my reputation. Feverish with desire for Manno, I wandered along with my daydreams, and turned to look out to sea. There he was, drifting across the flat water in the bay as if in a dream. He had turned off the engine and stood in the centre of the boat, facing the front, his arms held out from his sides. With an extraordinarily long pair of oars, he rowed forward.

I couldn't help myself! Bobbing up and down on my toes, I displayed my excitement by waving my hands above my head. I wanted him to know how I felt. Desire shimmered through my body. I would give myself to him and he would make love to me. I would allow it because there may not be another chance. If I had to spend the rest of my life in prison . . . or worse, at least let me have this day. Surely fate had thrown us together for a reason?

His sturdy wooden boat approached the quayside. My breath burned, my lips longing to press against his. I stood dangerously near the edge of the quay and waved. As soon as he could, my beautiful Manno leapt ashore, shouted a few words to his father, and hurried me away to the quietness of the backstreets.

'You came back to me!' he said incredulously. 'I love you, *koukla mou!*'

'I only have a few hours, Manno,' I whispered. 'Kiss me!'

He rose up above me, one hand behind my head, pressing me towards his mouth, his other hand against my derrière, pushing my hips against his. Oh, the thrills that raced through me. I wanted him so badly.

'Please, Manno, I think I'm falling in love with you,' I whispered.

'Come to my house?' he said in an urgent, questioning voice. 'We will be alone there.' Without waiting for an answer, he took my hand and pulled me up narrow, cobbled streets and steep steps. We arrived at a stone building with pale-blue louvre shutters and an arched door. He pushed it open, then dropped a hefty plank across the receivers on the inside. No one could enter. He started to pull the ties of my white apron, and I reciprocated, untying the kerchief around his neck. By the time we arrived at the huge, wall-to-wall bed, we were both almost naked.

'*Panagia mou!* I love you. I want to marry you!' Manno's face was close to mine. He slipped his hand inside my chemise

360

and stroked my bare skin. Oh, the thrill! I had dreamt of this moment so many times.

'I've never done this before, Manno.'

'God and all the saints!' he cried in a fit of passion.

I pulled off my black stockings and dropped my white, broderie anglaise combinations. The garment fell around my feet and for a moment, standing before him completely naked, I felt lost and embarrassed in the heat of a blush.

'I worship you with all my heart and soul,' he whispered. Staring at my body, he muttered something in Greek as he crossed himself, then he kissed me fervently and pulled me against him. In that moment, I knew he had done all this before with other women. To be honest, I was glad, being more than a little nervous about the size of his . . . erm . . . love.

'Be gentle with me, Manno. Truly, it's my very first time,' I whispered, too tender, too trustful, too much a woman to resist the handsome man who charmed me into longing for him. And I did, I wanted him so badly, nothing – not even the pain of losing my virginity – would stop me. His kisses were tentative at first, but my response left no question and as he understood that, he groaned into my mouth.

'You say what you like, *agapi*, you tell me if you want me to stop and I stop, yes?'

I was so shy, blushing and blinking like the virgin I was.

And so our first lovemaking began, united for the first time on an inconspicuous Tuesday morning in the deep shade of a little stone house in Syros. Both thrilled and afraid, and aching with longing, we made love all through the day. I could not get enough of him, nor him me. The experience was new to me of course, and I wasn't sure what I was doing; but Manno appeared more experienced. Crazy for more sensations, feasting on each other, deliriously happy, singing silently with Aphrodite's pleasures, until we were both desperate to go further than we had dared venture before.

Inevitably, at the point of no return, he growled into my ear and thrust passionately and desperately onward. I experienced a painful, stinging, but Manno's reaction was to cry my name so loudly I feared all of Syros heard.

'You are mine, *agapi*! Mine, my love!'

His words were overwhelming, primitive, yet loving; like balm to my discomfort. By late afternoon, we made love for the third and last time, I know I called out, but with no notion of what words. My body exploded with extraordinary violence after what started with a gentle feeling of perfect love. Waves of pleasure had built up to a fire and ice fit of uncontrollable passion. Closer, harder, stronger waves enveloped me until, God knows, I really do believe I lost consciousness in my euphoria. Then I was in his arms, tears of joy on my face, him rocking me, panting as he stroked my hair and muttered thanks to God and endearments to me in Greek and English.

'I have fallen in love with you,' I whispered.

'Stay, *agapi mou*! Stay, my love! Don't go back to the ship, stay and marry me and live here, on my island!'

I looked around, taking in my surroundings properly, for the first time after our bold and heated intrusion. The cottage was much the same as *Yiayá*'s on the island of Kea.

He mistook my interest in the cottage for disapproval. 'No, not here exactly,' he said. 'I will build you a house. A fine house with many rooms, on the side of the hill. I hear from my cousin in England you like to have many rooms. I have land, much land, all over the island my family have plenty land, *agapi*. You

362

tell me what you want, yes, I build it. I am a very fine builder. Stay, and we will marry, *agapi*!'

I blushed deeply. I had given myself to him, and he had begged me to marry him. There was justice in the situation. 'I can't. There is a war, I must help the sick and the wounded. It's my destiny, I swore an oath that I would do it for my brother and sister.'

'You are an angel. Where are they, your brother and sister? I will talk to them.' He lifted my chin and kissed me softly.

'No, you don't understand. They both died.'

'Ah, is OK then. They don't know what you are doing. You will be my wife.'

'Manno! What a terrible thing to say! Anyway, I hear talk that Greece is joining the conflict any day now, so I am sure I will be back in your country soon, Manno, but if not, swear you will come to find me in Dover.' Perhaps I would be locked in some English prison, my punishment for costing the British government thousands of pounds, perhaps even millions. We were at war, and I had caused the loss of their best ship and destroyed the lives of so many of our young men.

'I will come for you,' Manno cried dramatically. 'If I must sail my boat all the way to England, I give you my word: I will come to get you. Now tell me you love me. You are mine, do you understand, mine!'

As I climbed off the bed to dress, I saw a little blood on the sheet. 'Oh, Manno! I must wash that off before it dries, please, bring me some water.'

'No, *agapi*, no. It must stay. My father will be proud, he will hang the sheet out for all to see. In the *kafenio* they will say, see, Manno's wife was an English virgin! He is a lucky man!'

My face turned scarlet as the stain. I couldn't speak. What an awful idea! He must have read the horror on my face. 'Do not worry,' he said. 'It is something to be proud of. In the eyes of my family, it means we are married already.'

I had to get away, back on the ship. Return to my role as a nurse before I came face to face with Manno's father and died of embarrassment.

'Wait, wait!' Manno cried as I started to climb from the bed. 'Such an important occasion.' He opened a chest in the corner of the room and flung heaps of linen to one side, then he came to a wooden box which he placed on the table. Then he pulled a chair under the oil lamp that hung from the ceiling and, still naked, stood on it.

Oh, my!

I took the opportunity to admire his physique. He could have modelled for Michelangelo, except for that artist's understatement of David's manly attributes. Such a majestically round bottom, and his abdomen – solid ridges like Mrs Cooper's washboard. How I wished I had my sketchbook. He thrust his fingertips into the tray under the oil lamp and was clearly searching for something. Then he caught my look, peered down at his own body and grinned. 'You want me to come back to bed?'

'No!' I cried, blushing and looking away.

'Ah, I found it,' he said, finally producing a little gold key. 'My mother, she hide it here.'

Conscious of the time, I started to dress quickly while I watched him. Then I removed the plank that kept the door closed. He unlocked the little box and rummaged around. I heard him make a little, 'Ah, perfect!' while I was pulling my shoes on. He reached for my hand and pulled me up. 'Close your eyes,' he said, I did, and felt him slide something cold and lumpy onto my ring finger. Before I could see what it was, the door burst open, knocking me sideways. Manno backed up. A rotund

364

woman in heavy black skirts and scarf, brandishing a besom, set about walloping poor naked Manno. She screeched at the top of her voice while pointing to the jewellery box on the table. Unnoticed, I slipped out and ran down to the port as fast as I could, not slowing until I was up the ramp and safely on the ship.

I hurried around the deck until I reached the side furthest from the quay, hidden from the port. There, I examined the ring, a silver dolphin that curled itself around my finger.

'Hello, Delphi,' I whispered. 'You precious creature of the sea.'

CHAPTER 41
SHELLY

Greece, present day.

LATE AFTERNOON, SHELLY IRONED HER white linen pants and a matching shirt. Apart from a little mascara and lip gloss, she abandoned the idea of make-up, but then fumbled with buttons and smudged her eye make-up while fretting about Elias's remark. He'd been moody and begrudging all day and she hoped he wasn't going to try and embarrass her in front of the dive team, though she wouldn't put it past him. Had she understood correctly, that Harry had an endless string of girlfriends? The man was, after all, good-looking and surrounded by beautiful, half-naked women for much of the year. She would be naïve to think he lived like a hermit. Also, she wondered if Elias was perhaps a little jealous of her receiving most of Harry's attention.

At the dive centre, she found a long trestle outside the building, overlooking the sea. Petros was setting out thirty places with notebooks, pencils, upturned plastic glasses and bottles of water.

She found Harry inside, on his tablet and knew better than to speak to him.

Outside again, she noticed a place set with a label bearing her name. Feeling Petros's eyes on her, she looked up and gave him a smile. 'Thank you, Petros. It feels good to be an official part of the team.'

'According to my father, you've got more qualifications than several of the main dive team.'

Shelly felt him on her side, unlike his brother. She pulled out a chair and lifted a notebook and pen from her bag. The first papers were about the dedicated commercial dive support vessel; DSV for short. A solid hulk of ship that would show up well on any ship's radar, which was important as they were diving in a busy shipping lane. She started memorising the vessel's layout.

Once Shelly had the layout of the ship firmly ingrained in her mind, she found a sheet detailing the medical facilities on board. Then, she went through a 'worst case scenario' exercise in her head. Her local paramedic leader in Dover had given her the number of the Air Sea Rescue team nearest to the island of Kea, so she made contact and introduced herself and confirmed that they knew about the dive. Engrossed in making notes, she hadn't realised some of the dive team had arrived and felt herself blush when she looked up to see half a dozen men watching her.

Harry came out of the dive shop and introduced the team as they arrived, twenty-four men and five women besides herself covered every aspect of the dive, including technicians, boat crews, and dive management teams. They all settled down to the excitement of the pre-dive meet. For most of the team, using the bell for decompression was a new experience and, like Shelly, they had all studied the Standard Operating Procedure intensely. Several emergency scenarios were considered including oxygen toxicity, air embolism, and loss of consciousness. Everyone knew these were real dangers, and all those who would be in the water went through an unconscious diver drill. When Harry asked if there were any questions, Shelly raised her hand.

'I know it seems overly cautious, but as I'm assistant medical officer, can I have everyone's blood group, age, and any medical conditions before you leave this table?'

Elias piped up. 'Oh, come on! These are all very experienced divers, even those who are not going down. Don't you think you're being a bit over-dramatic?'

Shelly felt the heat of a blush rise in her cheeks and was determined not to look at Harry. 'No, I don't think you can be too careful. Don't forget, two very experienced divers have already lost their lives in the last decade here. Also, we must take into consideration this will be the first time we've all worked together, and accidents do happen.'

He tutted, took a beer from the fridge, and banged the edge of the cap against the edge of the table to remove it. Their eyes met and she saw nothing but hostility.

*   *   *

'That all went very well,' Harry said when they were alone. 'I must apologise for Elias, again. I'll have a word with him later. The problem is, he's very loyal and misses his mother, but won't admit it.'

Shelly shrugged as if it didn't matter, but in fact, she was still smarting.

An early night was the order, although sleep would be difficult with so much excitement bottled up for the next day.

'You must go home, Harry,' Shelly whispered, at the door of her apartment. 'We both need a good night's sleep.'

'Ten minutes?'

'Definitely not.' Her body temperature rose as he pulled her towards him. Dusk slipped toward night and the darkening shadows seemed to intensify the salty-spicy fragrance of him. Her heart beat faster as his face came inescapably close and for

368

a moment, urgent feelings of desire almost overpowered her resolve.

She longed to tell him how much she wanted him at that moment, but she resisted. People's lives depended on a clear head tomorrow.

His sweet mouth covered hers. Her hips pressed against his. She wanted him so fiercely that for a few seconds, she couldn't breathe – then she was panting. Her determination weakened; they were almost swaying in the erotic dance as old as mankind. 'Stop!' she said quietly. 'Not now . . . you really must go. We both need a good night's sleep. Tomorrow night, I promise we'll more than make up for this abstinence.'

'I'll hold you to that,' he growled, tugging her against his body one last time, before walking away.

'Tomorrow night, I swear you can hold me to anything you like.'

* * *

The next morning, everyone scuttled about doing their individual jobs. Little was said, no one wanted distractions, yet tension and excitement mounted with every passing minute. Although there had only been two deaths on the wreck in the past hundred and fifteen years, everyone feared another on their watch.

Divers would be on the *Britannic* for forty-five minutes with the remotely operated vehicle's camera watching and relaying its video to the dive boat monitors. The ROV would also keep check that the decompression bell did not shift in the current.

The ROV relayed images of the divers which were illuminated by the super powerful lights of two one-man submersibles. 'Look at that! The visibility's exceptional – it must be over a hundred feet!' Harry said. They all leaned closer to the monitors as one of the world's most magnificent liners loomed up out of the blue.

The *Britannic* lay on its starboard bow, facing south.

Shelly watched a pair of divers glide along the open and covered promenade deck. She recalled Gran Gertie's description of the area in a violent storm when a diver, swept off his feet by a giant wave, was saved by his lifeline. Difficult to imagine that squall while looking at the peaceful wonderland of the marine gardens, with colourful fish and delicate coral-encrusted railings. Powered by diver propulsion vehicles, the men moved effortlessly over the vessel towards the stern.

Like pairs of long-necked dinosaurs frozen in time, the gigantic lifeboat davits loomed above the divers. She imagined the lifeboats, each with seventy-five frightened passengers, swung out over the side of the ship, then lowered by the ropes. Would they see one? Or had all the lifeboats disintegrated? It was, after all, a hundred and five years since His Majesty's Hospital Ship *Britannic* went to the bottom of the Aegean Sea.

'I've never seen so much wildlife on a wreck,' Shelly said.

'That's because they're using rebreathers. There're no noisy bubbles to frighten the shoals of fish away. The only noise you hear is from the motors of the propulsion vehicles, which the divers use as little as possible, in order to save the batteries and also because they enjoy the silence.'

'Look at that. The divers apear so small against the propellers.' She remembered Gertie's description of the carnage they caused. 'Amazing marine life growing on the blades too. Saddle oysters, marine crustaceans, yellow sponges, they've all taken up residence, just how big are they, Harry?'

'The propellers? Twenty-four feet across and weighing thirty-eight tons,' Harry said. 'Can you imagine the noise, and the turbulence? They must have been a terrifying sight for those who saw them close up.'

'Look, we're seeing E deck from the outside. Those portholes are all open,' Elias said. 'Nobody was ever brought to justice for going against orders, were they?'

'What's going on there?' Shelly pointed to a screen where the dive camera was clearly deep inside the wreck. 'I thought there was only one video diver.'

'There is,' Harry said. 'What you're seeing is relay from an underwater drone. It's operated by the one-man sub. There are two. He's checking the watertight door between boiler rooms five and six. According to inquiry statements from the firemen, this door was jammed half open. Clearly, we can see it was all the way open. Nothing could have saved the ship with that open.'

'Even if the portholes had been closed, the *Britannic* was doomed when that door jammed,' the screen operator said.

Shelly wished her great-grandmother could have heard that statement.

The operator continued. 'Anyway, better she went down when she did. Just imagine if she'd got to Lemnos and embarked four thousand sick and wounded soldiers.'

'What's he talking about?' Shelly asked quietly.

'It's the minefield,' Harry replied. 'The full extent of it has only just come to light. Twelve mines were laid by German U-boat 75. The *Burdigala* caught the first mine, the *Britannic* caught the second, but if she hadn't, she almost certainly would have caught one on her return. The ship would be lower in the water, transporting four thousand casualties, many of whom had lost limbs and wouldn't have stood a chance. Add to them, over a thousand medical staff and crew. Can you imagine the carnage if she'd gone down under those circumstances?'

As the information filtered through, Shelly realised her great-grandmother had been vindicated after a lifetime of self-blame. She didn't understand why, but Shelly also felt she had in some way been released from a great weight too.

She had always blamed herself for not being able to rescue David when he needed her. Now, it was as if she had woken from a nightmare and saw the reality of the day.

If Shelly had been able to dive, and she had gone down to try and release David, she would almost certainly have become entangled too. She would have drowned and never known the tiny egg that was dividing and multiplying in the dark miracle of her womb. DJ would never have come into existence. She felt a tear slide down her cheek and, unnoticed, stepped outside for a breath of fresh air.

* * *

'What's happening on the other two screens?' Shelly asked. 'It looks like a tight spiral staircase. Is that another drone filming?'

'It's drone 2,' the operator answered.

'My grandmother talked about a spiral staircase behind her cabin on F deck. She said the boilermen made a huge racket in their hobnailed boots, changing shift.'

'Ah, no. This staircase is going up inside the mast to the crow's nest. We're looking for the ship's bell. It would be easier if the *Britannic* had settled on an even keel, then the bell would probably be at the bottom of that staircase. Unfortunately, she's on her side, so it could be anywhere. Look, the spiral's blocked with debris where the mast's bent. It may be in there, but he's giving up and going back out.'

'I guess it would be the icing if they found it?'

'Certainly would. The bell is the ultimate treasure.'

The drone came back into the open and took a 180 degree shot. The video diver appeared to glow in a great pool of light, like a giant radio-active spider. Attached to his body were six long, jointed legs, each carrying a powerful spotlight on the end. He was filming two divers collecting samples of marine crustaceans for analysis. The drone returned to the mast and travelled up its outside, then on an angle at the crow's nest where the mast had almost snapped in two.

A diver appeared and signalled he was going down to the sea floor directly under the mast. Shelly wasn't happy. It was a long way, almost fifty feet from the mast to the sand, and he was alone. Everyone was watching the other drone, which filmed the captain's bathroom with its beautiful Minton tiles, and roll-edged bath with four taps, clearly visible.

'I don't believe it. Is that the plug, still in the bath?' Shelly said with astonishment.

'It is,' Harry said. 'Remember, Captain Bartlett was about to take his bath when the mine struck.'

The lone diver went out of shot. Shelly's heart leapt.

'Where's he gone? The diver on screen 6. He was going to explore the sea floor below the mast. Now I can't see him.'

Then a pale light came into view. 'He must be on the bottom because he's kicked up some silt and it's drifted up, over him, so we can't see him so well,' Harry said.

Shelly thought of David and the fishing net, and felt sick.

Suddenly an awful screeching sounded. 'That's him,' Harry said. 'What's going on? Tell sub 2 to send his drone down.'

The operator spoke into his headset. 'He can't, he's running short of battery life. I'll try drone 1.' After a moment's conversation with sub 1, he said. 'He's going to check. Also, it's time to call everyone up for decompression.' The screeching started again. 'What the hell—' the operator muttered. 'Ah, got him on screen. Look, he's either in great pain or very excited.'

Shelly's mouth had dried so much she couldn't speak. The drone came around the diver's shoulders to get a better view of him. They could all see his eyes were wild and Shelly's first thought was that he was in pain. He lifted his gloved hand in front of the drone, then pointed it down to the sand. The drone operator in the sub manoeuvred the drone again. Then, they all saw it in the same moment.

Three-quarters buried in the seabed, the graceful curves of *Britannic*'s bell.

*   *   *

'They're starting their ascent,' Harry called from the prow. 'Unbelievable, after over a hundred years, to find the bell! I can hardly believe it myself. God forgive me and a dozen others for suspecting Cousteau might have had something to do with its disappearance. It's been there the whole time! I feel ashamed.' His eyes sparkled. 'Yes, shame on us all!' Excitement resonated in his voice. Shelly's grin widened. He swept her into his arms and kissed her fervently on the lips.

'Dad!' Elias shouted. 'You're embarrassing me!'

They broke apart, breathless and laughing.

'Divers' lives are at risk if we make a mistake up here.' He tore off his white cotton crew-neck and knotted the sleeves around his waist. Although he had a golden tan, Shelly could see his mother had been fair-skinned and Elias was destined to always be cautious of the sun. For a second, he glared at Shelly and she sensed his animosity gathering again.

'Let's prepare for the divers – we want to be ready when they surface,' he said angrily. 'They'll be exhausted after five hours in the water. Energy drinks, bottled water, and chocolate are top of the list.'

'Of course. What would you like me to do?' she asked.

'Just stay out of the way. Make us all an iced coffee while we wait.'

Shelly reminded herself that she was lucky to be on this monumental dive, and the trip was still full of excitement. She could hardly wait for the divers' return. Taking shite from Harry's son was little price to pay. Just a bit of jealousy, and actually, good to know Harry's son was so loyal. She descended to the galley and made *frappé* for everyone.

*   *   *

Carlos, descend-ascend team leader, called, 'All four divers are in the wet dive-bell! Oxygen particle pressure's confirmed. We're clear to raise the decompression bell to the next stage. Estimated time of arrival on deck, two hours from now. Elias, prepare to retrieve the shot lines and marker buoys. The sooner we clear the dive-site the better.'

'What's happening?' Shelly asked.

'Carlos is watching the ascending divers and checking the gas levels. Spiros is controlling the remotely operated vehicle.' Harry nodded at a serious man who stood before another series of screens.

'The diving bell's an advantage,' Harry said. 'Great for the divers to remove their mouthpiece for a while, and good for us to be able to communicate with them.'

'They'll be exhausted,' Shelly said, 'but it must be satisfying to see so many months of hard work and planning come together this smoothly. And, they've found the *Britannic*'s bell. Will they have it with them, Harry?'

'Absolutely not, it's against the law.'

They were all grinning, staring at the screens, when chaos erupted.

CHAPTER 42
GERTIE

Dover, 1917.

I ARRIVED BACK AT SOUTHAMPTON on a bitterly cold day. The wind whipped our cheeks, and the sting of salt chapped our lips. Matron Merriberry waited for us on the quayside. Josephine and I walked with a strange lolloping gait, the ground rocking and rolling under our feet. My stomach could not quite keep up.

'Land sickness,' Josephine told me. 'It will fade in a day or two.'

Matron escorted us to the Grand Hotel in Portsmouth where they would question us about our *Britannic* experience.

'Do you know, Gertie, I hardly remember anything from before the rescue,' Josephine said to me in front of Merriberry. She turned to Matron. 'Is that normal, do you think, Matron?'

'Absolutely. Even I cannot remember the minutes before we struck the mine . . . if that was indeed what happened. Some say we were torpedoed.' She stared pointedly at me, her face creased with worry-lines, and in a moment of panic I began to wonder if she knew what I had done. 'However, I was in the mess eating brown bread and jam. I remember that clearly.' She turned to me. 'Smith, do you remember eating brown bread and jam for breakfast in the mess that morning?'

'I do, Matron. Clear as day.'

'And do you remember anything about the portholes in the ward, Smith?'

'It's a blank, Matron. I went straight to my cabin and gathered my belongings, as you instructed, but I took too long because

I went back to get something I'd forgotten. You chastised me, as I recall, because we missed our lifeboat. Nevertheless, they made room for us on Lifeboat 2, Matron. I fell from the boat and almost drowned, but later, when I was back in the boat, I spotted Corporal Perkins unconscious in the sea. I pointed him out and he was rescued.'

She nodded. 'Good, that will do. You realise you saved his life? Don't forget to tell them about the blood transfusion. Another few minutes and his heart would have failed. Also, I'm reminded that inadvertently you saved *our* lives by causing us to miss that first lifeboat.'

I made a little nod. A great weight lifted from my shoulders, so suddenly I almost lost balance. Tears sprung to my eyes, which Matron, who never missed a thing, noticed. 'It will be all right, Smith, and the sooner this is dealt with, the sooner we can get back to our jobs. The past only has one purpose: to teach us not to make the same mistakes again.'

I wanted to turn and run away – flee from everything. The air around me was filled with my panic, my mouth wouldn't work, my brain was so confuddled that even my eyes wouldn't focus. Matron placed her hands on my shoulders, keeping me still while she stared into my face.

'Let me repeat that, Smith. The important thing to remember is: what has already happened, cannot be changed. However, the future can. We must strive to be the best people, the best example of prudence possible, in all things, from this moment on. Try to remember that, every day, on your walk through life, Miss Smith.'

I couldn't help myself; I leapt forward, flung my arms around her and gave her such a hug. 'I will, I promise I will. Thank you, Matron, thank you!' I gasped.

'Decorum, Miss Smith,' she whispered. 'Now, off to your hotel for an early night, then the inquiry tomorrow. I'll see you there, don't be late.'

* * *

I hoped with all my heart Father would come to Portsmouth. As soon as we got to our third-class room in the Sea Shanty Hotel, I posted three letters to Manno, and organised a telegram to my parents:

In Portsmouth for Britannic inq. on 14th. Hope home soon. Gertie.

* * *

The morning I'd dreaded had arrived and even my most fervent prayers would not stop the day progressing. Everyone's future depended on my answers in the inquiry. I had to think before I spoke, and lie convincingly for the sake of those on whom this country depended. Too many lives were destined to be lost because of HMHS *Britannic*'s sinking, but many more sick or wounded would perish if the *Britannic*'s senior medical staff lost their jobs because of my actions. They would be held responsible, I knew that.

However, I couldn't think straight, and my hands were trembling. In the mirror, I saw dark circles under my eyes and thought I looked half dead already. What was the penalty for lying under oath to a British Naval Tribunal? Probably death.

'I'm so afraid,' I whispered at breakfast.

'Why should you be afraid if you don't remember anything?' Josephine said firmly.

379

It became apparent they were all playing the same game, to protect me. I owed them so much. At the town hall, we sat in a corridor and waited, my hands spread on my knees like pale, wasted starfish. Merriberry joined us. She peered into my eyes and said, 'Remember the blood transfusion, Smith. It's important.'

She was called into the room where they held the inquiry. There must have been another exit because she never reappeared.

Josephine and I sat in silence although my stomach made terrible gurgling noises.

'You don't remember anything then, do you?' she whispered when the silence became unbearable. 'Only what you had for breakfast, and giving blood to the dying soldier, right?'

I shook my head. 'Not a thing.' Even as I said it, I wanted to confess. But Josephine, Matron, Staff Nurse, and perhaps even the Ship's Medical Officer might all lose their jobs in disgrace for leaving a trainee in charge of the ward. If I could take the entire blame, then I would, but I could not drop those who had placed their trust in me, in the mire.

'That's the spirit. Not surprising after all we've been through.'

* * *

I heard distant talking, then footsteps on the parquet floor. Two figures came around the corner, a man, and a woman. The woman was Matron Merriberry, and a moment passed before I realised the other was my father. My heart pounded with relief. I leapt to my feet, about to rush into his arms, when Josephine placed a hand on my arm.

'Steady now. We've got nothing to get upset about, have we?' A man stuck his head out and called Josephine into the

380

inquiry. 'You can't remember,' she said quietly one last time before leaving me.

I nodded, stood, and smiled as Merriberry and my papa approached. 'Hello, Father,' I said. Though the corners of his mouth twitched upward, he appeared tired. 'Thank you for coming to meet me.' I kissed his cheek. His dull eyes crinkled as he smiled.

'It so happens I was in the area on some business,' he said. 'A coincidence that means we can travel home together after the hearing.'

'I can't wait to see Mother. It's been so long.'

Merriberry turned my way. 'You'll be given the statutory leave after a sinking. You have thirty days with your family, Miss Smith.'

She tugged her tan cape around her body, reminding me of a brown cocoon our Arthur once kept in a box in his bedroom, waiting all winter for the beautiful creature to emerge the following spring. It didn't. I couldn't help thinking that Merriberry would never emerge as a butterfly either.

'Miss Smith, please!'

The call came from behind me. Merriberry placed her hand on my shoulder. 'Gertie, they *will* understand. It's normal to forget what happened after such a traumatic event. Relax now.'

I nodded rapidly, glanced at my father, then walked stiffly into the inquiry.

Inside the oak-panelled room, I was reminded of our courthouse in Dover. Six rows of spectators were tightly packed along the back of the hall; before that, men with notebooks scribbled frantically and I guessed they were the press. Before them, a row of men in uniform, and I dared not scrutinise their faces in case our captain was among them.

The official led me to a pulpit next to a row of men who had piles of documents in front of them, and a stenographer who recorded everything. My poor heart was thumping like the blazes. They made me swear to tell the truth, then asked me to repeat all the events of that day, starting with me waking up.

I told them everything in the most minute detail, and noticed some roll their eyes when I said I should get a new toothbrush because my bristles were becoming sparse.

'The problem is, I can't remember anything after leaving my cabin,' I said with conviction. 'It's all such a blank. As far as I can guess, it was the same as every other morning.'

'Do you remember what you had for breakfast?' one of the men on the bench asked.

I remembered Matron's words. Why would she make such a point if not for me to repeat it?

'Oh, yes. We had brown bread with raspberry jam.'

'So what time was this, Miss Smith?'

I'd walked into a trap and knew it immediately. 'I'm not sure, sir. In fact, that might have been the day before. We had the same breakfast every morning. The events of that day are all blurred. I was very frightened.'

'Were you in the dining room for the surgeon's meeting?'

'I can't remember, sir.'

'Do you remember what he spoke about?'

'No, sir. It's all a blank.'

'Where were you when the alarm went off?'

'I can't remember, sir.'

He sighed loudly. 'Did you open the portholes, Miss Smith?'

'It was forbidden to open the portholes, sir, so I can't imagine why I would do such a thing.'

'Yes, it was forbidden; but did you?'

My face burned. He knew, I sensed it. I couldn't lie under oath. 'I can't remember, sir.'

'You really expect us to believe you don't remember doing something that caused too many horrible deaths, and needless maiming?'

'Yes, sir. I mean, no, sir.'

'So which is it? Did you open the portholes?'

'I can't remember, sir.' My tears rose and I tried hard to keep my voice even. 'I nearly drowned, sir. I was pushed up from the deep by a dolphin . . . everyone saw it. I can't remember much else apart from saving Corporal Perkins. He was bleeding to death in the water.'

'So, let me see if I have this straight. You were on duty that morning and you cannot swear that you didn't open the portholes, an action that forced the Captain to sound abandon ship; an action that rendered the *Britannic*'s double hull and watertight doors useless, and caused the ship to sink faster, before she reached port; an action that led to the deaths of many brave soldiers, sailors, and medical staff?'

I lost track of his question and didn't know if I should answer yes or no. They saw through me, saw everything I was done for. 'I can't say anything for sure, sir, because I can't remember all that happened that morning.'

'I see. So, you may have opened the portholes?'

'I can't say, sir.'

'If you can't remember, then you *may* have opened the portholes, is that right? Just answer yes or no.'

'Yes, sir.'

He sighed loudly. 'Yes, what?'

I flinched. 'Yes, I may have opened the portholes, sir.'

'At last! Thank you, you may go.'

* * *

Outside the town hall, Josephine, Matron, and Father stood side by side staring anxiously at the entrance. As soon as I appeared, they strode towards me.

'How did it go?' Father asked.

I shook my head. 'I don't know. I told them I couldn't remember, but they went on and on until I don't know what I said.'

Matron and my father exchanged a worried glance. 'No use fretting about it now,' Father said. 'Let's go and eat, then start on our journey home. I don't like to leave your mother alone after dark. There's a Naval Train that runs, Portsmouth-Brighton-Dover. If we hurry, we'll just make it.' He turned to Merriberry. 'However, Matron, can I offer you some refreshment before we leave?'

Her cheeks turned pink and she stammered, lost for words! 'I . . . well . . . that would be lovely, but I think you'd be wiser to buy some food and drink to take onto the train, Dr Smith, to be sure it doesn't leave without you.'

He made a little bow. 'I want to thank you for letting me know about the inquiry, dear lady. You've been very kind,' Father said to her, deepening the blush in her cheeks.

She appeared flustered and said, 'Sorry to leave you, but I have an urgent appointment. Miss Smith, I have a little book I wish to lend you, in light of your recent work in the theatre. Please return it to me next time we meet. In the meantime, read as much as you can.' She handed over a brown-paper package tied with string. 'Safe journey to you both.' She turned quickly and rushed away.

'She seems a good woman,' Father said, watching her go. 'Now, as we walk to the station, tell me again what happened in the inquiry, and Matron's right, we'd better step on it.'

* * *

We boarded the train at one o'clock and dismounted at supper-time, taking a horse and carriage home. As we approached, my first thought was that there had been an accident, or perhaps even a bomb had fallen. A crowd of people stood in the lane outside our house. The police were there too, and people were shouting, though I couldn't make out what they were saying. Someone threw a small rock at the house and a window smashed immediately taking me back to the terror of the *Britannic*, when the lifeboat smashed the glass hospital sign on the hull.

It was already too dark to make out who these people were, until one stepped forward, yelling directly right into my face.

'You killed the only son I had left! He was fourteen! A sea scout with his whole life before him, and now he's dead thanks to you!' He up-and-downed my uniform with a glare. 'Call yourself a nurse? You're supposed to save lives, not murder the last of my boys because *you* can't obey orders.' He turned to the crowd. 'This is what happens when they let women into the war! It's a disgrace, she should be strung up for murder.'

My father put his arm around my shoulder and pulled me towards the garden gate. Someone threw an egg and by the strong fish stench that rose from the path, we knew it was bad.

'Go inside and lock the door,' Father said. 'I'll be in shortly.' He turned to address our assailants.

'Jacob Boniface, is that you? Was it not only two months ago I saved your daughter's life and gave you a fine healthy grandson?

385

Is this the way you repay me? Be aware that one day you will need me again, and when that happens, I'll remember this night!' There was a quieting of the throng. 'What on earth makes any of you think my daughter had anything to do with the *Britannic* sinking?'

'We've seen tonight's broadsheet, so we know, Doctor. The newspapers don't lie, do they?'

CHAPTER 43
SHELLY

Greece, present day.

An alarm sounded and a red light flashed over the monitors. Shelly jumped. 'What's happening?'

'A problem in the bell, please step way,' Carlos said, his voice tense.

'I'm a paramedic, if you need any help,' Shelly said, stepping back. Harry moved in next to Carlos.

'What's going on?' he asked.

'One of the divers, Matt, he's lost consciousness.' He turned back to the screens and adjusted the mic on his headset. 'Guys, go straight into the Unconscious Diver Drill. I'll talk you through. First, get any unnecessary gear off him. Making sure his upper body is in the airspace, then secure him to the side of the bell with the ratchet strap. OK? Confirm his airway's clear . . .'

A bone-chilling scream came from the back of the boat.

'I'll check it,' Shelly said, swiftly leaving the control cockpit. The moment she stepped onto the deck, the sight of Elias covered in blood made her heart thud. 'I need help! Now!' she yelled over the sound of screeching machinery.

Harry was beside her before she had reached his son.

'The back of his sweatshirt's caught in the recovery platform's line cogs. It's pulling him in. Turn it off!' she yelled, horrified that it was about to cut him in half.

Elias, weakened by loss of blood, gave up pulling away from the turning mechanism. Shelly grabbed the knotted sleeves at his waist and pulled with all her strength. In a matter of seconds, the winching gear stopped and both Elias and Shelly fell into a blood-spattered heap on the deck. Elias was unconscious, blood pumping from his side. Shelly tore off her shirt, rolled it, and thrust it at Harry. 'Press this against the wound with all your strength.' Two of the crew had appeared. 'You!' she said, pointing at one guy. 'Get the first aid kit.' She pulled her phone out and pressed rapid dial.

'Hello, this is paramedic Shelly Summer. We need an emergency helicopter ambulance for a patient who's bleeding out on a dive vessel.' She turned to Harry. 'Blood group and age?'

'O positive, twenty-one.'

'Blood group: O positive. Our coordinates are: 37°42'05"N by 24°17'02"E. Twenty-one-year-old male with open wound to the torso. I can accompany him up, I'm experienced on a 'copter lift, so if you have room for one more, just lower the cradle and a safety line. We have divers down and there's a critical situation below, so we need our aerials down for as short a time as possible. I'll have all loose items removed from the deck and prepare for your arrival, OK? Over and out.'

Shelly called to the other crew member. 'You! Move everything that's not fixed down, below decks. And I do mean *everything*! We don't want anyone decapitated by flying debris from the downdraught. Quickly!' To the other crew member, she said, 'Go inside and tell them we need to lower all aerials for five minutes, while the 'copter hovers above us, OK?'

She pulled a sphygmomanometer out of the medical kit, and put the blood pressure cuff on Elias.

'How is he?' Harry asked quietly when she had taken his blood pressure.

'Not good. He's bleeding out. Keep the pressure on that wound or else he won't make it.' She took the pulse in his neck. 'Very faint.' She glanced at the horizon, it would be another ten minutes at least. Suddenly, Gran Gertie came to mind. She was right here with Corporal Perkins dying in her arms, and what did she do?

Shelly tipped out the first aid kit, snatched a catheter and two syringes. 'Keep the pressure up!' she ordered Harry. Within thirty seconds she had a transfusion going from her arm, into Elias.

'The decks are clear, miss, what next?'

'Bring me a chair to sit on, but shift it inside the moment you hear that 'copter, and when you do, lower all the aerials. Once we're moving away, erect them again.'

Shelly felt slightly dizzy, but knew she had to stay strong for the helicopter lift. 'We need to strap that pad to the wound to keep the pressure up while they lift him. A couple of wide belts will do the trick. Quick as you can, guys, ask the crew for any sturdy belts, we need to be ready for that 'copter!'

'Leave the shirt in place and add the pad of gauze for extra pressure. It needs to be strapped *very tightly* in place.' She felt the pulse in Elias's neck again. 'If I'm not mistaken, it's no weaker. You can go, Harry. Find out what happened in the dive bell. You're needed there, even though Carlos knows what he's doing.' She caught the distant thrum of the 'copter and nodded towards it. 'Once I'm in there, I'm going to turn my phone off to save the battery. I'll turn it on for ten minutes, on the hour, OK?' Her head was spinning.

'Shouldn't you stop that now?' He indicated the tube that had become a lifeline to his son.

'Don't worry, gravity is a very slow business. I only know about it because I looked it up, out of curiosity, after one of Gran Gertie's tapes.' She studied Harry's son, who would almost certainly have been dead by now if it hadn't been for that cassette tape and Shelly's interest in all things medical. 'Odd how things turn out, isn't it?'

Harry gave a sigh and rubbed his eyes, then cupped her chin and kissed her gently on the lips. 'Thank you.' She could feel he was trembling, or perhaps it was her.

'Don't worry about things you can't change,' she said gently. 'I swear to do all I can for him, and you can thank Gertie for making the tapes, she probably saved his life. Please, go inside and check what's happening. I'd like to know before I leave.'

* * *

In the air ambulance, Shelly removed the catheter, placed a lump of cotton wool over the tiny wound, and bent her elbow.

'O positive, you said,' the medic queried before sticking the transfusion needle into Elias's arm.

She nodded. 'Same as me.'

'What you did was very unorthodox, and certainly not recommended, but I'm quite sure you saved this young man's life with your quick thinking.'

'He'll survive then?'

'Well, we'll do our best, but it's a bad bleed.'

Still feeling lightheaded, Shelly wondered what was going on in the dive bell. It sounded like a heart attack, but there was nothing she could do about it under the circumstances. Shortly, they landed on the hospital heliport and Elias was stretchered straight to A&E. Shelly confessed to feeling lightheaded and followed with one of the medics.

* * *

At ten o'clock that evening, Harry joined her at the hospital. She felt his rich brown eyes probing into her troubled soul wanting to see what was going on in there.

'Has anyone told you, Elias's going to be all right?' he asked.

With that information came a rush of relief, and her moment to fall apart arrived. 'Thank God!' She turned towards him. He slipped his arms around her and pulled her into his embrace, giving her permission to let the tension go. She cried onto his shoulder for a minute, then gathered her strength and sat up straight. 'Thank you, I needed that,' she said, taking his handkerchief and blowing her nose. 'Such a relief.'

'You risked your life to save his, so it's me who's thanking you; and Elias too. Apologies for bitching,' he said. 'From now on, you can do anything you want as far as my son's concerned.'

Shelly laughed limply. 'That's good. He's no longer angry with me for monopolising his father then?'

Harry lowered his eyes. 'I am really sorry for the way he treated you.'

'Believe me, I know all about conflicting loyalties.' There was a ring of bitterness in her voice. 'Sorry, it's just that I have been loyal to David since I was sixteen years old. It's so difficult to let go, and the awful thing is, I can't even talk about it.'

'Poor Shelly.' He placed his arm around her shoulders. 'I knew something wasn't right, and that you were in a lot of emotional pain. When you're ready to tell me, we can work through it together. No judgement, no worries. I'm here for you.' It was his hand upon her shoulder, the realisation, at last, she was not alone with her problems that gave her strength.

'Thank you. Is it that obvious?'

'Not at all, but you cry in your sleep, sometimes.'

'Gosh, how embarrassing. I promise, I'll tell all when we get back to Kea.'

CHAPTER 44
GERTIE

Dover, 1917.

MY FATHER FACED BONIFACE AND the mob fearlessly.

'The press might not lie, but sometimes by not telling the whole truth, the more gullible may jump to the wrong conclusions. My daughter almost drowned when HMHS *Britannic* went down. Nevertheless, she risked her own life to save the life of a British soldier, one of our very own boys. Corporal Perkins of the Royal Engineers. The people of Dover should be very proud of her – I am! You should be praising her bravery with a medal – not coming here frightening my wife by behaving like Luddites!' He stood taller and spoke over Boniface's head. 'You don't know the full story, people. Go home and let me do my job.' The distant clanging of the police bell rang out. 'Go back to your families now, before you get into more trouble.'

Once it was clear they were dispersing, my father called through the letterbox. 'Let me in, Gertie.' The first thing he noticed, as I had, was my mother, pale with fright. She huddled in the armchair with a blanket over her. Mrs Cooper held her hand while staring at us.

'Mrs Smith's taken a turn for the worse, Doctor,' she said. 'She's had nothing to eat all day, just a cup of beef tea. I put some oil of camphor on her chest to help her breathing, and goose fat and brown paper on her back, but she's still sickly.'

My father sighed, I knew what he thought of these remedies, yet he was too polite to reprimand Mrs Cooper for doing her best. He produced his stethoscope and listened to my mother's chest. After straightening he said, 'We must get you to bed, dearest. Now Gertie's here to look after you, we'll soon have you well again. I hear from the Matron our daughter's going to make a fine nurse.'

Oh! My father had never said anything so kind about me in my whole life, at least not that I'd heard. Although worried about my mother, I felt myself glowing with pleasure.

He turned to our three-day-domestic. 'Thank you, Mrs Cooper. After all your hard work, you may take a little time off now that my daughter's home.'

Mrs Cooper nodded at my father, then at me. I was not too sure that she was pleased, until father said she would still be paid, then a smile lifted her apple cheeks.

'Thank you, Doctor. I'll just help Miss Gertie get Mrs Smith into bed, then I'll be off.' She spoke to my father with such reverence, I thought she was going to curtsy.

* * *

I let Mrs Cooper out at nine o'clock. I had been into town for some supplies, and was pleased to see several acquaintances, but they treated me like a stranger. They were the same people I had left only six months before, yet it seemed their lives had moved on in my absence. Was I foolish to imagine the world would have waited, unchanged, for my return? Before I left, excited friends would rush to embrace me and chatter excitedly about the minutiae of their lives. Now, they were distant. This left me with a peculiar, yet intense, feeling of loneliness. That evening, my back ached and I was bone tired. I found Father in his armchair, reading.

'I'm going to bed, Father. I can't keep my eyes open.' I kissed his cheek.

'Wait, Gertie. Pour me a brandy, and a small one for yourself.'

'Me? Father! I don't think that's appropriate.'

'Stuff and nonsense. This is 1917. I do believe young people partake occasionally. Besides, I want to talk and there is nothing like a good cognac for loosening the tongue.'

I poured him a drink, and a small one for me too. This personal moment with my father strengthened my morale. For the first time, I realised he no longer considered me an irresponsible child. I found it difficult, even after all that had happened, not to grin like the organ-grinder's monkey.

'Matron told me she's very pleased with your progress, Gertie.'

'She's a marvellous woman and I wish to model my future on her. As I said in my letter, she promoted me to the theatre and though I'm not as yet a qualified theatre nurse, I've learned various sutures and it seems to have become my job to take care of the outer sutures, to close a wound after surgery and also apply the dressings. This leaves the surgeon free to move on to the next case. Through this recent work, I have discovered where my aspirations lie.' I stopped and took a breath. 'Can I tell you my dream, Father?'

'You can tell me anything at all, child,' he said, swirling his drink, then lifting his head to stare at me.

'I want to be a surgeon.' There, I'd said it.

'Ha!' he exclaimed. 'Don't look like that, Gertie! You've no idea what being a surgeon involves. When people die in your hands—'

'Excuse me interrupting, Father. I've assisted at one hundred and sixty-seven operations. Twenty-nine of our patients died on the table, but this was simply because their wounds were too catastrophic, or they had lost too much blood.' I put down my drink, turned my hand over, and pushed my sleeve above the small scars in my arm. 'Look, I've given direct blood transfusions, via the glass tube, to five patients, four of whom survived. The first one of those patients was in the lifeboat, and the procedure saved the man's life.'

Father lifted his eyebrows. 'Really? Well, I'm shocked. And you still want to be a surgeon?'

'More than anything in the world.'

'Then I'm proud of you, and relieved that you're home, safe. You have my total support, Gertie.'

This was not the response I expected. 'But there are no women surgeons. Where would I start?'

'Exactly where you are now, in the field hospitals. Do everything you can, show you are not afraid. Offer to take over. Most importantly, prove that you can lead a team of medics, because you cannot do the job alone. Get organised, get a reputation, and get all the knowledge you can absorb. Make people remember you because – and this is important for you to understand, Gertie – this war will not last forever! There will always be a shortage of good surgeons. This is an exciting time for women. An opportunity to prove yourselves. Be brave and rise to the challenge.' He went to the bookcase, pulled out a thick volume and handed it to me. 'Start with Matron's book, then this. Learn it cover to cover. I'll test you every evening over supper.' He handed me his wine-coloured tome. '*Gray's Anatomy of the Human Body*.'

I went to sleep feeling relieved. Did my father believe the newspapers? Did he believe I had opened the portholes? Merriberry must have guessed it was me, although it could have been any one of the patients while I was in the sluice room. Had she told my father? I got the impression they had spent time together. Not one person had asked me straight out if I had opened the portholes.

Memories of the mob outside the cottage concerned me. Clearly, they believed everything in the papers? Poor Mr Boniface, to lose his youngest son. I couldn't even remember seeing the boy.

* * *

I was having breakfast when the mob returned. The sound of hammering on the front door made me jump. 'Who is it?' I asked through the letterbox.

'The *Morning Standard*, miss. Can I ask you a few questions?'

'What? What about?'

'Were you on the *Britannic*, miss?'

Clattering from the fist-shaped brass knocker had woken Father. He appeared in his smoking jacket over his striped pyjamas. 'What's happening, Gertie?'

'There's a newspaper reporter outside, Father. He wants to come in and ask a few questions.'

Father opened the letterbox and called, 'We have nothing to say. Remove yourselves before I summon the constable.'

Mrs Cooper came in the back door. 'Here, there's a crowd outside again, Doctor. What's going on?' She placed the newspapers on the table.

Father groaned as he scanned the headlines. 'This is what's wrong!' He waved the paper, then dropped it onto the table and picked up a second tabloid. 'More headlines, and even more condemning than yesterday's. DOVER GIRL RESPONSIBLE FOR SINKING THE *BRITANNIC*?' He stared at me for a moment, then went on to the next one. 'NURSE CAUSES DEATH OF THIRTY MILITARY PERSONNEL, AND MAIMS FORTY MORE.' He glared at me again. 'What on earth did you tell them in that tribunal, Gertie?'

'Father, I told them I couldn't remember what happened before I was rescued from the sea. I said it was all a blank.'

He stared at the broadsheets again. 'Well, you might as well know, both Matron Merriberry and I have guessed what happened, but it is better if those words are never said aloud. You don't remember anything at all, you understand? Nothing will be changed by encouraging more problems.'

I turned my eyes away. 'Yes, Father.'

'Your mother has taken a turn for the worse and all this excitement is doing her no good at all.'

There was another knock on the door.

'Hello! *London Tribune* here. Dr Smith? Could we have a word with your daughter?'

Although Father directed his words at me, clearly, he was rationalising with himself. 'The best way to put an end to this speculation and harassment would be to make a statement to the press.'

He turned back to the door, placed his foot six inches from the jamb, and opened it. There was a crowd, jostling, voices all at once. 'Dr Smith!' 'A word, please, sir?' 'Is your daughter here?'

'Gentlemen, please step back and I will come out to talk to you.'

Then I saw my father do something I'd never seen before; one of the most important lessons he ever gave me. He paused before acting. I saw his chest expand and shoulders rise as he took in a long, deep breath. After a moment, he closed his eyes and let it out slowly. Then he stepped around the door and closed it behind himself.

I hurried forward and pressed my ear against the centre panel. Father's voice came through clearly.

'Each of you may ask one question. If anyone harasses me, you will all have to leave. Yes, you at the back with the trilby, what would you like to ask?'

'*Sunday Herald*. Was your daughter responsible for the sinking of the *Britannic*, sir?'

'No, she was not. At this moment, it is unclear if it was a mine or a torpedo that put a hole in the ship's belly.'

A different voice. '*Brighton Times*. Why did your daughter take so long to return to England, sir? Is it true she refused to come back?'

'No, it is not true. My daughter and one other crew member contracted influenza on the island of Kea. They were put into quarantine for two weeks, thereby missing the original inquiry and passage returning to Britain. My daughter did not take her due leave, she went on to nurse our fine boys near the Dardanelles. I'm very proud of her, and so should you be.'

'*The Express*. Does Gertie Smith remember seeing the open portholes, either from inside the ship, or from the lifeboat?'

'My daughter has some amnesia covering the time before she was pulled out of the water. She almost drowned, and such a thing often causes loss of memory.'

'*News of the World*. Is it true your daughter was rescued by a dolphin, sir?'

'Yes, she was. There were several witnesses including the ship's chaplain.'

'*People Newspaper*. Who was the soldier that Miss Smith rescued, Doctor?'

'I believe his name was Corporal Johnathan Perkins. She saved his life by bravely giving him some of her own blood.

I wonder how many of you have demonstrated that sort of courage?'

Once Father had answered a question from each reporter, he ended the exchange. 'Now, gentlemen, I'll thank you all to leave, apart from *The Express*.'

I ventured over to the window and peeped through the drapes. The mob dispersed hurriedly, leaving on horseback, in motor vehicles, and one on a motorised bicycle. I could imagine the queue for the telephone in town. My father was talking earnestly with a heavily whiskered gentleman. After a moment, they shook hands and he also left.

Father knocked on the door and I quickly let him in. He leaned his back against it and I noticed how his hand trembled as he pushed it across a brow.

'Sorry, Father. It wasn't my intention to make so much trouble for you.'

'Intention or not, we have to deal with it. I think we should play on the positive. Let's get the young man you saved to come here and talk to the newspaper reporters with us. Where will I find him?'

'I don't exactly know, Father.' Then I remembered Victoria Pimlet's letter, didn't she say she had seen him? Also, I considered perhaps Josephine, or even Merriberry would know his address. 'I can probably find out.' In the back of my mind was the nagging question, would he remember that it was I who opened the portholes?

When the mob had gone, I withdrew into the garden, embracing the breeze. I stood with my back pressed against the oak tree, feeling its strength, its support, and likening it to my strong-minded sister.

I stared out over the restless English Channel and remembered the sparkling, turquoise water of Kea. How I longed for my beautiful Manno again. He filled my dreams, and thoughts of our last meeting constantly interrupted my waking hours. He had asked me to be his wife, and now I feared I was carrying his child.

'I believe as one soul leaves another arrives, Gertie. Take strength in that,' my father had said after Sissy's funeral. 'For every death, there is a child born.' He would not be so comforted if he knew that child might be growing inside his daughter's belly.

I had not received a reply from my letters to Manno and although this still perturbed me a little, I felt confident he would write if he could. I returned to Mother's bureau and penned another correspondence. I didn't mention my fears in case I had misdiagnosed myself and it was simply my worrying that had upset my physiology. However, if I was wrong, having a child out of wedlock would destroy my father's reputation. I'd have to go away before my condition became apparent. If the truth emerged about the *Britannic*'s portholes, I could be in prison for deliberately going against orders . . . mutiny, which held the death penalty. Perhaps I should go back to Greece, run away and never return. But Father would be devastated if he and my mother were the sole survivors of our family. If I gave him a grandson his delight would be immeasurable, a small compensation for the losses he had suffered.

Before any of that, I needed a husband, and quickly!

Father came across the lawn and sat beside me under the tree.

'I thought you would be interested to know that your Corporal Perkins is coming for tea, tomorrow afternoon, Gertie. I have also invited Matron Merriberry, your friend the nurse, and the reporter. I hope to persuade the Corporal to speak to the press about your gallantry in the lifeboat.'

CHAPTER 45
SHELLY

Dover, present day.

BACK HOME IN DOVER, LIFE settled down to a new normal. Harry phoned most days. DJ came over most weekends. Shelly spent quality time revising with DJ on the run-up to his exams. Gordon stopped trying to set Shelly up with the postman, and a huge branch broke off the oak tree and blocked most of the road.

'Dad, don't forget we're taking DJ out for dinner tomorrow after he gets his exam results. I want it to be a special day for you too. We'll go early and stop for breakfast half way to Cambridge, is that all right?' Gordon nodded. 'There's something else.' Shelly sighed, then bit her lip and stared out to the magnificent oak. The yellow council wagon pulled up.

'Come on, spit it out,' Gordon said. 'At worst I can say no.'

'I'll be so sad to see that tree go. It's been there all my life.'

'All mine too, but that branch might have killed somebody, might have killed a whole family . . . how would you feel then?'

She nodded. 'I suppose you're right. Listen, I'd very much like to spend Sunday with somebody special, but I know you've got a race the next day and want to be back. If I drive you to the station in London, and get you onto the Dover train, do you think you could get a taxi home?'

'Let me think about it, all right? I'll let you know later.'

*   *   *

DJ got a first in every exam, and when she heard, Shelly found her eyes fill with tears of pride. She was so excited to see him. She and Gordon had offered to take him out for dinner at a restaurant in the heart of Cambridge, and DJ had shyly asked if he could bring a friend with him.

DJ was already there when they arrived, sat beside a young woman. He appeared nervous. He took the girl's hand and turned to Shelly. 'Mum, this is my best friend, Lilly.' He turned to the beautiful young woman. 'Lilly, this is my mother, Shelly Summer.'

Shelly smiled.

'I've heard so much about you, Ms Summer, it's wonderful to meet you at last.' Lilly blinked her baby-blue eyes that smiled from beneath pale lashes.

'Call me Shelly, please. Well done both of you for finishing your first year of university.' She turned to DJ. 'I couldn't be more proud, and if your father was here, he would be shaking your hand and congratulating you too.' Suddenly filled with affection for her boy, she felt comfortable sharing a personal memory with the girl he clearly adored. 'DJ's father. There was a tragic diving accident before DJ was even born.'

At that moment, Shelly realised a small miracle had taken place. For the first time in her life, she had spoken about David, the accident and her son, without so much as a tear or a tremor in her voice. All she felt was love, and pride, and hope for the future.

Gordon, who was sitting next to Shelly, grabbed her fist and squeezed tight. 'We're all right proud of yer, DJ, lad. Me included. An' I'm right sure yer dad is too. How could he not be?' His eyes met Shelly's in an emotionally charged moment.

DJ took Lilly's hand. For a second, they gazed at each other and then returned their attention to the meal. In an instant,

Shelly knew their first boy-child was destined to be named Dave. She smiled, filled with joy as she realised they would one day make her a grandmother. Could she live up to the standard that Gran Gertie had set? She would try. DJ's child, just the thought was overwhelming. A voice from the past echoed in her mind.

I come from a long line of Davids.

* * *

At ten o'clock the next morning, Shelly checked out of her hotel room. She had deliberately hung back to avoid the others. Deception did not come easily to her.

She had hardly slept, yet as dawn broke, she came to a decision that had eluded her for so long. Was she doing the right thing? She hoped so. The choice had been difficult to make, but she had to consider other people's lives. She *was* doing the right thing, she was sure now. This decision, the terrific burden of holding someone else's future in her hand had pressed heavily on her recently, especially since DJ had come into her life. However, after seeing her son with the young woman he loved, and after hearing the poignant words of Gran Gertie's first tape, Shelly knew her decision was correct.

DJ and Lilly should not be burdened with the past, and any parent who loved their child wouldn't want him overwhelmed by things he couldn't change.

* * *

After putting her father on the coach at Dartford, she headed towards Epping Forest. By the time she entered the rich woodland area, relief replaced those last niggling doubts. She had to stop the car, and let her tears go. In her mind, she spoke to Gertie, and to David, and then to her mother. With an overwhelming sense of relief, she confirmed she was doing the right thing.

Twenty minutes later, she pulled up in the drive of a majestic Victorian building. Grabbing her handbag, she got out and from the car boot, she lifted a white M&S bag that contained a complete new outfit. Bright, happy, casual clothes, although this regular occasion always broke her into little pieces. The gravel crunched as she walked away from the car.

Simon, her long-time friend and owner of Dover Divers, was reading his newspaper in the porch. He stood, took her into his arms and kissed her cheeks.

'How are you?' he asked softly.

She nodded. 'You know how it is, a bit emotional. DJ has just finished his first year at university. I so wish . . .'

He put a finger on her lips. 'I know. Shall we have some coffee first? Do you want to sit and talk for a while?'

She shook her head. 'I'd rather go straight to the room, if you don't mind, Simon.'

'I understand. We'll talk after.' He took her into his arms again and held her tenderly, rocking gently from side to side. 'I wish things could have been different, Shelly. I know it's only once every two months, but it's hard enough for me to handle our meetings. God knows how you've managed to accept the situation for so long.'

'It's love. Such a wonderful thing, but it also beats us up terribly.'

Simon opened the heavy oak door and Shelly went through, as she had every first Sunday of every other month for the past twenty years. 'I'll wait out here,' Simon said.

Shelly didn't hear him, her eyes were fixed on the overweight, middle-aged man at the toy table, his face, soft, rounded, and line free. A face that had seldom laughed or cried and had not known the frown of worry for twenty years. Shelly pulled a chair up and sat next to him.

'Hello, David.'

He cocked his head sideways, but didn't turn to look at her. He was trying to push a yellow brick into a triangular hole in the lid of a bucket. The brick was square.

'It's Shelly, David. I've come to tell you about our darling son. We had a baby boy, nineteen years ago. I told you, but you may have forgotten. His name's David John, like you. He comes from a long line of Davids, you know; though everyone calls him DJ.'

She bit her lip hard, her heart breaking, smashing into tiny pieces, yet she forced a smile. Longing to take his hand, touch his cheek, kiss his ear – yet she knew better. She picked up a triangular brick and placed it in front of him. He stared at it for a moment, then picked it up. After a few attempts, the brick clattered into the bucket, yet he remained emotionless.

'I've been on holiday, David. I went diving, to one of the most magical wrecks in the world. I always go diving, just for you, so I can tell you about it. This dive reminded me of our holiday together, when I was sixteen. I wonder if you remember any of that, at all. If you do . . . any little thing, me . . . your friend, Simon, who is outside right now, how happy we were?' Once again, she bit on her lip to clamp a threatening sob, then smudged a rogue tear away.

'Dear David, Simon came with us on that holiday. You got the tickets really cheap off Teletext, for you, Roger and Simon, but Roger came down with mumps, remember? Please try and remember. Poor Roger! I ended up going in his place. Oh my, as I said, I was only sixteen so it was a real adventure. I'd been so sad, so full of guilt because my mum had been killed going for my Christmas present on Christmas Eve.

'I was in love with you, desperately, head-over-heels in love, and you pulled my leg about it all the time. But in truth, I knew you were in love with me too.'

She watched his hands for a moment. 'Do you remember, you got that busker with the guitar at the airport to sing, "She was Only Sixteen", and you twirled me under your arm. "She was Only Sixteen" became our song.' She sang the first lines, staring at his face. 'It's still our song, my darling David. It always will be.' She swallowed hard. 'I wish you could hold me for a moment, just once. One hug. One.'

David picked up a cylindrical brick and tried to push it through the triangular hole.

'When we landed on the island of Paros, we got a bus from the airport to the town centre. Do you remember the promenade, that gorgeous little white church with the brilliant blue dome? And the big windmill with a thatched roof, David? Oh, those huge sails of white canvas, just next to the ferry port. Someone had painted PAROS CORNER in big blue letters on the wall behind the windmill. We lugged our cases onto another bus which took us to a beautiful little village on the edge of the sea . . . what was it called now?' She stared at him, her mind begging for him to say the word, or even glance up and acknowledge her. 'Naoussa, yes, I remember. How amazingly beautiful it was. All the pavements painted like crazy paving. Narrow alleys. Such a magnificent white church that towered above the village.' She recalled the scenes they'd enjoyed so much. 'We slept together, all night in the same bed, for the first time . . . for the last time. I remember snuggling up to you and thinking it was the happiest moment of my life, and it was.'

A nurse came in and asked if she would like a cup of tea. Shelly shook her head and returned her attention to David as she left.

'You made me get up to see the sunrise, David, you were crazy to photograph it. At first everywhere was a little dull and grey, and the air was so still, as if the world was holding its breath. Everything changed when that huge sun came over the horizon. What a drama, magnificent, the world turned golden, the water, the sky, Oh, my goodness, the sun moved so quickly. I wanted it to stop, wait for me to catch up. Does that sound silly? I've never forgotten that morning, my first sunrise, David.'

She swiped her tears away, sniffed, and forced a smile. 'Please, just look at me if you remember it. Just glance my way if you know who I am.'

He stared at the brick in his hand, turning it over and over and rocking back and forth slightly.

Exasperated, she said quietly, 'Then we stood on our heads and ate giant slugs.'

A reaction, something, please, oh, David, please. One small thing, just a glance, and then I'll come back!

Nothing, not so much as a pause or frown. She might as well not be there. The time had come.

'David, I have something important to tell you. I saved somebody's life, recently, and it seems to have changed me. Like the event restored a kind of balance to my own life, and now I can move on and stop living in the past. I'm sorry to tell you, David, I'm not coming back. I realise you won't miss me, and that you don't even know who I am, but I felt I had to come and tell you myself.' Even now, she longed for the smallest response, anything, please, even anger. There was nothing, and that nothing weighed so heavily on her, she gave up trying to hold back the tears that now ran freely down her cheeks. 'You'll always be in my heart, darling David,' she sobbed. 'You see, true love never dies. I'll continue to cover your extra costs here, but I do need to move on. I have learned the hardest thing is to let go, but I must.'

He took the block from her hand and tried to push it through the round hole.

'Our son, and I suspect in not too many years, our grandson, will also need me. And as for myself, I think I've found love again, after all these long, lonely years.'

Shelly turned and stared out of the window, seeing nothing but a blur of green through the tears that were still falling. After dragging one of Gordon's big white hankies from her handbag, she dried her eyes and blew her nose.

'Sorry about that. I really want to give you a hug, hold you close to me and kiss you – and the pain of not being able to – not once for twenty years, is more than I can take, David. Do you understand?' She sighed, frustrated. 'No, of course you don't, and perhaps it's just as well. So goodbye, my darling; be as happy as you can be.' She stood and watched him for a moment, his attention never wavering from the coloured bricks and the bucket.

* * *

Outside the care home, Shelly allowed the tears to run freely down her cheeks. She cried until her broken heart was completely drained, then she hurried into the Ladies just inside the entrance and tidied herself up. Simon had gone in to see David, as was their routine. Shelly had an appointment with the Matron, and told the woman that she was not coming back, but she would continue with David's upkeep expenses.

'A wise decision,' Matron said. 'To tell you the truth, Shelly, your visits confuse him, and he's unsettled for a couple of days after you've been.'

'Why didn't you tell me?'

'It had to be your decision. We'll let you know if there's any change, so you never have to worry about him, and you can still visit if you ever change your mind.' She picked up a pen and turned it over in her hand. 'There comes a time to stop living in the past, Shelly. If David understood, which he can't of course, he wouldn't want you to hold back. He loved you, still does in his way, so go and live a happy life while you still have time.'

*   *   *

Back home, Shelly slumped into a chair and wondered if she had the energy to listen to another of Gran Gertie's tapes. She thought about DJ, then David in the home. One day, she might tell DJ about David. Perhaps she would bring him with her to see him, if he wanted to. But not yet. It was too great a burden for a boy so young. She decided to tell Dad of her decision tomorrow, but for the moment, she owed herself a large glass of red, and perhaps she would listen to ten minutes of Gran Gertie.

Her great-grandmother's strength of spirit had helped Shelly to come to this difficult decision today, and she was

410

grateful. She glanced at the window. Light flooded in now that the big old oak tree had gone. Her spirits lifted; she must search for some acorns in the morning and pot them up. A new beginning.

CHAPTER 46
GERTIE

Dover, 1917.

Mother was not feeling very well the next day, but as we had already invited several people for afternoon tea, and Father had adjusted his busy schedule, he decided we should go ahead. He persuaded Mrs Cooper to abandon her chores and, along with her two daughters, serve afternoon tea, sandwiches and cakes to our guests. He had also invited Mr Hammersmith, the dentist, for reasons I didn't understand.

Everyone arrived within minutes of each other at three o'clock and I greeted them in the front garden. When my eyes fell upon Corporal Perkins's handsome face I almost forgot to breathe. I had forgotten how charismatic he was. Now, to see him in a smart suit, he appeared to be a gentleman of some standing and his slight limp only added to his allure.

'Thank you for coming,' I whispered, remembering I had kissed him. 'We welcome your presence at the house for refreshment.' Despite my self-consciousness, I relaxed in the knowledge that I could draw from his affection, so long as he did not remember what happened on that terrible day. Had my selfishness no bounds? My insides were in knots, and my mind desperate for something, someone, to cling to.

'I thank you for inviting me,' he said, lifting my hand to kiss the back. He went on to speak to Father, and although I spoke with Matron and Nurse Josephine, I was conscious of the Corporal's every move, as I suspected, he was of mine.

Matron was very astute. 'Decorum, Miss Smith.'

I pushed my shoulders back and stood taller. 'Yes, Matron. Sorry, Matron, I lost control for a moment.'

'Forgivable under the circumstances,' she said kindly. 'Corporal Perkins is an exceedingly handsome young man. I'm sorry to hear your mother is not well enough to join us.'

Corporal Perkins was never far from my side. I was distressed by the reporter drifting from one to the other, asking questions, being polite, and I guessed hoping to catch somebody off guard. He came to my side, and so did Perkins when he caught my worried glance.

'Do you know that to go against military orders, as the person who opened the portholes did, is regarded as mutiny . . . a *hanging* offence, Gertie?' Perkins said.

I clutched my neck. 'No, don't say such a thing, Corporal! I'm upset enough thinking about that terrible day.'

'Somebody has to pay, that ship cost over two million pounds,' the reporter stated. 'Please excuse me, I must speak with the Matron.'

In one swift movement, Perkins sat beside me on the sofa and peered into my eyes. 'Darling Gertie, how would you feel if I asked your father's permission to walk you out?' he said quickly, grabbing the moment.

'What do you mean? You're not making sense.'

'Gertie Smith, I would go down on one knee if I could. You know that I love you with all my heart, and I hope, one day, you will do me the honour of becoming my wife?'

'Corporal Perkins, this is hardly the right place or time! I can't think.'

413

He lifted my hand to kiss the back, then he noticed the dolphin ring. 'Why are you wearing a ring on your wedding finger?'

Surprised by the sudden cold tone to his voice, I answered. 'Oh, erm, yes, it rescues me from unwelcome advances, from male patients.'

'Am I making unwelcome advances?'

'No, of course not. Also, it's a dolphin, to remind me of my rescue on that terrible day when we all almost died.' My thoughts went to Manno and our afternoon in Syros when he gave me the ring. With burning cheeks, I remembered his words: *You are mine, agapi mou!*

'I can see I've embarrassed you, Gertie. Do forgive me,' Perkins said. 'Become my wife and I will tell the world it was not you that opened the portholes. Do you understand?'

Oh dear! In a flash I saw a solution to all my problems. I was a traitor, a Judas, selling Perkins out for deliverance from these scandalous accusations. Allegations that were true. Yes, I did open the portholes, but I was determined to deny it, difficult as that was. This was not only for my own good, but for Merriberry who had been so supportive to me and would surely lose her job if the truth came out.

How many more lives would be lost if Merriberry left the medical profession? Also, I would not confess for my father's sake. He did not deserve any more trouble in his life. And for my baby, who needed two parents. If I was prepared to surrender the man I loved for the sake of my child's reputation, then so be it. Perkins had offered me this solution and I was seriously considering it, only because I suspected Manno's baby grew inside me. The hole I dug for myself grew deeper and deeper.

* * *

The newspaper reporter was a stern looking man in his mid-thirties, all worsted suit, leather polish, and Brilliantine. He had a thick head of dark, glossy hair, and a mole with silver bristles on his jaw. He shook hands with father, Mr Hammersmith, and Perkins and half bowed towards me and the other ladies as an afterthought.

'Thank you for seeing me. I'll be out of your way as quickly as possible.'

Father indicated a chair at the dining table and as the reporter moved towards it, my father threw me a cautionary glance that said, *think before you speak*. I replied with a slight nod. He pointed to another chair and said, 'After you,' to me. A clever move, because it instantly made the sitting reporter slightly embarrassed for his manners. 'Thank you, Father,' I replied.

When we were all seated around the dining table with our tea, sandwiches, and cake, Father said, 'Do you have a list of questions for my daughter, Mr . . . ?'

'William Baily, at your service, sir. Yes, I came prepared so as not to waste your time.'

'And do you have a carbon copy for our records, Mr Baily?'

The reporter looked flustered for a second. I considered how much I loved my father when he insisted Mr Baily rewrote the questions out on double paper with a sheet of carbon between. I watched, considering each question as he wrote. No surprises. Another shrewd move of my father's.

'Please leave a space for my daughter's answers, under each question, and of course, a space at the end for her signature, and for the signature of the witness. Thank you.'

A slightly smug smile flickered across Father's lips.

The interview was on a par with the inquiry, except that he did not bully me. Mr Baily was surprisingly courteous. He wrote everything down, dated and signed, and asked my father and Matron a few questions too. I relaxed; fully confident the newspaper would not misrepresent me.

After, when the men lit their cigars and swirled their brandy, I wandered outside and found Matron and Josephine sipping sherry at a table set beneath the big oak tree.

'Gertie, come and join us. We were just talking about Kea,' Josephine said. 'Did you know Matron has just returned from there?'

Matron smiled. 'There was a memorial service for those unfortunate souls that were not found. The villagers remembered you. The nurse whose father kept the army's pigeons. They spoke fondly of you, Gertie.'

'Did you see the mailman and his father, the ones that saved us, Matron?'

'Manno was away to Syros. However, his father, Nikos, invited us to eat at his house with his daughter-in-law and his two grandchildren.'

'Daughter-in-law, and two grandchildren?' My mouth dried, what was she saying?

Merriberry nodded. 'Charming toddlers. Easy to see they would grow up to be spectacularly beautiful.'

Manno had a family on Kea! Now I understood why he had not answered my letters.

*　*　*

The next morning, Father paced up and down the drawing room muttering to himself. When he realised I'd entered the room he stopped and stared at me. 'Have you seen this morning's newspaper, Gertie?' he asked gravely.

416

'No, not yet, Father.' The broadsheet lay on the table. When I investigated, it was clear to see the newspaper editor believed I was at least partly to blame for the *Britannic*'s death toll.

TORPEDO OR MINE? the headline queried. Two paragraphs later, it went on to ask:

Who opened the portholes? An action that caused the two-million-pound ship to sink before it reached land. Below we have an exclusive interview with Voluntary Aid Detachment nurse, Gertrude Smith. Was this young woman responsible for the loss of so many lives, and also this great financial cost that our country must bear in these troubled times?

The reporter had only used half of the questions, which distorted the facts and made it look as though *I* had opened the portholes in defiance of the orders.

Mrs Cooper did not come into work until eleven o'clock.

'Is everything all right, Mrs Cooper?' my father asked, glancing at the clock.

'No, if you don't mind me telling you, sir, it is not all right at all.' Without waiting for any further discourse, she went on to explain. 'They, those local braggarts and fools, decided I was partly to blame for the loss of life on the *Britannic* because I work for you. They've harassed us all weekend. Jacob Boniface is amongst the worst. I couldn't step outside my own house today until they had cleared off.'

'But what did they do?' I asked.

'They threw rotten tomatoes at the window, and when I went outside to tell them to clear off or I'd call the peelers, well, that was when the real trouble began. They had put human excrement into a paper bag and set it alight on my doorstep. Well, I didn't know what was in it, did I? And what do you do when you find a small fire at your front door, well, you stamp on it to put it out, don't you? It's natural instinct, isn't it?' She appeared so glum, and then her chin shivered and I realised she was struggling to stay in control. 'I've never felt so humiliated in my life, me with kack all over my slippers and them laughing!' Mrs Cooper had hardly finished speaking when a crash came from the front of the house. Another of the small panes of glass shattered.

*   *   *

I returned home from shopping on Friday to find the constable waiting at my door.

'What is it? What's happened?' I asked, hurrying towards him.

'Your father, miss. A flying rock from a troublemaker struck Dr Smith while he was visiting patients. He swerved and drove his automobile into a tree. Don't be alarmed. He lost consciousness, but regained it on the way to hospital. His vehicle has suffered a little from the altercation, but that can be mended. He's recovering with nothing more than scrapes and bruises,' the constable told me. 'It could have been worse, so let's be grateful it wasn't.'

This was my fault! I returned to town in the cab and hurried into the hospital.

My father lay in a bleach-scented ward under clean, but thinning, sheets. After greeting him, I studied the head bandage and found the dressing nurse was competent. Quiet rage built up inside me. This was too much! Once Father was settled for the evening, I went to the police station.

'That thug Boniface could have killed him,' I said to Inspector Glassman. 'Surely there's something you can do to stop him?'

He ran his hand over his bald head, then down over his steel-grey moustache and beard. 'Feelings are running high, miss. People are demanding a public inquiry. They're not satisfied with the military one. They want someone to pay for their losses, and it seems they've decided that someone should be you.'

'Can't you speak to him, protect us?'

'In case you haven't noticed, there's a war going on. Our best constables are away fighting the Kaiser. What am I supposed to do with half a dozen *girls* in police uniform?' He raised his palms towards the ceiling.

'We've had three broken windows, Inspector. My own mother was injured by flying glass. Then Mrs Cooper was victimised in a horrible way, and now my father almost killed. These people have nothing to do with His Majesty's Hospital Ship! Boniface and his thugs are simply terrorising us because they are angry and feel useless. It's bullying, and if you can't put a stop to it, then I will try to end it by myself. It simply can't go on, Inspector. Will you come with me while I go and talk to Jacob Boniface?'

Where had I found the courage to speak to a policeman in this way? Thank you, Sissy, my darling sister.

He frowned and twisted the ends of his waxed moustache. 'I really don't think that would be a good idea, miss. The man's unstable.'

'Well, I can be unstable too. I am going to talk to him whether you come with me or not.'

Glassman closed his eyes for a moment and sighed. I noticed his clenched fists.

'Please, Inspector Glassman, isn't it better to talk than fight?' I stated vigorously.

419

He pulled in his chin and blinked at me. 'My thoughts exactly, but people are always eager to rush into an affray and fight. The sooner you lot get the vote the better.' He huffed and his shoulders dropped. 'Come on then, let's go and see the troublemaker.' He picked up a ring of keys from his desk and locked the police station once we were in the street.

Boniface was halfway between his delivery cart and the bakery when I saw him.

'Mr Boniface, can I have a word with you?'

He stopped, glared at me for a second, then hefted another sack of flour onto his back. 'You've got a nerve! Why are you here? Come to see what further heartbreak and damage you can cause?'

'Mr Boniface, you must understand, it was the *Germans* that sank HMHS *Britannic*! Now this has gone on long enough. My father could have been killed today!'

'Eye for an eye then, ain't it! You killed my youngest son. You don't know what it's like to lose yer boy. Fifteen 'e was. An' what about Fairclough's lad, 'is arm chopped off? What sort of a carpenter will 'e make now? Yer've got no idea what it's like, you in yer posh, White 'Ouse!'

'What! I've got no idea? My brother died fighting for the likes of you! My dearest brother!' Burning rage hissed through my body. I erupted like a volcano, my words venting inner fury. 'My most darling sister died far from home, nursing the boys that fought for us. How *dare* you! Yes, how *dare* you talk about sacrifice as if you are the only one who's suffered!'

Engulfed by wrath, I grabbed the scrubbed baker's paddle left to dry against the wall of the shop, and with all the anger in me, I swung it at Boniface. He stood there sneering, grasping the corners of a bulging flour sack on his back. Little did he know, I'd accumulated considerable strength, mostly in my arms, due to my work in Mudros. The wooden paddle twisted in my hands and the side of the spade chopped his arm and, I suspect, cracked his elbow.

He let out such a holler, dropped the flour, and we all disappeared in a dense white cloud. The Inspector made a grab for me and caught my shoulder. It took all my self-control to resist swinging a punch at the policeman's chin.

Boniface hollered. 'She's busted me elbow, little trollop, I want her arrested! Arrest her!'

'Oh, so sorry, Mr Boniface,' I screamed back sarcastically, pushing my face towards his. 'Perhaps we should call a doctor for you. But wait, of course we can't. Because you've put the only doctor in Dover in the hospital, you stupid, horrible, bad-tempered ogre!'

By then, Inspector Glassman had me so firmly around the waist that my feet were off the floor. 'Drop the paddle,' he said sternly.

I did, but Boniface rushed towards me yelling about his elbow, one big hand open and going for my throat. I picked up both feet and pushed him away with all the force I had in my legs. He staggered back, unbalanced, and landed on the cobbles on his backside, banging his elbow again, and roaring with rage.

By this time, a crowd had gathered. They started to point and laugh, and no wonder. A ridiculous tableau we were, covered in white flour, bellowing, and screaming, and flailing our arms and legs. However, the crowd's mockery further infuriated Boniface. 'Clear off, you nosy parkers!' he yelled, clumsily getting to his feet and rushing at them. His injured arm hung limply, while the other displayed a clenched fist that threatened to break any nose that came within striking distance.

Eventually, I found myself going to the police station to make a statement.

'You know I'll have to lock you up for your own safety, Miss Smith. The doctor in hospital . . . I could not let you stay out there on your own with Boniface on the loose,' Inspector Glassman said.

'No, Inspector, you have it wrong. You must lock me up for Mr Boniface's safety. Because I warn you, I cannot guarantee that I shall remain in control of my temper, should I find myself in the proximity of that despicable creature.' My insides trembled like Mrs Cooper's blancmange.

CHAPTER 47
SHELLY

Dover, present day.

SUMMER HEADED TOWARDS AUTUMN. SHELLY spoke to Harry every day and was relieved to hear that Elias had made a full recovery. Shelly ached to be with Harry and made him describe the weather, the dives, the landscape and the wildlife each time he phoned, dreaming she was right there with the man she loved.

'Come over before the season ends, while the water's still warm.'

Shelly sighed into the phone, remembering the bliss of an empty beach, a cloudless sky, warm smiles and welcoming faces.

'Let's get a dive in, and I can show you the rest of the island,' Harry said. 'Or, you said you wanted to go to Syros. We could go over for a few days. I'll go completely crazy if I don't see you soon, my darling.'

'Yes, oh, yes! I'd love to. I'll try to arrange it. Last week in October?'

'Perfect. Have you listened to all the tapes now?' Harry asked.

'I've one to go. Perhaps I could share them with you, what do you think?'

'Sure, I'd love to hear her speaking about Kea. You could fly into Syros. They have an airport.'

'Gertie went from Kea to Syros in a *caïque*, so I find that idea most appealing.'

'So, you arrange the first leg, to Kea, and I'll arrange the rest,' Harry said. 'I really can't wait to see you again.'

Shelly longed to see him too. She'd been thinking about inviting Harry and his sons for Christmas. With this in mind, she decided on a schedule of renovations and decoration. DJ insisted on doing any heavy work, and Eve was adamant she be style consultant.

It was the end of August, when Eve arrived at White Cottage with a party box of M&S sushi and two bottles of Grüner Veltliner. Eve watched Shelly zip herself into a disposable overall. 'I guess from the outfit, you're not joining me as one of the catering staff?'

Shelly laughed and fastened the strap on her yellow builder's helmet. 'Nope. Demolition squad, that's me!'

'Well, I hope you don't expect me to dress in that garb, because in truth, I'd rather die!'

DJ rolled his sleeves and grinned. 'We've got a pair of Gucci overalls for you, Eve, so you've got no excuse.'

'Oh, excuse me, young man, I'm pulling rank. Lowly builders are not allowed to interfere with the catering management, if you don't mind. We're an entirely superior breed. However, you are exceedingly handsome,' Eve said with her nose in the air. 'So, you can, in fact, interfere with me as much as you like.'

'Eve!' Shelly cried. 'Stop flirting with my son. You're old enough to be his mother.'

'Like you, you mean?' Eve replied in a flash, and they all burst into laughter.

Gordon came into the kitchen. 'I'm starving. 'Ere, d'you want me to stick those fishcakes in the microwave, Eve?' Gordon asked.

424

Eve placed her forearm against her forehead and faked a swoon. 'Touch them with those builder's fingernails and I will kill you myself, Mr Summer!'

Gordon turned to his grandson. 'What've these girls got yer doing now then, DJ? It looks like Armageddon in 'ere!'

DJ lifted his mask. 'We're taking the chimney breast down, Gramps. It takes up too much room. When it's gone, and we've decorated, Mum's going to take you into town to buy the biggest TV in the shop.'

Gordon's frown faded. 'Is that so? Then I'll give yer a 'and, lad. Do any of you know what you're doing?'

'Not without a mask and goggles, you won't,' Shelly said, thrusting a set towards him.

He threw her a dirty look, picked up the scissors and cut a small hole in the centre of the mask before putting it on.

'That kind of defeats the object, Gramps!'

'Don't care, I needs me smoke, lad. Be grateful I've given up the baccy and let me get on with me vape without a drama.'

DJ grinned with hero worship.

Gordon continued. 'Now, are you sure this is safe? Has anyone checked?'

'Yes, Dad, we got the professionals in. The surveyor said it's not supporting anything because the upstairs chimney was taken out thirty years ago.'

'Right then, no more shirking, people. Let's get on with the job. DJ, swing that mallet, lad.'

Shelly smiled, this was brilliant, the four of them doing a job together. She'd never have dreamt of such a thing and it made her tingle with happiness. She watched her son swing the long-handled lump hammer. It crashed into the chimney breast at

425

shoulder height. The whole house trembled but the chimney-breast stayed intact.

''Ere, yer needs to put yer back into it, lad.'

'Built to last, Gramps.'

Shelly beamed. 'Here, DJ, have a go at hitting my thumb.' She placed it a little lower, centrally, above the fireplace. 'Go on, go for it.'

He glanced at her nervously. 'You *will* pull it out the way?'

She grinned and winked. 'All you've got, lovey. Come on, now's your chance to show us what you're worth.'

'Stand back! Stand back!' Gordon ordered dramatically, suddenly in charge of the demolition and bubbling with fun. 'Wimmin under the table. Make sure yer gas masks are on. The Blitz is back an Gerry's goin' for a direct hit!'

'Now you've really lost the plot, Dad,' Shelly said, laughing at the fun in her father.

DJ hefted the lump hammer back and swung it at Shelly's thumb. She stepped away, he hit the spot and five rows of bricks clattered down in one great tumult.

'Well done, lad,' Gordon said, before puffing at his vape like a triumphant Popeye.

Shelly and Eve high-fived. Then they all, apart from Eve, shifted bricks into the barrow.

When the rubble was clear Eve cried, 'Break time!' and handed everyone a glass of white wine and a couple of sushi on a paper plate.

Gordon squinted suspiciously, first at the fish, then at his companions. When he thought no one was looking, he tipped his food on to DJ's plate.

Shelly said, 'I suspect there's a lintel, so a little higher this time, DJ.'

He swung the mallet again. She was right. The next five rows fell in, but didn't drop. They landed on a platform inside the chimney breast. Gordon and Shelly shifted them into the barrow.

'What's that, Gramps? It looks like a metal shelf with a trapdoor and a little chain.'

'That, lad, is the draught trap. When it's open, it draws the fire, and when the wood or coal's goin' good and proper, yer shuts it to stop the heat disappearin' up the chimney. Look—' He stuck his head in the chimney and pulled the chain. The little trapdoor almost closed.

'Dad, be careful, a brick might fall on your head!'

'Somethin's jammed inside, stoppin' it workin'. 'Ere, what's this?'

'Looks like one of those old camera spools, Gramps.'

'No it ain't. Yer know what this is, it's yer original YouTube.'

DJ threw an incredulous glance at Shelly. She bit her lip and shook her head.

'How do you mean, Gramps?'

'Well, this was how messages and pictures were sent from country to country in them there olden days, see.' He lifted the little container. 'It was strapped on the leg of a homing pigeon, so yer was limited on yer word-count, just like on yer Twitter. Shelly, sling us the torch, love.'

The torch hung next to the umbrella on the front door coat hooks. Shelly passed it to her father, then removed her helmet. 'Here, Dad, put this on while you're under those loose bricks.'

'Bloomin' wimmin,' he muttered, plonking the helmet on, then shining the torch into the depths of the chimney. 'Yes, here it is. Pass us the tea tray, will yer? And a cold beer wouldn't go amiss. Thirsty work all this demolishing.'

427

Shelly pulled the dustsheet off the kitchen table and chairs and they all sat around as her dad carefully sorted and aligned a set of fine bones into the shape of a pigeon skeleton.

'Poor thing, it must have fallen down the chimney after the fireplace was first bricked up,' Shelly said. 'Pass us the tube, Dad. Let's see if there's anything inside.'

'It's too heavy, that poor bird must have died of exhaustion lugging this,' he said, placing it in Shelly's hand.

She used a kitchen knife to get the tin lid off. Inside the spool, tightly rolled cigarette papers were held in place with a fine gold band. She slipped the ring off the paper and carefully unfurled the sheets. 'They're numbered, and they don't seem to have suffered much. The ink's faded to dark yellow, but it's still readable. Let's put them in order and see what they say.'

They spread them on the table.

'Go on then, I 'avent got me glasses on,' Dad said.

Shelly started reading the tiny letters.

Dearest Gertie, love of my life,

I wish to place this ring on your finger myself but – be brave my darling – the Hun has put an end to me with a blast from a mine. It got caught in my net, and went off as I pulled it in. I'm not going to make it back to England, agapi mou, so I'm sending Icarus with your wedding ring and my wedding vow. I know you are Catholic, so my father's called the priest to write these words to you, agapi.

Gertie Smith, I, Emmanuelle Psaras take thee to be my lawful wedded wife. Whatever your response is, 'I agree and declare, I do.' I want to say many things but fear the weight of this letter is too much for Icarus. I trust his brave spirit and pray this letter arrives at Lighthouse Lane. I wish to tell Adam how wonderful his mother is. Keep these cigarette papers and give them to him

428

when time is right. Tell him about his father, Gertie; that I love him, as I love his mother. He must grow strong and take care of you in your old age on my behalf, agapi. Your love fills my heart, Gertie, and makes my journey into the afterlife bearable. And when this shattered body gives up, as it will in the next days, I will take your love to heaven to comfort me until we meet again. When your time comes, you'll find me waiting for you at the gates of eternity.

All my love, for ever, Manno.

Silence filled the room, broken only by a very damp sniff from Gordon.

'How terribly sad. All that time Gran Gertie stood at the bottom of the garden, shaking her corn tin, poor Icarus lay dead in the chimney with Manno's wedding vow, his final goodbye, and her wedding ring. I've never wished there is a heaven more than I do at this moment,' Shelly whispered. 'I want to believe he was there for her when she died.'

'I think I'm going to cry,' Eve said, pouring herself another glass of white.

Gordon blew his nose noisily. ''Ere, you should have this,' he said, picking up the thin ring and passing it to Shelly.

She stared at it in the palm of her hand. 'It belongs with the next generation. Will it fit on your little finger, DJ?'

He pushed it on and lay his hand flat on the tabletop. They all stared at it. 'Just fits. Thanks, Mum. It's an honour to wear it. I can't believe it travelled across Europe attached to the leg of a pigeon. A bird that avoided gunfire and bombs; all for the sake of my great-great-grandmother, Gertie Smith. Amazing, isn't it? I wonder what happened to Corporal Perkins?'

* * *

Eight weeks later, Shelly found herself on the top deck of the ferry, staring at the port of Kea as the ship slid smoothly between the Church of the Trinity, and St Nicholas lighthouse. She saw a dozen people waiting for the boat and spotted Harry immediately.

'Harry, it's wonderful to be back,' she said, resisting the urge to throw her arms around his neck and kiss him on the mouth.

'Allow me help you,' he said, his brown eyes sparkling with pleasure as he kissed her cheeks and then took her suitcase. 'Let's get this to your room as quickly as possible.'

'Oh yes! I've got something for you.'

'I'm banking on it.'

She giggled. 'From my great-grandmother.'

'Ah, not what I was thinking, actually.'

'You're too naughty!'

'Mm, I do my best.'

By the time they got to her room, they were both laughing.

'I hope you're going to let me in?' he said.

'In what context are you speaking?'

'Now who's being naughty?' He bustled her into the room and locked the door.

Two hours later they came back into the real world, bright-eyed with their secrets and their love.

'I'm taking you to a taverna in my village.'

'Your village?'

He nodded. 'Over there in Vourkari. On the edge of the sea. The best fish.'

'Do you have a plan?' she asked.

'Yes, I'll drive there, we'll eat, and the rest is up to you.'

'No!' she laughed. 'You're teasing me, now. Is there anything you would like to do tomorrow?'

'We're going on a dive at midday, then we'll simply chill out, because the next day we're going to Syros Island as soon as it's light.'

'Oh, brilliant, I'm so pleased.'

'I'm quite excited myself. I have a big surprise planned for you there.'

'Intriguing; will I need my dive equipment?'

He shook his head. 'No, and don't interrogate me, I'm not telling you anything more.' He kissed the tip of her nose. 'Enough to say: you will be absolutely blown away, and probably in tears too!'

CHAPTER 48
GERTIE

Dover, 1917.

'YOU HAVE SPIRIT,' INSPECTOR GLASSMAN said, handcuffing me. 'I like a woman with spirit.' I made the walk of shame to the station, where he took the cuffs off and locked me in one of the two holding cells. I was to stay there until the hearing. 'You'll be safe down here,' Glassman said. 'This basement's stronger than any bomb.'

'It's not a bomb I'm afraid of, Inspector. I've seen the result of a gas attack, men coughing up chunks of their own lungs before they die. Will I have my mask with me?'

'I'll make sure it's brought in with your essentials.' The small room was about nine square yards, with a low ceiling, no window, and a barred door. A place in which to go crazy with claustrophobia. Her head was already spinning when she realised Glassman was speaking. 'Unfortunately, as it's Friday, there's no chance of a hearing until Tuesday, Miss Smith. However, we'll make sure you're as comfortable as possible. I'll bring some supper later, meanwhile, if you make a list of things you require, perhaps your daily will bring them in for you. There's a chamber pot under the bed, and a bucket of water behind the curtain.'

That was a grim moment, when he shut the heavy door at the top of the steps and silence fell around me.

In my solitary confinement, time stood still and I had no notion of day or night.

* * *

I heard the big door at the top of the stairs open and Mrs Cooper's protesting voice.

'Eeh, you're not keeping the poor girl down here? Come on now . . . what if she were your sister, is this how you'd want her treated, lad?'

'Oh, Mrs Cooper, thank goodness!'

'Now, now, don't fret, Miss Gertie. I've got all your creature comforts and we'll soon have you out of here. Your man friend is right behind me, and he'll be down as soon as I've relieved myself of your things.' She shimmied her shoulders and made a mischievous pout.

'Man friend? How are my parents, Mrs Cooper?'

'Your mother is ailing, but not much different. Your father's much better, miss. The people of Dover have really spoiled him. Everyone in town owes him a kindness, and here comes an opportunity to repay that debt. Folk have taken him special meals, and enough cakes for him to open a bakery. He'll be here tomorrow, once I've ironed him a fresh shirt and collar.' Mrs Cooper fussed about for ten minutes then bid me goodbye.

* * *

I heard slow footfalls on the stairs followed by Inspector Glassman's voice. 'So here she is, sir. I'm afraid we had no choice but to lock her up.'

Corporal Perkins appeared in full uniform, but not wearing his prosthesis. His trouser leg was pinned up, and he supported himself with two beautifully varnished crutches. He swept my heart away as he appeared on the other side of my barred doorway.

'Oh, poor Gertie!' He turned to Glassman. 'Aren't you going to let me in there?'

'I'm not sure the doctor would approve, sir.'

'Inspector, I'm a Corporal in the British army. Miss Gertie and I were both on the *Britannic* on the day she sank. I lost my leg in this war while fighting for you and my country. Also, I'm a close friend of the family. In fact, I was there for tea only last week.'

Glassman looked unsure for a second, then addressed me. 'What do you say, miss? Shall I let him in for half an hour?'

'Inspector Glassman, I assure you that Corporal Perkins is a soldier and a gentleman. I will be perfectly safe left alone in his company.'

'If you're certain, miss. I'll leave the door at the top of the stairs open, so just call out at any time and I will hear you. However, this does mean I will have to lock the Corporal in too.'

'Perfectly fine,' I assured him. Johnathan Perkins stood behind the inspector and wiggled his eyebrows in a comical manner and I struggled not to laugh. Oh, what joy, to have some company!

'Thank you so much for coming, Johnathan.'

'By all accounts, you caused quite an uproar. I came straight over when I read the newspaper.'

'No! It wasn't in the papers?'

'It certainly was, and it seems you struck a blow for all Dover. That Boniface is not a liked man.'

434

'He's just upset after losing his boy, and I shouldn't have lost my temper. The hearing's on Tuesday. As if I haven't got enough to worry about. How's my father?'

'I've been to see him, to ask his permission to visit you here, and I also asked if I could walk out with you. He's worried about you, naturally. Otherwise, he'll be fine once they've allowed him to attend to his precious car.'

I smiled, just imagining my father's concern for the Ford.

'Gertie, there's something else you should know, so you can prepare. Public opinion, driven by the press, has demanded another inquiry into the sinking of the *Britannic*.'

I felt my body deflate. 'Oh, no. They'll find out, won't they? I'm so afraid!'

'Find out what?' He blinked at me with what could only be an honest look of confusion.

'You don't remember?'

He shook his head. 'Remember what?'

I stared at him, unsure. Was he simply trying to make me feel better, or did he genuinely not remember? I had thought, when he offered to swear to the press that I did not open the portholes, that he must know what I'd done – but perhaps he didn't after all.

'It was my first hour in the ward. You and your fellow patients bullied and tormented me until I relented and opened the portholes.'

He stared at me, clearly shocked. 'We did?'

'You certainly did. I was almost in tears. Don't you remember?'

He shook his head again. 'You're telling me that it's I who is ultimately responsible for all that maiming and the loss of so many lives?'

'No, not you alone, it was also your friends, and of course I did go against orders. I told you it was against orders, but you

435

said that you'd heard Staff tell me to use my initiative, and that meant opening the portholes for ten minutes when the ward was stinking from fouled bedpans. In the end, I couldn't take any more, so gave in to you all and opened them.'

He stared at me, clearly horrified. 'Who else knows?'

'That I opened the portholes?'

'No, that we bullied you?'

'Nobody.'

He stood and paced two steps to the wall, and two back again. 'You and I, we must make a plan, Gertie.' He stopped and stared at me.

* * *

Perkins returned the next day, all suited up this time, and wearing his artificial leg. He used a walking cane, which gave him an ostentatious swagger that made me smile. As he approached, I felt my heart leap with pleasure to see him again.

'Dearest Gertie, I can't stand to see you in this place.' He took a deep breath and delved into his pocket. After a moment's hesitation, he struggled onto his one knee and thrust a small ring box into my hands. 'Tell me, may I ask your father for your hand, dear Gertie? Will you become my wife?'

'Oh, this is too fast. You must let me think, Johnathan. It's all . . .' Just at that moment, I heard footsteps scuttling down the stairs.

'What's going on?' Mrs Cooper demanded, clearly not recognising Perkins as the one-legged soldier she had seen the day before. She stared at Corporal Perkins who was trying to get up from his one good knee.

436

'If you must know, Mrs Cooper, I'm asking Miss Smith to become my wife. Now if you would kindly give us a few moments of privacy, I'd appreciate it.'

'I most certainly will not! Get yourself out of that cell, right at this instant!' She turned back towards the stairs. 'Inspector!'

Glassman came down to the cellar. 'Yes, madam?'

Mrs Cooper folded her arms beneath her ample chest and shuffled her breasts up into a more dynamic position. A clever ploy, as Glassman was clearly struggling not to glance at her bosom. He resorted to fixing safely on the explosion of ginger frizz that was attempting to escape the yellow satin ribbon securing her topknot. 'I'll thank you not to leave these two young people alone together down here!' she yelled. 'Dr Smith would not be best pleased!'

'Of course, madam. Except that the young man has a letter from Dr Smith permitting him to visit the young lady while she is in here.'

'Then make sure you keep that door between them locked!'

* * *

The next day my father came to see me. He sat next to me on the cell's cot. I was acutely aware of – and embarrassed by – the smell of urine from the chamber pot beneath my bed. I found it hard to meet his eyes when I said, 'I can't tell you how sorry I am, Father.'

'Let's not regret what can't be changed. I have every confidence in you, Gertie. Hopefully, after the hearing on Tuesday, you'll be released and we can put this behind us.'

Yet I felt his disappointment. 'Thank you for allowing Corporal Perkins to visit me. He was my very first patient, you know.'

437

'Yes, he told me. He came to visit me in the hospital to ask if he may visit you here.'

'May I speak frankly, Father?' He nodded. 'Corporal Perkins claims to love me, as he did on the ship, but I don't quite know what to make of him.'

'Sometimes, love is instantaneous, as it was between your mother and I.' He stared at the floor, for a moment lost in his thoughts, then he drew in a deep shaky breath. 'For many other people, love grows over time. If you enjoy his company, perhaps you should give him a chance to prove himself. Other than that, I can't advise you.' He glanced at my hand. 'He asked me about the ring you are wearing on your wedding finger, and to be perfectly frank, I had not noticed it. Is there someone else, Gertie?'

My mouth dried as my darling Manno came to mind. Why had he never replied to my letters when I had made it clear how much I loved him?

'The ring simply reminds me of the miracle dolphin that rescued me, Father. If that creature had not lifted me from the depths, I would not have saved Corporal Perkins. However, the enormity of these things still shakes me. Do you think God really orchestrated all this?'

His head tilted to one side as he smiled. 'Such an enormous experience? You think God had a hand in it all?'

I nodded, feeling a little foolish for even considering such a thing.

'How can we know?' Father concluded. 'Us, mere warring mortals who can set the world on fire with our bombs, and cause excruciating agony with our evil gasses. We who build great ships, Zeppelins and aeroplanes, and squabble murderously

438

about borderlines and areas of the great seas. Do we not think we are gods ourselves?'

I shrugged, unable to answer his questions. 'The thing is, Father, the man who gave me the ring – the ring that reminds me that a miracle dolphin saved me, so that I could save Corporal Perkins – well, that man is Corporal Perkins's rival for my hand in marriage. It's all too confusing.' My father shook his head so I tried to clarify. 'If I had not been saved by the dolphin, I could not marry anyone. But the man who put the dolphin on my wedding finger is not the man who has asked you for my hand.'

'I see . . . I think.'

'If there *is* a public inquiry, and I *am* found guilty of opening the portholes and causing the *Britannic* to sink before it reached the island of Kea, might they hang me for mutiny? I am so afraid . . .'

Saying my deepest fears aloud was too much for me. I gulped and hiccuped and choked on my anguish. The bodies in the sea, my drowning, the needle going into my arm to draw blood, the horror of having an amputated leg dropped into my arms. All of it . . . boiled up and scalded me. And now imagining the floor opening beneath my feet and a rope tightening around my neck, then snapping it at the end of my fall into the darkest place on earth. *Oh!*

'And if I was pregnant, would my life be spared, or would they still hang me after my baby was born?'

My father's eyes widened and his mouth fell slightly open, but he said nothing.

I was so overcome I could not draw breath. Darkness invaded from the corners of my eyes, and everything rushed away. Suddenly I was in hell, swinging from a rope in the void demanded by justice, all for my wrongdoing.

A burning sensation in my nostrils brought me back to now and the smelling salts that father wafted under my nose. Then I was in his arms, sobbing violently.

'We'll get through this, Gertie, poor, poor child,' he said, holding me against his chest as I wept.

Once Father had gone, I sat alone in my cell and studied *Gray's Anatomy* until I fell asleep. The muscles and bones, brains, eyes and organs on the pages all came back to me in my dreams as I had seen them in the operating theatre, then I saw them tossed in the water around the *Britannic*'s propeller. In the purple and black of a gangrene nightmare I fell through the hangman's trapdoor onto a heap of mashed bodies and gore and found myself screaming for all I was worth.

'Miss! Miss!' the sergeant cried. 'You're having a nightmare, wake up now!'

He was a decent fellow, and I could see he felt sorry for me. 'I'll make you some cocoa and we'll see if we can get you out of here tomorrow.'

* * *

When father returned to my cell, he informed me I had no post at home. My heart plummeted. So I would accept Perkins's proposal, even though we had little in common apart from the *Britannic*. He wanted to run off and fix broken vehicles, I needed to heal the wounded and nurse the sick. We were destined to hardly see each other before the end of the war.

'Gertie, I have some great news,' Perkins told me the following day. 'There's a shortage of mechanics now, and the government is accepting some amputees for certain posts that are not affected by their condition.'

'That's wonderful news, Johnathan.'

'I received my papers this morning. I long to go, but of course I cannot leave you while you are harassed like this. Marry me immediately, Gertie Smith, before I return to the war. Make me the happiest man on earth. If you do, I'll go straight to the press and I'll tell them I'm sure you didn't open the portholes.'

I stared at Perkins, then at the ring. I knew this would be the solution to all my problems and would make him immensely happy, but it would not mend my broken heart.

'Please, Gertie, do me the honour of becoming my wife. I can get a special licence. We can be married in the fortnight.'

I thought about the baby growing inside me and nodded.

* * *

The magistrate released me with a caution and Jacob Boniface was ordered not to come within half a mile of our house, or a hundred yards of me.

Back home – on a mattress where the flock-stuffing gathered in lumps, determined to quarrel with the contours of my body – I hardly slept, more confident by the day that I was with child. Each day became a struggle. Manno became my hero, an anchor in my sea of troubles, although I suspected he hardly understood the intensity of my feelings towards him. He was a simple village fisherman, only twenty-two years of age. Captivated by the unconventional man who had swept me off my feet and literally thrown me on the bed, I wondered if I had given my heart away too soon?

* * *

My father agreed with my wedding to Johnathan and because he was a soldier, we had special dispensation to marry, two weeks later, before a small group of friends which included Matron Merriberry and Josephine, and some distant relations of Perkins. That day I became the Corporal's wife in the town hall.

After the formalities before the registrar, we went back to our house. Mrs Cooper and her two daughters had prepared a wedding banquet – magnificent, considering we were in the middle of a world war. First, oysters, followed by a brace of pheasants with apple and walnut stuffing, roasted vegetables, and dandelion salad. Pudding was a luxurious apple charlotte with clotted cream.

After a little too much sherry, Johnathan and I left home, showered by the guests with rose petals and rice. Father drove us to a hotel in the town for one night. Someone had bedecked father's Ford in white ribbons, added a pair of old boots to the back bumper, and fixed a written sign that said JUST MARRIED to the rear of the car.

I was frantic, sure Perkins would realise I was not a virgin. However, my true friend, Josephine, was ahead of me.

'Gertie, come into the bedroom,' she said earlier that day.

I followed her.

'Look, I may be entirely wrong, if so, pardon me, but you may need this.' She handed me a little parcel wrapped in white linen.

'Thank you, but what is it?'

'Forgive me. You are probably intact.' Her eyes flicked down, then back to my face. 'I'm sure you are. But as you rode a motorbike in Mudros, such activities can rupture a woman's hymen. Do you understand?'

I nodded frantically. 'I think it did . . . I've been so worried.'

'Then, to save the tedium of explanations, use this gift and we'll say no more.'

'But how? I know nothing.'

'You will find a phial of fresh rabbit's blood and a small sponge. Saturate the sponge with the blood, and place it as high as possible in your secret place. Remove it and wash yourself as soon as possible after. All right?'

I need not have worried. For all Johnathan's flirting, I realised he was not experienced in the art of lovemaking. Clearly it was his first time, and he was as anxious about the event as I, until mother nature gave him a delirious shove in the right direction.

*   *   *

The broadsheets picked up on our union and the opportunity arose for my new husband to keep his word and exonerate me from any part in the sinking of the *Britannic*.

Three days after our marriage, Johnathan left for France. The press forgot me, and I personally visited the families of the lost and injured men. I talked about those brave fellows to their parents and wives which seemed to bring the mothers in particular some relief from their torment. I cried with them, genuinely moved by their grief.

With a heavy heart, I wrote to Manno and told him I knew about his family and I had found a father for his baby. I told him how heartbroken I was. He had betrayed me – but maybe I had betrayed him too, by marrying Johnathan. I tried to put it out of my mind but that was impossible. Now, I understood true love. No matter what he did, I loved him to the depths of my soul. There was no question, one day I would go back to that small Greek island and find the fisherman. I would feel his arms around me, and taste his lips on mine one more time. It seemed the saddest tears of were trapped in my heart, and would stay there until the day I met my one true love again.

I took work in the local hospital and saved every penny I could towards my trip back to Greece. When my pregnancy became obvious, I broke the news. Father congratulated my husband when he returned from France on leave.

Johnathan was thrilled and begged me to give him a son. He was such a dear man who clearly loved me. I tried to be the wife he deserved and kept my deceit to myself. I had made these two men, my father and Johnathan, very happy.

It was only in those darkest hours before dawn that I lay in my lonely bed and cried for my one true love.

As my girth expanded, so my mother's health deteriorated until she passed away in her sleep a month before I gave birth.

* * *

While my husband was away, I gave birth to a beautiful, blue-eyed son. I'm sure my father read all the signs that my baby was at least three weeks late, yet I claimed he was almost a month early. Johnathan came home for three days special leave, and was thrilled that we were now a proper family. We decided to call our baby Adam, after Johnathan's father.

'You've made me the proudest man, Gertie. Thank you. I love you both so much,' he whispered in my ear the night before he returned to the war. 'In an odd way, I am not so afraid of being killed now, knowing a part of me lives on, here.'

CHAPTER 49
GERTIE

Dover, 1917.

ADAM WAS SUCH A BEAUTIFUL baby, and with his birth all the powerful instincts of motherhood were born too. When his eyes found mine, I became lost in the wonder of him. This perfect little baby seemed to glow with love as he grasped my little finger.

My father doted on his first grandchild, buying him the best perambulator in the country.

With Father's encouragement, I took Adam out for a turn along Lighthouse Lane every morning after breakfast, once his thirty days of confinement was over. His eyes were already changing colour, and his porcelain pink skin had gained a golden hue. I saw Manno in every glance of my baby's wonderful eyes. As the weeks passed, I'm sure my father realised the dark-haired, brown-eyed baby was not the Corporal's child, but he said nothing.

My husband was due home in a fortnight. On several occasions, I feared he would see Adam's likeness to his Greek antagonist. I strolled along Lighthouse Lane, towards home, when I noticed a stranger walking towards me from the direction of The White House. The man stopped, staring in our direction, then suddenly, he tore off his trilby and started running towards us.

'Gertie! Is that you, *agapi mou*?'

'Oh, Manno! Manno!' I couldn't believe it. Overwhelmed, I longed to be in his arms, yet I remained frozen to the spot, remembering the woman and two children he had in Kea. I pulled the brake lever on the perambulator and turned towards him.

'Please, Manno, we can't be seen together. At any moment, someone might come down the lane. Go through the gate just ahead and wait for me in the field, behind the hedge.'

As usual, the fresh air had put Adam to sleep. Once Manno had disappeared through the gate, and there was no sign of traffic, I headed in his direction.

Tears welled in my eyes when I finally entered his embrace. 'Oh, my darling, I've missed you so much! What are you doing here? Why didn't you answer my letters?'

'I wanted to write to you, but I have a terrible confession, *agapi mou*.'

'I know, I heard. You have a wife and two little girls already.' I stared at the ground, unable to look at him, my tears coming dangerously close.

'What! No! Who has told you such a thing?'

'It's useless denying it. Your wife cooked a meal for Matron, only last month. Your children are beautiful, she says so.'

He cupped my chin and lifted my face so that I could not avoid his eyes. 'My *sister-in-law*, Katerina, looks after me and my father when we stay on Kea, and we look after her while my brother is in the army!'

I stared at him while the news went into my head. 'You're not married? Oh! Then what is your big confession?' He took a breath, his face colouring a little. 'Manno, you're blushing! Oh, my goodness, what is it?'

'I am ashamed, *agapi mou*, you see . . . I cannot read or write the English alphabet. My sister-in-law, she found your letters

446

two weeks ago. I kept them all, you understand. Katerina, she read some of them to me.'

'Manno, you break my heart.'

'I think your father has guessed the truth, that I love you, *agapi*, but he does not want his daughter to run away with a foreigner and live in another country. He told me I was too late, that my Gertie is happily married, and she has a child. He said if I really loved you, I would leave you alone. Is it true, *agapi*? Are you married to that *malaka* English soldier, Perkins?'

'What could I do? I was having a baby, and you never replied! I needed a father for my child, and that *malaka* English soldier, as you call him, saved me from going to prison and perhaps from being hanged. What a mess this is! What shall we do?'

'Leave him and come back to Greece with me.'

'I can't do that. If I leave him, he'll tell the authorities the truth. Besides, he really loves me. They could hang me, Manno, don't you understand? You see, it was me that went against orders and opened the portholes on the ship. Because of my action, the two-million-pound hospital ship sank before it reached the port. They could have saved it, repaired it, and gone on to save thousands of lives. I'm guilty of mass murder.'

'How can you be guilty of mass murder? You're a *girl*! This is crazy, you cannot stay with a man who blackmails you into having his baby!'

I stared at him, my heart thumping and my eyes full of tears. 'No,' I sobbed. 'No, you don't understand! Oh, why didn't Katerina read all my letters? This is too much, Manno!' Then I couldn't speak for the sobs that were jerking my chest. The pain gathered and rose until it escaped in a great howl.

Manno pulled me against him. 'Don't cry, please! I'll do anything you want, anything, but don't cry.'

'Manno, I love you! And Adam is *your* son . . .'

His jaw dropped, and for a moment he seemed frozen in shock. Then, he took me firmly by the shoulders and almost shook me, disbelief written on his face. 'My son! You are telling me that this baby, right here, is *my* son? My son?'

I nodded. 'I was a virgin, remember. You were my first love. I told you in my letters I was pregnant.'

Manno seemed too emotional to speak, then he exploded with joy. 'I have a son! Holy Virgin Mary, I have a son!' He crossed himself and then pulled me against him. 'This is a miracle. Let me see him. Does he look like me? My son . . . oh!'

'Yes, he's starting to look like you. I don't know how I'm going to explain his brown eyes and dark hair to my husband when he comes home, but it's clear to see he's changing to look a little more like you every day.' I unhooked the elastic loops on the perambulator's apron and pushed the hood down. Adam stirred and sucked his fist. 'It is coming up to his feed time. I must return home.' The pain of loneliness gathered in my chest. *Manno, my love.* I didn't want him to leave, but he must.

'He is so beautiful, yes,' he said breathily. 'Let me pick him up and hold him, my own son.'

'No, it's too cold. Come back to the cottage tomorrow morning. My father will be working at the hospital after eight o'clock.'

'I can't. My ferry ticket is for tomorrow morning. I must start back to the port. I don't have the money for another ticket back to Greece.' I could see he was distressed and it broke my heart.

'Then come back to the house. I will speak to my father.'

448

'I have spoken to him, *agapi mou*. He made it clear I was not welcome here. Thank the Virgin Mary I came across you, or I would never have known I have a son.'

'Trust me. My father's a good man. He's only doing what he thinks is best. Allow me to go and speak to him.'

'He will shoot me!'

'No.' I smiled. 'Fathers do not shoot boys who make their daughters pregnant anymore. Trust me.'

'I want you to know, I love you. When Katerina had read the first few letters to me, I went out and sold my boat to pay for a trip to come here.'

'Manno, you sold your precious boat? Oh, my goodness.'

'Well, to give you the truth, it was my father's boat, and now he is threaten to shoot me. But no worries, when I tell him about the grandson of his, everything will change.'

'You're crazy, Manno. Really crazy. Let me speak to Father. Come to the house with me.'

I pointed to the chairs under the oak tree. 'Wait there, Manno.'

'You're sure he will not shoot me?'

'I'm sure.' I pulled the front door open, wheeled the perambulator into the vestibule, and lifted Adam.

'Who is that?' Father asked as he turned away from the window. 'He was here earlier, looking for you.'

'Manno is the mailman who rescued us when the *Britannic* went down, Father.' I sat in the nursing chair in front of the fireplace. 'His grandmother looked after me, did my laundry and gave me her bed. A very special lady.'

Adam snuffled and gave a little cry, telling me of his hunger. As usual, the sound made my nipples harden painfully. I quickly unbuttoned the front of my dress and then opened the top of my combinations. My baby searched, open-mouthed, for my teat, latched on, and then nursed hungrily. His little fist opened and closed against the white skin of my breast, and his eyes half closed with contentment. There was something miraculous about feeding my little one, and the process filled me with wonder.

Father came over and, with an adoring look, peered down at us. 'One of the most wonderful sights in the world, Gertie.' Then he straightened up, and asked, 'What do you want to do about the young man?'

'He sold his fishing boat to come here and see me for a few hours, Father. His ticket to go back to Greece is for the morning ferry. I'm sure he will never return, so I would like to spend a little time with him. I know that's inappropriate, but still . . . who will know? Oh, Father!' And suddenly it was all too much. My tears broke free and raced down my cheeks. Adam stopped suckling and stared at me.

Father turned back to look out of the window.

'Oh, Father. I feel so ashamed. I've been nothing but trouble, haven't I? I'm so sorry. I try to do the right thing, but everything seems to go wrong. And now . . . and now I will have to bear the consequences of my actions for the rest of my life.'

'Do you love him?' I nodded. 'Where does this leave your husband?'

'Johnathan is a good man, really, and he does love me. He will provide a fine life for us, and Father, he deserves better than me. I will thank you to forget all this as soon as you can. Johnathan need never know. It would only hurt him.'

'I see. Gertie, as your father, I must advise you. Lies are never a good foundation on which to base a marriage. You must live with them for the rest of your life. However, I understand your reasoning.' He turned away from the window. 'I have to take the

Ford into town for a service, so I'll stay at the club after surgery and return home around noon tomorrow. Will you be all right?'

I stroked the downy hair on Adam's head. 'Yes, Father. Thank you.'

'Then I'll see you tomorrow, when I hope we can put all this behind us and forget it ever happened.'

* * *

Once my father had left, I called Manno in. He sat on the sofa and rocked Adam to asleep.

'He is magnificent, and so strong, like Hercules. Did you see how hard he gripped my finger? I feel so proud now, I don't want to be parted from him, Gertie. I should stay.'

'Don't frighten me, Manno. I've told you what will happen if my husband finds out the truth. Do you want me to hang?' I clutched my throat. The idea terrified me. 'Your son will grow up knowing his father caused his mother's death. He'd never forgive you.'

Manno's eyes widened. 'Forgive me, *agapi mou*, I didn't think of these things.'

'You are a good man, Manno, and I love you, but we have to think of what's best for our son. One day, I swear on my life, he will come to Syros.' I went to my mother's writing bureau and removed a small ivory box. 'Just to prove I am telling you the truth, look, here is the money I have already saved up towards my trip to Greece.' I hesitated, I had worked so hard for this, but then I thrust it towards him. 'As a demonstration of my love for you, I want you to take this money and buy your father's boat back.'

He reached out, I thought for the box, but instead he took my hand. 'You are still wearing my ring. The silver dolphin. That is enough proof for me, *agapi mou*. The boat is no problem, I sold it to the mayor of Kea. I'll win it back in a game of *tavli*. Also, the mayor has to get the mail from Syros, so he will lend me my own boat to get it. You see, is not so bad.' He looked tenderly into my eyes. 'Where is your bed?'

'No, Manno, I'm a married woman now. It wouldn't be right.' His face fell. 'Manno, you took my virginity, and I have given you a strong, handsome son, is that not enough?'

He sat in silence for a while. 'I have decided, I will wait until this war is over, then I will ask you to leave the Englishman and join me on my beautiful Greek island. While I wait, I'll build you the most wonderful house of stone that looks out over the sea. I'll plant olive trees, so we are rich with oil, and grapes to make the sweetest wine. There will be many almond trees, for their beautiful blossom in the spring, and walnut trees for fine nuts in the autumn. We will have beehives, full of golden thyme honey, and because you are English, we'll have roses . . . the biggest red roses.'

This was too much for me. I didn't want him to leave.

He lifted my chin. 'Why you cry, Gertie? I love you. One day we'll be together, *agapi mou*.'

'Oh, Manno, I wish with all my heart.'

We talked through the night, only stopping while I fed Adam. Manno watched, his face alight with awe. My heart was breaking as dawn approached. I knew I would never leave Johnathan. I had put his life in danger, made him lose his leg. I could not break his heart too. Manno's plan was all a dream, a fairy tale, doomed from the start.

At five o'clock, as dawn broke, I started to wrap Adam in a blanket with the intention of placing him in the perambulator.

'Wait!' Manno said, picking him up tenderly. He held him in front of his face and spoke seriously to our beautiful baby. 'My son, you must grow big and strong, and take care of your mother. You must do this for me, because I love her with all my heart. Your name is Adam, but I give you your Greek name. You, my son, are Hephaestus, blacksmith, god of fire and strength, because you were born from the fiery passion between your mother and me, your father, inside a house of stone, on the island of Syros. I don't know when I will see you again, but you will always be in my heart, and I will think about you every day, until I die. On this, I swear.' He gently kissed Adam's cheeks, his forehead, and his mouth, then lay him on the settle and kissed the palms of his hands and the soles of his feet. When he stood, and passed our baby back to me, his eyes were full of tears.

'I will walk to the gate with you, Manno.' I could hardly say the words for the pain in my throat. Would I ever see him again? 'Kiss me one last time.' My heart was breaking. All the love I had for him seemed to fill me in that moment. Oh, how I wanted to go back to Greece with him. We broke apart, and I tried to stifle my sobs as we stepped outside.

Sensing my distress, Manno said, 'Just promise me you'll wait until the end of the war, *agapi mou*. Give me a chance to prove I can give you and our son a better life.'

Unable to speak, I nodded. We were just under the big oak tree when a van came speeding down Lighthouse Lane.

Neither of us heard the collision, and I'm sure the driver was unaware of it, but there on the verge, as still as death, was one of my father's pigeons. I recognised it immediately. Icarus, a blaze of pure white feathers. I put the brake on the pram as Manno stooped to pick up the bird.

'It is a sign,' he said. 'Such a beautiful bird. It is like an angel sent by the gods. Look, it comes back to life in my hands!' The bird fluttered.

'It has a broken wing, Manno. Best to put it out of its misery. I don't want to see it suffer.'

'No, *agapi mou*, I told you, it is a sign, don't you see? There is so much I want to say, but the passion gets in the way and I can't find the right words in English. I will fix his wing and send him back to you with a letter. Katarina will help me with the English. Do you have a box?'

Aware of time ticking by, I hurried to the pigeon loft and brought Manno a pigeon backpack – a bamboo cage with two leather straps to hold it onto the shoulders of a soldier.

'Take care of my son, Gertie!' he cried, marching towards Dover port just as a huge orange sun met the horizon, silhouetting him as he turned with a final wave.

I waved back, hoping he could not see the tears racing down my face, or feel the pain of my broken heart. And for all I know, I could not see the tears on his face, or feel his broken heart either. I wanted to think that it was over now, but I knew the love between us was eternal.

* * *

I never heard from Manno again, but my love for him has never died. Even to this day, I think about him often. My storm-tossed soul still clings to the wreckage of life.

Let me give you this advice. If you find love, darling Shelly, grab hold of it. True love is the only thing you should never let go, regardless of the difficulties, it is a rare and precious thing.

Corporal Perkins loved me, of that I am sure, and I believe Adam and I brought him a great deal of happiness. However, it's a sad fact that he didn't survive the war. Although he was a non-combatant, he was often in the war zone. His end came when a jeep in his convoy broke down. He left his vehicle to take a look, and stepped on a land mine. He gave a message to another soldier, for me.

Dearest Gertie and Adam, I love you both with all my heart. Don't be too sad, you have made me happy beyond measure. I won't be coming home, darling nurse of mine. I leave you with the task of finding a good father for my boy. Someone who knows about discipline, and love, and the importance of affection and loyalty, Gertie. In the short time we have had together, I am grateful for all the joy you have given me. You know I've loved you from that first moment I saw you, on the Britannic. I want you to know that I'm not in any pain, but I will not make it back, my darling. I'll see you in heaven, beautiful Gertie. Hold my son tightly, for me. Kiss his sweet face, and talk of me when you take him to your breast.

All my eternal love,

Your devoted Corporal.

Adam had not been christened yet, and because his father had died, I insisted the boy had my family's name. This was an unusual thing to do, but times were changing and there was so much going on with women's rights, equality, and the vote, nobody was really surprised. Everyone knew I was a great supporter of Mrs Pankhurst, and Sissy would have approved.

Our son, Adam, grew into a fine young man, tall and handsome. In 1938, when he reached twenty-one, I told him about his father, Manno, how he pledged his love, but never returned.

Adam had a passion for travel. He had trained as an architect and specialised in bridge building, but he eagerly signed up with the army when they advertised for professionals, despite my objecting.

'Adam, I've lost almost everyone I loved to the war. I'm begging you, stay away from the forces.'

'Really, Mum.' He took me into his arms. 'Leave the drama programmes for the radio. *War of the Worlds* isn't real, you know, it's make believe, straight out of George Orwell's own head. I'm not going to be in any danger building bridges, now am I? Anyway, I want to try and find out what happened to my father while I'm abroad.'

'Honestly, you sound like my lovely brother, Arthur. He didn't believe anything bad could happen to him. "We'll show them!" he cried. Excited to join up and defend the Empire.'

'That was the olden days, Mum,' Adam said. 'Everything's different now. Nobody wants another war, do they? Stop worrying.'

He went to Syros, on a quest to find his father. So, it came about that I learned of Manno's death from our son. This was a dark time for me. The local people told Adam, Manno had pulled up a mine in his fishing net. The explosion killed him and his father.

Adam was working on a Greek bridge between the mainland and the island of Evia, the second-largest island in Greece. While there, he caught the ferry to Kea to visit his father's grave. He fell in love with a Greek girl, Anna, and in 1943 she came to England where they married. This was a time of joy.

Anna gave birth to Margarete in 1951. Unfortunately Anna became ill and died shortly after. I brought up Margarete, as my own. Not a difficult task as I loved her intensely, and still do.

At that same time, in 1951, Greece joined NATO and there were Greek elections. Adam went out with the army to support the new regime in what had become a very troubled country. Naturally, he went to Syros to see Anna's family. They took Anna's death badly. Adam was broken-hearted. He wrote to me from Greece and said he had a small job to do on Kea, then he was returning to his battalion, but I never heard from him again.

This, I knew, was all punishment for my wrongdoing. I had sworn to atone for my sins on the day the *Britannic* went down. How could I have foreseen this cruel twist, my son Adam being taken from me was the worst penance, but I had to bear it. I kept my pain inside, where it belonged, and when your mother grew, and married, I prayed God had forgiven me, and nothing else would happen to those I loved. To lose Adam, with no closure, no grave to weep over, was the worst punishment of all.

Eventually, Adam was listed as missing in action. Like any mother, this broke my heart. I refused to believe my beautiful son was dead. To tell you the truth, I still can't believe it. I tried to find out what happened, but to no avail. I had saved a little each year, always planning to go back to Kea or Syros. In the end, I managed to get to Kea in the Sixties. Time had passed, and people's memories are short. There were vague references to an English working on the island, but names were forgotten.

I visited Manno's grave, and wept the afternoon away. I had loved that man with all my heart.

The old cottage of *Yiayá* was still standing, although the door was locked, and rotting along the bottom. I placed my hand on the stone near the entrance, and remembered the pretty donkey and the sweet white goat. How we had laughed. I walked along the port. The chest had long gone, so I stood there for a while, leaning against the wall and looking over to the lighthouse, which hadn't changed a bit.

I had refused to tell anyone where I was going because I could not stand to be interrogated about my quest. All I wanted, was to remember Manno, my one afternoon of passion, and my beautiful son, Adam.

CHAPTER 50
SHELLY

Greece, present day.

Before sunrise the next morning, Shelly slipped out of bed and into a white linen bathrobe. After tiptoeing through the French windows, she sat on the balcony and stared out to sea. The lighthouse flashed reassuringly in the dawn light, and for a moment she stared at the quayside and imagined Gran Gertie, and Manno sitting on the chest. Poor Gertie, what an emotional turmoil to go through.

She smiled to herself and glanced back into the room, at the man sleeping in her bed; the man she had spoken to almost every day for months. Not only did Shelly know she had fallen in love, but she knew she had fallen for Harry's emotional warmth, the way he cared for her, and for the way he needed to be with her, be it for a week, or a lifetime.

Before Harry, she'd only had David. Oh, yes, there had been a casual affair or two, but she could not even remember their names, and as far as love was concerned, she had been too young to appreciate what she had with David, when they both lived for the moment. Now, on Kea, Shelly sensed this was a period for embracing the rest of her life. To put all her faith and trust in one man was a brave commitment, because she knew she could not stand to be hurt by Harry. All her emotions, especially love, friendship, and trust were invested in him.

The Greek light gathered, the town waking. The bakery drew its loyal customers with delicious aromas of fresh bread wafting on cool air.

Some Greek islands had sold their soul to the tourist's bankcard; prosperous islands where the locals were thespians, blatantly welcoming. 'Hello! So lovely to see you again, how long are you here for?'

Not Kea. On this island, the locals observed their foreign visitors with a slight air of curiosity. 'Why have you come here when you could go to Santorini or Mykonos?' Also, Kea didn't suffer fools lightly. This was not an island of nightclubs, expensive cocktails, or sunbeds. There was no *Demos* pelican with clipped wings, strutting the beach looking for tourists to be photographed with.

Kea was an island where you felt you belonged, or you left.

* * *

'Come on, no time for daydreaming!' Harry called. 'Shower, get dressed, then we're off. We'll have breakfast in a cove, halfway.'

In the dawn light, she saw their vessel was the beautiful white ridged inflatable boat they'd used before. The furiously fast and sexily sleek RIB was shaped like an arrowhead and powered by a throbbing black monster of a motor at the rear.

Harry's pride in the vessel was as wide as his grin. She climbed in and sat next to him in the cockpit. He told her to buckle up her life jacket and hang on.

A woman came over from a quayside taverna with a cardboard tray and a bag of pastries. 'Enjoy!' she called with a knowing wink. Harry pulled off slowly.

'Pull the fenders in, will you?' he called.

A little thing, yet it made her feel part of the team. As they crept out of the harbour, she pulled in the white bullet-shaped fenders that protected the sides of the vessel from its quay-side neighbours. Once she had returned to her seat, they had reached the open sea and Harry pulled the throttle hard back. The prow lifted and they planed over the crests of waves, out of the Kea Channel. She looked over to the calm sea on her left and imagined the *Britannic* beneath four hundred feet of warm, crystal-clear water. One day, she would dive that great ship. The mid-summer dive came back to her, and she realised she had not seen Elias yet.

Before long, the barren island of Yaros came into view. A coastline of tall cliffs with pleats and tucks seeming even more dramatic because of the early morning light. She remembered Gertie and the dolphins, Eleonora's falcon, and Manno and his teasing. The sky turned from grey-blue to peach, then Harry indicated the horizon to their right, just as the sun peeped over the line, rising like a great crimson fireball flinging a path of red light across the undulating sea, towards them.

She caught Harry's eye, and in a glance told him the sunrise never ceased to amaze her. He nodded, smiling, and she knew he felt the same. It was this similarity of spirit – the understanding they shared – that mattered to her as much as the spark between them, and their amazing compatibility in bed.

Harry lowered their speed, and they cruised into a shallow bay where he instructed her to drop anchor when the boat stopped. 'It's only chest deep here,' he said. She could see the bottom very clearly.

'Time for breakfast,' he said, his eyes lustrous with want. 'Let's eat on that rock.'

'Oh dear, I didn't bring my swimwear.'

He was grinning like a schoolboy. 'Then it seems we'll have to go naked.'

'But what if somebody comes?'

'Then they'll be the lucky ones.'

They pulled their clothes off and leapt into the water. Harry, with the food tray above his head, waded to the flat rock. Shelly swam, and once on the rock, saw herself as the little mermaid. He came to her side, and they fed each other flaky croissant, and drank lukewarm coffee, until they wanted each other so badly they slipped into the water and made love.

* * *

They arrived in Syros at lunchtime, and both were hungry again. They moored up, then sat at a quayside table.

Shelly stared around, trying to imagine the dancing bear, Gertie's first kiss, and searching the shops for *loukoumi*. She wondered about the house where Manno and Gertie had made love. Then she stared out to sea and wondered how many war ships had docked there, remembering all the ships came to fill up with water.

'What are you thinking?' Harry asked.

'I'm just trying to remember how it was when I came here as a child. My great-grandmother was here too. I was four or five, and she was an old woman. Every afternoon she'd disappear, and not return until dinnertime, all red-eyed and weepy. We never discovered where she went, but you've listened to the tapes now. I think she went to Manno's grave, or even Adam's grave, wherever that is.'

He shook his head. 'No, she didn't. I actually know where she went.'

462

Shelly sat up. 'What? Where?'

'Are you ready to order?' the waiter said.

Shelly blinked at him, trying to unravel the mystery and think of food at the same time. 'Er, village salad and lamb chops,' she said and turned to Harry. 'Where did she go?'

'One moment.' He turned to the waiter. 'The same for me, and a large bottle of water.'

'Where?' Shelly insisted.

'Well, that's my surprise, so don't spoil it now. I'll take you there as soon as we've eaten.'

'Give me a clue?'

'No clues. Now stop pestering me, and don't bother batting your eyelashes like that. I have a will of iron.'

Shelly's shoulders dropped. 'I think you're terribly mean, but I'll let you off just this once.'

* * *

'That was the most delicious food! Thank you.'

'You're welcome, now if you are up to it, we have quite a walk ahead of us.'

'So, come on, where are we going?'

'Still not telling. You just have to tag along, but, it will be worth it, and I promise you'll love it. First, we have to check in, but we're just over the road, so that will only take a minute. Then, I am going to show you something so amazing, I will have you under my spell forever.'

'I think you've managed that already,' she whispered.

He met her eyes and smiled. 'You bewitch me,' he said, grabbing her hand and pulling her up. 'Come on, we don't have all day!'

Ten minutes later, they were striding uphill, panting and perspiring. 'Slow down!' Shelly cried.

'I can't. We have an appointment. We're running out of time. Come on!' he called, taking her hand and tugging her onward and upward. They staggered up steps, panted up pathways, and blazed up backstreets too steep for cars or scooters. Finally, they arrived at the top of the hill and from outside the great monastery of St George, they looked down on the harbour town of Ermoupoli and the port of Syros.

'What an amazing view! Have I got time to take some photographs?'

'Not now, we're late,' Harry said quietly. 'Whatever happens next, I want you to understand that I have done this with your best interests at heart.'

Shelly nodded. 'I understand, but what have you done?'

'You're about to find out.' He knocked on the great oak door, and after a moment, it was heaved open by a hooded monk. 'Father, this is Shelly Summer, great-granddaughter of Gertrude Smith who died in 1998.'

'Welcome. Please follow me,' the old abbot said, lifting his head enough for them to see a clean-shaven chin and a kind mouth below his cowl. They followed him through the most beautiful church with cream marble columns and stunning murals on the walls that depicted religious scenes. After the church, they passed through cloisters to a row of monks' cells, and Shelly noticed one with the door slightly ajar. 'Please go in,' the abbot said.

Harry held his arm out, inviting Shelly to enter first. Her nerves jangled.

'Don't be afraid,' Harry said as she peered at the wizened monk sitting in an armchair, inside. 'Shelly Summer, I'd like you to meet your grandfather, Adam Smith.'

Shelly gasped. 'My grandfather, Adam? Gran Gertie's son? Oh, my goodness!' Completely overwhelmed, she felt her tears rise as she dropped to her knees at his feet. 'Grandad Adam, this is a miracle, to meet you after all these years of wondering what happened to you.'

Suddenly, she realised the truth. Gertie believed this was her punishment, to have her son taken from her. To believe he was dead, and then discover he had become a monk.

Shocked and confused, she turned to Harry. 'How did you find him?'

'I didn't. I've always known him, but didn't make the connection until I heard Gran Gertie's tape. I told you an English architect saved my father's life by pushing him out of danger, but the architect was badly injured himself.' Shelly nodded. 'That man was Adam. He was in a coma for a long time, and had no memory when he finally regained consciousness. The monks adopted him, and as he recovered, some of his memory slowly returned over the years; then, he decided to join the order.'

The old monk nodded. 'My mother came to visit me, long ago,' he said quietly with a distant look on his face. 'She said I had a daughter, Margarete, and a granddaughter, Shelly, and one day, when I was better, they would come here. They never came. I've been waiting so long. So long.'

'Dear grandfather, I am Shelly. My mother would have come, but Gran Gertie died before she told anyone that she'd found you. I'm sorry, but my mother was killed in a car accident more than twenty years ago. Gran Gertie, your mother, told me so much about you. How you loved maths at school and that you became a great bridge builder. She said you were very handsome, like your father, Manno. I'm so pleased to meet you. Did

465

you know, although your mother named you Adam, your father named you Hephaestus, blacksmith of the gods?'

He stared for a moment, and then smiled widely. 'No, I didn't know.'

'Your father, Manno, sold his father's fishing boat to the mayor of Kea and with the money, bought a ticket to England to see you just after your birth.'

'Why didn't they marry?'

'Well, they sort of did marry, actually. It was their intention, and Manno did put a ring on her wedding finger, it was shaped like a dolphin. Wartime, and the distance between them, made everything difficult. When the mine injured Manno and he knew he wouldn't live, he sent your mother a gold wedding ring, via carrier pigeon, and got the priest to write his wedding vows. He wrote a letter to you, too. Wait, I'll read it to you.' Suddenly overwhelmed, she turned to Harry. 'I can hardly speak. Thank you. Can you pull up a tape on your phone? I think it's side twenty.'

She sat on the edge of Adam's bed and took his wrinkled hand in hers. 'This is your mother's voice, a few years before she died. Harry nodded and passed her his phone and she pressed play. They all listened.

'*We went to Syros for a holiday. This was because nobody minded where we went, apart from me. That island, and the one afternoon I spent there in the arms of my darling Manno, had shaped my life, so I wanted to return, one more time, before I died.*

'*We all went to Syros, and it was on that holiday that I finally found my son, my precious Adam. I loved that boy so much, and wished things could have been different, but of course they could not. I had to do penance for my crimes because I did not want the*

466

sins of the mother to be passed onto her child. My boy was every-thing to me, and I pray I will see him in heaven one day.'

'I don't have a recording of your father's voice, but I do have the original letter with his wedding vows that he sent her when he was dying, and his heartfelt words to you. Gosh, it must be a hundred years old.'

'A hundred and three,' the old monk said.

Shelly blinked at her wizened grandfather. 'Let me try to remember what it said.'

'I've got it,' Harry said. 'You took a photo of it and sent it to me. Wait . . . yes, here it is.'

He passed the phone back to her again, And Shelly read it aloud.

Adam's face was hidden by his hood, but Shelly felt the splash of a tear on the back of her hand. 'I fear we've overtired you. We'll leave you in peace, and come back tomorrow, if that's all right?' She leaned forward, dipped under his cowl, and pressed her face against his wet cheek. 'I'm so glad I found you, Grandfather.'

* * *

That night, Shelly stared into the dark. Meeting her grandfather had changed her. She couldn't explain why. She didn't know him, had never met him before, or missed him in any way. Yet, after her visit, she felt complete, as if the last part of her jigsaw had fallen into place.

She wondered if her grandfather felt the same. Her answer came the next morning at breakfast, when the receptionist approached their table with a note that said she had to go up to the monastery.

'He simply didn't wake this morning,' the abbot explained. 'There was a note at the side of his bed and I'm sure it was meant for you.' He passed it over.

Shelly looked at the single word, written in Greek. 'I'm sorry, what does it say?'

'It simply says, "Thank you,"' the abbot said.

CHAPTER 51
GERTIE

Dover, 1917.

FOR MANNO AND ADAM I will wear black to the end of my days.

The rest you probably know. Margarete, Shelly, whoever you are listening to this story, I hope you are happy, and also find love. If you do, hold onto it with all the strength you have. Life is not easy, but it is a lot easier with someone who loves you standing by your side. Tell your children and grandchildren about me, about my story.

I only have one more thing to say. I don't know if you remember the holiday we all went on, together as a family. Gordon, Margarete and little Shelly. It was 1989 and Shelly had just started school. Gordon had a small win on Vernons football pools after correctly choosing seven draws out of eight in a line. Oh, my goodness, he was so excited he danced the polka around the garden with your mother, and I nearly split my sides laughing. The result was a second dividend of five hundred pounds; such a lot of money in those days, and certainly more than he ever had in spare change before.

We went to Syros, and I found my precious Adam. I loved that boy so much and wished things could have been different, but they could not. I had to do penance for my crimes, simply because I didn't want the sins of the mother to be passed onto her children and grandchildren. Adam was in the monastery, being looked after by the monks. I saw him, held his hand, and told him so many things.

I'm not sure that he knew who I was, and there was no way I could have transferred him to England, so I decided that this was the cost of my sins. To lose both the man I adored and his son. I believe I've paid for my sins, and nobody else will suffer because of my actions. My great wrongdoing, to lie about my age, and to disobey orders and open the portholes, had led to so much sadness and loss. If only we could see the future consequences of small actions, before we make our mistakes.

Go to Syros, dear listener. See the island and think of me, and all those I've loved so much. The place has a kind of magic that I can't describe, I think it must be due to all the churches, all those pockets of peace. I visited every one, walked through every door, and on that last trip, prayed for every person that I love, including you both, Margarete and Shelly. So, I hope God has answered my supplications and given you a blessed life. Whatever happens, just remember those words from Matron Merriberry: the past can't be changed, so don't waste your life dwelling on it. The past only has one purpose, to teach us not to make the same mistakes in the future.'

More than anything, I wish that you give and receive lots of love, through your entire life.

You have all mine.

CHAPTER 52
SHELLY

Dover, Christmas Eve.

'I'M REALLY EXCITED, DAD. OUR first Christmas in twenty years, what an occasion.' Shelly pushed a drawing pin through a red foiled decoration and into the beam. As she turned to come down the stepladder, she spotted the taxi pulling up outside. 'They're here! Quick, let's put the steps away. Can you turn the tree lights on?'

''Ere, why don't we make an occasion of it, like yer mum did? Glass of sherry, "Silent Night", mince pies, you know. Throw the switch . . . nothing works . . . ha-ha!'

Shelly laughed. 'You're right, we will. I'm so excited!' She shoved the steps under the stairs and answered the front door.

'Harry! Elias and Petros! I'm so happy to see you. Come in, come in.' Shelly kissed everyone and whispered, 'I love you,' into Harry's ear as she took his coat. The men huddled around the wood burner, rubbing their hands together.

'Hi, I'm DJ. Pleased to meet you guys.' He shook hands with everyone. 'You're just in time for the tree lights tradition.'

Harry grinned. 'How does that go?'

DJ said, 'First we have some toasts.'

'We ate on the plane,' Elias scowled.

'No, he doesn't mean a cheese and ham toastie, you're not in Greece now, bro.' Petros said. 'He means they say a few important words.'

'That's right. First we turn the lights on the tree, then all go to the pub and get drunk.' DJ poured out a tray of sherry and said, 'Alexa, Christmas mix.' Then, to the sound of 'Rockin' Around the Christmas Tree', he handed everyone a drink.

They all cried, 'Happy Christmas!' and chinked glasses. Harry, Elias, and Petros faced each other, tapped the bottom of their glasses on the table, and knocked back the expensive sherry in one.

DJ's eyes widened.

'Only the English would have *raki* glasses this posh!' Elias exclaimed, and they all laughed.

Shelly and DJ exchanged a glance. Shelly's eyebrows twitched, and she made the slightest nod at the sherry bottle.

DJ refilled their glasses. 'Sorry we don't have any *raki*. I must warn you, this stuff will give you the mother and father of all headaches. That's why everyone sips it.'

'Thanks, mate,' Elias said. 'I'd have brought you some proper *raki* if I'd known.'

Gordon stood and stuck his chest out. 'As head of this family, it's for me to make the first toast. Please raise your glasses to absent friends, especially my wife, Maggie.' He cleared his throat. 'This is the first Christmas we've celebrated since she was killed on Christmas Eve, twenty-one years ago.'

There was a second of emotionally charged silence while Shelly slipped her arm around her father.

'To absent friends,' everyone cried and took a sip of sherry.

Shelly raised her glass and thought about David and her first summer in Greece, and the years she had spent in a bubble of sadness and regret. *Thank you for letting me go, my darling David. I will never forget you, or the love we had.* She stood and glanced at everyone in turn. 'I'd also like us all to remember those who can't be with us today – friends, relations, mothers, fathers, lovers, grandmothers and *everyone* we care about – to wish them every happiness wherever they are.'

When each of them had voiced a toast, Shelly raised her glass again. 'Just one more, as we are all coming to visit you, in Kea, next: please all raise your glasses to summer in Greece!'

'Summer in Greece!' they cried in unison.

'Right, Dad, will you do the honours?' Shelly nodded at the Christmas tree.

Gordon plugged in and threw the switch. The lights flickered, went out, came back on and pulsed away. Everyone cheered and clapped and Gordon beamed like it was a personal triumph.

'Right, DJ, will you drive the boys and their cases to The Rose and Crown?' She turned to Harry. 'That's where everyone is staying, and also, that's where we're having Christmas dinner tomorrow. Too many of us to do it here.'

The doorbell chimed. 'Eve, come in!' Shelly cried. 'Harry, this is my business partner and best friend, Eve.'

Eve blinked at everybody. 'Wow! A house full of handsome men all to yourself, no wonder you kept going back to Greece!' Everyone laughed as Eve leaned towards Harry offering her cheeks for kisses and throwing an approving wink at Shelly.

''Ere, I want one of those, Eve love,' Gordon called, and everyone laughed again.

'I've come to see if you need lifts,' Eve said. 'Bill and Malcolm and DJ's girlfriend and her friends are already in the pub, organising karaoke.'

'Great,' Elias said. 'I'm not bad at karaoke, even if I say so myself.'

'Thinks he's Jay-Z,' Petros teased.

'Brilliant,' Shelly said to Eve. 'That would be a great help. If you could take Elias and Petros, Eve. Then, DJ could take Harry in the Beetle.' She glanced at the clock. 'I'll bring Dad in a few minutes.'

'You've got a Beetle, that's so cool, man!' Petros said as they went out of the door.

Suddenly, the house was quiet apart from the haunting melody of 'Silent Night'.

Shelly and her father exchanged a sad smile. 'It's Christmas Eve, Dad, come on. We have a wreath to lay.' She helped him into his coat and they stepped into the front porch at just that same time as her mother had, twenty-one years ago. Shelly lifted the beautiful Christmas wreath off the front door, the first one to hang there since. Then, she linked arms with her father and together, they carried it towards the bus stop on the bend.

'Rest in peace, my dearest Maggie,' Gordon whispered as they placed the garland on the seat.

'She was a wonderful mother,' Shelly said, hugging her father and feeling her tears gather.

Gordon gasped, then his gloved hand went over his mouth as he turned to Shelly.

'Bugger! I forgot to take the mince pies out!' he cried, breaking away from her arms and rushing back towards the cottage.

Somewhere in the back of her mind, Shelly heard her mother's last words: *Give me a kiss, my darling daughter, and don't let the mince pies burn.*

She looked up to the sky and started to laugh, and as her laughter flew in the frosty air, she experienced so much joy and relief, her feet seemed to leave the pavement and her heart floated towards heaven like a red foil balloon. 'Thanks, Mum. Happy Christmas,' she whispered.

ACKNOWLEDGEMENTS

WITHOUT THE HELP OF THE people mentioned below, *Summer in Greece* would not have been possible.

Sarah Bauer, Katie Lumsden and everyone else at Bonnier Books UK. Caroline Kirkpatrick, Sophie Wilson, Victoria Hughes-Williams, Jon Appleton and Linda Joyce. Simon Mills, the owner of HMHS Britannic, whose amazing books inspired me in the first instance; Jake Billingham, 'Mr Britannic', who tirelessly answered my questions; Yannis Tzavelakos and KiaDivers, for making me welcome on the island of Kea, for inspiring me, and also for their patience and encouragement. Thanks to all those divers who have travelled down to the *Britannic* on the seabed and posted their awesome underwater videos online for us to enjoy. Claire Wilson, for her medical advice. Tony J. Fyler, for his help and encouragement. Jill Dodgson, for pointing out I should leave the keyboard and exercise once in a while. JC Lee, for dozens of great pictures and videos of me, my readers and fans. Barbara and Ann-Marie, for their constant support, public relations, and translations. Patricia Castle, for accompanying me to Kea and Syros to research this novel, and for taking good care of me. My family, and most importantly, my husband, Berty, who brings food to my office when deadlines are tight, and always pours me an appreciated glass of red at the end of the day.

Thank you to each and every reader, especially those who have written such wonderful reviews. They really do make all the difference.

AUTHOR'S NOTE

WHEN I WAS RESEARCHING for my previous novel, *Greek Island Escape*, I was lucky enough to spend a few days on one of my favourite Cyclades islands, Syros. With its natural harbour and skilled boat builders, Syros is proud to be a working island. The capital, Ermoupoli, has the grand Miaouli square, paved in marble and surrounded by fine mansions. This is the best-preserved neoclassical town in Greece, where wonderfully ornate churches and delightful, white-washed chapels stand shoulder to shoulder. Built on a steep incline overlooking the port, Ermoupoli is dominated by its crowning glory, a magnificent monastery built on the summit of its highest hill.

I enjoy the larger Greek islands, Crete, Rhodes, Santorini and Mykonos – some of my books are set on them – and I try to visit them most years, but I am also fascinated by the lesser-known islands. While I was on Syros, I came across a day return ferry to the small island of Kea. This island was new to me, so I ordered a frappé at a nearby café and googled Kea on my laptop. Half an hour later, I could hardly wait to buy a ticket.

I had discovered that *Titanic*'s larger, grander and slightly younger sistership, the *Britannic*, lay on the seabed just a few kilometres away. All nine-hundred feet of her. I couldn't believe this wasn't more widely known – it was news to me. As a child, I was enthralled by BBC TV sea life programmes involving the great Jacques Cousteau, and captivated by the adventures of Hans and Lotte Hass. It is difficult to recall that they were in black and white, because I always remember them in glorious colour, such was my childish imagination. Those fascinating underwater scenes came back to me as I stared out at the inviting Aegean, under a sky almost too blue to be real.

The next morning, I boarded the ferry from Syros to Kea. On the top deck, taking pictures as we approached Kea harbour, I noticed an excited group at the railing and, on investigation, saw a young turtle heading the same way. What an amazing beginning.

I planned to do nothing but sit at a harbourside café, think about the wreck of the *Britannic*, and soak up the atmosphere (and the sun).

Kea is a small island, less than an hour's ferry ride from the mainland, and the harbour is lined with delightful cafés. At its most inland curve, a sandy beach is dotted with tamarisk trees and, on a rocky outcrop, I noticed the ubiquitous little white chapel of countless postcards. Further around the bay, a long promontory leads to the whitewashed lighthouse and church of Agios Nikolaus. Honestly, you could not design a more iconic Greek scene! I had to pinch myself. This charming little island, unspoiled by tourism, is a place of art and culture, perfect for year-round holidays. Its capital, a pedestrianised hilltop town in the centre of the island, is unbelievably pretty.

'On holiday?' the waitress asked as she brought my iced coffee.

'Not exactly,' I answered, 'I'm thinking of writing a novel about the *Britannic*. Did it go down near here?'

'You need to speak to Yannis Tzavelakos, from Kea Divers. He's the expert.'

She promptly pulled out her phone and called him. Within twenty minutes, the charismatic Yannis Tzavelakos, dive master, was at my table sharing his great knowledge with me. I was hooked! If you'd like more information, check out KeaDivers on Facebook, where you can see their great underwater films of local dives, including the shipwrecks of SS *Burdigala* and, of course, the HMHS *Britannic* which was only discovered in 1975. What a story they have to tell.

The *Britannic* was built in Belfast for the North Atlantic passenger trade. However, as she reached completion, war broke out and she found herself requisitioned by the British government as a hospital ship for the duration of the conflict. She sailed the much warmer waters of the Mediterranean Sea heading for the hospital clearing station on Lemnos island.

After saving many thousands of lives, disaster hit in the Aegean on the *Britannic*'s sixth rescue trip.

The sinking of the *Britannic* raises many questions. Did she strike a mine, or was she torpedoed? How could a vessel of this size and calibre – and, like the *Titanic*, deemed to be unsinkable – flounder in merely fifty-five minutes? Why couldn't she push on and reach the island of Kea?

I was fascinated, and so I watched real time video documentaries and Jacques Cousteau's dive down to the *Britannic* after he had discovered the ship. I also read letters from the nurses and medical staff who were on board when disaster struck. However, it was through reading Simon Mills very informative book, *The Unseen Britannic* (which I highly recommend), that I learned fascinating details of the ship. Simon Mills felt so passionately about the *Britannic* that he bought the wreck in order to protect it from marauders. By this time, I knew this ship had to be the subject of my next novel.

I went onto *Titanic*'s Facebook page and came into contact with Jake Billingham, sometimes known as Mr Britannic. His enthusiasm was contagious. I asked Jake what had first drawn him to the *Britannic*.

'My fascination with the Olympic class liners began at the age of five when James Cameron's *Titanic* movie was released in 1997. As a young boy, I knew much about *Titanic*, but I hadn't realised she had two sisters, RMS *Olympic* and HMHS *Britannic*. I went on to learn about HMHS *Britannic*, and why she ended her days on the Aegean seabed. Even today, the *Britannic* wreck is still as captivating. These ships and the people who sailed on them have become a part of me. The discovery of the HMHS *Britannic*'s crow's nest bell is a powerful reminder of the events that led up to the ship's sad and violent end. It also stands as a great archaeological find by an amazing dive team.'

I asked Jake how a few small portholes, twenty-five feet above the waterline, could have caused a ship that size to go down so much more quickly.

'One of the long-standing ambiguities concerning the loss of HMHS *Britannic* is the mystery of the open portholes on the lower decks. It's thought that somebody opened the portholes in an effort to air out the wardrooms to make them more bearable for the 3,000 to 4,000 patients that would soon occupy the bunks and cots which filled the decks.

'Most E-deck portholes were 18 to 24 square inches. We need six ports open to make twelve square feet, which would take on 400 tons per minute. Each 150 tons would pull the *Britannic* down by one inch. Assuming 16,000 tons of water came aboard in the first two or three minutes – perhaps longer – HMHS *Britannic* would have sunk by nine feet at the bow. Assuming she started at 32 feet, this would put her forward draught at 41 feet. Once the list developed then the E-deck portholes, normally 25 feet or so above the waterline but at 16 feet with the ship having 16,000 tons, could rapidly go under in ten minutes. It might not sound much, but this water is all coming from the starboard side; the water washes along the starboard E-deck corridor and seeps below to F-deck, while flooding from ports on F and G-decks increases the flooding. This continues to increase the starboard list. And all the time we have flooding increasing in the forward six watertight compartments.

'So, we may have – even with just a few portholes open – 24,000 tons of water aboard in 20 minutes. 40,000 tons of water is enough to pull the ship under and occurred by approximately 9 a.m. With those portholes open, the *Britannic* didn't stand a chance.'

WW1 Nursing

Investigations never revealed who went against orders and opened those portholes, but the general consensus seems to suggest it was a nurse. Before I started work on this novel, I had no knowledge of nursing in the First World War. I soon learned that First World War nursing was dangerous and exhausting work; remarkable women volunteered, many quite naive, yet brave beyond measure. They experienced the horror of war first hand, and thousands paid with their lives. The courageousness of these resilient young women – often scorned by men, and away from home for the first time in their lives – is still unrecognised. Thousands faced unimaginable horrors for the sake of their brothers and their country.

I had watched *Testament of Youth*, and read about Edith Cavell, but it was not until I read *The Virago Book of Women and the Great War* (a collection of letters home and diary excerpts) and *The Daughters of Mars*, that I realised the true horror that these women had to face.

My vision of the gentle young nurse, and the subservient VAD in her spotless, starched uniform was replaced by a much harsher reality: women struggling through the filth, discomfort, stench and lack of supplies to mend broken, dismembered and diseased bodies. Men writhed in agony in some of the most dreadful battleground clearing stations. In atrocious, dysentery-ridden conditions, these nurses and VADs attempted to ease pain and save lives.

Professional nurses were battling for recognition and proper training. Unqualified volunteers (VADs), most with total ignorance of medicine and the anatomy, found themselves pitched into military hospitals.

The nurses feared the VADs' arrival would undermine their efforts for recognition. Poorly paid VADs were used mainly as labourers, scrubbing floors, changing beds, swilling bedpans. However, because of a chronic shortage of trained nurses, some progressed to changing dressings and administering drugs.

The war produced medical issues largely unknown in civilian life and not previously experienced by doctors or nurses. Machine guns were still relatively new and due to the poor conditions in the trenches, wound infections were common. With no antibiotics or disinfectants, any injury could mean death. Instead, they used iodide or agonising salt to try and stop infection.

Thousands perished because of tetanus and gangrene. Towards the end of the war, some fundamental medical advances emerged; one of these was blood transfusions, performed simply by linking a tube between the patient and the donor for a direct transfer of blood. An example can be seen at the Florence Nightingale Museum in London.

Loggerhead Turtles – *Caretta caretta*

On a lighter note, we come to the beautiful turtles of the Mediterranean. The loggerhead sea turtle is the world's largest hard-shelled turtle. Adults have an average weight of about 298 lb (135 kg) with a maximum recorded weight of 1,202 lb (545 kg). The maximum recorded length of a loggerhead is 84 in (213 cm), though in the Mediterranean, the average is half that size.

Florida is the most popular nesting area for these turtles, with more than 67,000 nests each year. Greece is the most popular Mediterranean nesting area, with more than 3,000 nests per year, although the coastlines of Cyprus and Turkey are also popular.

Loggerheads spend most of their lives in the ocean and coastal waters, only coming ashore briefly to lay eggs. The turtles spend 85% of their day submerged. Dives usually last 15–30 min, but they can stay underwater for up to four hours. They feed on bottom-dwelling invertebrates, also sponges, urchins, starfish, jellyfish and other hatchling turtles, including their own.

Eggs are laid above the high-water line and the sex of the turtles is dictated by the temperature of the nest. Eggs kept at 32°C produce females, those at 28°C become males.

Incubation lasts 80 days. Hatchlings dig to the surface at night and head toward the brighter horizon created by the moon's reflection off the water. Then they swim for approximately 20 hours. Fascinatingly, an iron compound in their brains allows the turtles to use the earth's magnetic field for navigation.

When the sea cools, loggerheads migrate to warmer water, or partially hibernate by submerging for up to seven hours at a time, only emerging for a few minutes to breathe.

First reproducing after the age of 17, their lifespan is up to 70 years. In the Northern Hemisphere, loggerheads mate from March to June and lay between May and August.

The turtles display multiple paternity due to sperm storage. A single clutch may have as many as seven fathers, each contributing sperm to a portion of the clutch.

The females return to nest fortnightly, producing three or four nests on the beach where they themselves hatched. They climb the beach, scrape the sand away to form a pit and lay clutch of 112 eggs. After covering the nest, they return to the sea.

Sadly, the primary threat to turtles is humans – they drown after becoming entangled in longlines or fishing nets. Pollution also kills many thousands each year. Nearly 24,000 metric tons of plastics are dumped into the ocean annually; turtles can ingest this debris and loggerheads mistake plastic bags for jellyfish, a common food for them. The plastic causes suffocation or starvation, and those ingested can poison the turtles. The melting of the ice caps have an effect, too; the fresh water alters vital currents in our oceans, disrupting the natural journey of whales and many other sea creatures, including turtles.

Dolphins of the Mediterranean

Bottlenose dolphins are said to be the third most intelligent mammals on Earth, sharing close ratios with those of humans and other great apes.

The dolphin's shape allows it to swim very quickly, reaching up to 65 km per hour. This particularly playful dolphin is the one most likely to be encountered near the shore of Greek islands in the Aegean Sea. Here, an endangered population remains.

For me, dolphins are one of the most fascinating sea creatures on earth. The holy animals of Greek Gods, Apollo and Poseidon, as well as a symbol of friendship and solidarity, they have a special place in our heart. The relationship of Greeks with dolphins is as old as humanity. Homer's scripts, Minoan frescos in Crete and Santorini, and ancient coins all depict dolphins. Also, many myths and legends highlight the relationship between humans, Gods and dolphins.

The view of their glimmering bodies while chasing after food, or simply playing in the waves, or swimming near the bow of a boat remains etched in our memories of those who have been lucky enough to witness it.

Dolphins' gestation is 12 months. When born, the young dolphins stay with their mothers for three to six years and the mothers invent a special tune, a name for its baby, which the calf memorises for the rest of its life.

They breathe through lungs and can store enough oxygen to swim for 20 minutes at a depth of up to 500 meters. Dolphins barely sleep, and their hearing and visibility are incredible. Their role as hunters is crucial for maintaining a balance in the sea's ecosystem as they eat the unhealthy fish, thus preventing infectious diseases from spreading.

There are many anecdotes of dolphins defending humans from animals that attack them, like sharks. This behaviour is similar to that of mother dolphins protecting their offspring. Many swimmers and troubled divers claim they were held at, or transported to, the surface with the aid of a dolphin.

Why do they do this? While we can't be sure, one explanation may be related to the comparison between body characteristics of dolphins and humans since both are intelligent mammals. Thanks to its sense of echo location, a dolphin can hear our heartbeat, and so may realise when a person is very afraid. It is then that they act as they would with a traumatised mate or offspring.

In the old sea stories of Greece, there are dozens of claims of dolphins that helped drowning sailors, rescuing people from sharks, and making themselves useful as guides through treacherous waters.

Dolphins also help injured members of their own family groups, and new-born babies, to the surface by swimming under them and nudging upward. Remarkably, there are real stories of dolphins helping other cetaceans. In 1983 in New Zealand, a pod of pilot whales ran aground at low tide. The locals did their best to keep the whales alive until the tide returned. However, the whales became distressed orienting themselves. A nearby pod of dolphins seemingly realised the situation and swam into the shallow water. Despite the risk to themselves, the dolphins managed to herd 76 of the 80 stranded pilot whales back out to sea.

In the Gulf of Akaba, a British tourist was rescued from sharks by three dolphins, and there are several other examples of similar incidences in Australia.

In the Red Sea, 12 divers, lost for over 13 hours, were surrounded by dolphins for the entire time. The dolphins repelled many sharks that occupied the area. When a rescue boat arrived in the area, the dolphins led them to where the divers were, leaping in front of the boat.

As we can't talk to dolphins, we can't understand what their motives are in these situations. It is very possible that they are simply trying to help and protect fellow mammals in the ocean, something humans could learn from them.